PRESIDENT LINCOLN'S SECRET

STEVEN WILSON

KENSINGTON BOOKS
http://www.kensingtonbooks.com

KENSINGTON BOOKS are published by

Kensington Publishing Corp.
119 West 40th Street
New York, NY 10018

All Kensington titles, imprints, and distributed lines are available at special quantity discounts for bulk purchases for sales promotion, premiums, fund-raising, educational, or institutional use.

Special book excerpts or customized printings can also be created to fit specific needs. For details, write or phone the office of the Kensington Special Sales Manager: Kensington Publishing Corp., 119 West 40th Street, New York, NY 10018. Attn. Special Sales Department. Phone: 1-800-221-2647.

Kensington and the K logo Reg. U.S. Pat. & TM Off.

ISBN-13: 978-0-7582-3214-4
ISBN-10: 0-7582-3214-4

First Kensington Trade Paperback Printing: July 2009
10 9 8 7 6 5 4 3 2 1

Printed in the United States of America

Also by Steven Wilson

Voyage of the Gray Wolves

Between the Hunters and the Hunted

Armada

President Lincoln's Spy

To Angela for minding the cats,
and Jean for minding the commas

Prologue

Darkness followed the red mist.

Light returned gradually, accompanied by the heavy drumming of cannons and the flat crack of muskets. Fitz Dunaway heard his name being called, the words an indistinct drone. His eyes fluttered open in response. Above him was a bright sky with mare's tails for clouds, and dirty black smoke that rose in columns only to be torn apart by the wind.

His mind was clumsy, thoughts unfocused, and as he tried to turn his head to find out where he was he found that his body refused its orders. He searched for an answer to his predicament, but there was no solution. Sky blue trousers and scuffed brogans were all that remained of his world. He was on his back.

A bearded face fiercely streaked with dust and sweat hovered over him. "Colonel? Can you hear me? Are you all right?"

The man's words echoed and then, with a rush of water, became clear.

"Ripslinger?" Fitz managed.

"You just lay quiet, Colonel," the soldier said, comforting Fitz with a rough pat on the shoulder. "We'll get you back to the surgeon." Ripslinger disappeared, the horrible word lingering after him.

Surgeon, Fitz thought. He turned cold with fear. His eyelids closed involuntarily, and in that fraction of an instant, Fitz lost consciousness.

He awoke again, swaying back and forth, floating above the ground, suspended between four soldiers. Fitz's head hung limply. Everything was upside down—a battery of cannons thundered by, wheels a blur in the boiling dust. Infantry double-timed toward the front, officers mounted, shouting orders, trying to make sense of the madness that swirled around them. And dust. Dust hanging in the air; dust covering the dark blue sack coats of the soldiers; dust, and a dun-colored film, spurting from the soldiers' feet.

"Get his head," someone ordered.

Fitz felt a strong hand cradle his neck and hold his head up. The muscles ached from the strain of the unnatural position. He tried to say thank you but even that was too much.

He remembered what happened—or at least some of it.

Men were running, shouting—it was a rout. The Union line had broken, and Fitz was trying to rally his men when everything had turned black. Stop, he had wanted to say, turn and fight them—don't run away—hold your ground. He was floating now.

Darkness again, and this time Fitz welcomed it. He was tired and thirsty, and he thought that someone had set fire to his left arm and the blaze was just now feeding his flesh. He wondered why someone would do that.

"Colonel?" A surgeon stood over him, the man's coat caked with blood. Above the man's head was a tent, and Fitz knew he was at the surgeon's station. He heard men groaning, and the air was pierced by a sharp scream that ended quickly. Flies buzzed industriously around the tent, feasting on the residue on the surgeon's scalpel. "Colonel," the surgeon said again, his hand clamping on Fitz's chin. He shook Fitz's head until he was sure that his patient was awake. "I'm giving you chloroform." He interrupted his explanation to demand the drug. His eyes, ringed red with fatigue, found Fitz's. "Your arm is badly mangled and I must repair it. Do you understand?"

Fitz blinked once, a signal for yes, and then realized it made no difference if he understood or not—the surgeon would do as he thought best. Then he knew.

"No," he croaked. "No!" For God's sake don't do it. "Don't take my arm."

The surgeon, senses dulled from hacking arms and legs from perfectly good bodies, tried to focus his attention on Fitz.

"Please don't take my arm," Fitz cried out, but some imp snatched his voice away and replaced it with nothing more than a husky whisper. He licked his lips, hoping that would return power to his words, but his mouth was as dry as a vault. His tongue swept cracked lips in vain, and the surgeon, tired of this silly game, returned to his preparation.

"Water," Fitz thought to say. He could wet his mouth and speak so that this butcher would understand him.

A steward appeared alongside the operating table, holding a cotton cloth and a tin can. No. Not water. Chloroform.

Fitz shook his head in desperation as the man soaked the cloth. The cotton threads grew, and the heavy stench of the medicine drifted over Fitz.

"Water!" Fitz cried, loud enough to stop the surgeon and steward.

"Later," the surgeon said, irritated at the interruption.

"Now!" Fitz ordered. The surgeon responded with a flick of his chin at the steward.

It was a different cloth that descended on Fitz. It was heavy with hot water. The steward forced it between his lips and squeezed. It tasted sour but washed the dust from his mouth and replenished his strength. When it was pulled away, Fitz locked eyes with the surgeon. "Don't take my arm."

The surgeon's impatience was compounded by weariness, and he replied in a curt tone, "I may have to. To save your life."

Fitz propped himself up on his right arm, ignoring the searing pain from his wound. He was angry now and fed up with discussing the issue. "Surgeon. Bandage it. Drain it. Bleed it. But leave it attached to the rest of me. It's been at my side for thirty-four years. I've given you an order and by God, you'd better obey."

The surgeon eased Fitz onto the table, giving him a look of disgust. "As you wish, Colonel." He nodded at the steward to continue.

The cloth, stinking of chloroform, covered Fitz's mouth and nose. Before he felt sleep overcome him, he wondered what had become of the army, and his regiment. The rebels— ghostly shapes who rose out of a tangle of trees and fired from fewer than one hundred yards—had flanked them. What happened to the Union regiment on his right? Thomas? Why didn't Thomas protect his flank? Clouds drifted over his mind and the question remained, unanswered.

The Devil had the lowest bid. He and his fellow demons had contracted with the army to ship poor wounded soldiers, in condemned cars, over pitted iron rails that had been hastily laid on gravel roadbeds.

Fitz, like his fellow inmates packed in the crowded ambulance cars, rocked back and forth in agony as the train thundered on its endless journey north. Occasionally a steward would squeeze between the stacks of beds and wipe Fitz's face of soot and sweat, or glance indifferently at his heavily bandaged left arm. Sometimes water was provided, and twice a day broth, and bread for those who could handle the rock-hard substance. When the train stopped, a surgeon would sweep through the car, tossing out rapid-fire orders, and the stewards changed bandages or cleaned wounds or, if the patients were lucky, dispensed lemon halves to each man. Fitz sucked his down greedily, chewing at the pulp and even the bitter rind. If wounded officers are treated this way, Fitz reasoned, then how horrible must conditions be for the common soldier.

Some men died. Fitz would hear a hurried conference of nervous whispers and then several stewards would carry the blanket-covered body down the narrow aisle to the end car.

The stewards talked about the defeats. This general or that general was to blame, and the talk turned against the government and Lincoln. Fitz ordered them to stop that nonsense, but then realized he had not uttered a word. Perhaps he was dreaming.

"Get me water," an officer several beds down ordered. "My leg. Oh, it hurts so. Give me water, won't someone?"

A man across the aisle from Fitz, an officer with yellow skin and sunken eyes, glanced in his direction. "I wish someone would drown that creature." He lifted his head with great effort. "Your arm, eh? Well, you've still got it. I can't get rid of this sickness. I'm through with this war. Through with the army, and Lincoln, too."

Fitz was too weak to talk, but he was tired of the other officer already. He had seen despair creep through the camps, soldiers sullen and despondent because they had fought the enemy and lost. Officers such as the sick one next to him were no help. If they did not discourage the men, they did not encourage them either. The officer continued speaking—the next election would see Lincoln and the Republicans out, let the South have its way—there was no reason for Americans to fight Americans.

Fitz was awake enough to speak. "Shut up, you cowardly creature. If you can't pitch in fully then don't pitch in at all."

"I have a right to an opinion," the officer said.

"Yes, and I have a right to draw a pistol and shoot you,"

Fitz returned. "If you must talk, step out the nearest door and have at it."

The voices died down in response to Fitz's outburst. He felt good. He was a plain-spoken man—much more so than some people liked. Hot-tempered, one officer noted.

Fitz slid in and out of consciousness, gritting his teeth each time the train rattled over a worn rail.

The pain was almost unbearable, but Fitz also struggled with the other trials of being wounded. His body defied him. His wound would not let him turn, seeking a more comfortable position. His bowels refused to function, unless the steward gave him a coarse medicine that rocked his stomach before it produced a watery mix. Lice became his constant companions, hundreds of them. Setting up housekeeping in his bed, crawling over his body, and milling about in the foul mass that covered his bedding. They invaded his bandages, hiding in the wound that protected them from his efforts to dig them out with his dirty fingernails.

The pain never left him. The stewards gave him a teaspoon of a hideous concoction they informed him would help with the pain. It did not. It made him light-headed and filled his brain with warped dreams of Asia, and dead soldiers, and lice gnawing his arm from his body.

He kept his mind focused on Asia Lossing as much as he could. Her name suited her. She was as mysterious as the Orient, he had remarked to her. Yes, she agreed, but not nearly as distant. He took a carnal inventory of her hips, arms, legs, and breasts, and reminded himself of the times that they had shared in her bed. Fitz found himself aroused as he thought of her, and glanced down sheepishly to see if the bulge in his blanket betrayed his thoughts.

I will ask her to marry me, Fitz vowed. She had spoken about marriage before, and he had halfheartedly agreed it was the thing to do. His reluctant response had hurt her, and now he felt guilty he had not asked for her hand then. You must hurry, she had warned him; at thirty I am an old maid. He had surprised himself with his chivalrous response. At any age, Fitz had said, you are beautiful. *I will ask her when I arrive in Washington. If I arrive,* he reminded himself.

The surgeon—another one, not the man who wanted to remove his arm—had told him he would have to spend some time in the hospital. "You won't be able to use your arm for a while," the surgeon had said. He was a major with a thick head of white hair, far too old for his position. But Fitz liked him because he was profane and blunt. They had a great deal in common. "I'll send you up to the Armory Hospital. It's practically within sight of the Capitol." He examined the wound after carefully unwrapping it, and he filled the air with the curious physician's incantations of "mmm"s before scowling at Fitz. "You've given some of our people a hard time, Colonel, but here's my advice to you. Keep your damned mouth shut and do what the doctor tells you. This is a serious wound. We pulled enough lead out of it to build our own cannon. Hear me? Take your medicine and let it heal. Keep it clean. Once a day, new bandages."

Fitz awoke with the shuddering of the car. Men groaned or screamed in pain as shattered bones bit into flesh. Open wounds twisted as the car swayed to a stop, and men cried for stewards, water, or the relief of death. They were someplace in Virginia, Fitz heard one of the stewards comment—a day's journey from Washington. The stale air in the car stank of decay and the corruption of gangrene. Fitz turned his head toward a narrow slit in the car wall; beyond it, the full purity of summer. He saw trees fat with leaves that quaked with life in the faint breeze that teased them and carried into the car.

There was something else, an evil scent that reminded him of the dead carried on the train. He knew the smell—the thick and syrupy stink of flesh decaying, meat falling from bones, maggots swarming over vessels that had once been men.

They were carried off the train on stretchers and laid under tents as white as clouds. Surgeons and stewards moved among the long rows of wounded, replacing bandages, dispensing medicines, and giving the live-saving elixir of water. A male nurse, a gentle man with a bushy beard, slipped a soft hand under Fitz's neck and lifted his head. Fitz felt the smooth lip of a tin cup at his mouth. Cool water ran down his throat, and Fitz begged for more. He was given nearly half a cup, but the nurse stopped.

"The surgeon will have to look you over first, Colonel," the nurse said, guiding Fitz's head to the canvas. "There are some ladies from the Sanitary Commission who will stop by. They will write a letter to your loved ones."

"Washington?" Fitz asked, his mouth dry. He wanted more water. "How far?"

"Sixty miles," the nurse said. He glanced at Fitz's arm.

"How does it look?" Fitz asked, hoping the man would not answer.

The nurse smiled and stood. "The surgeon will be along. I'll come later with more water."

Fitz closed his eyes, sickened at the thought that he might yet lose his arm. He had seen the stacks of limbs near the surgeons' tents. Shattered arms and legs, inarticulate pieces of meat, skin sagging for want of life, streaks of blood still draining from gaping wounds. Marching past the sight for the first time he had thought of hogs scalded and butchered, their parts stacked for salting.

A large woman carrying a stool appeared and, placing herself next to Fitz, pulled a sheaf of papers and a pencil from oversized pockets sewn onto her dress.

She smiled at Fitz, and for an instant he saw a pity in her eyes that said she was looking at a dead man. He calmed himself and forced a smile in return.

"I'm here to write to your loved ones," the woman said, her voice surprisingly childlike. "What is your name?"

Fitz licked his lips. "Colonel Thomas Fitzgerald Dunaway."

"A colonel," she replied, impressed. "To whom shall I address the letter?"

Fitz told her and began an account of his condition. Asia must be informed of his wound and that he was in route to the Armory Hospital. He made light of his condition, hoping his description was not too shocking.

He did not reveal the truth. He was afraid he'd offend the woman scribbling dutifully. He could not bear to trouble Asia. She would know soon enough.

The pain was nearly overwhelming at times, knives piercing his flesh, scraping the muscle from his bone, but he knew if he could only get off that infernal train, he would feel better. He prayed to God that he would. It was an awkward effort; he had few conversations with the Almighty that weren't firmly planted in a string of oaths.

The woman left, assuring Fitz that she would post the letter, and the nurse returned with more water, although not as much as Fitz wanted. The surgeon, some pale balding man with a weak chin, followed. After examining Fitz's arm, he commented, "They'll tend to this in Washington."

Fitz felt hollow as the words echoed through his mind. *They'll tend to this in Washington.*

He awoke, realizing that he was moving. His stretcher was being carried onto a train. He watched with a sense of longing as the cool tents that had housed him for such a short time receded.

Fitz felt the train move steadily, the swaying now reduced from a sharp pitch from side to side to a gentle oscillation, the train calmed by its impending arrival at its destination.

They entered the city in darkness; Fitz was surprised by the rush of lights visible through the louvers. He was alarmed by the city's appearance. Lamps glowed in the darkness; wagons moved about freely, people behaving as if they had nothing to trouble them. He became unaccountably frightened by the disinterest and thought he would be pitched into a hospital and forgotten. His return to Washington plunged him into melancholy. It was no longer a city; it was strange and bewildering landscape of foreign sights.

He counted three changes, yard engines moving cars about, shuttling them to spurs that led to hospitals. He heard men shouting orders as cars were unhitched from the trains, and then the bump as an engine locked into the coupling. His excitement built at each movement, and he desperately wanted to scream at the voices to hurry, for God's sake, hurry. They took their time, however—more evidence that unfeeling dullards populated the city.

The rumble of the large loading door being thrown open frightened Fitz. He was not prepared, and he cried out in alarm, then gratitude. He was relieved, almost giddy, as two soldiers took hold of either end of his stretcher and carried him out into a night of sparkling torches. He wanted to thank them, to pay them for their compassion, but he could not trust himself to speak for fear he would begin crying. He lay still instead, squeezing his eyelids shut and thanking God.

A familiar, high-pitched voice brought him around. His eyes fluttered open. He wondered what time it was, and thought by the slant of the sun's rays through the open windows it must be well after nine o'clock. He caught sight of a black figure standing near the head of his bed, and as he twisted his head to make out who it was, a steward brought a chair over and sat it next to him.

Lincoln sat down in the chair, settling his long legs in the narrow space between the hospital beds. "If it isn't my old friend, Dunaway."

Fitz tried to pull himself up on his pillow.

"No. No," Lincoln said, patting him solidly on the shoulder. "Just lay there and rest easy." A doctor leaned down and whispered something in Lincoln's ear. "I understand you're banged up a bit. You're a young man; you'll come out of it. I did. Got kicked in the head once when I was a boy. Folks gave me up for dead."

"I'll be fine, sir," Fitz managed, hoping that he sounded better than he felt.

"I know you will, Dunaway," Lincoln agreed. "My, you gave me a start. I just stopped in to see how some of the boys were doin', and here you lie."

"I'll be well soon enough, sir," Fitz said. No one was listening to him. All they were doing was staring at his wound. How could people be such dullards? He had to get back to his regiment.

"You need anythin', Dunaway? Has your family been notified?"

Fitz managed a nod.

"You've got to rest up." Lincoln rose, his arms and legs locking into place. He towered over Fitz. "You get well, and we'll find somethin' for you to do. The Union can't afford to lose a fella like you."

Lincoln was gone, leading a pack of officers and doctors down the broad aisle that led out the door. The ward's customary noises returned—men moaning in pain, the clank of bedpans, the whispers of stewards dispensing medicines, the rhythmic squeal as wheelchairs rolled by. As Fitz lay in his bed, staring up at the joists of the whitewashed ceiling, he found the noises of the long ward reassuring. It was the stench of decay, the heavy odor of men's bowels failing them, and the sweet fragrance of blood that frightened him. He knew it was the smell of death.

Asia appeared on the afternoon of his second day in the Officers' Ward at Armory Hospital. Dropping next to his bed and calling his name, she kissed him on the forehead, mouth, and cheek. His tears came so quickly he wasn't prepared. He sobbed, throwing his good arm around Asia, and they rocked each other, finding comfort in the other's presence.

Asia drew back and, caressing his gaunt face, shook her head at his condition. "Oh, Fitz," she said, the tears coming again. "What have you done?"

He laughed, surprising himself, and then a thought struck him. She had not meant it to sound accusatory, but Asia's question had reminded Fitz of his childhood; yet the question wasn't the same.

Fitz's father, upon finding out that his son had no interest in farming, had fixed him with a hard disappointed glare and said, "What will become of you?"

Here it was again—what will become of you? His arm may take months to heal. Or it may never entirely heal. He knew of men whose open wounds still drained blood and pus years after the event.

He would become one of those pathetic old men who marched each Fourth of July, ignoring the taunts of vagrants and children. Or a neighborhood curiosity who droned on about his life in the army until the bored stares of those around him became too much. In short, he would live as an embarrassment.

He could go back to his regiment, if his regiment still existed. He would heal and return to the army and fight the enemy. But perhaps the war was over? Perhaps the mounting casualty lists sickened the nation and the soldiers were so disheartened they simply went home. Maybe the government was not capable of pursuing victory.

No. That couldn't be. Fitz knew brave soldiers and capable officers, and he knew that President Lincoln would never accept defeat.

Fitz was a soldier. There was nothing else to it. Ultimately it was a simple life of simple virtues, one that suited his nature. He fought, and led men in battle, and was well suited to the endeavor. *Goddamn it, Dunaway,* General Yardley had said after Stones River, *you're arrogant and hot-tempered, but I'd give my right arm for a regiment like you.*

The thoughts drifted out of his mind like the early morning autumn fog that rolled over the Tennessee mountains. It was time to stop thinking about anything except the woman he loved.

Fitz smiled at Asia. He would not think of it now. He was home. He was with Asia. He was alive.

Book 1

Chapter 1

Winter 1863
Twelve miles from Wilmington, Delaware

God spoke to Gantter on Tuesday. He thought at first it was Wednesday, but the Baltimore stage had passed him on its way to Wilmington, so he knew it was Tuesday. The people riding in the coach stared at him, disapproving faces, features plucked from the darkness by the vehicle's running lamps until distance and the darkness robbed the travelers of the strange sight of the man that locals called Preacher Jim. He knew he was the target of derision, and he dragged a trail of taunting children behind him on his daily crusade up and down the turnpike. But he was a soldier of God, God's instrument to warn the wicked of the eternal flames of damnation and prod the errant back to church. He set out each morning, long legs carrying a thin chest, spindly arms pumping, worn jacket and baggy trousers whipping in a stiff wind that meant nothing to James Gantter.

Especially after Tuesday.

He sat against the thirty-eight-mile marker, digging through the soiled canvas bag that held beef jerky and five or six apples, the stone fitting nicely into his narrow back. He decided instead to build a fire. The setting sun fell below the distant horizon, taking with it what pitiful heat it had once offered.

Jim was cold, and the Devil told him to go home, but clutching the battered Bible in his thorny hand he vowed to stay two hours more. The Devil lost interest and fled into the failing sun.

Jim was pleased with himself, despite the cutting wind and hands that shook so much with the cold that he could barely strike a flint. He had bested the Devil, and in doing so had proved God's power, which in turn validated his ministry on the Baltimore Turnpike.

He struck the flint a third time and sparks flew into the tiny nest of kindling he had prepared at the base of a dead log. The shavings glowed with hope and then sprang into life with a whisper of Jim's stale breath. He tended the fire carefully, laying dry twigs just so across the struggling flames. The fire was God's reward, he thought; he preached the Gospel and damned the sinners, and made the Devil turn tail and run. The fire stretched, its long fingers spinning tentacles of smoke into the night.

But Jim felt ashamed. He had given in to the Devil by reveling in pride. All that he accomplished was rightfully the Lord's. He stared into the fire, feeling its comforting warmth drive the cold from his aching hands, letting the heat rise to caress his numb face. He had made the fire, but it was God's doing as was all on the earth and in the heavens, so the pride that he had allowed to enter his heart was an effrontery to the Almighty.

Jim brought the heel of his boot down, crushing the life out of his fire. He fought back regret, knowing self-pity would follow close behind. The light was gone and with it the warmth that was a comfort on a miserably cold night. All that remained was the scent of wood smoke, taunting him.

He leaned back against the marker, fighting back the desire to curse himself and the Devil, and the desire to question God's wisdom. He glanced up at the stars, the Almighty's children, seeking guidance. When he saw the three lights, he cocked his head to one side, quizzically.

They glowed, these three lights, with a translucent yellow cast, moving in unison against the blackness. They were not stars; they were too large and did not have the clear shimmering light of winter stars. Jim watched them float toward him, so transfixed that he did not remember getting to his feet or walking into the middle of the turnpike for a better view.

The three yellow lights floated together, yet bobbed playfully, as if leaves sliding over waves. When he realized what they were, his legs failed him, and he fell to his knees.

He clasped his hands together, tears rolling into his greasy beard as three angels of the Lord passed above him. He prayed excitedly, the words running together in a wild stream, his eyes fixed on the angels. Preacher Jim was stunned by the wonder of the sight, filled with reverence and awe so completely that his actions were not initiated by command—he was moved solely by the spirit of the Lord.

The angels disappeared. Jim jumped to his feet, frantically searching the sky, hoping that he would find them again— God rewarding him with just one more glimpse of his wonders. It was God's judgment that the angels came to him, Jim knew. He had known pride, and God had commanded him to banish pride from his heart and smother the fire that had been the creator of pride, and in turn, as God's recognition of Jim's obedience, He had sent His angels.

"Glory, God, hallelujah," Jim said, the words floating away in pale clouds.

There!

He saw them, far away in the sky, their flight casual, unhurried, and God's children. Jim started to follow them, but the spirit of the Lord so gripped him that he could not force more than a few steps from his trembling legs. Emotion paralyzed him. He buried his face in his hands, sobbing in relief and gratitude. God was good, God was good. He had led man on the path of righteousness and, finding man tempted, had sent three angels to proclaim His glory.

When James Gantter raised his eyes toward Heaven to give thanks to the Lord, he vowed that he would rededicate his life in service to God.

He wondered, also, but in a respectful way, should God suspect he was plagued by doubts, why one of the angels had a flaming tail. It was not important, he reasoned. The Lord did as the Lord thought best, and Jim was to accept the miracles of God.

Jim set off for home, imbued with the power of belief, grateful to the Almighty for showing him the way. He marveled over what he had seen and the wondrous nature of the Holy Spirit. A marvel, he decided, and was so lost in the glowing memory of the incident that he forgot the cold, or even that God had made him deny the warmth of a perfectly good fire.

That miracle, his miracle of the angels, would have been enough to carry him for a decade or more in his crusade to save the wicked. But God in his wisdom, knowing that Jim was a product of original sin, and as such, unworthy, provided another glimpse of His power.

A bright light appeared on the horizon, a flash that illuminated objects so far away they had no identity. And then the heavens glowed, and Jim, frozen by the power of God's wrath, heard the voice of the Lord, deep and rumbling, rolling across the earth. The rapture. Lord Almighty had unleashed the thunderbolts to smite those who denied Him and His ways. Jim was witness to Armageddon.

He watched as the horizon pulsated with flames, so consumed by the sight that he forgot to pray. He figured the distance and direction, and was certain what lay under those flames. The knowledge was not troubling, but confusing, although he knew he should never question God's wisdom.

If God was intent on destroying the world, Jim thought, watching the flames spread in the darkness, why did he begin with Wilmington, Delaware?

Chapter 2

The Potomac River
Three miles above Fort Washington

Asia Dunaway. She forgot sometimes that she had been an Allen for many years until her marriage to Henry Lossing, and now she was Mrs. Thomas Fitzgerald Dunaway—the colonel's lady.

They balanced each other, the colonel and his lady. She was as outspoken as he but in a polished manner, taking time to think before she spoke. Many men were intimidated by intelligent women, and Asia had never met one she could not match in intellect. Fitz was different. His outbursts were usually followed by a flash of guilt for being brash and confrontational. He had a quick mind and was pleased when Asia bested him in trading quips, although he accepted her victory with a growl. They were honest with each other. That is, they had been until now.

She glanced over her shoulder, watching her husband navigate the crowded passageway between the steam engine and the launch's hull, making his way aft to speak to the able seaman at the tiller. Fitz was careful to keep his left arm close to his chest, the limb heavily bandaged, suspended in a gleaming white sling. She insisted on changing his bandages twice a day, discarding the fabric soiled with a light brown wash of blood but without, thank God, the stench of decay. Colonel Dunaway had been fortunate, the elderly surgeon at the Armory Hospital had told her—so many men with such wounds lose the arm, or their lives.

She pulled her purse open by its drawstrings, shielding her actions from Fitz. Asia was ashamed, wanting to tell Fitz, wanting to make him understand, and hoping to share the burden that lay on her heart from the letter in her purse. He was her husband, and a good man. She turned. Fitz and the seaman were deep shadows under the canvas awning of the steam launch, protected from the stiff gusts that whipped the river's waters into rippling whitecaps. It was cool, with a sharp wind despite the glaring sun in a crisp blue sky, and Asia fumbled with the letter.

She read the words again, foolishly hoping the angry message had changed, and the despair, that had clenched her stomach in a vise, was unfounded. The shock she had felt as she sat in the parlor, puzzling over the return name and address as she opened the letter, her eyes falling on the contents, had long since faded. It was replaced by the dull ache of knowing she was powerless to help him as she had in the past.

The steam engine's gentle chug kept pace with the words that jumped from the page, each piercing her breast. She angrily crumpled the letter, but dropped her head in regret. She could not abandon him. She smoothed the wrinkled paper on her lap, folded it, and slipped it into her purse, once more making sure that Fitz could not see her.

"Well, Mrs. Dunaway." Fitz's voice startled her. "Are you enjoying your regatta?" He sat next to her, easing his wounded arm into a comfortable position. He was still gaunt, but his skin had lost its sickly pallor. His sudden appearance filled her with guilt. She struggled to speak.

"I don't know if 'regatta' is the word, Colonel Dunaway, but I am enjoying myself."

He grew alarmed. "Why, my dear, have you been crying? Have I done something?" He was solicitous, if clumsy with expressing himself, Asia knew, and was apt to lose his temper with matters that he did not understand.

She had been crying, Asia realized. "Oh," she said, removing a silk handkerchief from her sleeve. "It is the wind. It is a blustery day."

"It is," Fitz agreed. "But the seaman tells me we should have the vessel in sight at any moment. I would have preferred meeting the president in Washington rather than taking this boat trip. There." He examined her eyes as she slipped the handkerchief back into the cuff of her sleeve. "Still a bit red, but not teary-eyed." He shifted his arm again, wincing. "I can't seem to find a position that works."

"Let me see," Asia said, pulling the sling to one side with care.

"Asia," Fitz whispered in alarm. He looked aft. "I can't have you pawing after me where that fellow can see. It's indecent."

"Fitz. I'm well north of the equator. It's evident you are in pain. Now quit bouncing about."

"Of course I'm in pain," Fitz said. "I've been shot. And the cold causes my arm to ache. And I'm sure that being on the water is of no help."

She looked at him patiently. "Are you done, Colonel Dunaway? If so, kindly assist me by closing your mouth while I examine your wound."

Fitz turned his head away, waiting as Asia delicately pulled the sling from his arm and eased the bandages to one side.

"You're bleeding again." She was trying to control her emotions, but it was obvious she was frightened.

"The surgeon said to expect—" he began, hoping he could convince her that her concern was unwarranted, but she cut him off.

"The bleeding has increased. It's dark and thick." She held up her hand, her eyes betraying fear. She removed her gloves, straightened the bandages, and withdrew her hands. Her fingers were smudged with blood—they were strangely vibrant under the muted shadow of the canvas awning.

Fitz shook his head, dismissing both her evidence and alarm. He pulled the bandages and sling back into place and was about to tell her it was nothing when he saw an island in the middle of the Potomac River.

"Good Lord," he exclaimed, forgetting his wound. It was a ship, a double-turreted monitor—a long, black vessel that stretched halfway across the green river. An island all right, but one of rust-streaked iron and oak timbers as thick as a man's body. Her two turrets, topped by conical canvas awnings that gave them the exotic look of Chinese pagodas, shared the low deck with a delicate platform of railings and ladders, wrapped around a squat smokestack. A column of brown smoke drifted from the stack, only to be snatched by the wind and carried across the river.

Fitz turned to Asia to find her as awed as he at the sight. "She is majestic," Asia said.

"Only a woman would declare a warship thus," Fitz said.

"Yet warships are always referred to as 'she,' " Asia returned. "Why is that, my dear husband?"

"I refuse to answer, wife," Fitz said. "I'm calculating." He squinted, using the height of a nearby river bluff as a measuring stick. "She is two hundred to two hundred and fifty feet from end to end."

" 'She,' " Asia said.

"We will come round to her starboard side," the helmsman called out. "Kindly wait till we're tied off before you board her."

Fitz watched sailors moving into position as the faint commands of officers traveled over the choppy water. She was an island unto herself—a hunk of iron moored in the middle of the Potomac, several hundred seagulls swooping above her, chattering for attention. The *Alchemist*, Lincoln's note had said. *I will be aboard the navy's newest acquisition—come see me immediately. I need you.*

I need you. Lincoln's words surfaced in Fitz's mind as the steam launch approached the ironclad. Fitz's response had been a muttered "Thank God." He cherished his time with

Asia, and his chest grew tight with pride when he introduced her to the many visitors to the boarding house as "my wife." But he soon tired of the endless calls of politicians and well-wishers, and the silver salver mounded nearly to its rim with calling cards. "The Secretary of State visited this morning at 10:00 AM and would be pleased if Colonel and Mrs. Dunaway would accompany the Secretary and Miss Fanny Seward to the play this Friday night." "The Honorable Thaddeus Stevens requests the presence of Colonel and Mrs. Dunaway at dinner the 14th inst. At 8:00 PM."

It was all Lincoln's doing. It was the president who gave Fitz his regiment and Mr. Lincoln who led the crowd to the Lossing Boarding House to inquire after Colonel Dunaway's health. Fitz saw it well enough. People made a show of concern for him because the president had. Lincoln was sincere—the others were pleasant because they thought it required of them.

He loathed the social requirements of being a hero, partly because his wound troubled him, but mostly because he couldn't stand people fawning over him. Then came Lincoln's note—*I need you.* Thank God there was something to do besides listen to fat politicians spout platitudes.

Fitz felt Asia at his side as he read the note at their home on 20th Street. He sensed her reluctance. "I shall go and speak to him and that is that," he said. He already knew of her fears.

"What if he sends you on a mission? Your health will not permit it."

"The Washington cliff dwellers do not encourage me remaining," Fitz said, and regretted it.

He began to suspect that marriage required a good husband to consider his words before he said them. No—that was unkind. Asia was frightened. It was a bad wound.

"My dear," he said, finding that his love for Asia gave him patience and a surprising gentleness. "I must have something to occupy me. You have tended to my every need, and there is nowhere I would rather be than at your side, but I swear I will go mad if I don't have at least a trifling duty to attend to."

He folded the note, slipped it into his pocket, and took his wife's hand, leading her to dinner.

The boat nestled against the hull of the ironclad, amidships, coming to rest alongside a rank of smartly uniformed sailors.

A burly officer extended an arm from the ironclad's deck. "Your hand, Mrs. Dunaway." He assisted Asia as she stepped from the launch to the iron deck and under the shadow of a canvas awning.

Fitz waved away the proffered hand, steadied himself, and made a short hop to the deck. The movement jarred his arm, and he clamped his eyes shut as waves of pain rolled over him. He opened them in time to return the deck officer's salute. Asia's hand slid into the crook of his right arm, and he felt her squeeze his forearm in reassurance. He hoped that she hadn't seen how much pain he was in.

"The president is this way," a heavily bearded officer said.

Fitz and Asia followed him, passing the massive forward turret, its iron plates pinned in place by rivets as large as a man's fist. Two fifteen-inch cannon poked their ugly snouts from gun ports. Under a broad awning covering the forward section of the ship, they found President Lincoln in deep conversation with a naval officer. The president smiled when he saw them.

"Why here is Dunaway, and his lovely wife," Lincoln said, striding forward, his broad hand seeking Fitz's.

"Mr. President," Fitz said, letting his hand slide into Lincoln's. For once Lincoln's grip was gentle, the handshake restrained. Fitz was relieved. "May I present Mrs. Dunaway."

"You may indeed," Lincoln responded with a stiff bow. "This is Dahlgren." The navy officer approached. He was thin, his face dark and covered with wrinkles, and he was impassive, Fitz noted—strangely like the vessel on whose deck they stood.

"Your wound, Dunaway?" Lincoln inquired.

"Healing well, sir," Fitz said.

"Good, good," Lincoln said. There was an awkward pause before he continued. "Dahlgren? Will you escort Mrs. Dunaway—"

"Mr. President," Asia said, her interruption as seamless as if it had never happened. "I must inquire what you intend to do with my husband—"

"Asia, please," Fitz said.

Her tone was playful, but there was an unyielding nature to it. "I am quite certain he is as valuable to me as he is to the country."

Lincoln looked thoughtful. "Well, you've got me there."

"So you will pardon me for insisting, respectfully, that wherever you dispatch my husband, so too must you send me." Lincoln and Asia were smiling at one another. It was a contest skillfully cloaked in a light jest. Fitz was about to speak when Asia stopped him with a sharp look. "I have invested too much time in Colonel Dunaway's recovery to see him jeopardize his life on a hazardous mission for you." She settled herself and added, "I look ghastly in black."

"God grant me the forbearance needed by all husbands," Fitz said.

"No, no, Dunaway," Lincoln conceded. "The lady's right. You are valuable to me, but more so to Mrs. Dunaway. Although, I hope you don't think me too bold to remark that any color would suit you."

"Why, your excellency"—Asia smiled—"what a charming thing to say. Many men would be well served to take a lesson in flattery from you." She shot a meaningful glance at Fitz. She was teasing him, and it pleased him. Lately she had fallen into dark moods—becoming pensive and reluctant. He assumed it was something he had done or said, and he grew sullen at her reluctance to answer his questions. Sparkling, he had once described her manner—her green eyes flashing, her soft features framed by auburn hair. Her quick wit, each barb accompanied by the ghost of a smile. But she had changed.

"Dahlgren," Lincoln said. "Stay close by to see that I get

everything just right. Colonel, have you ever been to Wilmington?"

"Delaware," Dahlgren clarified. "The DuPont Works."

"I have not," Fitz said.

"The powder works," Lincoln continued. "Mighty important to us. So important we got a regiment up there whose only job is to mind the place. Keep Confederate agents away."

"They didn't," Dahlgren said.

"No," Lincoln said, "they didn't. They had an explosion up there the other night. Lost a quantity of powder, powder we can't afford to lose, and several buildings. That'll cut down on production. The folks at DuPont said they could make it up. They've got a place up in Pennsylvania. That's their problem. My problem, and yours, Dunaway, is to find out what happened."

"Are you sure it was the work of Confederate agents?" Fitz said.

"Pretty sure," Lincoln said. "I'm not telling you all I know, Dunaway, because I want you to go up there with a clear mind. Talk to the DuPont people and the army folks up there and let me know what you find out. I hate to be mysterious, Dunaway, but you'll have to trust me on this."

"That powder was consigned to the navy," Dahlgren said. "Powder is hard to come by, Colonel. We can't afford to lose even an ounce of it. We're sending our man to Wilmington." He spoke as if he were in a hurry to be heard. Or, Fitz thought, to make sure that the navy was well represented in this endeavor. Perhaps he had little confidence in the army. "Phillip Abbott," Dahlgren continued. "He's one of the navy's best men. You've heard of him, of course?"

It gave Fitz a hint of satisfaction to say, "No."

Dahlgren was nonplussed at Fitz's reply. "Brilliant man. Just brilliant. Master inventor. He is responsible for the improvements to Ericsson's original design."

"Indeed?" Fitz said. "Who is Ericsson?"

"Of *Monitor* fame," Asia explained to Fitz. "Colonel Dunaway feels it best not to trouble his mind with surplus information."

Fitz suppressed a smile. He missed her biting humor, even if it was directed at him.

"Our ironclad fleet," Dahlgren said, "owes much to Professor Abbott. This vessel is a product of his. There is no subject the man cannot conquer. I am confident that his investigation will reveal the truth behind the DuPont incident."

"Go up there, Colonel Dunaway." Lincoln smiled at Asia. "In the company of your lovely wife, of course, and keep in touch by telegraph. I need to know what you learn. Wear the wires out, Colonel, no matter how insignificant the matter may seem." He took Asia's hand in his with all the affection of a father. "You must take care of our colonel, Mrs. Dunaway, but you must look after yourself as well."

"I? Mr. Lincoln," Asia said, surprised.

The tall man, towering over Asia, leaned close to her. "Something troubles you, Mrs. Dunaway. Remember that you must be your own best friend. I hate to see such lovely eyes filled with sadness."

Chapter 3

The Laconte Theatre
Quebec City, British Canada

The audience exploded in applause as the curtain rose for the third encore. Shouts of *bravo, magnificent,* and *brilliant* delivered in a confused mixture of French and English showered the actors. They clasped hands. Othello, his dark skin glistening with sweat in the harsh footlights, radiated majesty. Desdemona, arrogant, her alabaster breasts swelling about her low-cut bodice, swept the first few rows for her next likely conquest. "Royal and Victoria January, the brightest stars in the galaxy of actors," the critic of the *New York Herald* gushed. To others, the Januarys were devils.

"The finest swordsman the stage had ever seen," John Wilkes Booth had taunted him. Booth was drunk, and he became a madman when he was drinking, surly and vindictive. He had followed Royal January and members of the company into a tavern just off Broadway one evening.

January, surrounded by his friends, had lifted his glass in return. "I'm glad that you recognize your betters, John. Now go away and let us celebrate our triumph."

The insults were too much for John Wilkes Booth. "Better?" He staggered forward, his eyes flashing in rage. "You're a charlatan, January. A rank amateur." He kicked a table to one side as he advanced. Some of the actors stepped back.

"The handsomest man in America," January had said. "Isn't that what someone said of you? My how the drink has taken its toll. Your youth, ability." He waited to gauge the impact of his words. "Tell me, John, can you still handle a sword? Or has yours been permanently sheathed?"

Booth had waved his cane at January like an imaginary sword. "I can still spit a pig." Two men had quickly grabbed Booth's arms, holding him back.

"Let him go," January had said, reveling in the opportunity. He selected a man's walking stick with, "May I?" and tested its weight and balance. He had slashed the air several times, taunting Booth, and lowered the walking stick in his direction, challenging the actor.

Booth had broke free of his captors, removed his coat, and seizing his own walking stick, took a final drink from his glass and advanced toward January. Chairs and tables had been pulled to one side, clearing an arena of sorts, while the tavern keeper's shrill protests were ignored.

The two actors approached one another.

"I've had your sister," Booth had said, his breath hot with alcohol and rage.

"Indeed?" January had said. "She told me you did not rise to the performance."

Booth pushed January back with a shout, twisted the handle of his walking stick, and withdrew a sword from the cane scabbard. He had brandished it at January amid shouts from the other actors, begging both men to stop the fight.

"Mr. January?" A young man January recognized as an understudy had pushed his way through the crowd and tossed him a sword cane. January smiled his thanks, withdrew the blade, and prepared himself for Booth's attack. The other actor had lunged at January's chest, withdrew, circled to the right, and lunged again. The crowd fell back, forming a rough circle. Booth attacked again, and January parried the blade, following with a riposte and then a feint to the left.

Booth had still been drunk, or near drunk, but he was still dangerous. January edged to the right, keeping well clear of the other man's blade. His opponent was reckless, mad some people thought, and that made him violent.

"Do you have a wager on the contest?" January had asked the understudy. Robert. His name was Robert Owen—an earnest boy. "Put your money on me, Robert." January struck at Booth, who stumbled away from the sword point, colliding with a chair. He kicked the furniture out of his way and returned the blow. It had been an awkward response, and he lost his balance. Some of Booth's companions had pleaded with him to sheath his sword, and one man attempted to insert himself between the two combatants, hoping to reason with them. Enraged, Booth slashed at him and then pushed him aside, rushing for the kill. January had waited a moment to gauge Booth's action, pivoted, and brought the flat of the blade across the back of his attacker's hand. Booth cried out in pain as his sword clattered to the floor. He cradled the back of his hand and stooped to pick up his weapon, when January slid the tip of his sword under Booth's chin.

"I believe the event has been settled," January had said. The other man glared up at him, his eyes dark pools of rage and humiliation. John Wilkes Booth stood, and nodded. His friends rushed in and pulled him away to safety. January had turned to find Owen at his side, sharing in the actor's triumph.

"Your sword, Mr. Owen," January had said, returning the weapon. "I am at your service."

Royal January now bowed again, basking in the admiration of the audience. His sister curtsied deeply.

"For God's sake, must you show everyone your breasts?" he muttered under his breath.

"They must have something to entertain them," Victoria January smiled, rising. "Your performance tonight had little to offer."

The curtain descended and the other actors made their way off the stage, leaving the principles to their applause.

January wasn't done with his sister. "You could have been reading your lines, for all the passion you generated."

The curtain rose and January extended his forearm, leading Victoria downstage.

"Perhaps I should learn to garble my words," she smiled, offering her slender hand as a parting token to the audience. "I thought at first you were speaking an unknown tongue."

The manager of the house appeared and presented a bouquet of yellow roses to Victoria in appreciation, stood back, and led the audience in another round of applause.

"What about your clumsy efforts to upstage me?" January said through a tight smile. "You behaved like a rank amateur tonight. It was positively pathetic." He bowed once more, sensed the applause waning, and with his sister on his arm, withdrew as the curtain descended.

Victoria dropped the bouquet on the floor and broke free of her brother's arm. She crossed backstage and entered her dressing room. Royal January pushed his way through the stagehands and actors for his dressing room.

A young actor stepped in front of January and proclaimed in a burst of admiration, "Sir? Sir? Magnificent. Amazing."

January's cold eyes searched for the stage manager as he sidestepped the actor.

"I cannot tell you how much this performance means to me. To be a member of your company, sir."

January lost his patience. "Jessup?" The stage manager appeared. "How many times must I tell you? How can I state it other than to plainly say I will not be approached by anyone before or after a performance?"

"I'm sorry, Mr. January," Jessup said, trying to drag the young man away.

"But you're my idol," the shocked actor said. He was betrayed, his golden moment was really brass. "The greatest living American actor."

"Get him away from me," January ordered Jessup. "Out of my sight, out of this theater, out of this company. Do you understand?"

January disappeared into his dressing room as Jessup led the shattered young man away.

"But I wanted to tell him. Didn't he understand?"

Jessup tried to ease the actor's pain. "He understands only what he wants, and nothing else, boy. The world is a stage for Royal and Victoria January, and we are merely players."

January sat at his makeup table, fuming over his sister's performance, worse still her inability to recognize how slovenly she was. Her pale efforts poisoned his, undermining all that he attempted to give to the audience. He poured a glass of whiskey, downed half of it, and went to the door that adjoined his dressing room with his sister's.

He threw it open with a bang. She spun to face him, just closing a silk robe over her bodice. "Get out!" she demanded.

He was gratified to see she feared him. "We're not finished yet."

"I will call for the manager—"

But before she could say anything else he had her pinned in his arm, his mouth covering her. She fought his advance, struggling to break free, but the firmness of her full breasts against his chest and her resistance only inflamed him. He felt her hands seeking him, her fingernails clawing at the bulge in his costume. She returned his kisses, each one a mounting explosion.

January pushed her onto a divan, tore away his heavy costume, and freed his swollen penis. Dropping to his knees, he pulled out the dagger used in the performance, slipped it under the silk ribbons securing Victoria's bodice, and with an upward sweep released her breasts from their confinement.

She parted her legs, readying herself, and said, as if in a dream, "Slowly, my lord. Oh, so slowly."

Chapter 4

Eleutherian Mills
Near Wilmington, Delaware

Major Bloom was a liar, Fitz thought. Or at the very least he was doing a very poor job of avoiding the truth. The major had met Fitz and Asia at the Hagley Yard of the E. I. du Pont de Nemours and Company site on Brandywine Creek. The meeting had started badly with Bloom being disagreeable about Asia's presence.

Fitz silenced him with a curt, "She is not your wife but mine. And even I do not presume to tell her where she may or may not go."

Bloom relented, either because Fitz outranked him and carried a warrant from the president or because Asia's cold gaze caused him to reconsider his position.

"Very well," Bloom had grumbled, "but this is a dangerous place and I will not be held accountable for her."

"No," Fitz said. "That is why *I* married her. Has a man from the Navy Department named Abbott arrived?"

"Not to my knowledge," Bloom said.

They traveled a short distance in a carriage to the scene of the explosion. Fitz smelled the desolation before the vehicle stopped. It was the heavy stench of burned wood, and damp earth mixed with the sharp, stinging scent of fired powder.

When the carriage stopped Fitz was first to dismount. He said nothing as he surveyed the destruction. All that remained of the three buildings were charred timbers jutting from mounds of shattered bricks. The steady pillars of smoke that floated into the afternoon sky and the remnants of fires that glowed within the rubble reinforced the notion.

As Fitz studied the macabre landscape, Bloom spoke, stacking explanations and observations atop one another so effortlessly that no seams were apparent in his conclusion.

"One of the workmen was smoking," Bloom said. "There are several hundred here, and you don't expect a man to be denied a cigar. There were no rebel agents." He laughed at the thought, adding, "For God's sake, Colonel, this entire area is safeguarded by the 178th Michigan."

"You command the regiment?" Fitz asked.

The question startled Bloom. "What? No, sir. Colonel Greenwood."

"I would expect Colonel Greenwood to have met us with his explanation," Fitz said. "Where is he?"

Bloom grew defensive. "Called away, sir. Important business."

"Gentlemen." A man hurried toward them. Seeing Asia, he amended his greeting. "Oh. My apologies, madam." He removed his hat, and nodded in place of a bow. "I am Kinnane, the mill manager."

Bloom introduced Fitz and Asia but did not continue explaining his theory.

Fitz spoke to Asia, to spite Bloom. "That makes perfect sense, doesn't it, my dear? A moment of inattention, an unguarded flame, a clumsy attempt to light a cigar?"

Kinnane's eye's widened before he blurted, "What is this? What are you implying, sir? What have you told them, Major Bloom?"

"I?" Bloom said, offering the appropriate amount of innocence.

"A workman's doing," Asia said. She aimed her charms at Bloom. "Isn't that what you said, Major? Oh, silly me. My woman's brain is often unable to grasp such complex theories, but I believe, Mr. Kinnane, the good major plans to lay this fiasco at your feet." She cocked her head to one side, as if she had just noticed something. "You were a lawyer before the war, weren't you, Major Bloom?"

Bloom's face reddened. "What of it?"

"I've spent my life among lawyers, Major Bloom," Asia said. Her tone was cool. "I can tell when a lawyer is forced to argue a weak case."

"Bloom," Fitz warned the major. "Do not banter words with my wife. She has a sharp mind and a quick wit. I can testify to those traits personally." He turned his attention to Kinnane. "What happened?"

The mill manager, relieved to have his chance to talk, barely drew a breath before the words tumbled out. "The fire started there, at the Number Two shed, I think amid the wagons ready to be loaded."

Fitz saw a string of bright red enclosed wagons in the distance, the du Pont name painted in gold letters over the word *explosives.* A driver sat under a shelf that extended from the roof of the wagon. "Like those?"

"Yes. Yes," Kinnane said. "We're very careful." He tossed Bloom an accusing glance. "Our men are very careful. They know what one spark will do. The buildings are well separated to prevent incidents such as this. One building setting fire to another."

"And yet it happened?" Fitz said.

The idea puzzled Kinnane. "Yes." He looked over the rubble. "But I don't know how. Unless the fires were set at once."

"But the major assures me the mill is safe," Fitz said. "Surrounded by a regiment from Michigan." Kinnane had no response, so Fitz continued. "It was either an accident or the work of traitors. Why are you reluctant to offer any details, Mr. Kinnane?"

Kinnane hesitated. "We had a report, you see. A very puzzling event. I did my very best to investigate the explosion, but—" He decided on a solution. "We must speak to Gideon."

A large black man sat on an upturned bucket in the shadow of a drab, brick building, wrapping a soiled bandage around his hand. He stood when he saw the party approach, touching his knuckles to his forehead in salute.

"Hello, Mr. Kinnane," he said in an English accent. He moved his bandaged hand behind his back.

"Mr. Gideon," Kinnane said. "This is Colonel and Mrs. Dunaway." A moment passed before he was compelled to add, "This is Major Bloom."

Bloom was incredulous. "A nigger? We bring this incident to a nigger?"

"Mr. Gideon knows more about powder than virtually anyone here. Mr. du Pont himself has said as much."

Bloom turned to Fitz, outraged. "Colonel, surely you cannot place any value on the word of a common nigger. He could be the very cause of this horrible accident. Look at his hand. Show us your hand, boy. I'll wager it's burned."

"Major," Fitz said. "Shut up."

"I beg your pardon, Colonel. I see no reason—"

"It's because you're ignorant," Asia explained. "That is the reason."

Bloom stiffened but remained silent. Gideon had been examining his injured hand while the conversation took place, waiting for an appropriate moment to speak.

"I caught it on a bit of iron," he said, offering his hand to Bloom. "But you may look it over if you must."

"What can you tell us about the explosion?" Fitz asked.

"We had the line ready," Gideon said. "Six wagons. Three and three. That is to say, three up to be loaded and three well back on the off chance that an accident occurs. One can never be too safe in dealing with explosives. The first set had been loaded, and the driver took them one hundred yards from Building Number Two."

"That is how we load and transport the powder through town," Kinnane said. "The wagoneers are steady hands."

"What could you possibly know about explosives?" Bloom asked.

"I was nearly a decade a gunner in the Royal Navy," Gideon said. He returned to his account. "I came down the line and handed each driver two copies of the bill of lading. I had just signaled for the first wagon of the second set to move forward, when I noticed a glow in the night sky."

"See! See," Bloom said. "A cigar, no doubt. Or someone trying to keep warm. It was near midnight, wasn't it? And very cold out?"

"It was," Gideon said. He remained polite despite Bloom's interruption. "A cold night. But closer to ten. The glow, a yellow light, came from above."

"A lantern, then," Bloom tried. "A clumsy attempt to illuminate the area."

"Above me, sir," Gideon said. "From the sky."

Bloom was stunned into silence, giving Fitz time to speak. "Explain yourself."

"Sparks," Gideon said, searching his memory. "A stream of fire. Like wax dripping. The first wagon of the second set caught fire near the tailgate. Then the roof of Number Two. Bill Ward was driving the wagon and he must have seen the fire because he whipped his horses into a gallop, away from the building and the other wagons. His wagon exploded about fifty yards from the building. I was knocked to the earth but arose in time to see the building on fire. There was another explosion, and I was blown clear."

"Fire from the sky," Bloom said.

"Major Bloom," Fitz said, taking the officer by the shoulder and leading him away from the group, "a word with you, please." He placed himself between the others and the startled major, and kept his voice low. "This is what I think. I think your Colonel Greenwood knows damned well that this is somehow the work of Confederate agents, and rather than take the responsibility, he has excused himself from the scene. I further think that you are here deflecting any accusation that your colonel's incompetence, or the entire regiment's for all I know, led to this catastrophe."

"Colonel! I must protest."

"I carry a warrant from President Lincoln," Fitz said, fighting to control his anger, "with instructions to determine the cause of the explosion. Your actions indicate you haven't the slightest idea what happened, but you will make certain to lay the blame at someone else's feet. I don't have that luxury. This is what I recommend. Go away. Go away now, go far from my sight."

All Bloom managed was, "Sir?"

Fitz sighed in exasperation. "For God's sake, man, are you that thick? Leave now, or I will shoot you." Fitz returned to the group.

"I do hope you weren't too harsh with him, dear," Asia said. She smiled at Gideon and Kinnane. "The colonel and civility are distant cousins."

Fitz slid his arm carefully from the sling, lifted the fabric over his head, and handed it to Asia. Unbuttoning his tunic, he slipped his arm in, settling it in place. "Your bandage needs replacing, Mr. Gideon. If you don't keep burns aired out they will putrefy."

"Burns?" Kinnane said in shock. "I thought you told the major—"

"He was irritating me, Mr. Kinnane," Gideon said, dropping his bandage in the dirt. He allowed Asia to dress his burn with the sling.

"The fire?" Fitz prodded.

Gideon winced as Asia tied off the bandage with an apologetic glance. "I haven't seen anything to compare to it in twenty years. I was a boy, on H.M.S. *Hesperus*. We were in a gale off the Land of Fire. Between the wind and heavy swells we were all convinced the sea would swallow us. I heard the men shouting, and then an able seaman next to me cried out, pointing to the rigging. The sheets and spars were ablaze, glowing in the darkness like a fiery cross of old. I was struck dumb, and could do nothing but watch the flames leap from spar to mast, race down the ratlines and sheets, covering everything aboard that good ship."

"Saint Elmo's Fire," Fitz said.

"It was," Gideon confirmed. "Harmless, but a frightening event nevertheless. Especially for poor, ignorant seamen in times of peril."

"But this fire?"

"From the heavens as well," Gideon said. "But terrible. It flowed like the other, but there was heat to it." He sought a way to explain. "It appeared to be raining fire."

"Could someone have gotten close enough to throw a bomb? Or an infernal engine of some sort?"

Gideon gave the question careful thought before answering. "No, sir. These buildings are spaced apart. Each set is surrounded by an earthen bank. Where I was, at Number Two, I could see everything. It was a clear sky. The fire came down, straight down from the sky. A giant could have been pouring molten lava from his boot." He dug in his pocket, remembering something. He pulled out a scrap of fabric and handed it to Fitz. "I found this a short distance from Number Two."

Fitz took it. It was a bit of silk, no larger than his palm, scorched around the edges. Its surface was smooth, and almost liquid in its texture, but the odd thing was its reverse. It was coated with something that was tacky. He put the fabric to his nose. Fumes from the silk stung his eyes, and the stench was that of machines. He looked at Gideon, seeking an explanation.

"That has no business on these grounds, sir. It's not the remains of a powder bag."

"I hope you have an explanation, Colonel Dunaway?" Kinnane said.

"I have a speculation," Fitz said. "But it doesn't make any sense."

"Don't be modest, Fitz," Asia said. "We have more than our share of mysteries here. Let us hear your theory."

"Arrows," Fitz said. "I've seen Indians use flaming arrows to fire prairie. They fire them nearly straight in the air. They travel in a high arc, on their target." It was obvious that the others weren't convinced. Fitz understood their reluctance—they thought the idea just shy of ridiculous, but he had nothing else to offer. "Let us not waste time talking about Indians and flaming arrows. I hope that Mr. Abbott, when he finally appears, will condescend to give us his opinion. He should have been here by now."

"Don't belittle the navy, Colonel Dunaway," Asia said.

"They are not punctual. To me that means unreliable. Unreliable and unseemly."

Asia smiled. "Be patient, dear. Not everyone is fortunate enough to be as infallible as you."

Fitz noticed an army courier riding toward them. The soldier called, "Colonel Dunaway?" as he stopped his horse.

"Yes?"

The soldier pulled a folded dispatch from his tunic and handed it to Fitz. "From Washington, sir. The War Department."

Fitz took the message, stepped away from the others, and read it. He slipped the message into his coat, nodded to the messenger that he was dismissed, and turned to the others.

"Phillip Abbott has disappeared," he said.

Chapter 5

The President's Office
Washington, DC

"Stanton," Lincoln advised his Secretary of War, "if you don't settle down you'll contract apoplexy."

The gnomelike man with a jutting gray beard answered with an enraged glance. Secretary of the Navy Welles sat at the long cabinet table, surreptitiously sliding the blunt end of a pencil under his full wig to chase an itch. Seward lounged at the far end. The Secretary of State enjoyed watching Stanton sputter around the table, throwing off excitement like sparks from a fireworks display.

"This is a catastrophe, Mr. Lincoln," Stanton cried in frustration.

Seward lit a cigar, leisurely waving the match back and forth just to watch the dancing flame. Stanton hadn't learned the secret of handling Lincoln. The Secretary of War exploded about every subject until just the sight of his demonstrations wore everyone out. Lincoln remained calm. Even when Lincoln was not calm, he remained calm. Often the president would pull out a volume of humorous stories, read out loud for a bit, and then chuckle.

"The finest mind we possess—" Stanton listed the extent

of the disaster "—equal to Ericsson in his ability to design ironclads—"

"I shouldn't let Mr. Ericsson hear that if I were you," Welles said, his eyes rolling back in ecstasy as he found the source of his torment. He worked the pencil feverishly, dislodging the wig.

"He has been gone a month," Stanton snapped.

"How is it that we are just finding this out now?" Seward said. He prepared himself for Stanton's onslaught.

Surprisingly, Stanton dropped into a chair, exhausted. "Abbott is a difficult man. Temperamental. Irascible. He is also an expert on everything. Guns, ships, powder—anything he turns his mind to."

"Well then, Mars? What can the rebels make of him?" Lincoln asked, willing to talk now that Stanton had calmed down. He knew his Secretary of War hated the nickname.

"I don't know," Stanton returned curtly. He was submerged in defeat.

"What can *he* make of the rebels?" Seward asked, standing. "He has a remarkable mind, and the ability to turn it to any subject under the sun. He knows our secrets because he was there at their birth."

Welles tossed the pencil on the table. It rolled to a stop against a sheaf of papers. "Midwife to every one of them," he said, following the analogy. "Whatever Ericsson designed, Abbott made better. My concern is beyond that the rebels have our man—"

"Isn't that bad enough?" Stanton said.

"It's—did he go to them willingly?"

"Well," Lincoln said, intrigued by the idea. "I'd like to hear more, Welles."

Seward was impressed—he'd almost considered Gideon Welles nothing more than a capable government employee. Now he showed flashes of insight that revealed a fine mind at work behind those dull eyes.

"Abbott is a madman," Welles said. "He's made it known

to me that other men are constantly at work to steal his ideas. He is convinced that others, Ericsson included, are plotting his downfall. He is virtually impossible to deal with unless he receives the glory he feels is rightfully due him. We've given him everything we could, and still he demands more."

"Not a Union man," Seward observed wryly.

"Not any sort of man except his own. I truly believe if the rebels offered to proclaim him Caesar, he would turn Confederate in an instant."

"Good God!" Stanton exclaimed. "Have you ever seen such vanity?"

"Not outside of this room," Seward quipped.

"Is it as bad as you let on?" Lincoln asked of everyone, turning the subject back to its origin. Seward noticed that some of the levity had gone out of Lincoln's voice.

"It is," Welles said, "if the man has gone over to the rebels. They cannot match our manufacturing, but they have shown themselves to be highly innovative. *Virginia* demonstrated that."

"*If* he has gone over," Stanton said.

"That reminds me of the story of the man on his way to the gallows," Lincoln said. He ignored Stanton's groan. " 'If I go willingly, or put up a fuss,' the man said, 'I'll be just as hanged.' "

Stanton lost his patience. "Yes, Mr. President, but this is a damned sight more serious than a hanging."

Seward burst out in laughter, followed by Welles. Stanton, angered by their response, stomped off to one corner of the room in defeat.

Lincoln smiled, but the emotion faded. "Come back to us, Stanton. No offense was meant."

The Secretary of War spun around. "This is bad business, Lincoln, and it's no time for stories. That man has secrets locked in his head that can do the nation great harm. Welles knows that. Or at least he ought to."

"What do you propose?" Seward asked.

"Find him, and be quick about it," Stanton returned.

"It's reported he's gone to Canada," Welles said. "Quebec City."

"My God," Stanton gasped. "He's in the clutches of those rebels already."

"No," Welles said. "His family has a lodge or something up there. On the St. Lawrence. Every time his feelings are hurt he flies north, vowing never to return."

"Now the British are involved," Stanton said. "Goddamn their meddling in American business." He turned on Seward. "You ought to begin diplomatic action to have him return. And while you're at it, warn those damned British—"

"No, gentlemen," Lincoln broke in. "Let's not twist the lion's tail. You said the man was difficult. He may have just gone north in a fit of temper. Let's not wring our hands just yet. Not until we know the true circumstances behind the man's departure. There is no reason to believe the British are involved."

"I don't trust them," Stanton snapped.

"You don't trust anyone," Seward said.

"You were the one who wanted to keep the Confederate emissaries, plucked from a British vessel," Stanton huffed.

"Let's leave the past in the past. We need to keep a lid on this," Lincoln reminded his cabinet. "I have a fellow in mind who can do just that. Let us dispatch him and await his report."

"Mr. Lincoln," Stanton said grimly. "We mustn't wait too long. Abbott is worth fifty thousand men to the rebels. If his *Monitor* secrets are made known to them they can be turned against us in any number of ways."

Seward saw Lincoln's shoulders slump and his face collapse in melancholy.

"He is worth those same fifty thousand men to us," the president said. He asked Welles, "Does he really possess that much intelligence about our ironclads?"

"I'm afraid so, Mr. Lincoln," Welles said. "Every secret of their construction. But that is not my only concern, sir. What troubles me is the excellence of his mind. His scientific skills are beyond comprehension—military inventions pour from him like milk from an overturned bucket. Were he to turn his brilliance against us for whatever reason, it would be a disaster."

Lincoln shook his head, walking away from Welles. "Then we must intercede. For I believe this poor nation is just one disaster short of defeat."

Chapter 6

Crehan and Sons, Watchmakers
Brooklyn, New York

Politics held no interest for Robert Owen. For that matter, nothing did except acting and the South. The two had combined to captivate him, to seduce his soul and turn him into the worst possible romantic—the passionate youth. He had gone to Richmond as the lowest member of an itinerant band of actors and, on the fourth performance of an unwieldy melodrama, had been approached by the Januarys. His help was needed, and he would be expected to travel.

Strangely, the journey began in Brooklyn some months ago.

The doorbell announced Owen's entrance into the cluttered watchmaker's shop, and signaled the tall Negro behind the counter that he had a customer.

"Good day," the Negro said, nearly obscured by the gloomy interior of the shop. "I am Crehan."

Owen nodded in return, uncertain about how to proceed feeling, despite the fact that January had sent him to Crehan, foolish and very nervous.

The watchmaker stepped from behind the counter, visible now in the light of the afternoon sun that filtered through a grimy window.

There was a heavy closeness about the cramped confines of the shop. Owen was surrounded by counters and shelves—cluttered with watches, clocks, mainsprings, keys, faces, plates, and frames. And the man himself, Crehan—the black skin on his face sagging, his shoulders barely supporting his head, and his eyes, lumps of coal amid fields of snow, gave no sign of life. The man was stupid, Owen decided, and yet did not have the sense to realize it. It was the nature of his race. Owen found his courage, and stiffened it with arrogance.

"Mr. January sent me," he said, looking for any sign that the mention of the great actor's name would rouse the watchmaker's interest.

It did not. "I thought you would be along shortly."

Owen was startled. "How did you know I—"

"Someone," Crehan corrected Owen's misunderstanding. "He told me he would have someone come by."

"My name is Robert Owen." He was careful to state his name in a slow manner, keeping his diction clear. Be proud of every word, January instructed. Deliver your lines so that each word stands as importantly as its neighbor. Your audience will note how each is prized and presented to them.

"How do you do, Mr. Owen?" Crehan said.

"Very well," Owen returned, and then grew impatient. He should not be passing the time of day with this Negro. He was here for a purpose. "I am instructed by Mr. January to retrieve a package." He felt he was being stern enough.

Crehan did not bother to respond. He returned to the counter, searched through some cabinets, and carefully removed a box hidden among a nest of parts. He placed it on the counter, gently opened the box, and looked at Owen—a signal to approach.

Owen kept his face expressionless. He had no idea what to expect, was too timid to ask January what the device was, but was certain he did not want a Negro questioning January's trust in him.

Crehan lifted the machine—it was a clock of sorts, Owen could see that—and set it on the counter. He held up a brass key. "Insert this key here, in this keyhole." Owen was irritated to note that Crehan moved with deliberation, as if teaching an idiot. "Rotate it four times." The Negro did so, counting. "One, two, three, four. Remove the key." He pointed at a tab jutting from the frame. "Engage the gears." There was a muted click as his finger slid the mechanism forward. "Set the clock, and the timer."

"Timer?" Owen said, forgetting his vow.

"I followed the drawing exactly," Crehan said.

"Yes," Owen replied, embarrassed he knew nothing of the machine. It galled him that a Negro had to instruct him. The act violated every notion of his superiority.

Crehan returned the clock to its box, closed the lid, and pushed it toward Owen.

The young man took it, trying to look confident, and said, "Our business is done, then?"

"Except," Crehan said, "for the others."

"Of course," Owen said, feeling foolish. He fought to retain his dignity. "I meant this device only."

"We are done, yes."

Owen turned and left the shop, relieved to be out in the sunlight, away from the dull nigger, out of the dusty shadows of the watchmaker's hovel. He despised men who did not know their place—men who did not have the common decency to accept the task that God had laid out for them. He did not acknowledge it—Owen was too young to accept the responsibility of life's truth—but men such as Crehan threatened his superior role. There was no question that his class as a gentleman entitled him to deference from the coloreds, and the Irish. His color, the skin of the ruling class, his God-given role as guardian of humanity, guaranteed his station above his inferiors.

Then why, Owen allowed the troubling thought to slip through, did he find that nigger's manner insulting? He corrected himself—why did he feel that Crehan was, in that brief exchange, superior?

Owen retreated to the familiar territory of his instructions.

He would travel to Quebec, carrying the strange device that was so important, to Royal January, and in doing so prove himself worthy of January's favor. The warmth of Victoria January's smile, rising as the sun over her brother's shoulder, filled Owen with expectation. She captivated him with her beauty—he was thrilled when she spoke to him, unashamed to blush when her hand fell lightly on his as she sought his attention. Owen knew that Royal January was pleased with his interest in Victoria; he had seen the famous actor out of the corner of his eye, smiling. Yet he was careful to observe the proprieties when he spoke to Victoria. She was a lady and could not be approached except with all the courtesy due her class.

Owen fumbled for his watch, aware that he had lost himself to a swirl of intoxicating daydreams. He must find a cab and get to the station. He slid the watch into his waistcoat pocket, smoothed the material, and set out.

Crehan went through the routine of closing his shop. He pulled the flimsy green shades and unfolded the louvered shutters across the windows. He lowered the lamps, turning the keys until the last glimmer of flame disappeared from the edge of the wick. He lit the remaining lamp, the one that always sat on a small, round table near the stairway, and carried it up the steps. His footfalls were slow, burdened, the steady thump of a heart that had nearly reached its end.

He entered the second story of the shop, stopping in the first of two adjoining rooms. Setting the lamp on the floor, he opened a window facing the street. The sounds of carriages, wagons, and the clack of horses' hooves striking the paving stones flooded the room. The cool air followed, dispersing the stench of sickness that hung in the dark room.

He did the same in the other room—the bedroom—used to the stink of soiled bedclothes. He knew that the smell would soon dissipate, although not completely. Its shadow would linger, a reminder of the sickness that consumed Charity.

He spoke to her, gently removing the defiled gown that clung to the wasted body. There was little of his wife underneath the garment—sagging brown skin, the surface distorted by the rounded shape of protruding bones. Her vacant eyes never moved; her mouth, lips stained with drool, was a ghoulish reminder of the passion they had once enjoyed.

On the table next to her bed was a tin bowl filled with water, a thin scum of soap residue coating the surface. He began washing her, lifting her arms tenderly. It was his ritual of caring, of love.

"There was a young man come in just a moment ago," Crehan said, dipping the cleaning rag in a bucket of water, wringing it out with a twist of his powerful hands, and then washing her. "Near a boy. He reminded me so of Michael. Proud. He had a purpose like Michael." He stopped for a moment in thought. "Red hair, too. Sandy colored in a way, but his manner was like Michael's."

Crehan slid his hands underneath his wife's naked body and turned her. He did so four times a day. If he didn't, the sores would set in. He cupped her head in his hands and twisted slightly. Her mouth and nose were free of the mattress, and she drew in faint breaths.

"He wasn't nearly as tall. More like Matthew. Heavier though. He fancied himself a gentleman but he tried too hard." Crehan chuckled. "Young men are that way, ain't they?" He wrung the fabric out, and the droplets danced on the water. "He come for Mr. January's clock. The one that other fellow drawed. He must be smart, that other one." His voice hardened. "No smarter than me, though."

Crehan finished cleaning Charity, stuffed the soiled bedclothes in a sack for washing, and dressed her in a gown he had made. He would feed her later, some broth he had coaxed from the remains of a chicken, and turn her once more before he went to bed. He slept on a pallet spread on the floor in the other room.

He planned to work on January's clocks. He would make ten more, because he thought of ways to improve them. He forgot his grief, forgot the woman who lay close to dead, as he examined the intricate drawing. It was made by a smart man—a man who knew machines. Not clocks, but the mechanics of clocks. Crehan could make it better. He was sure of that.

Crehan went downstairs, sat at his worktable, adjusted the oil lamp, and picked up the beginnings of another January clock. He liked to hold the piece as he studied it—maybe the weight added something to his understanding of the machine. Whatever it was to be used for did not matter to Crehan. He was a clockmaker—the instrument was all that concerned him. The complexity, gears, rods, springs, tooling, hands, and the finish of the face—he was a clockmaker.

His reflection in the windowpane caught his attention, but he looked beyond the tired face with the melancholy eyes to the images of his sons. His face softened at their memory, producing a hollow smile that was nearly lost in the dying light. He turned away from the window to his clock, concentrating on the complicated device in his hand.

That is how Crehan found relief from torment. There were no memories of the deaths of his boys in the hard, polished surfaces of the clockworks; no reminder of his wife, dying from grief; no intrusion of any kind. Not even the thing that Royal January had planned.

Chapter 7

The Canadian Northern Railway Terminal
Quebec City, British Canada

Fitz shrugged his cape over his good shoulder and stepped from the coach to the station platform. The vast station was a field of steam floating just over the heads of the crowd. It was the product of a sharp cold that caught a person's breath, and then tossed it in the air in celebration of winter's power. The train engines added to the clouds, injecting violent bursts of steam at the feet of passersby. The hundreds of horses that lined the loading dock, waiting for freight to be transferred from the train to the long line of wagons, snorted spurts of steam from their nostrils.

"The bags, Fitz," Asia reminded him.

"Yes," Fitz said as a porter with a handcart appeared. The man began loading the luggage without waiting for instructions.

A short man in a fur hat approached them. "Colonel Dunaway?" The man's thick beard parted in a friendly smile. "Davis Tooke, Assistant Consul." He bowed to Asia. It was then Fitz realized that the man was portly, not just heavily bundled against the weather.

"Welcome to Quebec City," Tooke said. "If you'll follow me we'll find someplace a bit warmer. The wind comes through this old barn of a station." He glanced at Fitz and Asia. "If you don't mind me saying, you may want to find heavier coats. I learned immediately not to underestimate the winters here."

"Have you been here long?" Asia asked as they trailed behind him.

"Two years," Tooke said. "Right out of college. Harvard, class of '60." They passed an ice-covered girder and veered to avoid a cluster of passengers. Just beyond, Fitz saw the crowd flow around an obstruction, and in the midst of that, a wall of red.

A company of British soldiers, dressed for winter campaigning, formed ranks under the bullfroglike croaks of a sergeant major wielding a swagger stick. The men moved quickly, falling into rank, stiffening to attention, their Enfield rifle-muskets clamped against their shoulders, soldiers and weapons perfectly aligned.

Fitz eyed them appreciatively and realized with a pang of disappointment they paid no attention to him. He would have appreciated the courtesy of professional recognition— one soldier to another.

"Here we are," Tooke said, stopping at a carriage. He said something in French to the porter. "He'll take your bags straight to the hotel. We have rooms for you at the St-Denis. I suspect that you'll want to freshen up. " His eyes flicked to Fitz's arm. "Do you require any special assistance, Colonel?"

"That is a lovely hat, Mr. Tooke. Did you make it yourself?" Asia spoke before Fitz exploded. She knew the idea that Fitz needed any assistance, at anytime, under any situation, was anathema to him. What generally followed a question like Mr. Tooke's was a tirade.

Tooke, confused, said, "No, Mrs. Dunaway. It is rabbit. I purchased it."

Fitz cooled enough to respond. He appreciated Asia's intercession. "I need no special consideration whatsoever, Mr. Tooke. I wish merely to do as ordered by the president."

As they took their seats in the carriage and started off,

Asia leaned close to Fitz. "I think we would need a whole family of rabbits to make a hat for Colonel Dunaway's head."

Fitz pretended to ignore her but he responded with a warm smile. She had told him once that she knew him well—that he ran on emotion, which, despite his reluctance to admit it, often overwhelmed his good sense. *But, Colonel Dunaway, she had said to him after they made love, I wonder how well you truly know me?* He had no answer.

"What do you know of the circumstances that brought us here?" Fitz asked.

"Everything," Tooke said. He was, despite his portly frame and slow manner, a levelheaded young man. "Professor Abbott's disappearance is of the utmost concern to everyone. We have been informed he had a violent argument with the superintendent of the Brooklyn Navy Yard just prior to this latest episode. It is rumored"—his face reddened in embarrassment—"that he enjoys the company of a certain type of woman."

"Presbyterians?" Asia said.

Tooke, shocked, tried to reply.

"Is he here?" Fitz said, saving the youth. "In Canada?"

"We think so."

"Think so?" Fitz said.

"Every report places him here," Tooke said. "That's what I've been able to learn. When he has traveled to Quebec City before, he stayed in various hotels, under assumed names." He pulled a notebook from his pocket and glanced at Fitz apologetically for the interruption. "I want to be sure of my facts," he explained, refreshing his memory and continuing. "Just over six feet, heavy set, white hair, in his midfifties, very belligerent and impatient. Very particular about his meals, and prefers the company of—"

"Yes," Fitz said, "Presbyterians. Where is he now?"

"We don't know," Tooke said. "I don't know. He does have rooms at the St-Denis, but no one recalls seeing him for some days."

"How long, exactly?" Fitz said.

"That's just it," Tooke said. "He was so secretive about his comings and goings that no one is certain."

"Have you searched his rooms?"

"Yes," Tooke said. It was clear he found the idea troubling. "I don't like snooping about another man's room. It is ungentlemanly."

"Advance to spying, Mr. Tooke," Fitz said. "See how you feel about that."

"Did you find anything of substance, Mr. Tooke?" Asia asked.

"Well," Tooke said, "there is one thing." He pulled his heavy coat to one side and dug through his clothing. He held up a small, leather-bound notebook, about four inches by six inches. The edges were worn, and the cover was speckled with stains. He handed it to Fitz.

"What is it?" Fitz asked, trying to open it with one hand. Asia took it from him and opened it. As she turned the pages, one after another, Fitz saw on each a wild array of numbers, drawings, and indecipherable notations.

"I have no idea," Tooke said. "It's his, Professor Abbott's. I found it in his valise, but—" He stopped, letting the mysterious contents of the book finish his explanation.

"You found the valise in his rooms?" Fitz asked. "Then he was close by, or had been so recently?"

"No, sir. I had the place under observation. Several of the hotel staff were paid to keep me informed should he return. He never appeared. He abandoned the valise."

"Was there nothing else in the valise?" Asia asked.

"No," Tooke said. "Nothing of importance. A few personal things. Books. Newspapers. Unfortunately, Inspector De Brule has the valise."

"De Brule?" Fitz said.

"The Crown Inspector. I approached him several times to assist us. He was very polite but absolutely useless. He is a very odd person. "

"This adventure is filled with odd people," Fitz said, prepared to be unimpressed.

"De Brule is quite wealthy, and he counts many influential people as his friends. People say that he has his position because of his ability to gather information, embarrassing information, about high-ranking officials. He is also decidedly anti-Union, and vocally pro-Southern," Tooke said. "He always appears to be helpful, but in the end it is only an appearance."

"How did he come to have Professor Abbott's valise?" Asia asked.

Tooke hesitated. "He took it from me, as I was leaving Abbott's rooms. It was by good fortune that I had slipped his notebook into my pocket." Asia was about to hand the book to Tooke, but the young man shook his head. "Please keep it. You might be able to divine some meaning from its contents. I can't."

"Do you know the Southern agents in the city?" Fitz asked. "Could they be involved in Abbott's disappearance?"

The carriage stopped, and Tooke wiped the condensation from the window and looked out. "Here is the St-Denis."

The carriage bucked as the driver alighted. The door flew open and a blast of cold air announced they must abandon the warmth of the vehicle.

The lobby of the St-Denis was small, Fitz noted, not as luxurious as Willard's but comfortable, inviting, with a scattering of divans, tables, and surprisingly, given the intense cold outside, potted plants. Fitz was about to ask Asia what kind of plants could possibly survive this extreme weather, but decided against it. She had chided him on his lack of knowledge about flora. In a pique his only reply had been, "I know grass and trees. That should suffice."

"I'll see to your rooms," Tooke said, hurrying to the front desk.

"How are you?" Fitz asked. He had been planning his questions carefully the entire trip, knowing that his efforts to inquire after Asia's well-being often had ended in disaster. She would lapse into silent periods, sometimes emerge in a defensive mood, and then seeing that he was hurt and confused, become contrite. He had been watching her closely, sensing that whatever troubled her in Washington had made the trip with them. When her attention drifted away from their journey to the passing countryside, he began to develop his strategy. He vowed to keep his temper in check and to mask the irritation that arose when he found himself sinking deeper and deeper into the morass of misunderstood emotions.

Asia Dunaway looked at her husband, surprised at the suddenness of the inquiry. "Well, Fitz. A little tired, of course." Her smile told him she was aware there was more lurking behind that question. "Why?"

Fitz stepped aside as a cart bearing their luggage passed by.

"You were—" Fitz began. "You don't seem yourself."

Her sadness returned. "It is nothing," she said. "The length of the journey."

"It was before we came to Quebec City," Fitz said, trying to keep his thoughts in order. He would be logical about this, he reminded himself, and not let his feelings intrude. "Sometimes I find you as you have always been, but then a cloud comes over you, and I suspect I have done something."

"It is not that, Fitz. Let us not speak of it now."

"But when I ask, you change the subject, or—"

"Well, here we are," Tooke said, suddenly appearing. "Room 221. Your bags should be there now. All we need do is follow the porter. Is something wrong?"

Fitz felt defeated. He was tired and his arm throbbed, and he knew he did not have the reserve to wage a campaign that required delicacy and understanding. And yet here was the woman he loved, at times so distant she might have been a stranger, deflecting his attempts to reach her. He realized he had failed her somehow, and for the first time a thought emerged he had done his best to keep submerged: Was there someone else?

"Perhaps if you retire to your rooms for a brief respite?" Tooke suggested.

"Why don't you go on," Fitz said, struggling to remain calm. He was angry at Asia, with her secrecy, with his inability to return his wife to the person she was.

"Yes," she said, following the porter.

"Let us go to the consul offices," Fitz said before Tooke had a chance to speak. "I want to know about Southern agents, and I must inform my superiors of my arrival." Fitz could not stand being at the mercy of doubt. He needed the comfort of acting without hesitation, of bringing a situation to a quick resolution. Doubt was an illness, a creeping, insidious sickness that weakened a man to the point of inactivity. And now, it had a firm grip on him.

Chapter 8

The Beaufort Asylum for the Insane
Five Miles from Quebec City, British Canada

The artist worked in limited colors, painting five dark figures on a canvas of bright snow and lining the umber trunks of regimented naked trees on the edge of the frosted field. Dominating the background was the dull gray bulk of the asylum, heavy with misery, two-story stone buildings facing one another across a commons. They were joined by palings—stout wooden posts that denied the inhabitants entrance to the world that had discarded them. On the left were three comfortable houses, the largest belonging to the superintendent, and smoke curling from chimneys into a sky that was nearly as white as the fields. The only true colors that existed in the scene were those of the two sleighs—red for one, and yellow for the other.

Silence could have been another color, all sounds muted to whispers on the monochromatic canvas—those that escaped did so in respectful hushed tones.

Goodwin stood with two men, far enough from January and the Confederate agent Provine to give them privacy. Sorrel was a small squat man, angry about something, everything. Locker was taller, even tempered—the kind who paces easily through life. They were both a good head shorter than Goodwin, as were most men.

Goodwin offered the two men cigars. "How long have you been up here?"

Both men took the cigars, Sorrel jerking his from Goodwin's hand. "Too damned long," the shorter man said, waiting for a light. He puffed on the cigar, drawing smoke from the tip that mixed with his frozen breath. "We don't do nothing but talk. All we do is talk."

"A little over a year," Locker said, rolling the cigar over the match, patiently nursing the tip until it glowed red. One more speck of color on the canvas.

"And we've done nothing," Sorrel said, watching January and Provine talk near the sleighs. It was obvious he wanted Goodwin to understand their trials. "Mr. Provine there isn't the kind of man who wants things done quickly."

Locker was prepared to be more charitable. "He's thoughtful."

"Do they pay you well?" Goodwin asked.

Both men answered, "No."

Sorrel elaborated. "I think Mr. Provine's feathering his own nest." He looked at the landscape in disgust. "He likes it up here."

Provine and January stopped some distance from the others.

The Confederate agent marveled at the scene. "Isn't it beautiful, Mr. January?"

"Cold," January concluded. "Desolate." He shivered. "This is a long way from Quebec City."

"No. No," Provine corrected him. He was dressed in an expensive topcoat and a beaver hat. His face was chapped from the chill wind, his mustache stiff with frost. His eyes gleamed with opportunity. "It is the perfect place to discuss business. No one will discover us here." He felt it necessary to tutor January. "They spy on us constantly, you know. Union men, English men in the pay of the federals. Everybody must know what everybody else is doing. We cannot simply go about without taking precautions. I've told Richmond this. And yet all of the resources go to Montreal. Look. See my two agents there? Incompetent, but they are all I have."

"I don't need men," January pointed out, once again. Provine didn't seem to grasp his need. In fact, he never acknowledged it. "I need to transport my goods to Baltimore. I would like you to approach Mr. Ledford for me."

"There are other shippers," Provine said.

"Not men who are friendly to our cause. Ledford is discreet. He has a network in place."

"Ledford is a valuable man," Provine noted, almost incidentally.

"Yes. I know," January said.

Provine skillfully slipped away from the object of the discussion. "Mr. January, I'm sure you will find a shipper with Mr. Ledford's level of sensitivity. Unfortunately, Mr. Ledford, and I concur with him on this matter, is reluctant to involve himself with Confederate activities unless he knows the participants well. I could advocate you and your need, truly I could, and I will. You have my word on that, but he is wary of such efforts."

"Except those proposed by you?"

"He is cautious," Provine confirmed. "I will speak to him, but I have little hope that he will accede to your wishes." The landscape captured his attention. "It truly is breathtaking. Not like that hated swamp. I tell you, between the heat and pestilence, Richmond could claim ten years from a man's life."

"Will you speak to Mr. Ledford for me?" January asked. "We have very little time."

"I have a house picked out. In the Upper Town. You must come and visit me." Provine grew sympathetic. "I will speak to Ledford. I can promise you nothing, but I will convey to him your need for his assistance." His interest drifted. "I lived in one tiny room in Richmond. In the summer the air stank of sewers and in the winter it was choked with wood smoke."

"We all had to endure," January said, signaling for Goodwin. They watched in silence as Provine and his companions climbed into one of the sleighs. In a few minutes the vehicle had disappeared over the white landscape, the only evidence of its passage the thin shadows of its runners.

"His men aren't happy with him," Goodwin said.

"They have company," January said, taking a cigar from Goodwin, followed by a lit match. He waited for the cigar tip to glow before continuing. "I have to have Ledford. He is the only trader I can trust. I cannot get those items south without him."

"Will Provine represent you?"

"Provine—" the word followed by a burst of smoke "—is far more concerned with establishing his home in Quebec City. I suspect he feels if he does nothing, he will suffer no harm." January said, "What of those two? Will they come to us?"

"Yes. They can be bribed, although they don't know it."

They walked to their sleigh, and as January stroked the horse's mane, he asked, "Can you do it? All of it?" It was complicated, he knew. Perhaps far more so than Goodwin was capable of understanding. He was intelligent, and with time and examination there wasn't a machine he was incapable of comprehending. But this was more than machines, and Wilmington proved that control was not always possible.

"Yes," Goodwin said. He added, "I know as much as he did. I've got copies of everything. I never let a thing pass that I didn't ask questions. What about Provine?"

" 'Either betray'd by falsehood of his guard, Or by his foe supris'd at unawares.' "

Goodwin waited patiently. He never understood how a grown man could dress up and pretend to be someone else.

"Kill him," January said, his talent unrecognized.

Chapter 9

Tooke introduced Fitz to Abel Chamberlain, the American Consul to British Canada. The harried man spoke a few words of greeting to Fitz, drew Tooke into his office for an extended visit, and left Fitz to his own devices in an anteroom. A young man, a secretary of sorts, felt sympathy for the stranded officer.

"They might be a while," the man said. "Mr. Chamberlain is particularly vexed today."

Fitz, irritated at being abandoned and tired of trying to find a position where his arm didn't hurt, said, "Why is today different from any other day?"

"The British are landing more troops. Can I get you a refreshment?"

Fitz remembered the company of soldiers forming ranks in the train station, a swath of bright red against the dull bodies of the train cars—greatcoats, packs, blanket rolls, white leather belts and harnesses—these men had come to stay. "How many troops?" he asked.

"Five to ten thousand. Relations are very strained, you know. We've all been given orders not to antagonize the British in any way."

"Oh, good," Fitz said. "I am particularly adept at not antagonizing people or foreign governments." The secretary, catching his caustic tone, offered a polite smile and disappeared behind a desk covered with papers.

Tooke retrieved Fitz, led him to an unimposing office near a set of stairs, and sent for coffee.

"Mr. Chamberlain is distressed," Tooke said as he hung up their garments and slid behind his desk.

"The British army." Fitz supplied the reason for the counsel's fear. He didn't realize how tired he was from the trip. Or maybe it was his concern for Asia, or the fact that he seemed never to have been without this wound. He knew he needed rest—four hours of good, deep sleep would refresh him.

"How did you know?"

"The young man told me. And I saw a company in the station. He has every right to be frightened. The British army has a habit of treating its rivals badly. I'm sure there's a fair amount of diplomatic square dancing going on, trying to keep the two nations from coming to blows."

"Yes," Tooke said. "Mr. Chamberlain was insistent that we do nothing to jeopardize the fragile relationship between the American government and Her Majesty's government."

"Mr. Tooke," Fitz said, feeling a bit devilish, "I am the soul of propriety. You were about to tell me about the Southern agents in the city."

Tooke recalled the conversation in the carriage. "Oh, my, yes. We know of three—Sorrel, Provine, and Locker. They have never been active. A common rumor is Provine prefers the company of society to the intrigues of conspiracies. I've never met the man."

"Those three? No one else?"

"None have caught our attention. Of course there is always talk. Most natives up here, French and English, detest Lincoln and distrust the North. It's fashionable to make demonstrations on behalf of the South."

"Demonstrations?"

"Parties celebrating Southern victories, dinners with mock

Southern regalia decorating the dining room. The Januarys dedicated a performance to the brave men of the South. Their Southern antecedents are well known. Maryland, I believe."

"Has Abbott ever been seen in the company of these people?" Fitz asked.

"Not to my knowledge."

A knock on the door interrupted them, and a clerk appeared.

"Colonel Dunaway?" He handed Fitz a telegram.

Fitz read it, and then handed it to Tooke. "It's from the War Department. They are absolutely certain Abbott crossed the border several weeks ago, heading for Quebec City." Another clerk delivered two cups of coffee. "Well," Fitz said, after taking a sip of the brew. "It appears he is here, and we are here, so now it is simply a matter of finding him." The coffee was bitter but Fitz was glad for its warmth. He watched the steam rise from the black liquid. "But why would the man come to Quebec City? You said he's been here before?"

Tooke said, trying to be helpful. "Several times I understand. Let me ask about."

"All right," Fitz said. "It's in our best interest to proceed as if Abbott will be, or already is, in the hands of Southern agents. In any case, he came willingly or by coercion. It's down to cases, and ours is simple; find and return the good professor to the United States."

Chapter 10

A sia had seen to most of the unpacking with the assistance of a hotel maid, a stout Frenchwoman who managed to decipher Asia's instructions in textbook French. She'd used little of the language since leaving boarding school and traveling to the continent. She was seventeen then, and had never been so homesick in her life. London was dirty and Paris was wonderful, and it seemed to her that Rome was a city frozen in the past. When she returned home, more than ready to be rid of the foul-smelling aunt who had been her chaperone, the first thing she told her father was that she never wanted to leave Washington. He had thrown back his head in laughter and promised that he would never ask that of her again, but he pointed out the obvious—every country and every continent has contradictions. As do people.

The night of her return she snuck out of her house and made her way three blocks to the west. Asia was bursting with stories of all she had seen.

She had always loved Robert's house. It was a stately Georgian of refined proportions. Everything balanced—chimney-to-chimney, dormers, windows, and thick columns crowned by scrolled capitols. The porch was bordered by holly bushes speckled with red berries.

Asia had spoken to Robert for hours, while his mother, a beautiful woman with golden hair, sat quietly on a nearby settee, lost in the latest Walter Scott novel.

Now she remembered Robert's letter, waiting until the maid had closed the suite door behind her, before drawing it out of her purse.

Dear Asia, he began. She smiled as his writing changed to match the intensity of his emotions, letters half-formed, and ink smudged as his thoughts fought one another to be included in the letter.

> *We have been too long out of each other's lives and thoughts, so I found it important to tell you of my decision.*

Her heart sunk, reading the letter, knowing what he had decided. He had always been impetuous, and deep within he battled the twin demons of inferiority and arrogance. The end result was anger—a result of the circumstances of his birth.

> *Washington holds no interest for me unless I return a triumphant conqueror. The south is my country, the nation holds my heart. I turn my passion toward something good, and pure, knowing that I can do no better than to fall at the shrine of southern liberty.*

Asia folded the letter, remembering the boy who had played Romeo to her Juliet, and his mother, strangely sad and alone, their only audience. Robert was the director, stage manager, and Hamlet, or occasionally Richard III. He had lost himself in his performances, escaping for a short period from the house that saw few visitors and only fleeting moments of joy. She had watched the tenderness and comfort, which mother and son shared, as if they held a secret too delicate to expose to another soul.

Asia continued reading.

> *I have thrown myself in with a courageous band—heroes that will strike a blow for the south, and pierce the heart of the hated north. You must console yourself with the knowledge that although we may not see each other again, our bond will never be severed. I trust my soul, I give my life, and bind my will to companions of like thought. We are involved in a crusade of the highest order—a holy adventure.*
>
> *Love, Robert*

She slid the letter into her pocket, knowing she should have told Fitz. He knew something was wrong, and his poor attempts to learn the source of her pain did nothing but lead to even more turmoil. But Asia had decided, on the trip to Quebec, that it was not necessary to speak of the letter, or Robert. If she did, Fitz would take it upon himself to do *something,* and most likely any action he took would be wrong. There was no reason now—Robert had gone south from Washington, probably to Richmond, and was now probably leading troops into battle. A larger stage, Asia thought, so much grander than the day parlor.

She worried about him. He was such a passionate young man, a boy really, if only five years younger than she. She had seen him fight for every measure of respectability due him. She could have been describing Fitz, she realized. Except that Fitz Dunaway had been hardened by adversity, and tempered with the fires of conflict. Fitz fought wars, while Robert played at them.

They were enemies. Fitz was sworn to protect the Union, and Robert sworn to destroy it. Asia loved them both, and she feared her heart could not bear the strain.

The knob clicked and the door opened. It was Fitz, looking tired but happy to see her. She stood and went to him, feeling guilty over her treatment of her husband and her thoughts for Robert.

"You look all in," she said, slipping his cape from his shoulders.

"I am," he said, wondering if he was forgiven for whatever wrong he had committed. He watched her as she poured a cup of coffee and brought it to him, looking for any signs that her mood might change and she would fall into the melancholia that had become so much a part of her life. And his as well.

"Thank you," he said, taking the coffee. After a few sips he decided the coffee at the St-Denis was far superior to that at the American Consul.

"What did you learn?" she asked, settling next to him.

He told her, wishing at the same time the suite had a piano so he could relax as she played. He relayed the War Department's telegram, and added that he had sent one to Lincoln that said no more than "Arrived Quebec City. Investigating." For the first day in a strange city, there was little else to be said. He saw the trunks were unpacked.

"Where are my quarters?" he asked, hoping she would see he was teasing her.

"There, Colonel Dunaway," she replied. Her eyes brightened. "And mine, are there." She indicated a door across the suite.

"So far away," Fitz said. "I may have cause to reconnoiter."

She leaned over him, brushing the dark hair off his forehead and kissing the bridge of his nose. The presence of her breasts so close to his mouth and the sweet aroma of her perfume filled him with desire. He guided her lips to his and kissed her deeply.

Asia stood and shook her head, cautioning him against any ill-considered action. "You are confined to quarters, Colonel Dunaway. Your arm needs time to heal properly."

"What I had in mind," Fitz said, "has nothing to do with the condition of my arm."

Asia answered a knock at the door, saving herself the trouble of responding to Fitz. A white-gloved bellhop bowed, spoke something in French, and handed her a small envelope. She closed the door and found a letter opener on a desk.

"What is it?" Fitz asked.

"From Inspector De Brule," Asia replied, reading the note. "He has invited us to the theater this evening as his guests." She looked up at Fitz, her eyes shining with delight. "Oh, Fitz. We are to see the Januarys."

Chapter 11

The lobby of the Latrobe Theater
Quebec City, British Canada

Fitz thought Asia was lovely and continually told her so, from their suite, through the hotel lobby, into the cab, out of the cab, and under the brilliant chandeliers that sparkled over fields of diamonds surrounding the throats of plain-looking women whom wealth had made beautiful. Still, she could not accept his opinion. He was, after all, only her husband.

"I had no idea I would be going to the theater," Asia said.

"Nor I," Fitz said, trying to keep his arm away from the blundering crowd. "And there was no reason for us to attend the theater tonight. We could have told De Brule—"

"But the Januarys, Fitz. It is practically impossible to find tickets."

"What is so special about these actors?" Fitz asked.

"But they are not actors," Inspector De Brule said, appearing next to Asia. "Flaming stars across the blackness of the night sky. The pathos of a thousand setting suns—the promise of those same suns rising. In short, celestial beings, children of the gods." He bowed to Asia. He was much taller than Fitz, elegantly thin with a fox's face, and dark eyes. Fitz detested him immediately.

De Brule took Asia's gloved hand in his and kissed it just above the knuckles. He smiled, but did not release her hand. "Christopher De Brule, at your service."

"You've already met my wife's hand," Fitz said. "I am Colonel Thomas Fitzgerald Dunaway."

De Brule's smile to Fitz was without warmth. "And this is Asia Dunaway, of course." He released her hand and glanced at Fitz's bandaged arm. "I had no idea you were injured, Colonel Dunaway. Perhaps the evening will prove too taxing for you. I will be most happy to accompany your lovely wife should you desire to return to the hotel."

"The wound is a trifle," Fitz said. "A cannonball's glancing blow. I, myself, sewed my arm back on with a bayonet and a shoelace."

"Fitz!" Asia exclaimed.

"A true American hero," De Brule said, with a courteous bow.

Fitz found De Brule's cultured manners hollow and false. He did his best to hide his contempt for the man. It did not help his mood that Asia was apparently infatuated with De Brule.

Fitz heard a delicate chime sounding above the crowd's chatter.

"We must take our seats," De Brule said, slipping his arm under Asia's. He looked over his shoulder at Fitz. "This way if you please, Colonel."

Fitz tried to protect his arm from the crowd ascending the broad steps to the second-level boxes. He fixed his eyes squarely on the back of De Brule's head. It would be easy, even in the crowded environment of jostling theater patrons. A shape rap with the butt plate of his Colt, and all of De Brule's sophistication would crumble to the floor.

He had that image happily planted in his mind when a large woman with frightening red cheeks stumbled into his arm. She apologized in a flurry of unintelligible words but hastily backed away when she saw Fitz's face contort in agony. This was no place for a soldier, Fitz thought, as the waves of pain subsided.

George Goodwin listened to the music escaping the tavern several doors down. It was comforting on a cold night to hear the sound of guitar and the melancholy singing. The French in Canada were a sad people, Goodwin thought, longing for a time when they would have their own country, lamenting their fate at the hands of the victorious British.

He stood in the recessed doorway of a bakery. The only lights that existed in the frigid night spilled into the street from the tavern, and even those were knife-blade thin, slipping through the cracks in the shutters.

Goodwin dipped his head to light a cigar. He cupped his hands around the match, keeping it close to his chest, out of the stiff wind. Half a dozen scars appeared in the wavering light that shone on his face, the largest disappearing under the collar of his jacket. The match died, as clouds of pale smoke drifted into the Rue de Canal.

Provine lived by the clock, going here or there when the hands of his watch told him so. *Uncreative*, Royal January had explained to Goodwin, and Goodwin trusted everything that January told him.

"He is not careful," January had declared as he applied his makeup for that evening's performance. "Every other night, after visiting his whore, he goes to that tavern."

"I know the one," Goodwin had said. He'd followed Provine several times before, marking the man's route and stops as opportunities.

January had tested the fastenings of his cloak—Othello's cloak—was satisfied that they were securely attached, and then smiled at Goodwin. "I know you do."

The cigar smoke settled in a languid wreath around Goodwin's face. Provine would have three glasses of beer and perhaps some bread and cheese, leave the tavern, and turn left onto the Rue de Canal.

Goodwin thought he recognized the tune that drifted down the narrow street, but then gave up trying to recall the title. He settled for snatches of the soft melody and decided that knowing what it was called was of no consequence.

He felt in his coat pocket for his cigars, and counted by feel—six. He found the best cigars in Quebec City at a little shop with red shutters. He made a point of stopping at the store, wedging himself into the confines crowded with barrels, boxes, and crates of tobacco, to buy thirty Nicaraguan cigars. Very good, the elderly owner said, confirming his taste in tobacco. Very good.

Goodwin's fingers stopped. He had fallen into his own routine, and from that someone could easily plan to ambush him. He sighed, regretting not only his mistake but the comfort of his habit.

Fitz was seated next to an unexpected guest. Madame De Brule was probably eighty, constantly squinting at the audience below her, and smelled of cloves.

De Brule had maneuvered Fitz and Asia into a box overlooking the dress circle and, before Fitz could protest, had swept Asia into one of two chairs placed in the extreme left of the box. Two other chairs, far to the right, were reserved for Fitz and Madame De Brule.

"My dear colonel," De Brule said, by way of explanation. "My mother seldom has an opportunity to attend the theater. And in the company of a handsome man such as yourself. But you must forgive her. She knows not a word of English. She considers it a vulgar language. I've afraid her hearing has completely failed her. You must make allowances, if you would be so kind. She will insist upon speaking to you. Please be kind enough to listen."

Fitz wanted to make sure he understood De Brule. "She can't hear, and she can't speak English." He glanced at Asia in frustration.

Asia gave a tiny shrug of helplessness.

"Of course, Mr. De Brule," Fitz said. "I will be the perfect gentleman. Perhaps I'll have an opportunity to repay the kindness."

"It is very kind of you to invite us to the play, Inspector De Brule," Asia said, hoping to stop Fitz before he went too far.

"It was nothing," De Brule replied. "After all, our association need not be entirely official. My good friend Mr. Tooke mentioned that you were arriving, and I thought the least I could do is treat you to the Januarys as the Moor of Venice and Desdemona."

Madame De Brule rapped Fitz on the shoulder with her fan, followed by a deluge of French in a shrill voice. She punctuated every fourth word with a blow and ended the tirade in what had to be a question.

"Madame," Fitz said, amazed that any voice could be that high. "I'm sure I don't know what you said. Even if I did, I'm sure I wouldn't care."

De Brule leaned forward in his chair so he could look around Asia. "Mama is being inquisitive, Colonel Dunaway. She wishes to know if you are a Confederate officer."

Fitz glared at De Brule for the question and his proximity to Asia, and then turned to answer the old woman. "I am not," Fitz snapped, his words just below a shout. He had fallen into the habit most people adopt when speaking to the deaf—volume could overcome infirmity.

"It's no use, my dear colonel," De Brule explained. "She is quite deaf. Simply nod or shake your head when you deem either an appropriate answer."

"Fitz," Asia whispered across the intervening space. "Please don't be rude. This is a rare gift for me." Her eyes begged him to understand.

Fitz, defeated, nodded. "Just watch out for your champion," he whispered.

She looked at him in mild reproach. "Why Fitz, I married my champion."

The house lights began to dim, and the crowd fell silent. Fitz watched Asia's excitement grow. He loved her. Her happiness was all he desired, and when she smiled, or made a joke at his expense, he thought she had returned. Her strength was in her intelligence and humor, and the fire that consumed her when they made love.

He considered himself a poor husband. Not a bad man, but a man who stumbles through a relationship because he is ill prepared to undertake the complicated journey of marriage.

Madame De Brule swung her club again, catching Fitz on the hand. She directed a torrent of words at him in that high-pitched voice that pierced his brain. She stopped, obviously waiting for a reply.

Fitz accepted the challenge, and keeping his voice low, added, "Yes, he is a jackass, but what could one expect from a shrew like you?" He beamed at her.

Madame De Brule's face softened in gratitude, and she turned her attention to the stage.

Fitz turned to Asia, who was much too enthralled by her surroundings to notice Fitz. But his interest wasn't in his wife—it was in De Brule. Inspector De Brule, Tooke had warned him, was a friend to the South, and virtually the moment they arrived the good inspector invited them to the theater. Was it a scouting party, Fitz wondered? Certainly Abbott's disappearance and the possibility that Southern agents were involved had diplomatic impact. The arrival of additional British troops and the fear of an American invasion were all-too-real signs of a strained relationship. But was Abbott abducted, or had he simply run off in a moment of pique? He was in Quebec City, the telegram said with certainty—but where?

Would Inspector De Brule help them find Abbott, Fitz thought—or would he hinder them? A thought struck Fitz. This was about more than finding an errant professor—if it was not done with delicacy, Fitz might find himself directly between two nations on the verge of armed conflict.

Then the truth of the matter became obvious—if he handled this as clumsily as he did his marriage, he could be the cause for war.

Fitz was aware of thunderous applause, and as it died away, men's voices filled the theater. Actors—the play had begun.

Provine listened politely as the two men argued in French. He had been very methodical with his plans. Quebec City would be his home after the war. Well, it was his home now, and he certainly had no intention of returning to Richmond. He hated the insurance business, but he was trapped by his allegiance to his father, and spent his time talking about risks, fees, and percentages to dull men with plain wives. Only the war saved him.

His father, a bitter old man whose blood steamed at the thought of Yankee aggression, offered his son's services to the Confederacy. It was the best thing that had ever happened to Provine.

"Here! Here." The little Frenchman slapped the table with the palm of his hand. He was drunk and insistent, but in a friendly way. "Go to St. Vallier Street, in St. Roch. The houses are sturdy, and the women have big breasts." The other men at the table laughed.

Provine had paid a woman to teach him French. She cleaned his rooms, told him about the city, and, after pocking a pound note, taught him a few phrases in French. If he had extra money, she lifted her dress and tutored him in other subjects.

"St. Roch?" Provine asked.

"You want a house," the Frenchman said. He wrapped his fists around imaginary timbers as if testing their strength. "A strong house, eh? Go to St. Roch."

His companion, a man with a cloudy right eye, slapped the idea away as nonsense. "He's a gentleman. Can't you see that, you old fart? That's a working man's district. Go to Beaufort."

"The insane asylum?" Provine said.

"No, no," One Eye grumbled. "Beyond that."

"Look at this. Look at this," the little man observed in disgust. "He offers Beaufort only because that's where the distillery is."

The others laughed again, and even One Eye grinned in appreciation. "Well? So? If the gentleman builds a house in Beaufort we will go and visit him. And perhaps the distillery as well."

"You come to stay?" the Frenchman asked Provine.

"Yes. After the war as well."

"What do you do?"

Provine had thought of that. He was certain it would not be insurance. "Shipping."

The Frenchman wiggled his hand in response. "It is not as good as it used to be. Men build ships still at the St. Charles, but not so much as before."

"What do you do?" Provine asked.

The man swelled with pride and slammed his fist on the table. "I am a carter. In the winter I drive the sleigh and in the summer the wagon." He held up four fingers, one of them misshapen. "I have four fine horses, young and healthy, and when I say go—we go." He leaned closed and slapped Provine's arm in comradeship. "If you go three houses down," he said, his breath heavy with drink, "there is a woman who will take your money, and in return"—he belched softly—"she will lay with you."

"Thank you for the advice." Provine stood. "But, no. It's late." He paid the shopkeeper for his drink and more to buy the table a round. He shook the sawdust from the hem of his coat and tipped his hat in good-bye.

He went into the cold night and took a deep breath. His new friend misunderstood him—he would not build ships— he would own them. He had embezzled enough money from his accounts to buy partial ownership in a shipyard located in Lower Town between the Queen and King's wharves. With any luck, he decided, he would not see Richmond again.

*   *   *

Goodwin saw light flood the street in a narrow arc as the tavern door opened. The shadow of a solitary figure emerged, and the light disappeared, swallowed by the darkness. He dropped his cigar on the low stoop and slid his hand into his coat. It was Provine. There was little light to distinguish any features, but the man's round bulk, and ambling gait, told Goodwin who he was.

The Southern agent walked with his head down and his hands stuffed into the pockets of his long coat. His belly was full, and he had pleasured himself with his whore. Now, Goodwin knew, he would make his way home, satisfied in every way, seeking the comfort of a soft bed.

Goodwin felt the reassuring touch of the knife's handle. He kept it safely hidden in a leather sleeve, strapped across his chest, until he needed it. A dagger, January had called it. Thin, deadly, easy to withdraw and employ in a fight—a delicate instrument of mortality. January's words.

Iago was handsome, Asia thought, and his voice was deep with passion, but Royal January as Othello outshone any actor on the stage. She watched him, listened as every word, crisp and strong, filled the theater. They dueled, the two actors, Othello the Moor and Iago his Ancient, entering the stage accompanied by attendants bearing torches.

"Those are the raised father and his friends: You were best go in," Iago warned Othello, but the Moor refused.

"Not I; I must be found: My parts, my title, and my perfect soul shall manifest me rightly." Something captures his attention. "Is it they?"

Iago, following his gaze, replies, "By Janus, I think no."

Enter Cassio and certain Officers with torches.

She recognized him, her heart catching in her throat. He was Cassio, and she felt herself trembling as he spoke to Othello.

"The duke does greet you, general." His voice was stronger, deeper, and he moved on stage with all of the assurance of a

veteran. "And he requires your haste-post-haste appearance."
He looked in her direction, and Asia froze thinking that
Robert would somehow notice her and forget his lines. She
willed him to look elsewhere.

"What is the matter, think you?" Othello asked. Cassio
was so long in responding that Asia thought he had forgotten
his line, and she remembered how Robert became angry
when he could not memorize his lines after the first reading.
His mother had to sooth his rage, and Asia would make
jokes until Robert decided to try again.

"Something from Cyprus, as I may divine," Cassio said,
capturing the moment, striding downstage left. "It is a business of some heat; the galleys have sent a dozen sequent mes-
sengers."

She lost herself in his delivery, amazed that Robert Owen
had finally realized his dream—her dream as well, for they
shared that goal from their child's plays in the day parlor.
The stage was his, and for the length of his speech, hers as
well.

Asia was so enthralled with the performance that she
nearly forgot his letter. She was afraid Fitz could sense her
anguish and that he suspected the actor whose words traveled over the heads of the audience was his enemy. She knew
as surely she was being foolish.

She took a chance, glancing at Fitz, and saw him looking
at her. He smiled, but then his eyes questioned her, and she
saw a familiar expression that asked, *Why are you troubled?*

Goodwin moved smoothly, stalking his prey. You should
have been on the stage, January had told him, but Goodwin
believed the man was jesting. Nothing took the place of a
good killing—a well-planned action that culminated in a
shocked look, crumbling into pitiful disbelief, sinking into
the desperate realization that death was stealing life away.
Well planned of course, well thought out and conceived so
that all eventualities are accounted for, and yet knowing full
well that things can always go awry. Not tonight, Goodwin

knew, his boots whispering over the wet cobblestones. Provine, head down, continued to approach, unaware of the other figure on the Rue de Canal.

Tonight Goodwin would shorten the distance between his round target and himself, with measured steps, advancing until Provine looked up. By that time, it would be too late for one and just right for another.

Cassio turned to Iago, the exaggerated motion of a man who has had too much to drink. "For mine own part,—no offence to the general, nor any man of quality,— I hope to be saved."

Iago smiled, and responded with a courtly gesture. "And so do I too, lieutenant."

"Ay," Cassio said, "but, by your leave." Robert was subtle, with a touch of irony, capturing the character and circumstances perfectly. He was not Robert, Asia realized, but Cassio, and the impatient boy had long since disappeared and, in the time away from her, had matured. "The lieutenant is to be saved before the ancient." He dismissed the debate, growing magnanimous. "Let's have no more of this; let's to our affairs. God forgive us our sins!"

Goodwin pulled his knife from its sheath, seating the handle firmly into the palm of his right hand. He glanced over his shoulder and then past Provine, making sure the street was clear. It made no difference if there were witnesses—the attack would be quick, two shadows approaching, one bearing death, the other unsuspecting. There was no one on the street, and Goodwin tightened his grip on the knife.

Victoria January was beautiful. Her makeup was muted, defining her cheekbones, the line of her jaw, and the gentle breadth of her forehead. And she was graceful, her delicate hands imploring, pleading, and begging for understanding. Her voice was the early morning sun on a summer's day, soft and hopeful.

Asia saw something else.

"Bounteous madam," Cassio said, bowing. "Whatever should become of Michael Cassio, he's never anything but your true servant."

Desdemona paused. "I know't; I thank you," she added, knowing that there must be no misunderstanding. "You do love my lord; you have known him long, and be you well assur'd he shall in strangeness stand no further off than in a politic distance."

Robert barely lifted his gaze from Victoria's lovely face, and when he spoke his words were infused with passion.

Robert Owen was in love with Victoria January.

Provine raised his head, looking in Goodwin's direction for the first time. Goodwin maintained his pace. Provine's senses were dulled by alcohol; he probably wouldn't recognize the man approaching him. He barely noticed Goodwin when he met with January—why should a gentleman acknowledge his inferior? Besides, Goodwin always hung back, letting others call attention to themselves by talking. He never spoke unless January spoke to him.

He could see Provine's eyes narrow even in this dim light. He was on the edge of recognition, a face that had no place or name but had a presence in his memory. Provine's steps continued; there was no hesitation because Goodwin did not exist, and if he did not exist, especially to a gentleman like Provine, then there was no danger.

Goodwin turned the knife blade away from Provine. Even a random piece of light sliding along its edge might frighten Provine, and the man was steps away.

Goodwin smiled. Provine, seeing the smile, returned it, knowing there was no mystery to the man approaching, and certainly no danger because—

Goodwin slapped his hand over Provine's mouth and jammed the knife into his chest.

Provine's muted scream died under Goodwin's hand as the two staggered back to the shuttered window of a bakery.

Goodwin's arm came back, covered with black blood in the freezing air, and then he plunged the knife into Provine's chest again. More blood cascaded down the front of Provine's elegant waistcoat, dropping silently on the cobblestone.

Pinned back against the wooden shutters, Provine saw the bakery sign overhead. A mother goose trailed three goslings across a field of blue. There was no pain, but he was tired and cold, and he desperately wanted to sleep.

A mother goose and three goslings.

Goodwin stood back and let Provine's body collapse on the street. He wiped his knife and hands on the dead man's coat, glanced around to make sure he had not been seen, and walked away.

Chapter 12

The Latrobe Theater
Quebec City, British Canada

"We're invited to meet the Januarys," De Brule said, escorting the party down the grand staircase to the lobby. "I know you've had a busy day, but this is a rare privilege. They are a most private pair, gracious to be sure, but they seldom entertain visitors."

"You know them well?" Fitz said, remembering Tooke's warning about De Brule and the Januarys. Asia clung tightly to his arm, silent as they navigated their way through the buzz of theatergoers. Bodies collided into one another as the audience fought for the exits.

The play was barely understandable to Fitz. He had spent most of his time parrying Madame De Brule's constant assaults with her fan, with an occasional glance to make sure that De Brule wasn't taking liberties with Asia. The inspector had no hope of diverting Asia's attention from the play—she did not take her eyes from the stage. It was worth it, Fitz thought, worth the wretched old woman and her foppish son to see Asia enjoying herself.

"Well? Does anyone know well the most exciting duo on the stage?" De Brule discounted his influence.

"I believe I asked that question," Fitz said.

"Oh, no. No. I am one of many charmed by the January." He glanced at Fitz. He wanted to be understood. "But from a distance."

A stage manager intercepted them as they entered the vast cathedral of flats and ropes backstage.

"Monsieur De Brule, the Januarys beg your indulgence for thirty minutes."

De Brule turned to his party. "Ah, there, you see? Their time is not their own."

"Fitz?" Asia whispered. "I think I shall return to the hotel."

"What?" Fitz said, caught by surprise. "But I thought you wanted to meet these people?" He guided her to one side so they could speak privately. "What is it? I thought you were having a wonderful time."

"Yes," she said. "I am, Fitz. Really."

"But why must you run off like this? Aren't these the very people you wanted to see? Asia—"

"I do," she said, her voice low. "But I'm so very tired. You need not accompany me. Please, Fitz. Try to understand."

"Understand," Fitz said, stunned. Now she had swung the other direction—she was a pendulum swinging from darkness to light. "I've been trying to understand for a month. First you want something, then it means nothing."

"My dear Mrs. Dunaway," De Brule said, finding his chance to be the gentleman. "I know it's bold of me, but my carriage is just outside the stage door. Would you accept it to return to your hotel? And perhaps, forgive me for asking, allow my mother to join you?"

Fitz saw Asia's face fall in relief, and he knew he could say nothing else. He was so hurt by her inconsistencies that he didn't trouble himself to work up a good rage against the Frenchman.

"Thank you," Asia said to De Brule, and when she moved to kiss Fitz on the cheek he saw his moment to exact revenge. He backed away, denying her. It was a mistake, and he knew it immediately. He was acting like a child, but he was hurt.

Her eyes told him everything. He had wounded her as surely as she had him, and he accepted his triumph. She was calm, loving, distant, sullen, a swirl of emotions that Fitz found impenetrable.

De Brule escorted his mother and Asia to the carriage, and returned, without the façade of a host.

"Tooke is a young man," De Brule said. "I don't understand his concern about this man, Abbott. As I understand it, he comes and goes. First here, then the United States. The man is unbalanced. I urge you to forget all of this nonsense. I myself give the whole thing little credence."

"You must believe at least a bit of it," Fitz said, surprised at how cold De Brule's manner had become. "You took Abbott's valise."

"A precaution. Tooke reported the American missing." He shrugged. "I investigated. Besides, this business has made everyone very uncomfortable."

"How do you stand on the war?"

"The war?" De Brule said. "I am French-Canadian. What do I care how the United States settles its affairs?" He noted Fitz's wound. "Look at you. A brave young man wounded by his countrymen."

"The enemy did this," Fitz corrected him. "At the time I didn't consider them my countrymen. I had a decidedly different opinion of them."

"Oh, yes," De Brule said. "The rebels. But the war need not have happened if the Confederacy had been granted their God-given right to govern themselves. All this death, all this waste for nothing. We live in peace here in Canada. We are civil and prosperous."

"You're speaking as a French-Canadian?"

"Yes."

"Under British rule in British Canada?" Fitz asked. De Brule flushed.

"The Januarys will receive you now," the stage manager said.

"We are unfortunate enough to be occupied by our former

enemy," De Brule said. "One day it may come to pass that this is no longer the case. There is talk that some in your country want to invade Canada. The United States may find itself less successful than the British. In fact, may I suggest this is already the case. Particularly since it is apparent to the world you are losing the war."

Asia let the carriage window down. "One moment, please," she called to the driver, her heart beating wildly. She motioned to one of the actors, just exiting the stage door. "This is most important," she said. "Has Robert Owen left the theater yet?"

"Robert?" the actor turned to his companion. "Why, no. I saw him backstage just a moment ago."

Asia pulled pencil and paper from her purse and, holding the paper to catch the pale light of a street lamp, wrote quickly. When she finished, she folded the paper and handed it to the actor. "Please. I know this is most unusual, but please return to the theater and make sure Robert gets this." She handed it to the actor.

He took the note and glanced at it curiously. Then, happy to be a player in a romantic farce, saluted her with the note. "I will be delighted."

Royal January rose effortlessly and shook hands with Fitz. The actor was tall and lithe, his dark hair brushed away from his broad forehead. His face was youthful, but his black eyes reflected the harsh maturity of a worldly man. Fitz did not trust him.

"Colonel Dunaway," January said in a mellow voice. "This is a pleasure. Let me introduce you to my sister, Miss Victoria January."

Fitz thought, guiltily, that she was the most beautiful woman he had ever met. Her blond hair was brilliant, capturing the light of the candles scattered around the room. He felt her large blue eyes examining him as if she intended to catalog his every feature. She remained seated, of course, as Fitz bowed, and he had an unobstructed view of the remarkable expanse of her full, white breasts. They rose and fell with each breath, as naturally as the constant rolling of moonlit waves against the sand.

As he stood, his face was on fire in embarrassment.

"Please," Royal January said, indicating two chairs in the richly furnished dressing room. When De Brule and Fitz were seated, January looked at them expectantly. "Well? You must tell me how you enjoyed the play."

"A triumph," De Brule said. "How can anyone expect to play Othello, or delude themselves into thinking they would play Desdemona, ever again?"

Victoria, lounging on a fainting couch, one arm thrown seductively over the back, said, "And you, Colonel?"

Fitz's mouth went dry. He struggled to think of something. "It must be hot in those clothes."

"Hot?" January said. He gave De Brule a pained expression. "Hot?"

Fitz felt himself slipping into embarrassment. "In those actor's clothes. With those lights. Walking about on stage."

Victoria was gracious. "It appears the colonel has little knowledge of the theater. One does what one must to carry the play. Costumes are never uncomfortable. They are endured for the sake of the performance. We must, we actors, draw upon every device, don't you know. Our voices, the costumes." There was a beat before she added, "Our bodies." She didn't give him time to respond. "Your wound? Is it painful?"

"Not at all," Fitz said. He was relieved to talk about anything but actors. She was beautiful, he thought, and she exuded desire. He had not slept with Asia for some time. His arm and her moods conspired to keep them apart. This woman could turn a man against everything he held dear.

"What do you think of Quebec City, Colonel Dunaway?" January asked. "But I have been remiss in my duties. Would you like a refreshment?"

"Nothing, thank you," Fitz replied.

"A sherry," De Brule said. "If you please."

January rang for a servant, so Fitz directed his answer to Victoria. She leaned forward in expectation, exposing more flesh.

"From what I've seen of it, the city is lovely," Fitz said, ignoring the desire to stare. "A bit too cold for me. I prefer moderate weather."

"One becomes accustomed to the winters in the city," Victoria said. "There is something enchanting about spending one's day indoors, warmed by a vigorous fire." Her eyes questioned Fitz. "Where is your home, Colonel?"

"At present, Washington," Fitz replied.

"Oh, no, no," Victoria said. There was a gay trill to her voice but the tone bordered on disdainful as well. "I mean, where were you born? You're Southern, aren't you? Oh, my. I hope I haven't offended you, that blue uniform and all."

"You haven't," Fitz said. How easily Asia's memory slipped from his mind. "Tennessee. East Tennessee, near Cumberland Gap."

"Very mountainous, is it not?" De Brule contributed to the conversation.

"Most places," Fitz said. "I was raised on the Powell River. My father owns a large farm."

"But not a plantation?" Victoria said. "No slaves?"

Fitz shook his head.

"I thought everyone in the South owned slaves," De Brule sniffed. "Am I mistaken?" The Januarys' attention had shifted from him, Fitz was pleased to see.

"But have you been home, Colonel?" Victoria said, ignoring De Brule. "Certainly you've gone home to your family lands?"

"Not in some time."

Victoria was about to speak when her brother interrupted. "I suppose that would be complicated for you now, wouldn't it, Colonel?"

"East Tennessee, at least some parts, are occupied by the rebels," Fitz said. "If that's what you mean?"

"I could not stand it if I were prevented from returning to

Mayfield," Victoria said. "I draw my strength from our home. Royal and I return whenever we can. We love riding over the fields, and the sound of laughter in the cool evenings." It was clear she pitied Fitz. "To refute one's heritage is a punishment beyond this poor child's comprehension. I mean to declare one's people, one's family, the enemy? Would your friends and neighbors not consider your actions those of betrayal? Your family, Colonel? They must be crushed. Oh, how I pity you for having to choose cause over kin."

"I believe Colonel Dunaway suggested that if he returned home," January explained, "he might be hanged." He turned his attention to Fitz. "And yet here you are, amidst the snowy fields and arctic air of Canada. May I be so bold as to ask why?"

"He's on the trail of a countryman of his," De Brule offered. "Abbott? Isn't it? A runaway madman of some sort."

"Yes," Fitz said. "His name is Abbott, Phillip Abbott, and what he is remains to be determined."

"On his trail?" Victoria said. "You're not a detective, are you?"

Fitz glanced at his uniform. "No. As far as I know, I'm still a colonel of the Regular United States Army. Abbott is reported to be in the city. A friend is concerned about his well-being."

All three looked appropriately sympathetic. Actors, Fitz thought, and now he had joined the cast. "You haven't seen him, have you?"

"I?" January said. He looked at his sister, who shook her head. "No. Not I. Of course we see so few Americans here. Most of our friends are, by circumstance, other members of the company. I'm afraid I wouldn't know the man if he was sitting across from me." He stood, his long frame graceful— a feline movement. "Gentlemen, you must excuse us. The performance was taxing and sleep is a necessary ingredient of an actor's life."

Fitz and De Brule rose, the Frenchman favoring Victoria's hand with a kiss, Fitz bowing slightly from a safe distance.

Outside, snow had begun to fall, thick feathery flakes that drifted in a moderate wind. De Brule signaled for a cab.

"I'll have Abbott's bag delivered to your hotel tomorrow," De Brule said. He pulled the fur collar of his coat close around his neck. Fitz threw his cape over his shoulder, fastening the frogs with one hand. "I'll have my men look for Abbott," De Brule said without enthusiasm. The meaning was clear—*you can expect little or no help from me.*

"You have been most gracious," Fitz said. De Brule offered him the cab when it slid to a stop in the snow, but Fitz waved the opportunity aside. "I'm not that far from the hotel. I'll walk."

De Brule stopped, one foot on the iron rung of the vehicle. "I thought you detested cold weather?"

"I do," Fitz said. "But I get along under most circumstances."

De Brule looked up, letting the falling snow pepper his face. "Snow is a different matter entirely. One may leave a trail in the first falling, but one's passing may be entirely obscured in minutes. In fact, any number of events can lie hidden under a vast field of snow. Years could pass"—he turned to Fitz with a meaningful look—"before any evidence of one's behavior is detected, hidden, as it were, under God's blanket. It hides even the ugliest of truths under a chaste field of purity."

De Brule regarded Fitz for moment and then swung into the cab, closing the door.

Fitz rapped on the cab door. The window slid down with a rattle and the detective's face appeared, partially obscured by the darkness.

"Inspector De Brule," Fitz said. "Snow melts."

Chapter 13

Hotel St-Denis
Quebec City, British Canada

Fitz awoke after a restless night. He had dreamed of battles, and men dying, and the long, dreadful journey to
Washington. His men marched to certain destruction across
a wheat field, ignoring his cries to stop. His mind reacted
with a flurry of images, all tumbling around one another in a
frantic mixture. Asia would appear and then disappear before he had a chance to call her name.

Asia had been asleep in her room when Fitz looked in on
her after his return from the theater. She appeared to be
sleeping deeply, and he thought about going to her, but he did
not. He was afraid that, rather then being asleep, she was
awake, only pretending so she would not have to talk to him.
He turned silently, closed the door to her room, and thought
for a moment he heard sobs. He did not go back.

In the morning, when he opened her door, he found that
she hadn't moved. The idea irritated him. He was still angry
with her from the night before, and his night had been so
miserable.

After his morning toilet and rebandaging his arm, he
dressed, careful not to disturb the bandage. He was surprised
to see a note that had been slipped under the door. It was

from Tooke, inviting Fitz to breakfast in thirty minutes so that he might share fascinating information with him.

Fitz tossed the message in the fireplace, plopped his garrison cap on his head, and closed the parlor door behind him with a soft click. He hesitated, wondering if he should have awakened Asia, thinking perhaps to leave a note to tell her where he had gone. It was to assuage the guilt he felt over his petty behavior the night before. He decided against it, settling on the excuse that he would not be long, and Tooke might have very little to offer anyway. The real reason, however, was that he felt like a fool for his impatience with her. It was because he did not know what caused her to change. Being unsure of his emotions, Fitz feared that somehow, for some unexplained reason, he might lose Asia.

He was directed to Tooke's table near a large window looking out on the street. The snow that began falling last night had increased in strength, turning the world into a wild jumble of snowflakes.

Tooke noticed Fitz's gaze. "Thrilling, isn't it? Here, sit down please. Coffee? You'll want coffee." He waved at a waiter and ordered for Fitz. "It amazes me, the snows we get up here. It piles up like white mountains. Everything looks like a fairyland. Everything softens under a heavy cover of the stuff. Getting around can be a challenge, but the people pay it no heed."

"Yes," Fitz said, when the coffee was set down before him. "Inspector De Brule and I discussed that last night." He told Tooke about the visit to the theater and conversation with the Januarys.

"That's one pair I wouldn't trust," Tooke said. He looked at Fitz expectantly. "Rumor has it after their next performance they're going south."

"Are they?"

"They're advertised through the month. Did you know they make nearly twenty-five thousand dollars a year?" The idea appalled him.

"No," Fitz said.

"Rumor has it—"

"More rumors? Isn't anything certain up here?"

Tooke said, "Nothing reliable. Anyway, it's common knowledge they buy up medical supplies and ship them south. Are you going to eat?"

It was easy for Fitz to see the rotund young man's point—money and a cause went hand in hand. Shipping medical supplies or even gold could be readily accomplished with a little bit of luck and daring. How much of each were needed, Fitz wasn't certain. Tooke cleared his throat and glanced at the menu board on the table. He was hoping that Fitz would join him so he wouldn't have to eat alone. "I think I will eat," Fitz said.

Tooke grinned in relief. "Yes. Good. Good." After the waiter had arrived and taken their order, Tooke leaned toward Fitz, locking his fingers together on the table. "Have you been able to make any sense of that book?"

Fitz had forgotten about the mysterious object. "Not a bit," he said. "I have no head for science or mathematics. If Billy had two apples and Tommy had two apples, my answer would be applesauce."

Tooke gave him a blank look. "But the military academy? Surely you—"

"Passed by the skin of my teeth. Textbooks do not necessarily make a soldier, Mr. Tooke."

"Of course," Tooke agreed. "The contents of the book are well beyond my capabilities."

"I certainly can't offer much," Fitz said. "My apologies to Billy and Tommy."

Tooke laughed. "I went to the Department of Deeds and Properties. I was able to secure some information about Abbott's property. He has a farm on the Ile d'Orleans. It's in the St. Lawrence." An occasional dark shape would slide by the window, a carriage braving the blowing snow. "Do you think the rebels have him?"

Fitz rubbed his shoulder, settling his arm in the sling. "I

don't know. Coming to Quebec City in the dead of winter makes no sense, unless he was made to. I don't know. What struck me last night," Fitz added, remembering the conversation, "is De Brule went out of his way to mention Abbott when we were in the company of the Januarys. I didn't have to say a word. The Januarys denied knowing the man, or even hearing of him."

"Are you certain—"

"Inspector De Brule was far too polite. If Abbott is supposed to be here, or so you have heard, we may have a chance to find him. And as he is not at the St-Denis, then the possibility remains that he is at his farm. What the Januarys have to do with this, if anything, I have no idea. In other words, Mr. Tooke, I have no answers." Fitz saw De Brule weaving between the tables in the crowded restaurant. He smiled a warning at Tooke. "And here is the inspector."

"Good morning, gentlemen," De Brule said. His shoulders were covered by a thick layer of snow. He hadn't even bothered to shake his coat clean before entering the hotel. It would be a short visit.

Fitz noticed he carried a worn valise in his hand. "You've arrived bearing gifts. How kind of you."

De Brule was not amused by Fitz's attitude but he remained civil. "Abbott's famous luggage." He set it on the floor next to Fitz.

"Won't you join—" Tooke began.

De Brule held up his hand, forestalling the invitation. "Duty calls. But I have some good news. Your lost friend has returned to the United States."

"Abbott?" Tooke exclaimed.

"How do you know?" Fitz asked.

"One of my officers," De Brule said. "He was making his customary inquiries at the terminal. We do our part to keep track of the comings and goings of all interesting parties, Colonel Dunaway, contrary to what you may have heard. My officer, remembering Mr. Tooke's original request to my office, was told that a man named Phillip Abbott purchased a ticket not two days ago. His destination was New York City."

"Two days?" Fitz said. He gave Tooke an amazed look. "Virtually the moment we arrived."

"Ironic if it were true, Colonel," De Brule said, "but of course we have no way of determining that."

"Your man is certain of this?" Fitz said. "It was our mysterious Phillip Abbott?"

"He is," De Brule said. "And therefore, I am. Your journey to Quebec City was in vain, I suppose." He remembered. "Except of course, your visit to the theater." He became solicitous. "Your charming wife? I hope she is recovered. I would never forgive myself if I were somehow the cause of her discomfort."

"Ease your mind, inspector," Fitz replied. "You didn't make her sick." He leaned back in his chair, taking a thoughtful attitude. "I can't get over how coincidental it is that your man was able to obtain and confirm that information. I must admit I am most fortunate. There is no longer a reason for me to remain in Quebec City."

De Brule's face tightened, but quickly relaxed. "You have a sharp mind, Colonel Dunaway. It's a shame that it is not better employed. Good morning, gentlemen."

Fitz picked up the valise and set it on the table, after De Brule left. "If I had a big dog I'd sic him on De Brule." He snapped the cover off the clasps. "Or even a small dog."

"I'm amazed he returned it," Tooke said. "Abbott returned to New York. This whole affair has been for nothing."

"This valise is a token, probably because it has no value," Fitz said, laying several newspapers on the table. "And if I were you I would give no credence to that story."

"He was lying?"

Fitz looked at Tooke. "You don't find it a bit of a coincidence that I show up and Mr. Abbott departs for the United States? You must not be so trusting."

"Then where is Abbott?"

"I haven't the slightest idea," Fitz said. He fanned the papers on the table, and counted them. "Well, that's it. Seven papers. All *Harper's Illustrated Newspaper*. Apparently Abbott likes to read the news. And nothing current at that." Fitz flipped through them. "McClellan, Peninsular Campaign, Army of the Potomac, the James River." He gathered up the papers and dropped them in the valise in disgust. "Worthless." He knew what he had to do next. "How can we get to Abbott's farm?"

"On Ile d'Orleans?" Tooke said, surprised. "Not for some time. A person could get lost outside of the city in this weather."

"Can we hire a boat?"

"The river is frozen in deep winter, Colonel Dunaway. People travel on sleds. There are ice roads marked across the river. Broad avenues."

"Ice? Are there no bridges in this town?"

"They are absolutely safe this time of year." Tooke glanced out the window to add weight to his warning. "But we'll have to wait until the weather clears. It is far too dangerous to travel in a blizzard outside of the city. "

"I just can't sit here and do nothing," Fitz said. He realized that Tooke's suggestion was the only sensible option open to him. "Will you send a telegram for me when you return to the consul?"

"Of course," Tooke said. He produced a pencil and paper. "It will go out in State Department Code. That is if the lines are not down. In that case we shall have to rely on courier, but he cannot leave—"

"Yes, I know," Fitz said. "Until the blizzard subsides. Have you thought about using polar bears as gallopers?"

Tooke gave an apologetic shrug.

"The fastest way," Fitz said. He glanced to make sure no one was close enough to hear him. "To A. Lincoln. Unable to find Abbott at present. Weather curtails search. Reports that he has returned to the United States unreliable. I will contact again in two days." He nodded, and Tooke ended the dictation.

"The weather might not clear in two days," Tooke offered, slipping the notepad and pencil in his pocket.

"In that case," Fitz replied, "I'll think of another way to say there has been no progress."

A puzzled look crossed Tooke's face. "Isn't that Mrs. Dunaway?"

Fitz twisted in his chair and caught a glimpse of Asia, bundled against the cold, passing the dining room doorway. He stood. "Where's your coat?"

The shocked Tooke said, "What?"

"Your coat! Give me your coat, man."

Tooke pointed to a row of coats hanging from pegs on the far wall. "There. Third from the right."

Fitz was halfway across the dining room when Tooke cried, "What shall I do about a coat?"

"If I'm not back in two hours, steal one," Fitz said, yanking a coat and hat from the rack. He raced outside, throwing the coat over his shoulders and pulling the soft cap down on his head. The wind battered him, snow—combined with tiny slivers of ice—driving into his face. He quickly surveyed the nearly empty street, knowing once Asia disappeared into the blizzard, she was lost to him.

He wasn't sure why he had to follow her. It was fear, mostly. She could be going to meet someone; the notion that anyone would go for a walk in this miserable weather made no sense. There was no other reason. And that reason would explain why she had been so distant these last weeks.

He saw her, a rough form, no more than a shadow, but the walk told him it was Asia. He set out after her, hanging back so that she would not see him, but not so much that he was in danger of losing her. He had come to Quebec City to find a man and, he thought ruefully, he might just accomplish that task. But the man, he thought, might be the one who had stolen his wife's heart.

He silenced his mind with a sharp command, reminding himself that his mission was to find Abbott, but he did not stop walking—he did not turn away from the woman who moved like a ghost through a white mist. He could not, and yet he feared that to continue would be more painful than a dozen wounds. To give up now was to admit that he had truly lost his wife—the woman whose love, whose touch, meant so much to him.

The snow slackened enough for him to see that the sidewalk was barren of people. He felt cold, abandoned, and he recognized the hollowness in his chest as a sign of the loneliness that lay in store for him.

She stopped at a storefront, looked at a slip of paper in her hand, and entered.

Fitz's heart raced, and his mouth was dry. His legs carried him forward, until he passed the shop window. He caught a glimpse of the scene inside. It was a shop, perhaps a small café, dark and inviting, with tiny tables set around the interior. Asia hurried to one of the tables, smiling as she threw off her coat. A young man stood expectantly and they embraced. They held each other tightly, and parted reluctantly.

Fitz continued to walk, too stunned to think, numb to the snow that peppered his face or the cold that tried desperately to pry his heart from his body.

Chapter 14

Rue du Bois
Quebec City, British Canada

All of his life there had been a grim voice that welled up in him when things appeared too desperate for solution. *There has got to be a way.* The voice had been Fitz's companion at the U.S. Military Academy when the intricacies of mathematics conspired to overwhelm him—on the plains when Cheyenne Dog Soldiers had him and a thin squad trapped on the Republican River. At Bull Run, and again in Washington when he was falsely charged with murder, he resolved to win. *There has got to be a way. Stubborn,* his superiors had written on his fitness reports; *obstinate,* a rotund colonel had tossed at him.

Fitz shifted in the seat, smiling at Asia as the sleigh passed silently through the snow. She returned his smile, oddly relaxed.

If there were another man, Fitz vowed, he would find himself in the fight of his life. Asia would not be given up so easily. *I love her.* For some reason or other she was drawn to this other man. *Well, so be it. I can just as surely draw her back to me. I will win her again,* Fitz thought. *There has got to be a way.*

"Here is the Consul," Asia said as the sleigh slid to a stop.

Fitz alighted, blinking in the bright sunlight. The sky was the cleanest blue he had ever seen—the color of innocence, he thought as he held out his hand for Asia. A blue of promise.

"Good morning," Tooke said, exiting the building. "Beautiful, isn't it? I see you received my message."

"It feels positively warm in the sun," Asia noted.

Tooke looked up. "No clouds. No wind. A remarkable day. I thought we could make for the Ile d'Orleans. Do you feel up to it?"

"If you mean me," Fitz said, irritated at the question, "I am here. How far is it?"

"About five miles," Tooke said. "I've taken the liberty of hiring a sleigh."

"Have you a driver?" Asia asked.

Fitz recognized the true reason behind her question. "May I remind you, Mrs. Dunaway, that I already have one injury?"

Tooke looked from Asia to Fitz. "What?"

"Colonel Dunaway," she said playfully. "You speak as if I am careless."

Relief swept over Fitz. Everything was going to be all right. Despite what he saw, and what he knew to be true, everything was going to be all right. He felt like a boy whose love had taken his hand in hers.

"Careless?" Fitz replied. "Not in the least. But you are damned dangerous."

A frightened look crossed Tooke's face. "What?"

"She wants to drive the sleigh," Fitz said. He exchanged a warm look with Asia. Nothing could come between them—could it?

"But—"

"Mr. Tooke," Fitz said, gently removing all doubt. "She will drive the sleigh, because she *will* drive the sleigh. My wife is resolute."

Asia kissed Fitz on the cheek. "And my husband is most perceptive."

Asia was at her best behavior, guiding the two-horse team with a gentle hand. Even Tooke was forced to concede she was a talented driver, despite his misgivings. For Fitz, the ride down a snow-packed road and onto the ice was the smoothest he had ever experienced. He felt little beyond the slight tremor of the blades cutting into the snow. Heavily bundled in carriage blankets, the journey was more a pleasant outing on a gleaming field of white than a search for the elusive Phillip Abbott.

Fitz, sitting next to Asia in the front seat of the sleigh, shifted so he could speak to Tooke.

"Have you had any correspondence from Washington?" The blizzard had blown itself out after trapping the city in its grip for nearly two days.

"Nothing," Tooke said. He gave Fitz a puzzled look.

"What is it?" Fitz asked.

"I am completely perplexed by this event. Abbott took his usual rooms at the St-Denis. Of course he wasn't there, but why take rooms in the city when his farm is barely five miles away?"

"You said he desires the companionship of questionable women?" Asia tossed into the conversation.

"Such women," Fitz conceded, "are unlikely to be found on a farm. Another question becomes, did he leave his room of his own accord or was he abducted?"

"He left his belongs behind," Tooke ventured.

"Nothing of consequence. Correct?"

"That's right. The valise—"

"Filled with outdated newspapers."

"And the notebook."

"Which I carry"—Fitz patted his breast pocket—"and for which there appears to be no key. I believe Mr. Abbott left without violence, but left expecting to return."

"There." Tooke pointed, leaning over the back of the seat. "Go up that bank, and at the crossroads, turn right. It shouldn't be more than a mile." He settled back in his seat. "But if Mr. Abbott left his rooms on his own, why hasn't he returned?"

"Well," Fitz said, fishing through his coat pocket for his pipe. "He's either on a fast packet to the South"—he slipped the pipe stem into his mouth—"or he's taken that long voyage across the River Styx."

"Oh."

The sleigh rode easily up the bank, its team finding enough purchase for ample footing.

"Look at the trees," Asia said in wonderment.

The bare branches were coated in thin bands of snow, sparkling in the stark rays of the sun. Every bit of the landscape was blanketed, robbed of any distinction by the brilliant cover. Mounds of snow banked against walls of buildings, wrapped itself around fence posts so that only the tops remained visible, and ran in deep drifts up to the edge of the road. The roofs of the houses were bare, snow having melted away from the heat within.

"It is a beautiful place," Asia said, "isn't it?"

Fitz remembered the blizzard and the scene in the shop. "It is," he returned in a whisper.

"Here, I think," Tooke said, pulling a sheet of paper from his coat pocket. He examined it, glancing up to get his bearings. "There. Down that lane." He pointed to a small house, shadowed by several outbuildings, and a large barn.

"This place is abandoned. No one's been here for some time," Fitz observed. "The lane is snowbound," he added in reply to Tooke's questioning look. "There's been no fire in that house recently. The roof is covered in snow."

"Do we go on?" Tooke asked.

"We do," Fitz said. "All we have to show for our efforts thus far are a book, some newspapers, and a missing man. We might yet be rewarded at Mr. Abbott's farm."

Asia snapped the reins and the team picked up its pace. The snow was much deeper on the lane leading to Abbott's, and the sleigh body bottomed out several times as the horses struggled to make their way. They got within a hundred feet of the house before a drift denied them passage.

"We walk," Fitz said, stepping into a snowbank. He sunk up to his knees, steadied himself, and turned to Asia. "I think it best you remain with the sleigh."

"I haven't seen this much snow in my life," Asia said, tying off the reins and then climbing out on the blade support. She stepped down, her dress billowing around her as she sank.

Fitz laughed at her shocked face, but she gave him a defiant look and fought her way forward.

Tooke joined him, rolling from leg to leg as he stepped into the snow. "She is a remarkable woman."

Fitz felt a pang of regret. The secret that hung between Asia and him was almost too much to bear. But his love for her gave him strength. "I pray more so than I know," he said, allowing himself a moment of weakness.

They struggled toward the front door of the modest farmhouse, but it was blocked by a snowbank.

Fitz brushed the crusted snow from his trouser legs. "The barn, I suppose." Asia and Tooke removed as much of the caked snow as possible from their garments, then followed Fitz's path through the snow.

"I long for warm weather," Tooke said, struggling after Asia. "I've had enough snow and cold."

The barn's ancient door hung open, balancing on rusted iron hinges. They entered the dark interior. It was free of snow except the patch that had managed to blow in through the doors. Fitz found a lantern, lit the wick, and held it out to cast a light.

He saw several tables cluttered with tools and half-finished baskets scattered to one side. "A workshop," he observed as he examined the items on the tables. Burned scraps of paper were littered around the tools. "These won't tell us anything," Fitz said. He picked up several baskets, examined them, and tossed them back on the workbench. "I suppose these are for gathering apples." What he found eminently more intriguing was that the tools appeared to have been heavily used.

"This is odd," Tooke said, catching Fitz's attention.

"What?"

"Here are bits of silk."

"Fitz!" Asia called in alarm. "There's a dead man in the corner."

The man lay propped against the wall, legs outstretched, arms dropped to his side, strands of his white hair littered with dust.

"Abbott," Fitz said, approaching him. "Shot in the chest." He knelt down. "Dead for some time."

"But he looks so natural—" Asia began, and realized what she had said. "Aside from the gunshot wound."

Fitz stood. "Frozen. Or as close to it as he could be." What did Tooke say? He turned. "Silk?"

"Yes. There. A goodly quantity." Tooke gave Fitz a perplexed look. "But, see here. It's covered with something. Pitch or something."

"Fitz?" Asia said.

"The DuPont Powder Works. Remember? They found scraps of silk there as well." He stopped, trying to assemble all that he knew but finding that it was a puzzle without a solution. Worse than that, it was several puzzles, all the pieces intermingled. "None of this makes sense," Fitz said, confused. Everything was laid out for him to examine, but his mind refused to cooperate. He was defeated, at least for the moment. "Let us go back to the city and I'll inform President Lincoln of my findings, such as they are." He picked up a piece of Tooke's silk. Rubbing it between his fingertips he added, "I feel foolish telling Mr. Lincoln that I am as perplexed now as I was when I arrived."

Asia glanced at the body in the corner. "I'll say a prayer for poor Mr. Abbott."

"Say one for me as well," Fitz said, leading them out of the barn. "I'm still surrounded by mysteries."

They reached the sleigh after stopping several times to catch their breath. Fitz helped Asia into the vehicle.

Tooke, catching his foot on a blueberry bush partially hidden by the snow, stumbled into Fitz.

Tooke's head exploded, spraying blood and tissue into the air. Fitz jumped into the sleigh, shouting, "Go!"

Asia screamed at the horses, snapping the reins and at the same time pulling them hard to get the horses turned. The animals, frightened by the smell of blood, struggled, but bolted forward, fighting their way through the snow. Asia jerked the reins, forcing the team back onto the track they had broken to the farm.

There was a high-pitched whine and a crack as a bullet passed over them. Fitz pulled his .44 out of its holster and got off two shots in the general direction he thought the fire was coming from.

"Are you hurt?" Asia called, urging the horses on. Chunks of snow and mud were flung into the air by their hooves. The animals' legs were an excited blur, their heads extended as they gulped in the cold air.

"No," Fitz said, trying to find their assailants. "If that poor man hadn't tripped I'd be lying back there. Not him."

He saw a sleigh coming out of the tree line behind the barn and outbuildings. The driver found Asia's path and accelerated. There was another man with him, and he was holding a carbine. Fitz aimed his pistol but knew any chance of hitting them was remote. Still, he could hope. He cocked the hammer back, aimed, and fired.

The sleigh continued after them.

"Is there someone following us?" Asia said, betraying her fear for the first time.

"Can you get us to the river?" Fitz said.

"Hold on," Asia shouted, pulling hard on the reins. The sleigh plowed through a drift and whipped heavily to the right, as Asia fought to keep it on the main road. All they had to do was drive straight to the river's edge and onto the ice.

Fitz turned to see the other sleigh expertly take the turn and pick up speed on the snow-covered road.

"Speed up," he said, climbing into the backseat. He knelt on the nest of carriage blankets, used his knees to lock himself into place, and cocked and carefully aimed the pistol. He squeezed the trigger, and the revolver jumped in his hand with a sharp bark. He saw the sleigh waver, but the driver regained control.

Fitz saw the drift line at the edge of the river in time to prepare himself. They were going too fast.

The horses plowed through the bank, sending a cloud of snow spraying into the cold. The sleigh bounced once, left the earth, and seemed to float above the ice.

Asia, belatedly, called, "Hold on."

Fitz, in the midst of climbing into the front seat, was thrown into the air. He caught the seat edge as the sleigh landed with a bang on the ice. It slid sideways, but Asia regained control and turned the horses to match the direction of the runaway vehicle.

"Are you all right?" Fitz asked.

"Are *you* all right?" Asia replied.

They gained some distance as the other sleigh slowed, descending the snow-covered bank with caution. Fitz watched as the driver drove his horses faster. The man with the carbine, now just a vague figure, steadied himself.

It's a Spencer, Fitz thought. *He's fired twice*—he realized he couldn't be sure, but he decided it was twice—*and he's got five more rounds.* Their only defense was to outrun their pursuers.

"How are the horses?" he asked Asia.

"Winded," she replied. "They aren't made for this sort of thing." She tossed him a frightened smile. "Neither am I."

Fitz turned. What he saw heartened him. "Hurrah! You've put more distance between us." He watched, unbelieving, as the other sleigh slowed, then stopped. "They're giving up. You've done it, Asia."

Her smile was worth a fortune to Fitz, and he impulsively kissed her on the cheek. "There's never been a man or woman who could handle a team of horses like you."

There was a loud crack and the sleigh pitched to the left. The horses screamed in terror as the ice fractured below their feet and the sleigh lurched to a halt, throwing Asia and Fitz nearly out of the vehicle. Fitz watched in horror as fissures raced crazily across the ice and under the blade. Green water rolled up between the pieces of ice.

"Get out," Fitz cried. "Get flat on the ice and crawl toward the shore."

Asia threw herself out just as the sleigh sunk to its body. Icy water rushed into the sleigh as Fitz jumped from the vehicle. White-hot pain rushed over him. He had landed on his wound. He tore the sling off and sought out Asia.

Thin lines raced across the ice, crackling like a vengeful fire. Flows began to separate from one another as Fitz hurriedly crawled toward Asia.

"Fitz!" she cried. "Fitz, the horses. They'll drown."

The weight of the sinking sleigh had the animals trapped. They fought frantically, trying to pull themselves out of the hole that had opened beneath their feet. Screaming in fright, they thrashed helplessly in the freezing water as the sleigh shifted.

Fitz pulled himself to the vehicle, cursing himself, the horses, and the murderers who tried to kill them. That was why they had stopped—they saw Asia drive off the marked road and onto thin ice.

He got as close to the edge of the ice as he dared and, reaching out, grasped hold of the tongue pin. He twisted it back and forth, hoping to work it loose. The two horses, worn out from their struggle, could barely kick at the water.

Fitz checked to make sure the reins were free, and then jerked on the pin. He felt it move. The ice cracked beneath him and frigid water rush over his shoulders. He heard Asia scream, and he pulled on the pin. It broke free of the tongue, and the horses, renewed from the release of the sleigh, fought their way over the edge of the ice and galloped unsteadily toward the bank.

Fitz crawled to Asia. Standing, he helped her to her feet. "Follow those dumb animals," he gasped, shivering. "If the ice will hold horses, it will hold us."

They trotted across the ice. The cold water had taken more from Fitz than he realized, and he had difficulty keeping up with Asia. When she started to slow to allow him to catch up, he waved her on.

He glanced over his shoulder to make sure they were not being followed, but there was no sign of the other sleigh. He saw Asia resting near a stand of trees, gulping in air—they had reached safety.

When Fitz joined her, she threw her arms around him and laid her head on his shoulder. He held her tightly, ignoring the pain in his arm and the sharp cold that swept over him.

"We must find some warmth," he said. He remembered they had passed a string of houses on their way to the river. He knew they were nearby. He pried her arms from around his neck and forced a smile. "As enjoyable as I find this respite, we need shelter."

He took her by the hand and led her toward the road. The words were out before he could stop them. "I thought I'd lost you." She misunderstood, glancing back at the river. "No," he said. "I mean the man in the restaurant, the other night. I thought you had found someone else."

"Oh, Fitz," Asia said, laying her hand on his cheek.

He watched as her eyes filled with tears and felt her soft hand caress his face.

"Don't you know how much I love you?"

He was too confused to respond.

"Fitz," Asia said, stopping him. "He is my brother."

Chapter 15

Railway station
Burketon, New York

The old man picked his way through the crowded dining room, his black walking stick leading the way. No one paid the slightest attention to his stooped figure. The din was overwhelming as passengers devoured their meals to the discordant music of slurping, silverware scraping over plates, and the loud hum of conversation.

Nothing disturbed the old man's progress to his table and the company of an elderly woman, dressed in the heavy black garments of full mourning. She stirred cream into a cup of tea and did not acknowledge his presence as he sat down.

"Don't you think you've milked that performance a bit more than necessary?" Victoria said, keeping her voice low.

"Try not to stir that tea into oblivion," Royal January returned, stifling a racking cough with his handkerchief.

"Consumption?" Victoria said. "A nice touch."

January handed his sister a telegram, as the table next to them burst out in raucous laughter. Salesmen, January knew—vile, dirty men.

"Is it good news?" Victoria said, taking the document. She laid it on the table and read as she stirred.

January returned a disgusted expression. "Do I look like

good news? No. It was a bungled mess. How I despise amateurs. They were supposed to follow Colonel Dunaway only."

"Who?"

"The late Mr. Provine's men. Follow, nothing else."

Victoria's hand trembled slightly as she brought the cup to her mouth.

"For God's sake, do you have to overplay every part?" January whispered.

"What was the 'else' they did?" Victoria said, ignoring him. She patted her lips with her napkin.

January said, "Shot them. Killed them."

"Them?" Victoria said, exchanging a lascivious glance with one of the salesmen.

"Remember your age," January said. "Your *supposed* age. Dunaway, his wife, and that impertinent fellow, Tooke."

She returned to grieving, but grew weary of the façade as she said, "The colonel was such a handsome man. Does this alter anything?"

"Nothing," January said. "Goodwin and Owen are well on their way to Baltimore on the packet. We will proceed to New York."

"De Brule? Have you heard from him? Will you hear from him?"

"He won't say anything," January said, slicing off a sliver of butter and spreading it on a roll. "He can't say anything. Sentiments for our cause are one thing but if the crown government were to discover one of their officials was actually supporting a foreign agent—"

"He's a fool," Victoria said. "He's done little to help us. His performance at the theater was so transparent I believed at first I was watching you."

January ignored the slight. He had other things on his mind. "He is a fool, yes, and he knows far less than he suspects."

They ate in silence before Victoria said, "I wonder. Should

I dab the corner of my eye once or twice before we depart? The grieving mother's tears, you see."

January found the question legitimate. "Once, I think. But when you arise, be a bit unsteady on your feet."

Victoria considered his suggestion. "Yes, I think that will do nicely."

Her brother returned to other issues. "We had assumed that Dunaway would follow us. If not us exactly, then our path. There may be others. I will say that we must be very careful from now on."

An idea struck Victoria. "You know, Royal, you must direct. Your knowledge of stagecraft would lend itself well to that endeavor."

"Director." The suggestion pleased January. "Do you think so? Well, it's something to consider. First, we must see to our furies."

Chapter 16

Hotel St-Denis
Quebec City, British Canada

Fitz closed the door, then poured himself another cup of coffee from the urn on the cart. He had summoned the concierge to the room and given him a sealed envelope and a ten dollar gold piece. "This goes to the American Consul," he instructed the man. "On the double-quick and unopened."

The concierge nodded, his eyes locked expectantly on the coin in his hand, and hurried off.

Their refuge after nearly dying on the ice had been the home of a young cobbler and his pregnant wife. She hung back, embarrassed at her condition, as the shocked man ushered them into the tiny cottage. He never ceased his endless stream of excited French as he guided them to the fireplace and shouted orders at his wife. She returned shortly with two steaming mugs of tea. Asia did her best to thank the two as a rotund gray cat draped itself across Fitz's boots. He didn't care. His feet were wet and cold, and the obese cat could lie there all day for all he cared.

They stayed an hour, until Asia could convince the cobbler it was urgent for them to return to Quebec City. It took Fitz's animated gestures and a five dollar gold piece to convince their rescuer to rent them his sleigh. Fitz would have pre-

ferred to bask in the heat of the roaring fire, but he had to report to Lincoln.

Asia and Fitz returned to the hotel, raced upstairs to their
room under the stares of startled guests, and ordered hot
water, a bathtub, and coffee. Fitz called for a porter to take a
message to the consul telling him about Tooke and Abbott.
He enclosed a short note to Lincoln.

The porter had barely left when more arrived with a tub
and buckets of steaming hot water. Fitz ordered them taken
to Asia's room, and tipped the men.

Asia appeared from his room, ran across the parlor, and
disappeared into hers, calling, "I couldn't let anyone see me
like this," behind her. She added as she disrobed, "I claim the
first bath as a lady, and I tell you now, Fitz, I fully intend to
soak until the cold is driven from my bones."

Fitz could hear her sigh as she slipped into the bath. They
spoke through the partially open door. Fitz did not ask her
about the man she called her brother. He never knew she had
a brother, and now, on top of everything else, the information stunned him.

"I sent to the consul, telling him about poor Mr. Tooke,
and Abbott," Fitz said, taking a moment to steal a glance at
his wife. He saw smooth shoulders and soft white arms. He
remembered his duty. "And a telegram to Mr. Lincoln in-
forming him of the proceedings."

"Now what do we do?" Asia said, running a washcloth
over her neck.

Fitz turned away. "I must think this over. Abbott is, or
was, the key. He may yet lead us to his murderer."

"What do you expect to learn from him?" Asia said. "Are
you still watching me, Fitz?"

"Watching?" Fitz sputtered.

"Yes. Should I get out now or are you enjoying yourself
too much?"

"Get out," Fitz growled. "Heaven forbid that I should find
a moment of pleasure."

She was out of the tub and into a robe before Fitz had a

chance to appreciate the view. "It's not you, dear," she said, touching his cheek. "It's too cold to be improper. Now it's your turn."

Asia was waiting for him on the settee when he finished dressing. She patted the cushion—a signal for him to join her. She gathered herself before speaking. "His name is Robert Owen," she said, "and he is the only family I have left. He sent me a letter several months ago."

"That is what has been eating at you," Fitz said.

"No. Not his reemergence." She turned grave, and spoke only after several attempts. "He has thrown in with the rebels."

"How do you mean?" Fitz asked, and then answered his own question. "As an agent, working in Canada."

"I don't know," Asia said.

"What else could it be?" he said.

"Fitz, I don't know. I didn't know he was here."

"It's the logical assumption. He is here with the Januarys and they are rebels. If not actively, at least in spirit."

"Robert is not the sort of man to harm anyone," Asia pleaded. "I know him."

"We were nearly killed," Fitz said. "What do you call that? Abbott is dead. Where is the game in that? Young men are not always aware. That may be the case with your Robert Owen."

"Please don't be sarcastic. I've been nothing but honest with you."

"Except for this."

The words stung Asia. "Do you trust me?"

"What?"

"Do you trust me?" Asia said again. "Will you put your life in my hands as I put mine in yours?" The words were calm but insistent.

Fitz gazed at the woman who was so much a part of his life. "Yes," he said.

She locked her fingers together on her lap, readying herself. "My father kept a mistress. It was common knowledge to everyone but me. Mother accepted it. She preferred not to be troubled by Father's adventures. Mother's only interests in Father, after a time, was the entrée that he provided to society. I followed Father one afternoon. It was in the fall. I remember the way I kicked my path through the leaves. They exploded in the air and rustled to the ground. Father must have heard.

"I saw him enter the house and waited at a distance until I grew bored and returned to my home. Later that night, Father came to me and said, 'The next time, walk with me.'

"My father took me to Mrs. Owen's house. It was a beautiful home, and Mrs. Owen was the loveliest creature I've ever seen. She was an angel with blond hair, and a sweet face." She smiled at Fitz. "A widow, Father told me, with a child. Robert. We would go and visit, Father and I, and then sometimes I would walk to the house where Robert and I played. Mrs. Owen always welcomed me, keeping treats for my visits."

"When did you find out he was your brother?" Fitz asked.

"I was twelve," Asia said, remembering. "Robert told me. We had been fighting, and he wanted to hurt me, I suppose." She glanced at Fitz. "I probably deserved it. I can be a wretched person. So he told me. He was very cruel about it. I ran home, crying. Father found me in the gazebo. I told him what Robert said. I told my father it was a lie. I made him swear to me it was a lie. He refused. Even before that I knew in my heart it was the truth. Hating my father for loving another child. He told me it was true. An indiscretion, he called it. I thought, what a terrible way to describe a little boy. He made excuses. He was honor bound to provide for Mrs. Owen and Robert. It was a month before I went back. Mrs. Owen welcomed me as if nothing had happened, and Robert bullied me into performing as Juliet to his Romeo. We vowed to become actors."

"He may have something to do with Abbott's murder," Fitz said, knowing what her response would be.

"He could not," Asia said.

Fitz wanted her to be right. "Probably not." He rose. "We must pay a visit to the Januarys."

"Why are we going to see the Januarys?"

Fitz began buttoning his tunic. "Because I don't know what else to do."

Chapter 17

The Good Lady
In the Cabot Strait

Robert Owen was relieved when Mr. Goodwin tossed his spent cigar out the porthole. He despised the stench of Goodwin's cigars, and the crowded confines of the cabin reeked of unwashed bodies and stale air. Owen found, to his embarrassment, that he was seasick. He fought back the nausea, declaring it a weakness and not worthy of a gentleman's attention. He had nearly succeeded until the cigar's fumes enveloped him. The bucket at the foot of the bed, meant for night soil, beckoned.

He vomited, his stomach twisting in agony, until it seemed that he must have filled the bucket with puke. His head throbbed as he wiped his mouth with a handkerchief and slid to the farthest end of the bunk from the bucket.

Goodwin emptied the contents of the bucket through the porthole, following the cigar into the cold swells of the North Atlantic.

Goodwin tossed the bucket on the deck and slid back into his bunk. "You're an educated man, aren't you?" he asked.

Owen stifled a surge of bile. "Yes. Columbia." He steadied himself, letting a wave of sickness pass over him. He thought talking would take his mind off his condition, although initially the last thing he wanted was to endure a conversation. "I graduated from Columbia."

"Where's that?"

Owen felt the ship slip to one side, but she quickly righted herself. "New York," he said. "New York City."

"Acting?"

Owen clamped his mouth shut, swallowed, and waited until it was safe to talk. "The law. My father wanted me to be a lawyer. My mother as well."

"A lawyer," Goodwin mused. Spray came through the open porthole, but as he stood to close it Owen said, "Would you leave it open, please. I find the cool breeze relaxing."

"I don't think it will sink us," Goodwin said, peering out the window. "I've been with the Januarys for fifteen years. I do all they ask of me without question." The wind flung droplets into the cabin. Goodwin's face glistened, but he did not notice the spray. "I wonder if you can do that, Mr. Owen?"

Owen shivered a bit but was reluctant to now ask Goodwin to close the porthole. "What is that, Mr. Goodwin?"

"Do what is asked of you without question?"

Owen sat up, annoyed at Goodwin's tone. He didn't like to have his integrity questioned. He finally settled on a gentleman's response. "I am a man of honor."

Goodwin, water streaming down his face, looked at him. "What does that mean—a man of honor?" He made the question an accusation.

"I gave my word to Mr. January," Owen said. He knew better than to engage in an argument with one's inferiors, but often his temper got the best of him. "I will do what I am instructed."

"Without question?"

"Yes."

"Regardless of the consequences?" Goodwin pressed.

"Mr. Goodwin," Owen said. "I did not take half an oath."

Goodwin's gaze was locked on the white foam boiling across the wave tops. "I saw torches long ago. At night. Far away, mostly hidden in the woods." He spoke as if something had come back to haunt him. "A long line of them. I was a boy, nearly a man, man enough for my father to work me like a man. I thought it strange to see torches late at night." He slammed the porthole cover closed and dogged it down.

"Mr. Goodwin?" Owen began, curious about his recollection.

Goodwin opened the cabin door. "I'm going to see to the crates."

Owen rose slowly from the bunk, staring after Goodwin. *He can do anything,* Royal January had explained to Owen. *Put a machine before him and he understands its complexities in an instant.* Because he respected the Januarys, Owen agreed, although he'd never seen evidence of Goodwin's intelligence. And when he did speak, he was an enigma. He spoke well enough for an uneducated man, but he was no gentleman. Despite that, there was a bond between the famous acting duo and the man who was as silent as a tomb.

Of course I am an honorable man, Owen thought.

He had told Asia the same thing. She had come into the little shop in Quebec City trailing the scent of cold, her face radiant. They held each other in greeting, until Owen guided her to a chair opposite him. A waiter appeared, laying menus expectantly on the table, but Owen shook his head, ordering coffee and a pastry for each.

"Look at you," she said, overwhelmed at the handsome young man who had replaced the boy.

"And you," he said, grinning. "You have become a beauty."

There was an awkward moment. Owen knew she wanted to ask him about his decision, but they had so much to say to each other, so many questions begging to be asked and answered.

"I saw you the other night," Asia said.

He blushed under her admiration. "Last night," he corrected.

"Yes," she said. "So much has happened, I've lost track of time. You were magnificent."

Owen smiled in response. "I've learned so much from the Januarys. They are amazing." He noticed the ring on her finger.

"I've remarried," she said, irritated at herself because it sounded like an apology.

"Are you happy?" he asked, and then saw her face fall. "The frown hardly becomes you, Asia. Is it because of me?"

"I'm afraid for you," she said.

The waiter brought the coffee and pastries. He set them on the table. His hopeful smile disappeared when Owen dismissed him.

"I am no longer that boy in my mother's parlor," Owen said.

"But I will always love you," Asia said. "I'm afraid that you're involved in dangerous business."

Owen tried to make light of her concern. "The only dangers in acting are bad reviews and indifferent audiences."

"Don't dismiss me, Robert," Asia returned. "This is serious business."

Owen grew angry. "Always the big sister. Did you come to Canada to beg me to return home? If you did, you've come on a failed errand."

"No," Asia said, "I came with my husband. I didn't know you were here."

His love for her softened his words. "Well, whatever reason, I'm glad you've come." He picked apart one of the French pastries. "But you mustn't be concerned about me or anything I choose to do. What I'm doing is important. I've finally found something to dedicate my life to." He gave her a wry smile. "Besides acting, of course. The South is my home, my cause. I've always known that in my heart, but it took the Januarys to shake the notion free. I am certain, Asia. You must know that."

"Fitz is a colonel in the Union army," Asia interrupted.

The statement surprised Owen. "Fitz?"

"My husband," she said.

Owen tossed the roll on the plate. "Unfortunate."

"Am I an enemy as well, dear brother?"

He could not fight her tenderness. She had always disarmed him with soothing words, or a kind gesture. It was a game—he retreated into his anger, and her gentle love retrieved him.

"You must know that no matter what, you are my sister," he said. He shrugged, signaling that it no longer mattered to him. "Even if you married a Yankee. The other one was a fool. But at least he was a Southerner."

"Fitz is a good man," Asia said. "A decent man."

"An honorable man, I suppose?"

"What decent man is without honor?" Asia asked.

Owen conceded the point with a nod. Then he became suspicious. "What is he doing here? What is your husband's business?"

"You must give me a promise," Asia said, ignoring his question. "You must promise me that you will always behave as if I am at your side."

"What?"

"I am your sister, Robert Owen. You know me as well as I know you. Promise that you will do nothing I would not approve of. You are a good, gifted man, but you are headstrong, and I think"—she hoped her words would not sting him—"easily taken advantage of."

"I am not a child," Owen said. "I do what I do for the honor of my country."

"Yes," Asia said. She had grown weary of talk about honor long ago. War dimmed honor until the only residue of that noble sentiment was heartbreak. "Will you give me your oath? That I will be constantly at your side."

Owen let his annoyance pass. He loved her, and what she asked of him was so little. Besides, she had always been his guide in life, the one whose rational approach tempered his anger. She was the one who comforted him as a boy when life became too confusing or painful. And she required nothing in return.

"You have my oath," Owen said. "I will behave as if you stand next to me."

Goodwin followed the narrow passageway to a ladder leading down to the cargo hold.

At the bottom of the stairs he found a ship's lantern, lit it, then closed and locked the glass door. The hold was stacked from deck to overhead with crates, barrels, tubs, and boxes, all lashed in place by a web of ropes. He had bribed Captain Douglas to make sure his crates were loaded last and therefore they would be first off-loaded when they arrived in Baltimore. Douglas had demanded more so Goodwin could inspect the crates during the voyage. "I can't have just anyone wandering about my ship. Call it insurance."

"So I'll get the money back when we arrive," Goodwin said.

Douglas appreciated the comment. "No, but it's a lovely sentiment nevertheless." Something about Goodwin struck Douglas. "You're one of those careful men, aren't you? Methodical. That's good. Now give me my money and you scamper from keel to top main at your pleasure."

Douglas had been right about Goodwin. He was careful in all accounts; some mistook it for slowness, but they were mistaken. He studies things—people, circumstances, and events. Goodwin trusted the accuracy and certainty of machines, and mathematics. Numbers came naturally to him, not out of books or lessons but from the complexities of his own mind.

He found the crates and tested the lashings, inspecting the ropes that tied the crates in place. He held the lantern so that he could see the knots. He pulled on them to make sure there was no slippage. He took his time examining each crate, and when he was convinced that they were intact, he returned to the ladder, extinguished the lantern, and climbed up to the passageway.

He went on deck and saw the rolling waves again, their white tops barely visible in the dark. He wondered why they had reminded him of the torches in the night, but gave up trying to find an answer. He pulled a cigar from his pocket, bit off the tip, and lit it, holding his coat as a buffer against the wind. He wrapped his arm into the ratlines to steady himself and enjoyed his cigar.

Two children, brother and sister, holding each other in the carcass of a fallen elm tree. They trembled so from the cold, and from fear, that their sobs came in pitiful little gasps. Their nightclothes were soiled and ripped from running blindly through the woods. Goodwin found them. The others, patrollers and neighbors, his own father and brothers, had spread out looking for the murderers, and Goodwin, stumbling through the thicket, saw a movement to his left. They were pale ghosts in the deepening shadows, holding one another so close that Goodwin thought they were just one.

"Mr. Goodwin," Captain Douglas said. "The sea is a bit excited tonight, is she not?" He kept his hands jammed in his pockets as he approached Goodwin. "The winds out of the nor'east. Is that what's got you roamin' about my vessel? You've got no worries. She'll kick up a bit but nothing will come of it.

Goodwin knew the captain's type. Having once gotten the taste of ready money, he hung close for more. "No," he said. "The air feels refreshing."

"But not for your companion, eh?" the captain said with a chuckle. "He turned green the minute he set foot on deck."

"You'll have to ask him," Goodwin said.

"Well, when we arrive in Baltimore all will be well," the captain said. He phrased his question carefully. "You have people waiting for you in Baltimore?"

"No," Goodwin said.

"The federals are very careful about Baltimore. Always

looking after who is coming and going." He leaned next to Goodwin. "Mr. Ledford's a smart man. Knows his business. He recommends to avoid any federal entanglements."

"That seems the thing to do."

"It is. And easy enough when you've done it many times. Not so easy when you haven't. "

He had a point, Goodwin thought. Now he had to find out how much it was going to cost. "Have you a way around that?"

"I have," Douglas said. "We'll pick up my pilot at Honor's Point. He knows a place just beyond that. We can stop off, unload your cargo, and no one will be the wiser."

"What about the other passengers?"

"They will be told it's a government shipment. As for the pilot and my crew, the pilot is discreet, when he's well paid. The crew will say whatever I tell them to say."

"I'll need wagons and horses," Goodwin said.

"This isn't the first time I've done this. Everything that you need is there." Douglas paused long enough to gauge Goodwin's response. When he was satisfied he could continue, he said, "Three hundred dollars."

Goodwin concentrated on his cigar.

"For three hundred dollars," the captain said, "I'll make sure that Mr. Goodwin, his companion, and your cargo were never on this good vessel. Bills of lading, passenger manifest, everything." He opened his hands as if he were a magician. "You may as well have been spirits."

"Done," Goodwin said. He stuck out his hand and the captain took it, sealing the bargain. "You know what happens if you do me wrong?"

"Mr. Goodwin," Douglas said, "I'm not in the habit of going about making unnecessary enemies." He touched his fingertips to the bill of his cap. "Good night, then."

Chapter 18

The Latrobe Theater
Quebec City, British Canada

Fitz, stunned, said, "What is this?"
Broadsides were pasted over the front door. The remaining performances of *Othello* had been cancelled.

Fitz jerked on the front doors as Asia joined him. He found one that was open and stepped aside as she entered. He was close behind her. He stopped in the middle of the lobby. There was no one in sight.

He shouted, "Hello?" There was no response. He shouted again. A little man with a heavily waxed mustache appeared through a doorway near the cloakroom. He chattered rapidly in French and waved his arms about excitedly. He came at them in a loping half trot.

"Wait, wait," Fitz said. He turned in desperation to Asia. "Can you tell me what this man is saying?"

"I was the worst French student at Madame Szell's Boarding School, but I can tell you he's not happy to see us."

"Mr. Malott?" a man called from the top of the grand staircase. He had a thick German accent but at least he spoke English. "Who are these people?" He addressed his next question to Fitz and Asia, the words echoing in the empty lobby. "Who are you? What do you want?"

Malott turned his assault on the gentleman rapidly descending the stairs.

Fitz waited for an opportunity to explain but Malott did not give him the chance, tossing rapid-fire invectives in every direction.

"I am Ebert," the man said, impatient with the interruption. "This is Malott. We are the owners of the Latrobe." He waved Malott to silence and glanced at Fitz, a signal to explain himself.

"I am Colonel Thomas Fitzgerald Dunaway. This is my wife. We are here to speak to the Januarys on a matter of importance."

"Oh. The Januarys," Ebert exclaimed. He described the situation to Malott in a burst of bitterness. Malott was about to respond when Ebert launched into Fitz. "I will tell you about the Januarys. Charlatans! Dilettantes! One week left on their contract. Sold out, I may say, and they disappear."

"Where?" Fitz asked.

"Home," Ebert cried. "New York. The United States. Gone, leaving every member of their company stranded in Quebec City."

"Robert Owen," Asia said. "Did Robert Owen remain?"

"Gone as well," Ebert said.

Malott, feeling left out, began a new tirade. Ebert waited a respectful length of time before silencing him.

"When?" Fitz said.

Ebert dismissed the question as inconsequential. "Two days. Three days. Gone with that specter of a manservant."

"Who?" Fitz said. "What's his name?"

"He's a servant," Ebert said in disgust. "Why should I trouble myself with a servant's name?"

"Do you know a man named Abbott?" Asia said.

Malott attempted to brush aside Ebert's attempts to silence him but accepted his partner's efforts.

"He says that Professor Abbott was a constant visitor to the Januarys," Ebert said. "He was particularly fond of Miss January, although I doubt you would not find a man under eighty who isn't." He listened with patience before convincing Malott to draw a breath. "They left very suddenly, the Januarys. I have no idea why, nor do I care. My reputation is ruined. My theater is ruined."

"Did they take the train?" Fitz said.

"Of course they took the train," Ebert said. "One that will eventually deliver them to New York."

"Mr. Malott," Fitz said, trusting Ebert to translate. "Do you know what the Januarys and Abbott discussed? What was the nature of their business?" He knew it was a lost cause. "Did you overhear them talking?"

When Ebert was done translating, Malott shook his finger at Fitz in rebuke. Ebert, equally offended, spoke for both of them. "I am a gentleman, sir. Gentlemen do not listen in on other gentlemen's conversations."

"Come on," Fitz ordered Asia. "Maybe we can find some gentlemen who aren't gentlemen."

"Thank you," she said to the owners.

"Madame?" Ebert said. "You are not perhaps an actress, are you?"

Asia beamed. "No. But thank you for asking."

They were outside before Fitz spoke. "We've got to find them." He could read the anxiety in Asia's face. "We'll find your brother as well. Don't worry."

"What if he's fallen in with them, Fitz? He's guileless. His head is all filled with noble causes."

"We'll take this journey one step at a time. We have to find the Januarys and bring them to justice for their part in Abbott's murder."

"But you don't know if they had a hand in the poor man's demise."

"You don't think it's a coincidence that Abbott is murdered and they flee?" Fitz waved for a cab. "I'll send a telegram alerting the president. We'll have the trains bound for New York stopped and searched. They shouldn't be hard to find."

"And Robert?" Asia said.

Fitz knew he couldn't lie. Asia would know before the words left his mouth. And no matter what he said, he knew Robert Owen would have to stand for his part in this. He had just gotten his wife back, and now he was likely to lose her again. "I will do all I can." It was weak, a way to avoid stating the obvious—he might have no control over what happened.

He was in the middle of a windstorm. Events spun around him so quickly that he could barely see them. If the Januarys killed Abbott, and Fitz was certain they had a hand in it, then why flee? Asia was right, there was no evidence to link them to the murder. If they left two days ago as Ebert had said, then they couldn't have been involved in the ambush at the farm.

But Owen and the manservant? Could it have been them? They had never gotten close enough for Fitz to see, and even if they had, there had been no opportunity to identify either one. He had seen Owen only once, through a frost-covered window, and to his knowledge he'd never seen the mysterious man-servant. It could have been them. That meant they left after the Januarys.

"Fitz?" Asia said. "The cab."

Fitz assisted Asia into the vehicle and climbed in after her.

How was Abbott linked to the Januarys? Romance? It was easy enough to see how Victoria January could capture any man's interest. If so, why kill him? Something to do with the strange baskets and patch of silk they found at the farm?

It was the windstorm again, bits and pieces flashing by him so quickly that he could not grasp their significance. So be it. Pluck from the whirling mass what you can.

The Januarys are famous—they cannot travel without being recognized, and between Quebec City and New York there are dozens of terminals and depots. If they stopped at a few, just a handful, they could be identified and detained for a crime that thus far was murder. Only murder, he thought wryly, but there is more behind that.

Suppose Abbott's murder was not the real crime, the reason behind this event? He could have gotten too familiar with Victoria January, and her brother, in a fit of righteous rage, could have killed him. An act of honor. In a barn? Far from civilization?

No. This was a skirmish, Fitz decided. The battle would come later—how and when remained a mystery.

Chapter 19

Secretary of the Treasury Salmon Chase watched Representative Thaddeus Stevens digest the news. The lawmaker had a bitter nature about him—his rounded shoulders and persimmon face bore the marks of a man whose life had been a profound disappointment. One of the most zealous of Radical Republicans, Stevens had no use for people who did not hate the South as much as he. It might have had something to do with his black mistress, Chase thought—one of the worst kept of Washington's tantalizing secrets. But Chase didn't care. All he wanted was the Executive Mansion in 1864, and he knew the only way to do that was to discredit Lincoln. As Lincoln had stolen the nomination from him in Chicago, so now would Chase work to retrieve it.

There were a few other representatives in the room; all except Chase and Stevens gathered close to a liquor cabinet, principally because of their thirst, but their desire to avoid Stevens running a close second. The room was provided for their comfort between calls. Here they sat, surrounded by bookcases, sitting in comfortable chairs with stacks of newspapers at their feet. The true business of the country was conducted in this room, away from the public galleries.

"Dead," Stevens said, his voice as coarse as his face. "I thought Lincoln sent that fellow to find Abbott?" He recognized the irony of his question. "I mean alive. What good does the man do us dead?"

"I urged the president to send someone else," Chase said. *You are truly the most ambitious man in America,* his daughter Kate had observed with a mixture of pride and awe. He smiled at the memory. Kate was the only person who understood him. "That man is a Tennessean. He served well enough in the army, but this matter was beyond his capabilities."

"So a man most valuable to our cause is now dead?" Stevens said. He was a zealot and he despised those who weren't. "Was he able to accomplish anything up there? This Dunaway?"

"No, I'm afraid not," Chase said. He calculated every word as he spoke, adding just enough regret to his words to convince Stevens of his sincerity.

"Well, where is he now?" Stevens demanded. "This soldier, Dunaway?"

"Still in Canada, I suspect," Chase said. "With his wife."

Stevens's mouth flew open. "Wife! What is God's name is his wife doing with him? Do we send our officers about on official duties trailing their wives?" Chase watched as Stevens's rage grew. "That incompetent baboon. Does he know what he's doing?" The question exploded at Chase, who understood it for what it was—Stevens venting his hatred of Lincoln. A clever man, a keen politician—but a president? "We have lost a man whose valuable service to the Union is well known. What is worse, we have lost him because of our bungling efforts to secure his safety. I am sickened."

Stevens dropped in a chair, the color leaving his face to return to his customary waxy complexion. For a moment Chase was afraid that Stevens would become physically ill. The thought disgusted him. And pleased him—Thaddeus Stevens, one of the most powerful men in the government, now had a new enemy. Delivered by Secretary of the Treasury Salmon

Chase. It would not take much to link Dunaway's failure to Lincoln.

"How do the other members of the cabinet feel about this misadventure?" Stevens muttered, so drained of strength by rage he could barely talk.

Chase became contrite, talking as Stevens stared at the carpet in thought. "Seward is indifferent, of course. Welles was greatly disturbed but reluctant to confront the president. Bates has no role in this, and Blair, other than an occasional curse, remains silent."

Stevens looked up. "What about Stanton, man?"

Here Chase had to be cautious. An understanding of sorts had developed between Lincoln and Stanton. They still battled, but it was evident the contests were conducted from bases of mutual respect. What about Stanton, indeed?

"He is terribly disappointed in the outcome of this affair," Chase said. He constructed his sentences with a politician's skill, remembering that Stevens was as competent as he at saying all that could be said without saying anything. "He pressed Lincoln for stronger measures. I believe he expressed doubts about Colonel Dunaway."

Stevens rose, reinvigorated with righteous indignation. "Have the man recalled," he ordered.

"I believe the investigation is still ongoing."

"Oh?" Stevens was at his most vicious when he unsheathed his sarcasm. "Abbott isn't expected to rise, is he? Does the good colonel possess skills of biblical proportions?"

"I meant to say that he has identified suspects in Mr. Abbott's murder."

Stevens grew cool, a snake with his quarry in sight. "What suspects?"

"The Januarys. Royal and Victoria January."

"The actors?" Stevens became cruel, his tone mocking the idea. "What has the president to fear from actors? For God's sake, this is an embarrassment."

"Dunaway telegraphed the president," Chase began, playing the reluctant messenger. "He named the Januarys as suspects, stated that they were fleeing to New York, and insisted that warrants be issued for their arrest. He also insisted"— Chase liked the way Stevens stiffened when he heard the word—"that all trains between Quebec City and New York be searched. He also said he was proceeding to New York with all speed."

Stevens's face twisted in contempt. "With his wife."

Chase shrugged. The whole fiasco was completely beyond his power to right. He watched Stevens seethe, cold violence steadily building in the diminutive man. "Recall him."

"Sir?" Chase said.

Stevens's eyes flashed at Chase. *"Recall him."*

"Colonel Dunaway was dispatched by the president," Chase pleaded. "I have no authority to do so."

Stevens looked at Chase as if he were an imbecile. "Then I will have the Joint Committee on the Conduct of the War subpoena him," he spoke deliberately, taunting Chase, "and Honest Abe will have to produce him immediately."

"You think that is the course of action that should be taken?" Chase asked.

The silence that followed was ominous. "I think," Stevens declared, "this is one of many such events for which that Illinois ape will be held accountable."

Fitz turned the book back and forth, hoping the sunlight streaming through the train window would reveal some clue about its contents. Asia sat across from him, dozing. *She would make a good soldier,* he thought. *She can sleep anytime, anywhere.*

The book claimed his attention again, and he began to page through it. Drawings—boxes of some kind with hoses or pipes leading out of them, machines with cogs and wheels— and calculations. Numbers, letters, and short bursts of cryptic notes filled the pages. There were endless calculations, so many that they filled the inside back of both covers.

Fitz hated mathematics. At the Academy his instructors had quickly determined that neither the artillery nor the engineers would have the pleasure of his company. *You will not require the principles of Euclid to sit a horse,* a disgusted instructor had informed him. He was marked for duty with the cavalry, where it was generally accepted that dash, not decimals, was required.

He closed the book and retrieved his pipe and tobacco pouch from his coat lying next to him on the seat. His arm was stiff, and occasionally a sharp pain reminded him of his wound, but it felt wonderful to be done with that confining sling and to have at least partial use of his arm. He lit his pipe and wondered how successful he would be. The Januarys were certainly far ahead of him, but Fitz hoped the telegram to President Lincoln and his request to have the New York trains searched would prove successful.

Asia shifted; her eyes fluttered open briefly, and then closed.

Her brother.

She was far too hopeful, Fitz knew. Robert Owen had thrown in with the Januarys, and the acting couple had likely killed, or caused to be killed, Phillip Abbott. A question emerged to trouble Fitz—why?

Abbott's body had been frozen, or as close to frozen as could be, and Fitz, who had seen battlefields littered with bodies, could not tell how long the poor man had lain in the barn. He could have already been dead when Asia and he arrived in Quebec City. But if the man was so valuable to the Southern cause, why kill him? And what was Abbott constructing in the barn?

He flipped through the book again, hoping for a revelation. The pages stopped, revealing two pieces of silk—one from the DuPont Works and the other from Abbott's barn. Fitz examined them. Different colors and sizes, and the DuPont swatch was badly charred. He laid them in his palm, then turned them over. There was a thin coat of some tarlike mixture covering one side. He dropped the two bits of fabric between the pages, closed the book, and slid it into his coat pocket.

He'd find out when the Januarys were captured. He'd telegraphed information about their general appearance ahead, and there had to be plenty of *carte de visites* available in New York with their likeness. He was reduced to adding "accompanied by Robert Owen and a manservant." He could not bear to ask Asia for a description of her brother, and the other man appeared to be a stranger to everyone.

"Lost in thought?" Asia asked, waking.

"Yes," Fitz said. "Sleep well?"

"Well enough." She stretched and glanced out the window. "Where are we?"

"Near Saratoga, I believe."

"Will we catch them, do you think?" Asia asked.

"Yes," Fitz said, knowing what she really meant. "If their destination is really New York, they can reach the city only by crossing the Hudson. There will be men posted at the ferry crossings along the New Jersey shore."

"I mean—"

"I know what you mean," he interrupted. "He is a part of it, and if he is captured, he will have to pay."

"Robert could not have harmed anyone," Asia said.

"He is still involved—"

"I know, Fitz," Asia said, pleading for understanding. "But his only fault is he is passionate and unthinking. He would never have knowingly done anything to warrant punishment. You make him out to be a cruel person."

"No," Fitz said. She was afraid and wanted reassurances that no harm would befall her brother, but he had none to offer. "No, I believe him to be as you describe him, but he has made an unfortunate choice. A man is dead, Asia, and Robert is a part of it." He thought of the book. "There is more to this, I fear."

"What do you mean?"

"The book," Fitz said, and then wondered aloud about the connection between it, the two pieces of silk, and the DuPont explosion.

"I don't understand," Asia said, rubbing her eyes. She covered a yawn with her long, fragile fingers. "Never mind. I'm too tired to comprehend."

There was expression in her hands—love, irritation, tenderness—and when she crossed her arms, her hands disappearing in the fabric of her dress—defiance. Now, Fitz saw helplessness.

"When this is done," he said, hoping even that innocent statement did not reignite her concern for her brother's fate, "I would like to go back into the field."

"The field?"

"My arm is nearly healed," he said, flapping it as if he were a bird testing a damaged wing. She smiled at his silliness. "And I would be far more useful to the Union in command of a regiment. Or perhaps a brigade."

"I can't stand to have you away from me," Asia said. She reached across the narrow aisle and took hold of his left hand. "Are you certain that your arm is healed?"

He leaned forward and whispered in her ear, "So much so I think I can pick you up and carry you to the nearest bed."

Asia drew back and scolded him with her eyes. "Colonel Dunaway, such conduct. I shall be the judge of that." She gave him a coquettish smile. "Soon, I hope."

Chapter 20

Saylor's Creek, Maryland

Two steam tugs pulled *The Good Lady* alongside a broad wooden dock set on thick pilings covered with a thick coating of slimy algae. Some of the passengers, bundled against the cold wind blowing off the Chesapeake Bay, came on deck to watch the activity. The others remained in their cabins, determined not to emerge until they reached Baltimore.

Had they done so, the sight of Saylor's Creek would have cruelly disappointed them. If there was creek it had long ago disappeared in the rocky shore that ran beneath a thick forest. The only sign of civilization was a decrepit ship works, occupied by the rotting hulks of three unfortunate inhabitants, and a smattering of buildings. Evidence they were occupied were thin streams of smoke that came from their chimneys.

Owen joined Goodwin. An ancient seaman followed, depositing their luggage on the deck. His presence goaded Owen into digging into his pocket for some coins. The seaman accepted them without any outward sign he was grateful.

Owen heard Captain Douglas's orders over the rumble of

a freight wagon being pushed into position over the worn decking of the dock. It stopped below the sides of the ship, wagon tongue toward the shore, surrounded by men ready to off-load the ship.

"Mind your noggins," a sailor shouted as a spar, trailing a sling, swung over their heads.

Goodwin pulled on Owen's coat sleeve. "Take the luggage ashore. I'll see to the unloading."

"I thought we were going to Baltimore," Owen said. "Why are we here?"

Goodwin watched as the hatch cover was removed and the sling disappeared into the hold. "Later," he said. "Go ashore." Four sailors manned a windlass and began the laborious journey round the deck to raise the load.

His eyes shifted from the spar to the pulleys, to the thick ropes pulled tight with the weight of the crates. One of the smallest crates came first. The pumps and hoses, he knew, were likely to be set aside until the larger boxes were brought up.

"Captain?" Goodwin shouted. "I want the other crate just like this brought up next."

Douglas, lounging with another sailor on the quarterdeck, shouted, "Mr. Landers? Be so kind as to fulfill the gentleman's wish."

A man dressed in filthy canvas trousers and a heavily patched jacket waved his acknowledgment. "You heard the captain," he bawled at the crew. "Load this one's twin on next."

A team of four mules was led down the dock, turned, and backed over the wagon tongue. They stood patiently as they were harnessed to the wagon. Another crate materialized from the deck, and the sailors on the sway rope made ready to swing it over the ship's side and lower it onto the wagon.

Goodwin watched the men and the spar. He saw it bend with the weight of the crate as it strained to carry the load. It was the other crates that he was concerned about. They were larger than the first crates, but most of that was to accommodate the thick layers of sawdust. There was no weight in saw-dust, but there was in the thick glass jars that rested within the crates.

As the sailors were swinging the spar back into position, Goodwin beckoned the mate over. "That spar is too weak to handle the other crates."

The mate cast a critical eye at the spar. "Eh? Well, we'll see." He turned to go when Goodwin stopped him.

"Replace it."

The mate shook off Goodwin's hand. "Don't lay hands on me, mister. I'm doin' my job as I see fit."

"Mr. Goodwin?" The confrontation brought Douglas off the quarterdeck. "Kindly unhand my man. I give the orders on this vessel. Release him and stand aside."

"Replace the spar and I will," Goodwin said.

"We don't have the luxury," the captain said. "The more time we spend here the more questions people ask. Questions you want to avoid, as I see it."

A man drove the first freight wagon off the dock. Another one was quickly pushed onto the dock, awaiting the largest crates.

"That spar won't support the weight of those boxes," Goodwin said. "If they drop, your ship won't see Baltimore."

Douglas, enraged, moved closer to Goodwin. "What have you brought about my ship? No one said anything about ex-plosives." He looked to see if anyone was listening and then lowered his voice. "Look here, I don't deal with that sort of thing. I value my life and my ship too much for that non-sense. Well, it's onboard now, so we'll do what we must." He gathered courage. "But that will be another one hundred dol-lars for my inconvenience, and your damned cargo."

"I'll pay you nothing more," Goodwin said. "It's not ex-plosives. But it'll be worse than that if those crates fall."

The captain stepped back, trying to fathom Goodwin's warning. He turned to the loading gang. "Mr. Baldwin," he shouted to the mate. "Trade out that spar and be quick about it. Find a good one, you hear. And see you do everything as this gentleman orders." He glared at Goodwin as he added, "I want no accidents here."

Owen found a grimy shack that served as a restaurant. A slovenly woman with ponderous breasts, barely hidden by homespun, pinned him with an impatient look. Her greasy hair was tied back in a bun, but it was so matted it was impossible to tell the color.

"Do you have coffee?" Owen ventured, preferring not to touch the counter that separated him from the woman. "Something to eat?" His seasickness had departed long ago and his stomach complained of being empty.

"Ham, pickled eggs. Pork. Crackers," she replied in a monotone.

"Do you have bread?" Owen said. He noticed her fingers were caked with filth. "For a ham sandwich."

"I'll put ham on a cracker," she said, searching under the counter. "You can call it a sandwich if you like."

Owen paid fifty cents for two pickled eggs, a cup of coffee, and a thick slice of ham trapped between two slabs of cracker. He drank the coffee first, then took his food outside to inspect it in the sunlight. He flicked bits of dirt from the eggs and pulled two stringy hairs from the ham before eating. He had finished and had time for a cigar before Goodwin drove up.

A man who had driven the first wagon up came out of a small building. Owen saw Goodwin approach a man near one of the vehicles. As Owen watched, the two men talked. Both wagons were loaded with the crates that he had seen loaded above Quebec City, far enough down the St. Lawrence to escape the winter ice.

But when he asked Goodwin what they contained, his only answer was an uncomprehending glance. Either Goodwin did not know, and Owen found that unlikely, or he declined to tell Owen.

Owen found that insulting and was about to take Goodwin to task, but decided against it. He excused the action as being on orders of Royal January. He also knew that Goodwin was a dangerous man. He took solace in the knowledge that the man would never be a gentleman.

The man continued to talk with Goodwin, and soon he turned and called to one of the sheds. A boy appeared, some years younger than Owen but big, with a thick chest and wide shoulders. Owen watched Goodwin shake his hand, and the youth removed his cap and ran his fingers through a tangle of blond hair.

Goodwin caught sight of Owen and waved him over. Owen picked up their luggage and joined the men.

"This is Mark Hurlock," Goodwin said of the young man. He introduced Owen as "Bob," a nickname Owen hated. "This is his pa."

"Mark'll take good care of you," Hurlock said. He was an older, shorter version of the young man. "I taught him all there is about being a teamster. When you get done with him, just send him back to me."

Goodwin counted out fifty dollars in gold pieces to Hurlock.

"What are you fellas haulin'?" Hurlock asked in a casual manner.

"Nothin' of consequence," Goodwin said. "Why?"

"Oh, nothin'," Hurlock was quick to reply. "Just don't want my boy mixed up in anything improper."

Goodwin smiled, looking at the boy. "It wouldn't be the first time now, would it?"

Hurlock chose not to answer the question. "You take good care of my boy now, won't you, mister?"

Goodwin said. "As well as if he were my own."

Chapter 21

Hoboken, New Jersey

The train slowed to a crawl with a piercing squeal followed by a burst of steam. Fitz hopped from the train as it pulled under the roof of the station. Asia was at his side as he scanned the vast throng of passengers. A black porter set their bags beside them as another porter appeared and, scooping them up, said, "Where are you folks going?"

Distracted by his search, Fitz said, "Wait. Wait a moment."

"There," Asia said, pointing across the heads of the crowds trying to fight their way to or from trains. "There are soldiers over there."

"Come on," Fitz ordered the porter, and taking Asia by the hand, pushed his way to a knot of blue uniforms gathered at a food stand. One man, an officer sporting a thick brown mustache, glanced up as Fitz approached.

He caught sight of Fitz's shoulder straps.

"Come to attention," he shouted, setting his coffee cup on the food stand's stained counter.

"Never mind that, Lieutenant." Fitz dismissed the formality. "Have you any news of the Januarys?"

"No, sir," the officer said. "None, sir."

"Nothing?" Fitz replied, stunned. "But the New York train comes through here, am I right? Don't you have to switch trains here for the city?"

"Yes," the lieutenant answered. "Here to the Hudson. You can take the boat-train over or one of the ferries."

"You have not seen the Januarys?" Fitz said.

"No, sir. No reports at all."

Fitz exploded in frustration. "Will you tell me how it is possible for any one of you to see anything, when you're all tied to this wagon?"

The lieutenant's face reddened. "With all due respect, sir. You don't know of what you speak."

"I don't," Fitz barked. "I don't. For God's sakes, man, I came right up to you before being noticed. It would have been just as easy for the Januarys, trailing a brass band, to walk right past you."

"Fitz?" Asia cautioned.

Fitz ignored her. He was angry, but at himself and not at the hapless lieutenant. He had grown certain the Januarys were the masterminds behind Abbott's death, no matter what roll the unfortunate man himself played. Their reason escaped him, but not their guilt. "I specifically ordered that these and other stations leading to the city be posted. God only knows how well the others are guarded."

"May I speak, sir," the lieutenant said, his voice trembling.

"Yes," Fitz snapped. "And I had better be satisfied with what you have to say."

The young officer took a deep breath before beginning. "All the exits from this station are guarded. If you look behind you, sir, you will note sentries posted at intervals along the platform."

Fitz followed the officer's glance. Soldiers, wearing sky blue greatcoats and holding muskets with fixed bayonets, stood at ease, examining the passing throng. He turned back to the lieutenant.

"You would have been stopped, sir, regardless of your uniform. It is highly likely that the Januarys are in some kind of disguise. We stop all young couples traveling alone. These men here"—he nodded to the men gathered around him— "have just been relieved, after four hours on duty. "

"I saw them as we came up, Fitz," Asia said of the soldiers on the platform.

Fitz fumed at his own stupidity. If there was one trait he could pluck from his body forever it was his temper. It was far too quick and terrible to do him any good, and, he admitted to Asia when she scolded him over the explosive rages, he vowed to curtail his emotions in the future. He realized wryly that he would have to redouble his efforts. "Lieutenant," he began his apology. "What is your name?"

"Miles," the young man said. "Terry Miles."

"Well, Lieutenant. All I've managed to do is make a fool out of myself."

"I'm sorry we weren't successful, sir," Lieutenant Miles said. "But it doesn't take much for anyone wanting to get to New York to do so unnoticed."

Fitz nodded. "Go back to your rations," he ordered the man, and walked a short distance in thought.

The porter arrived, pushing a cart bearing their luggage.

Asia opened the drawstrings on her purse, handed the porter a quarter with, "Leave them here," and waited. A few minutes passed before she nudged her husband. "I am hungry and my feet are sore, two conditions a lady learns to avoid at all costs."

Fitz gave her an irritated glance that turned apologetic. She was right. It was time to rest and eat. But he knew what he wanted to do. "Very well, then, I shall take you to Brooklyn." He spied the porter. "Here! Follow us."

"Brooklyn?" Asia said. "What's in Brooklyn?"

"My good temper for one thing," Fitz replied. "I seem to have misplaced it. I'm certain we'll find someplace to eat as well."

"Then Brooklyn it is," Asia announced.

Mr. Conroy, superintendent of the Brooklyn Navy Yard, was startled to see a woman in his office. Fitz and Asia had been waiting nearly thirty minutes when the big man with a coarse brown beard arrived. When he opened the door leading to the yard, the din of steam engines, hammers, drills, and drop forges followed him in. Fitz was convinced that the conversation would be carried on in a half shout.

"This is no place for a lady," Conroy said in a booming voice.

"My wife, confidant, and nurse," Fitz said. The sentence was punctuated by the piercing wail of a steam whistle. He cringed as the horrible noise penetrated the office, and then abruptly stopped. "How can anyone possibly endure that?"

"It never stops," Conroy said. "The fleet needs attention. Wood or iron, they come here and we make them whole again. We build new ones, too. That noise? You'll get used to it. Everyone does. We all go a little deaf, I suppose. Speaking of enduring, I don't know how you fellows stand it on the battlefield. Seems to me that things would be worse there."

"We aren't as loud as you folks," Fitz said, "but we make up for it by trying to kill one another."

Conroy shrugged. "I never thought of it that way. Here, sit down. You must have come over on the ferry. How did you find the trip?"

"I'm surprised that we made it here in one piece," Fitz replied as he and Asia took two chairs. "I had the wits frightened out of me on that treacherous ferry run from Hoboken to here."

"New York ferry masters are crazy," Conroy said. "If their boilers don't blow up then they run into each other, or their own ferry houses. They race one another for the privilege of being first across the river." He gave Asia an awkward smile. "I'm sorry I have no refreshments for you, Mrs. Dunaway."

"There is no need to make an apology, Mr. Conroy," Asia replied.

From Conroy's window overlooking the East River, Fitz could see several double-turreted monitors tied off to refitting barges. "You knew Mr. Abbott?" Fitz said.

"Knew him?" Referring to Abbott in the past tense confused the superintendent. "I worked with him," Conroy said. "I told him to go to the Devil—pardon the expression, Mrs. Dunaway—at least a dozen times a day."

"Difficult?"

"On a good day, difficult. Most of the time I would have shot the man if I had a gun handy."

"I have the unfortunate duty to inform you," Fitz said, "that Abbott is dead."

"No." Conroy said, surprised. "Dead, you say?" He hesitated, his eyes searching for the best way to continue. "Colonel Dunaway, I'm sorry for the man's family, if ever he had any, and for the Union because of his service to the cause, but—" He scratched his chin, parting a wave of whiskers. "The man was mad. Nothing satisfied him. Nothing. He had a violent temper. Anything would throw him off."

"My," Asia said, "how I despise a man with a temper."

Fitz ignored her. "Did he ever mention an association with the Januarys?"

"The actors? No. Nothing. He would frequently disappear. Go into Manhattan and seek the company—"

"Yes," Fitz said, sparing him the embarrassment. "I'm aware of that. But never to the theater? No contact with the Januarys?"

"Not that I'm aware of," Conroy said. "But I spoke to him only about work, and as little of that as I could get away with. I thought Ericsson was difficult to contend with. He's most proud of himself, John Ericsson, and idea-for-idea there's no one who could match him but Abbott. But they despised each other. I suppose that's why Abbott kept running off." A question occurred to Conroy. "How did he die?"

"He was shot," Fitz explained. "In Quebec City, Canada."

"Canada?" Conroy said. "Well, I suppose nothing should surprise me about that man's life or death. Insane. The most bizarre human being I ever had the misfortune to deal with. You know, he insisted that we save iron filings for him."

"Filings?" Fitz said.

"From the ironclads plating. Some of the iron sheets come

in with burrs on the edgings. And of course we have to round out the rivet holes. Abbott demanded that we save iron filings when we cleaned off the burrs. Mad. Absolutely mad."

"Did he tell you why?" Asia asked.

"No, and I made the mistake of asking him," Conroy said. "The man had a fit. 'I shall show Mr. Lowell how it's done,' he said."

"Does Lowell work here?" Fitz asked.

"I've never heard of a Mr. Lowell," Conroy said. "And I can't see how iron filings would impress anyone." He fell back on the earlier subject. "Dead. I am amazed."

"It's an amazing situation," Asia said.

"Why would he want iron fillings?" Fitz asked. And then added, truly mystified, "Who is Lowell?"

Chapter 22

Crehan and Sons, Watchmakers
Brooklyn, New York

Royal January opened the door for his sister and stood to one side as she entered the dark shop. They had abandoned their characters to walk in Brooklyn as themselves. Like most people, they remained anonymous on the crowded streets.

"Mr. Crehan?" January called. "Are you about?" He held a cane in one hand and slipped the other into his waistcoat pocket, laying his fingers over a pepperbox pistol.

Crehan appeared out of the darkness near the back of the shop, his black skin blending in perfectly with the deep shadows. "Yes?" he said, resting his hand on the counter.

"Mr. Crehan," January said. "Good day to you, sir."

"Good day," Crehan returned. He noticed Victoria for the first time. "And to you, lady."

"My associate stopped by some time ago," January said, "and retrieved the first device. We were pleased. Quite pleased. You have the others done?"

"The young man," Crehan said, remembering. *Like Michael,* he thought. *So much like Michael.* "Yes. He was here. He came and got the first clock. I'm glad."

"Glad?"

Crehan walked behind the counter. "That it worked. I always guarantee my work." He dug through some boxes under the counter, and then looked up. "The man who made the drawings?"

"Mr. Abbott," Victoria said, and corrected herself, "Professor Abbott." Her brother shot her an infuriated glance. Her response was a coy, "Oh, I'm sorry. Wasn't it my line?"

"A teacher," Crehan said, placing a small wooden box on the counter. "They can't do everything, you know. Teachers. They may be educated but they don't know everything." He removed ten intricate clocks from the box and arrayed them on the counter. "Here they are. All you wanted."

January removed his black suede gloves, picked up one of the clocks, and studied it, turning it back and forth to catch what little light came through the front windows of the shop. "Remarkable," he said, the word escaping him in a breath of admiration. He set the first clock down and held another up.

"They aren't very complicated," Crehan said as Victoria laid her hand on her brother's shoulder and shared in his appreciation of the machines. "Once I had done two, the others came along well."

"Look how delicate," she observed. "Like little jewels."

"It reduced the weight. Abbott thought of everything." January set the piece on the counter. "Do they work as specified?"

This time it was Crehan's turn to pick up one of the clocks, directing his answer to his creation. "The man's drawings were good and clear. I tested them, adjusting the balance until I got them just right." He was lost in the device. "Wouldn't it be something if we could fix each other up like this. If we all had gears and such, and we just replaced them when one wore out. Or maybe if we got sick, or something."

The clock's intricacies charmed Victoria. "How do they work?"

"I told the young man," Crehan said.

Victoria smiled, not used to being denied. "Tell me."

Crehan held up a clockwork mechanism and showed Victoria a key that hung from its frame by a bit of twine. "Two of the clocks have a key. They will fit all of the machines." He flicked a small lever near a set of gears. "Make sure the brake is set." He inserted the key. "Turn it clockwise four times." He did so. "Release the lever. That engages the gears." The clock's whirring was barely noticeable as he turned it around to expose the back. "After several minutes, you set the time here, the hammer will strike this pin." His finger stroked a brass shaft. "This will pierce into the bladder." He looked up. "The man who made the drawings called it a bladder. *Gutta purcha,* I believe. The flint"—he showed them a wheel suspended on a shaft—"is struck here." He became lost in the beauty of his craftsmanship before he returned to his explanation. "Which creates the spark." He set the mechanism on the counter. "All as the man who made the drawings wanted."

"It looks too complicated," January said. "Fragile."

"There's nothing to be concerned about," Crehan said. He was certain of his work. "They're strong, and very reliable. They will do what they are supposed to do."

"You should have lived at the height of Athens," Victoria said. "You would have rivaled Aristotle."

"Do they have my kind there?" Crehan said, packing the clocks away. "In that place?"

"I'm going to give you twenty dollars extra," January said, laying a gold piece on the counter. "I want this transaction to remain a secret." Something occurred to him. "When I was here before, there were children. And your wife, I believe. Where are they?"

Crehan's eyes fixed on his hands as if they held the secret of his sorrow. "My boys have passed. Brain fever." He would not tell them about Charity—he could not shame her by letting anyone know that she had died inside long ago.

Victoria assumed a sympathetic attitude. "Oh, how tragic. Isn't it tragic, Royal? To lose one's children. It makes my heart weep. Truly it does."

January counted out several coins. "Yes. Tragic." He slid

them across the counter to Crehan. "Pack them well, if you please, and we'll be on our way."

Crehan seemed not to hear.

"Mr. Crehan, if you will, please?"

The clockmaker responded with a blink. "Yes, Mr. January. Of course." He pulled several rags from a box under the counter and, folding them, carefully wedged them tightly between the clocks. "I would like to have met the man who made the drawings."

January took the box and tucked it under his arm. "He is on an extended journey. But I've no doubt that you'll run across one another in the distant future."

"Yes," Crehan said. "But it doesn't matter anyway." The Januarys were about to leave when he asked Victoria, "Miss? That place you said? Athens? Is it very far from here?"

Victoria was pleased to find a dramatic moment in such a dusty little shop. "Indeed, Mr. Crehan. Some ten thousand miles and a millennium at least. But with your skills, you would have been a giant among giants."

"And my children?" he asked.

"Kings, Mr. Crehan. Kings in a land of princes."

They left, stopping to let a carriage slide by on the cobblestone street.

"Why do you waste your time on a nigger?" January said, searching for a cab.

"An audience, brother," Victoria said, "even an audience of one, even a single nigger, deserves the very best performance I can provide."

"You have no shame?" January asked, partly in appreciation. "Have you?"

Victoria answered with a sweet smile, that of a woman who has accepted her faults. "Are we going home now, brother?"

January's face became a mask—hard, expressionless, filled with hate and determination. "Home, sister. Truly home." His love for Victoria emerged. "And from there we observe the destruction of Sodom."

* * *

Crehan waited until the door of his shop closed, and then locked it. *Kings,* he thought, *kings in a land of princes.* He would have settled for boys who lived into manhood.

"You see," he spoke into the gloom as he cleaned off the counter, "in this land there isn't even room for my kind." The clocks, scattered on dusty shelves around the small store, watched him. "To the white man we will always be niggers." He closed the drawers beneath the counter, pulled over his head the thin leather apron that he always wore, and hung it on a peg on a beam butted against the end of the counter. Michael and Matthew, as fresh as if they had just come in from the cold air, stood in the center of the shop, holding hands.

"Who were those people, Papa?" Michael asked. Matthew looked at his older brother, deferring to Michael's boldness.

"Some people," Crehan said, thinking it odd that his boys should be standing in front of him.

"I know that," Michael said with youthful impatience. "I mean, *who* are they?"

"Actors," Crehan responded. "Great actors. They just came by to purchase a clock."

"I want to be an actor," Matthew said to Michael.

"You don't want to make clocks?" Crehan asked him.

Matthew reconsidered. "I want to make clocks."

"Are you going to do it now?" Michael said, his head turned like a little bird.

Crehan frowned. He did not want to discuss such things with his boys. But they were dead. A year next month. He approached a doctor when they fell under the fever's spell— when they slid into delirium and their sweat stained the bedding. The doctor was white, a man who had praised his clocks, and he had said, "I don't tend to your kind."

The frustration that had boiled within Crehan, as he watched his children waste away and his wife's mind shatter. He struck the doctor and then the policemen who had been summoned, and when a friendly roundsman had opened the cell door with a cautionary, "Go home," Crehan had no fight left.

He had gone home and found his boys lying side by side in a disheveled bed, heads touching as if to share one last youthful thought, lifeless fingers intertwined, slipping into the dark land.

Charity had thrown herself over their slender bodies, hoping to shield them from death. Crehan, stiff from the beating he had been given, hot tears slashing over the tiny forms on the bed, lifted her, guiding her to the other room. That night, as he made arrangements to see to his children, she slipped into grief so profound that it consumed her mind, and smothered her soul.

Crehan climbed the stairs, looking back to make sure the boys were following him. Michael led Matthew, and Matthew became interested in everything along the way, until Michael pulled on his hand impatiently. Crehan felt a sense of well-being, knowing that his sons were with him and soon Charity would be free of the body that failed her.

"You two best come along now," Crehan said.

"Can I be a soldier?" Matthew asked, trying to pull away from his brother.

"You can't be no soldier," Michael said. "You're a nigger. Everybody knows there ain't no nigger soldiers."

Crehan stopped, trying to remember. He looked down on his sons. "But there were. The Moors. They were as black as you and me. They were great soldiers. Shakespeare wrote a play about them."

Matthew gave his brother a defiant glance. "Then I can be a soldier."

"Yes, you can," Crehan said, leading his dead children up the stairs. He stopped them, a hand on each imaginary tiny shoulder. "Now you two just wait here, and your momma and I will be along shortly."

"Will it hurt?" Michael said.

Crehan read the concern in his son's eyes. "Why, not a

bit." He found the pillow at the foot of his wife's bed, the one he had freshly laundered, and stood over her. "You go to sleep," he said. Her beauty had been distorted by the illness and her black hair had turned gray. He lowered the pillow and watched as her chest rose and fell slowly. His eyes were fixed on the soft swell of her breasts, those that she had freely given him in a bond of love so complete that they withheld nothing. From those breasts had sprung the life milk that fed their babes. Her body shuddered and became still.

"Is she dead?" Michael asked.

Crehan looked up to see his sons standing in the doorway. He dropped his head, and the pillow slipped out of his hand. He searched his pockets for the pistol.

"Don't be afraid, Papa," Matthew said, in a tiny voice that was almost a whisper.

Crehan smiled at his two sons, placed the muzzle of the pistol against his temple, and pulled the trigger.

Chapter 23

On the Washington Road
South of Baltimore, Maryland

There was no seat on the freight wagon. The unwieldy vehicle was a crude timber box set on a thick frame with huge wheels. The steering wheels were four feet high, Owen estimated, but the rear wheels were three times that. The vehicle was massive, and it rumbled over the road like faraway thunder. The teamsters rode on the inside mule of the first span of animals, one hand on a jerk line, the other holding a whip nearly eight feet long. Four spans, eight mules, pulled the wagon at a steady pace, just barely below a walk.

Goodwin had instructed Owen to ride with Mark Hurlock, and to watch him. "It may be that you'll have to drive the wagon," he had said, but refused further explanation.

Owen rode an ancient mule, out of harness, alongside Mark. He watched the young man skillfully guide the mules without moving the jerk line threaded through his large fingers. He had never watched a teamster drive a freight wagon before—he had considered any pursuit requiring manual labor beneath him, but Goodwin was insistent that he learn the complex task of guiding a slab-sided, cumbersome freight wagon.

He finally decided that he would prepare for a part—that

of a wagon driver—and to do so required that he study the situation. To pass the time, and because he knew nothing about trade, he asked Mark. It was a mistake to do so.

The young man with the flowing blond hair and the broad hands born to dominate a band of stubborn animals loved to talk.

"It helps to know the mules," he began, and to Owen's dismay continued without interruption. "The eight belong to my pa, and the other ones up there your friend is drivin' belong to Old Man Ruddel. He don't treat his animals the way they ought to be treated." He spat a stream of tobacco juice in a graceful arch to the side, just missing Owen. "Each one of my pa's is picked out special by him, and he names them, too." He nodded at the lead, inboard animal. "That's Ben, and next to him is George, and Mike, and Jesse. And up ahead is Tom." He glanced at Owen. "He's oldest and he's got more of a temper than the rest, but by God they all got enough of a temper to suit me." He returned to his introduction. "James, but we always call him Jim, because James is far too grand for that animal, and Mordecai." He stopped his narration long enough to dig a plug of tobacco out of his cheek with a dirty finger. "Pa said he never read the Good Book, but he always likes Bible names like Mordecai."

"James is a Biblical name," Owen said, hoping to break into the young man's speech long enough to ask a question. He shifted in the saddle to improve his position. Most of the leather was worn off the saddle, and stitching stuck out to jab him as he rode. The only saving grace was that his mule needed no guidance from him. It plodded along, next to its companions.

"James?" Mark was surprised. "James is? I bet my pa don't know that. Well, it don't matter. He knows mules and oxen, and he knows drivin' a freight wagon, all right. He had me and my brother in the saddle once we was old enough to sit still. My brother went and joined up, and Pa was fit to be tied because he said there's more than enough money to be made here and a fella don't need to go off and make a little when there's a lot to be made."

While Mark talked, Owen watched the motion of the mules as they plodded along at a steady pace, never bothering to break the steady gait they had maintained from Saylor's Creek, through the crowded streets of Baltimore, and onto the Washington Road. Ahead of them, keeping a distance that never varied, was Goodwin. Owen watched the bulk of the man's back, a dark shape that reminded him of the boulders heaped atop one another at the Falls of the Potomac. Solid, immoveable, capable of stopping any man-made force sent against them. They had found a big mule for Goodwin—a big animal that could carry his weight. He sat on the mule—jerk line trailing through his hand, appearing to ignore the teams, the road, and the weather. The only movement from Goodwin was the few times that he removed a cigar from his pocket and lit it. A pale cloud of gray smoke dashed over the man's shoulder, swept up by the winter wind. Sometimes Owen caught an acrid scent that reminded him of the airless cabin on *The Good Lady,* stinking of cigars and his own vomit.

He had been disappointed when Royal January told him to go with Goodwin, explaining that he, rather than the Januarys, counted now on Owen's help. He would have preferred staying with Victoria, stealing an occasional glance at her bewitching eyes or the gentle sway of her breasts under the fabric of her dress.

He knew she loved him, her manner told him as much. Owen knew also that Royal January was highly protective of his sister's virtue and, it was rumored, had fought three duels to protect her good name. He suspected that January knew of his feelings for his sister, and he was certain that the famous actor accepted his intentions as honorable.

"What kind of man is your friend?" Mark asked.

"Friend?" Owen came around. "Oh, Mr. Goodwin. He's not really my friend." He stopped his mule, slid from the saddle, and decided to walk for a few miles. His ass hurt. He felt as if he had been split in half.

"Goodwin? I thought he had another name. I thought he told my pa that his name was Shell or something like that." Mark concluded that it wasn't important. "I don't hear well. When I was a boy I nearly froze to death, and I don't hear well since then."

"How do you manage the line?" Owen said, to divert the conversation to his needs.

Mark toyed with the thick, leather jerk line. "Keep it loose. See how it drops? Don't ever pull them up tight. Them mules got more strength than you got. They're trained, don't you see. I rub a bit of tallow on the line. Don't cut into your hand so much."

Owen listened patiently, trying to remind himself that Mark was only a boy and boys seldom understand why they do things.

"It takes some time to train good wheelers. That fella there on the inside, that's Sadie. He's worth his weight in gold. He knows the line so well it don't mean nothin' to him."

Owen wondered why anyone would name a jack after a woman.

"You give a jerk," Mark said, "and they go one way. Give a pull, and they go the other." He hefted the whip in his hand. "I never use this unless they get out of hand. I just snap it over their heads and they get the message. It's a warning."

Owen studied Mark's hands and noted his commands, and watched as the mules responded to what he thought was an almost imperceptible pull of the line. Mark talked to the mules, soothing them in a gentle voice. Owen decided the boy was almost graceful in his management of the eight mules and the rumbling wagon.

Owen also decided, after having his spine jarred from his tail to the base of his neck, that he was done studying Mark. The young teamster, apparently glad for the company, kept the air between them filled with an endless stream of inconsequential chatter. He could walk to where they were going,

Owen thought in frustration, and arrive before the lumbering parade. He asked himself the question he had posed at the start of the journey—where were they going? He had no idea, and Goodwin made no effort to take him into his confidence.

The worst of all, Owen realized, staring at his fingernails, is that his hands were getting filthy. He folded his fingers into his palms, hiding the dirt-encrusted nails, and for good measure slipped his hands under his coattail. He could not stand dirt on his hands, and he virtually shuddered in horror when dark, half moons of grime appeared under his nails. He hated feeling unclean. Every part of him called for the healing effects of a warm bath, soaking the weariness of travel away and washing off the scum that had, over the days, accumulated on his body.

He was sick of this affair. He watched Goodwin's bulk sway on the big mule. He hated Goodwin because he was within sight. If we are smuggling this load south, Owen asked himself, then why not leave it on the ship and chance the blockade? Now that would be an adventure. Not this hopeless, painful caravan to some unknown destination. Running a blockade! Owen's thoughts shifted to a blue-green sea under a cloud-laced brilliant sky. He was called to the stern gun, the gun captain having been wounded, to take his position. He knew nothing of cannon, he admitted outside of his dream, but that was a trifle—he was called to duty. He took his place alongside the gun as his valiant crew strained to load the huge ball in the cannon's muzzle. A faithful servant, a Negro boy with flashing white teeth and an adoring expression, handed Owen a spyglass. Settling the eyepiece in place he saw, at less that half-a-mile distance, five Union frigates bearing down on them. Owen, confident the enemy would be his, trapped the spyglass between his palms and snapped it shut.

The front right wheel of the wagon skipped off the edge of a rock, dropping the wagon with a crash. Owen stumbled in surprise, and tasted blood. He had bitten the inside of his cheek. He gave Mark a disgusted look, but the young man was too intent on guiding the animals to notice.

Owen tried to return to his dream, but reality had shattered it so completely that he was unable to reassemble the pieces. He on a ship, with other ships chasing it—everything else was gone.

But what are we smuggling? he wondered. He drifted back and let the wagon pass him until he was just behind the tailgate. He was a spy, he decided, sent to infiltrate the enemy. He peered through the cracks in the high tailgate. He saw nothing except the huge crates, expertly tied down, filling the wagon bed. He had seen them before, and they were just as innocent. There were larger crates in Goodwin's wagon. Heavier, too, Owen thought, although he knew it was only a guess. By why take such a cumbersome load overland? He knew they were going south, southwest at least. He read the signs and mile markers as they passed. This was a ruse, he offered himself. We will go south by land and then turn off to one of the nearby rivers. There the crates will be loaded on vessels that will steal along the coast and take them up into Richmond. Owen knew there would be bands, and lovely young ladies gaily waving their handkerchiefs—thousands of white doves fluttering over the heads of an adoring crowd.

Owen contemplated the crates in Goodwin's wagon. What did they contain?

Lincoln, the heels of his boots locked against the porch railing, leaned back in his chair, balancing on its hind legs. Soldiers of the Invalid Corps, clothed in sky blue uniforms with matching greatcoats, drilled on the vast lawn of the Soldiers' Home.

Seward leaned against the column of the small President's Cottage, savoring a cigar. Stanton, indignant, paced back and forth. Lincoln often came to the cottage on the grounds of the Soldiers' Home, but his practice was to escape Washington's infernal heat and take up residence in the shaded grounds in the summer. Today it wasn't the seasonal heat he had escaped, but the hellfire of Congress, and perhaps an occasional scorching from Mary. Lately, according to Seward's observations to the pugnacious Stanton, he was coming here more often.

"What are we doing in this desolate place?" Stanton barked, suspicious of any change in routine.

"For God's sake, man," Seward replied. "If you were married to that shrew, wouldn't you want to get away?" The secretary of state was certain that wasn't the cause of Lincoln's flight, but he liked to outrage Stanton. Now they had both come to see Lincoln, leaving the noise and congestion of Washington for the soft rustle of pines and the distant call of orders.

"Chase," Lincoln mused, his long legs angled to span the distance between his chair and the railing. "He's carrying tales to Stevens."

"It was Chase." Stanton leaped on the name. "He tells everything he knows to the Radicals. What he doesn't steal away from cabinet meetings, he makes up."

"This reminds me of a story," Lincoln said.

"For heaven's sake, Lincoln," Stanton erupted. "Can you not concentrate on the matter at hand?"

The president ignored him. "There was this fella who walked down a road. Same road every day for nearly five years. Every one of those days this dog came runnin' out of this farmhouse, just a snappin' and barkin' at this man. And every day the man did his best to avoid the dog's teeth. One day the dog comes out after the man and the man pulls a pistol from his pocket and shoots the dog dead."

Seward laughed, choking himself in the process. He doubled over and regained his breath. Stanton, dumbfounded, looked at Lincoln. "I don't understand it."

"Mr. Secretary," Seward managed. "Lincoln is the man and Chase is the dog."

Stanton understood. "Oh. Then by all means, shoot Chase."

"What does the Joint Committee on the Conduct of the

War want?" Lincoln asked, balancing from one leg to another.

"I have no idea what the committee wants," Seward returned. "I doubt they know. But Stevens, and probably Ben Wade and others, are unhappy with the agent that you sent to Canada. Especially since his express instructions were to find Mr. Abbott."

"Well," Lincoln reasoned. "He found him."

"Yes," Seward noted. "But dead. I don't think we can consider that a successful conclusion."

"This isn't about Abbott or Dunaway or any of that," Stanton said, shaking his finger at Lincoln.

"Of course not," Seward said. "Chase is stoking the fires and any log will do. I'm sure the committee will make a big noise until they can convene and question the good colonel."

"They won't waste their time on that," Lincoln said, dropping his feet with a thud on the floorboards. "They'll bark a bit and make demands, but there isn't enough meat and damned little bone for them to gnaw on. We'll take that away from them as well. Abbott is dead, and so far as I know even the rebels can't suck knowledge out of the poor man's brains. So he can't hurt us. I think we can allow the rest of it to drop quietly." He hooked his boots on the railing again and became lost in an attempt to balance himself on the hind legs of the chair. "Stanton, would you be so kind as to send a telegram to Colonel Dunaway, thanking him for his good work and recalling him to Washington. We'll give him a post hereabouts." Lincoln's long arms went out. Stanton's scowl caught his attention. "Well?"

"If you don't shoot Chase," the secretary of war asked, "can I?"

Lincoln's head fell back as he emitted a high-pitched laugh. Even Seward joined in as the squat Stanton awaited an answer.

"By God, Stanton," Lincoln said, wiping tears out of his eyes. "We'll make a humorist of you yet."

"Lincoln," Seward said, wanting to be clear on the issue.

"The committee will call Dunaway. If they can't find just cause, they'll make up something."

Lincoln let the chair drop forward but expertly caught it before it touched the floor. "Yes, they will." He held his arms out as if flying. "There's nothing to be gained from confronting the committee. Not with things going as badly as they are. That's just playing into their hands. If they want our friend Dunaway, we must give him up."

Chapter 24

Hotel Oriental
Philadelphia, Pennsylvania

They had gone from Brooklyn to Hoboken, taking the ferry around the tip of Manhattan, an elderly couple enjoying each other's company as the smoke-shrouded island passed to starboard. He kept a tight hold on his carpetbag, with all the suspicion of an old man whose few remaining valuables had to be carefully guarded. His wife—she had to be his wife for the way she doted over him—still looked remarkably young, and several of the male passengers thought she appraised them as if she were selecting a mate.

Of course the idea was ludicrous; her gray hair and wrinkles dispelled any such notion.

The train south to Philadelphia had been wearing, and Victoria had been angry with her brother for most of the trip, since Hoboken in fact, for his constant need to enlarge his role. He, lost in his character, approached a young Union officer at the station. She was locked on his arms, furiously trying to hold him back.

"Young man?" January had said, his voice feeble with age. "Why are all these soldiers about?"

The officer, happy to oblige the old man, had smiled and

said, "Nothing to be concerned about, sir." He was their protector. "We're looking for some fugitives."

"Murders!" January said, glancing in alarm at Victoria. She gave him a sharp look that cautioned him. One misplayed speech and they were lost.

"No. No," the young officer said. "Nothing like that." He leaned into them. "The Januarys. Isn't that remarkable?"

"Who are they?" January said.

"Actors," the officer had replied, charmed by the old man's innocence. He glanced at the carpetbag. "Would you like some assistance? Which train are you on?"

"Trenton," Victoria had answered. "We are off to see our poor daughter." She lowered her head in grief but recovered. "Her husband was lost in the war."

"Let us hurry, dear," January said. The officer reached for the carpetbag, but January had shook his head. "No, thank you. It's most gracious of you, but I can manage." He barely managed a civil, "Come along, Beatrice," to Victoria. She had responded by giving the inside of his arm a sharp pinch. "I loath that name," she whispered.

"I know," January had said, shuffling to the line of passenger cars.

Victoria's cries awakened him. They had made love, and she had fallen asleep first. Her nails had dug into his back and she cried out as her passion mounted. He lost himself in her demands for more, until she fell away with a single soft cry and he buried his face in her soft breasts, spent.

He threw on his robe, pulled back the heavy curtains on the window, and watched Philadelphia sleep under a white moon. He slid the window up an inch or two, letting the cold air rush into the room. He studied the shadowing buildings, wondering if any of them existed when Washington crossed the Delaware River with his brave men to attack the Hessians. His father had bought the book for him, Parson

Weems's *The Life of Washington,* well before he was old enough to read it. But as a child he kept it close by as he slept, his fingers tracing the leather spine and his mind exploring the wonderful life that Washington had lived. He would be a soldier, January thought, and had told his father so. *Be an actor,* his father had suggested, his clear blue eyes tinged with red from constant drink. *Become an actor, and for once an evening and twice on Saturday, you will become anything you desire.*

Royal January watched the constant glow of the lights scattered about the dark town and wondered who tended the lamps. Tradesmen, machinists—he thought of Goodwin and his knowledge of machines—blacksmiths. He was about to give up the exercise when he saw a distant line of streetlights. His soul slipped away, and that night came back.

The fire had tried to suck them in, to destroy his sister and him as it was destroying the house. Flames licked around the thick columns that were once white, boiling the paint until it blackened. He had reached out, his hand finding Victoria's, and they ran. He heard glass shattering, and wood, dying in the grasp of the fiery monster, cracked loudly from behind.

He heard people screaming as he and his sister had run into the woods. He looked over his shoulder and saw demons bearing torches, racing over the grounds of Mayfield. He remembered his father saying that word with such pride, Mayfield. That was the name of their home, their plantation, and when their father and mother weren't traveling with the company they returned, exhausted, to Mayfield. "I draw my strength from this place," Father had announced in his deep baritone. Now, as they ran, the beautiful house melted, and devils raced over the grounds.

They had hid in the woods, far from the terror of the night, listening to the screams as people died—Mother, beau-

tiful Mother, wild emotion followed by despair so profound, January thought she was lost forever. Father, large, powerful chest and thick arms. His hands suggestively caressing the faces of the young actresses who came for visits.

January had thought he saw his father on the porch, drunkenly wielding a sword, trying to drive off the slaves.

Royal and Victoria had collapsed in the thick underbrush, crawling until their hands bled, finally slumping against the rotten trunk of a fallen tree. Their nightclothes were ripped and caked with dirt. He had tried to be brave for his sister, but he trembled violently. It was fear, he knew, and cold, and he held her as much for his comfort as her security.

Screams echoed through the darkness, and heavy smoke rolled out of the woods, obscuring the trees. There had been nothing recognizable in the thick veil, just vague outlines that writhed in agony.

Royal January, gasping for air, had covered his ears with mud-covered hands. Victoria had buried her face into his chest. He had become the protector, and he would be the father. He saw his mother's face, stiff with contempt, and inches away from his father's, accusing him of unnatural liberties with the slave children. His father, drunk, denounced the stories as rumors. He slurred his words, and January watched his father's eyes fill with self-loathing.

"It's too cold," Victoria said from the darkness. He saw her shape move in the bed. "Close the window."

January returned to the bed and slipped under the bedclothes. She drew close to him, laying her head on his shoulder, her hand playing over his abdomen.

She whispered, "It's too cold." She could not stand the cold. It was this memory that had come into her dreams and made her cry.

January flung the bedding to one side, revealing her pale, naked body. He removed his gown so he was naked as well, and she threw her leg over his, searching for warmth. Her muffled sobs were those of a child's and he could feel her hot tears rolling down his side.

Royal January stroked his sister's hair, and said, "Don't worry. They won't come for us, sister. I promise."

Chapter 25

"Recalled," Fitz said in disbelief as he showed Asia the telegram. They were about to leave the hotel when a clerk, barely a boy, stopped them with a breathless, "It's for you, Colonel Dunaway."

Asia took the telegram and read it. "President Lincoln directs Colonel Dunaway return to Washington at once and call upon him at the Executive Mansion. He thanks the Colonel for his superb efforts."

They had tracked a couple they believed to be the Januarys to Princeton, although Fitz became more uncertain about their quarry as they traveled west.

"Why in the world would they go to Princeton?" he wondered out loud, hoping that Asia had a logical answer.

"I don't know," was all she offered, and then buttressed his doubts with, "I'm not convinced they are the Januarys. We have rumors and nothing more."

Fitz hoped his disgusted look would silence her, but she continued. "It would have been better for them if they had fled to Richmond. They could have crossed the border at any point, or slipped in through the blockade."

All Fitz could offer was, "Let us find a train to Washington."

Fitz and Asia booked seats on the first available train and set off for Washington, after only an hour's wait. Neither one said anything of substance for some time until Asia asked, "What do you think it means?"

Fitz, lost in thought, really didn't hear the question. "What?"

"The fact that you are recalled," Asia said.

"I don't know," Fitz said, and briefly lapsed into silence. "I suppose they find my efforts to capture the Januarys a waste. Or they have already been captured." He sunk down in the seat and threw his arms over his chest. "It can't be to inform the president of my progress. I've kept him duly informed from the beginning. I've practically burned up the wires with telegrams."

"I am forewarned," Asia said.

"Forewarned?"

"Yes, husband. You've slipped into your redoubt, and no assault can drive you out." She tapped his crossed arms. "Now you are fully entrenched, every inch of bone and sinew prepared for battle."

"Would you kindly say what you mean?"

"Of course, dear." Asia was being coy now. "In a nutshell you're ready to fight anyone, anywhere. Why don't we determine who the enemy is before we begin the battle?"

He couldn't stand her being right. "This situation infuriates me." Before she had a chance to ask, he continued. "Abbott and the Januarys. That damned business at Wilmington." He slapped his chest. "This silly book and snippets of silk, and now we are to strike our tents and move on."

"Have you any suggestions?" she asked. Her calmness irritated him, but there was nothing he could do. She saw things so clearly that he was convinced she had a sixth sense, while he struggled with unwrapping circumstances until everything had been reduced to a shambles, and he was still without an answer.

"I do not," he conceded.

"Then we will go home, and you can continue your convalescence in your own bed." She stroked his arm tenderly. "How is your wound?"

He glanced at his arm. "Much improved. I recommend anyone with a wound take the waters at Quebec City."

Asia laughed, and settled next to him, slipping her hand under his arm.

"Your brother is safe," Fitz said. He ventured into the subject with trepidation. He had acknowledged early on in his relationship with Asia that he trampled over people's emotions like a clumsy mule. *I have no sense when it comes to those matters,* he warned her. And now he broached the subject of a man who was his sworn enemy, and a man Asia loved.

"Is he?" Asia replied.

"Long gone," Fitz said, watching the countryside pass. "Whether with the Januarys or not, he has disappeared."

"But you can't be sure?" Her hand gripped Fitz's arm, tightening as she spoke. "If he were here in front of you at this instant, would you arrest him?"

"I would."

"If I begged you not to?" Asia said, the words hopeful. "If I said 'Fitz, please let him go,' would you?"

Fitz lifted her chin so she could see his eyes. "You know I must do my duty. I would rather lose my arm than cause you pain, but I cannot turn my back on an enemy of my country. You knew that before asking me if I would let him escape." He hoped she understood what was in his heart. "I know so very little with any certainty. I love you, this I know, beyond all reason. I took an oath to my country. That is unalterable. If I am ordered, I will go after something until the thing is got."

"Perhaps," she said, running her fingertips over his lips, "you will find, on the right occasion, that compassion outstrips your sense of duty."

He straightened, breaking the mood. "Perhaps." He

looked down at her, smiling. "But I don't ever recall changing my mind about anything."

She resettled her long skirt. "My dear husband," Asia said with a playful glance. "You have never changed your mind. But I recall changing it for you many times."

Chapter 26

The Senate Hearing Chamber
United States Capitol
Washington, DC

He looks like a child, Fitz thought, as Ellwood Omwake lounged in the chair next to him. It had all, Lincoln had remarked to Fitz as he bid him good luck at the Soldiers' Home, gone to hell in a handbasket.

"Now see here, Dunaway," Lincoln had said, escorting Fitz down the steps and along the driveway to the carriage. "Those fellows are a bunch of politicians who've got a burr under their saddle, and at present, that burr is you. I never thought it would go this far, committees and all, but you can stomach this, can't you?"

Fitz had tried to restrain his temper. "Mr. President, I didn't shoot Abbott and I was trying to do my best to catch the people who did when you summoned me here. Now I find out the Joint Committee on the Conduct of the War is investigating me."

"No, no," Lincoln had said. "They're just doing this to feel important. No one thinks you shot that poor man. Anyway, as far as I'm concerned, the matter is closed. Just go up to the hill, answer their questions as truthfully as you can, and that's that. Stanton's counsel will accompany you."

This was incredible. "Mr. President, why do I need a lawyer?"

Lincoln had laid his big hands over Fitz's shoulders. "Son. That's the trickiest bunch of she-wolves I've ever seen. They could get Gabriel so mixed up he'd claim he was playin' a banjo instead of a trumpet. Omwake is your man, in any case, and I want you to listen to his advice. Go and do this for me and things will work out for the best."

"Can't you," Fitz had said, weary of official Washington, "tell them I'm not coming? I beg your pardon, sir, but I should be after the Januarys instead of this—" He couldn't think of a word that wasn't offensive.

"No, I can't, Dunaway," Lincoln had said, opening the carriage door. "A man might not want to do what his wife wants but by damn, he'd better listen to her." He wanted Fitz to understand his predicament. "The Januarys and their bunch are probably in Richmond. They may be on their way to England or France. If they're out of the country, that's as good as them being out of our hair. Abbott's dead and that's that. Let's tie this other up as quickly as possible. Go up there, say as little as possible. They want me a sight more than they want you." He managed a smile. "Don't pistol-whip anyone."

There was nothing else for Fitz to say except, "Yes, sir."

Neat rows of chairs, rank and file with a broad aisle in the center, sat mostly unoccupied behind Fitz and Omwake. There were a few spectators waiting for the hearing to begin—news-papermen, toying with notepads or exchanging pleasantries with their colleagues, and, Fitz was surprised, several couples who apparently thought the events would be entertaining. Other men, some dressed as gentlemen and half a dozen or so as laborers, were scattered about, drawing on cigars, arms thrown over the backs of their chairs, bored already.

Fitz turned back to the tables arrayed before him. Clerks—sharpening pencils, filling inkwells, readying stacks of notepaper—concentrated on their duties, never once looking over the room. A few scurried about, whispering in their comrades' ears or bringing supplies that could not be done without.

Clerks—Fitz dismissed the breed. They bustled about like vermin, taking and giving, so intent on their purpose they forego any interest in what transpires around them. He glanced at the heavy oak table, set on a platform just in front of them. That is where the committee would sit, pondering all they hear, and hearing only what they choose. The Joint Committee on the Conduct of the War. Officers not well versed in politics came before it and were, if they were lucky, sent packing with a harsh warning about prosecuting the war against the rebels with more vigor. Some unlucky ones were carried away to prison, accused of traitorous activities. Others were sent home, cautioned to hold themselves in readiness to be called before the committee in the future.

Union Generals Pope and Fremont had fared well before the committee. They spoke the language, reserving their harshest criticisms for officers who functioned poorly against the enemy—or officers they deemed to be blocking their advancement. Pope and Fremont were generals whose ineptitude killed soldiers, but their talent with patronizing rhetoric guaranteed their professional lives.

Four civilians entered, each trailing a pack of clerks, and each took his place. The long table in front of them was covered with a green velvet cloth with ashtrays and pitchers of water placed strategically for their benefit.

"You may expect to see and hear anything in this room," Omwake had said as they walked down the aisle and took their seats.

Zachariah Chandler, a tuft of whiskers sprouting from his chin, sat to the far left. The only remarkable thing about his plain face was a pronounced scowl. Ben Wade of Ohio, his gray hair matching bushy eyebrows, exchanged comments with Chandler. Next to him, looking like a befuddled teacher, was Daniel Gooch. He turned the pages of a massive document, entranced by its contents. Andrew Johnson was the last member of the committee. He looked like a brawler.

Fitz noticed Omwake slumped in his chair as if the whole affair bored him. The only time he stirred was to take a pinch of snuff and sneeze delicately into a stained handkerchief. Fitz rubbed his left arm impatiently—a habit since his arm had began to heal.

Omwake discreetly laid a hand across Fitz's knee. "Don't fidget. Don't bounce around," he said under his breath. "The committee will take that as a sign of disrespect."

"I don't respect them," Fitz returned.

Omwake looked at Fitz in surprise. "Oh, don't tell me you're one of them."

"One of who?"

Omwake dropped back in his seat in realization. "The Legion of the Innocent, Colonel Dunaway. Those poor souls who speak their mind and then are surprised to hear a rush of air as the guillotine blade falls." He shook his head. "You are a troublesome breed. Can't you just tell one little lie? Bend the truth? Would you, in your heart of hearts, have the sense to withhold a fact?"

"Are you counseling me to be dishonest with the committee?"

Omwake's face softened in amusement. "No. Be circumspect."

"I can be nothing more than I am," Fitz said. The suggestion, that he could so easily be turned into the sort of person he despised, angered him. "I am honest and forthright."

Omwake, leaning toward Fitz, kept his voice low. "I know that, you dunderhead. Just don't give them any ammunition."

"This thing is not done yet. There are too many unanswered questions," Fitz said. "While we waste our time here, the enemy is getting away."

There was a sharp rap as Senator Wade brought the gavel

down on a block of oak. Several secretaries prepared themselves.

"Mr. Chairman, if I may?" Chandler said.

"By all means, Senator," Wade replied. He slipped a plug of chewing tobacco into his mouth. His cheek swelled as he chewed the tobacco into submission.

"Mr. Omwake," Chandler said. "May I ask the purpose of your presence here?"

"Senator," Omwake said, not bothering to straighten in his chair. "The colonel and I are good friends. Since his business is fighting, not politics, I offered my services."

"Ah," Gooch said in a soft voice. "That's just our business as well. Fighting. More specifically, to make sure that our soldiers do fight."

"Then we are in accord, Congressman," Omwake said. His swept his hand dramatically toward Fitz. "Here sits a true hero of the Union. No one can question his courage or skill."

Fitz felt his anger growing. He might as well be on the auction block, going to the highest bidder. He wanted to speak for himself, and he was not convinced that Omwake could do any better than he in explaining his actions. He wanted to be after the Januarys.

"Well, you see," Gooch responded, "we have you there. Our purpose is to question. Our questions deal specifically with the death of one Phillip Abbott, and the escape of his murderers. Mr. Abbott's service to the Union was immeasurable, and his death a profound loss."

Wade spoke for the first time, his voice booming from his thick chest. "And the villains responsible got away." He looked at Fitz as if he had already heard his answer. "Tell me, Colonel, how many of the rebel party responsible for Abbott's death did you capture or kill?"

"None," Fitz said, "sir."

"Wound any?" Wade returned.

"No, sir."

"Didn't get close enough to bloody their noses, eh?"

"No, sir."

"You're from Tennessee?" Chandler asked.

Johnson spoke before Fitz had a chance to reply. "Surely, gentlemen, we're not going to hold that against this man?" The others laughed politely.

"My apologies, Senator," Chandler said. "But not every Tennessean is a good, loyal Union man like you."

Fitz was stung by the collegial banter of the four men facing him. They had no idea what he had seen, the horrors he had endured. They were not fit to clean the boots of the good men Fitz had seen die on the battlefield. They were politicians, and nothing worse could be said of them. "I was born and raised in Tennessee," he said. "But I'm a graduate of the military academy and I took an oath of allegiance to the United States."

Gooch blinked, as if handed an unexpected gift. "Exemplary. As was McClellan, Fitz-John Porter, and a dozen or so others whose patriotic rhetoric was never matched by accomplishments on the battlefield." He bore down on Fitz. "Why, after having been sent by Lincoln to Quebec to locate and safeguard Mr. Abbott, did you fail to do exactly that?"

"I couldn't find him," Fitz said, and regretted the answer.

Wade rolled his head at Chandler, and they exchanged sympathetic glances. "Well, that much is obvious, Colonel. Why couldn't you find him?"

"He didn't want to be found," Fitz said, developing an intense hatred for the men seated in front of him. They looked down on him, pitied him, and at the same time found talking to him somewhat distasteful. That, to Fitz, was certain. He would rather stand toe-to-toe and fight a man until they were both bloody pulps than be placed at the mercy of fools.

"Senator," Omwake said. Something caught his attention. "I wonder if I might trouble you for a glass of water?"

Chandler glanced an order at a clerk, who rose, filled a tumbler from the crystal pitcher on the table, and set it in front of Omwake. The little man took a long drink and set the glass down on the table.

"Now," he said, his thirst quenched. "Here it is. Abbott was just as likely an agent of the rebels as not. His death is regrettable, but it could be nothing more than a falling out among thieves. Colonel Dunaway was hot on the trail of the conspirators, sparing no effort, despite being seriously wounded in service to his country, to find and bring these criminals to justice."

"Yes," Chandler began.

"So rather than take the poor man to task," Omwake continued, "and since, I might add, a wound he suffered on the field of battle has not yet fully healed, I respectfully suggest that you release him from this inquiry so he can go about his business." He glanced at Fitz. "In all honesty, gentlemen, he is, after all, a little fish in a big war. I can think of half a dozen generals"—he hid a burp behind his fingers—"and maybe a politician or two who need investigating."

Andrew Johnson laughed, and Chandler and Wade offered a smile. Fitz felt the tension in the room melt away as Johnson whispered to Chandler.

"Colonel Dunaway," Wade said, taking a paper from a clerk at his elbow. "Let me understand you." He took a moment to read and handed the paper back to the clerk with a "Yes. Yes. All right." His dark eyes sought out Fitz. "The president sent you to Wilmington, Delaware, to investigate the explosion of the DuPont Power Works?"

"Yes, sir," Fitz replied.

"What did you determine to be the origin of that explosion?"

"A rebel action of some kind," Fitz said.

"How did you determine that, Colonel Dunaway?" Johnson asked.

"I spoke to several employees of the works," Fitz said. "I believe their account to be true and accurate."

"With whom did you speak?" Chandler asked.

"Mr. Kinnane, the manager of the works, and one of his trusted employees."

Chandler moved a slip of paper about on the table. "One Gideon, a Negro?"

His question startled Fitz. He had sent the report mentioning both men to Lincoln, but he did not expect it to fall into the hands of these jackals. The committee was also known as the Jacobean Club, Omwake had remarked. Fitz preferred to think of them as jackals. "Yes."

"Both employees of the works?" Wade snapped. His tone was sharp, unforgiving, and it signaled a new level of questioning.

"I just said they were," Fitz replied, feeling his anger rising.

"Down, Colonel. Down," Omwake whispered out of the side of his mouth.

"So you did," Chandler said. "Did you speak to Major Frederick Bloom, or Colonel Henry Greenwood?"

"I spoke with Bloom," Fitz said. "Greenwood was unavailable." He continued. "Bloom's explanation was there was an accidental explosion. He was most insistent on that. I didn't find the theory plausible."

"Then you can tell us," Wade said, "how the rebels managed to avoid a regiment of infantry, gain access to the works, and set explosive devices?"

It was a trap, and Fitz had walked into it. He knew it was going to sound ridiculous but there was no way around it. "I believe the rebels used some device to deliver fire to the works." He heard a tittering behind him. "It may have been something as simple as flaming arrows." Someone behind him burst out laughing. Omwake had nothing to offer.

Wade leaned forward, playing the moment for all it was worth. "Flaming arrows? You mean the rebels have enlisted Indians into their cause?"

"It could have been another means," Fitz said, but he knew he was lost.

"What means?" Gooch said. Until this time he had been busily reading from a ledger of some sort. Fitz had nearly forgotten he was there.

"I don't know."

"Colonel," Wade said, sitting back in his chair. His manner said that he was more than willing to believe Fitz but there was so little to base his support on. "We have Major Bloom's and Colonel Greenwood's signed affidavits detailing what they believe was the true cause of the explosion. I'm sure had you bothered to conduct an in-depth investigation, you would have concluded, as had they, that it was an accident, nothing more."

"I disagree, Mr. Wade," Fitz said.

"*Senator* Wade, Colonel. As much value as the army puts on titles, I should think you would be sensitive to the proper way to address elected officials."

"I still disagree, Senator Wade. Bloom had no desire to find out what really happened, and Greenwood was conveniently out of the area. I can't tell you how they did it, but I'd be willing to bet the rebels had something to do with the incident."

"Colonel?" Gooch said. "Who is Robert Owen?" The others turned their attention to the congressman and then to Fitz. Omwake remained calm, but it was obvious the question caught him unaware.

Fitz felt his stomach fall away.

"I'm pronouncing the name correctly, am I not?" Gooch pressed. "Robert Owen? An actor?"

"A companion of the Januarys," Fitz said. Did he know? He had to know. "A member of their company in Quebec City."

"He," Gooch continued, toying with a pencil, "disappeared at the same time. Is that so?" He let some silence pass before pleading, "Come, come, Colonel. You have nothing to fear. It's a simple question." He was Fitz's friend, his guide. Answer the questions and be shown the way to safety.

How did he know? "He did."

"Don't keep us in suspense, Gooch," Wade said, irritated.

"What Colonel Dunaway is apparently reluctant to disclose is that Owen and he are related."

"What?" Wade turned his fiery gaze on Fitz. "Is this true?" He glanced at Gooch, furious that the congressman had not shared the information beforehand.

"Robert Owen," Fitz said, "is my wife's half brother."

Chandler directed his question to Gooch. "Are you telling us this rebel is the colonel's brother-in-law?"

"He is my wife's half brother," Fitz tried again. He knew it was no use.

"What does that make him?" Wade thundered. "Half a traitor? Half as dangerous? The question is, has any of that rebel sentiment rubbed off on your wife? Or on you, for that matter?"

Omwake tried to soothe Wade. "Senator, may I point out that Mrs. Dunaway comes from a fine family. Many of us knew her father, the late Caleb Allen. No finer patriot existed. The colonel himself has the president's confidence."

"So did McClellan," Chandler growled at the mention of General George B. McClellan. He was the darling of the radicals until he revealed a single, glaring flaw—he could not win battles.

"A confidence misplaced, as we all know," Omwake said. "We all regretted General McClellan's failure on the battlefield, none more than the president. But surely, as well prepared as you are for this hearing, you must be equally well versed in Colonel Dunaway's service to the union."

Gooch posed his question to the committee. "Why does he hesitate to answer my question?"

"He is my brother-in-law," Fitz snapped. "I've never met him. I'm not even sure I could pick him out if he were sitting in the audience behind me." That was a lie, but it made no difference now.

"Calm yourself, Colonel," Johnson suggested.

"Then let me fall back to your position," Gooch said. "Your wife traveled to Quebec City with you."

"I required her assistance," Fitz said. "My wound—"

"You look perfectly recovered now, however you were wounded," Gooch interrupted. He drew strength from the revelation. "So. She travels to Quebec City with you, and her brother, or half brother if you prefer, just happens to be in the city. In the company of known confederate agents. And you yourself reported that these agents may have murdered poor Mr. Abbott. This is no Gordian Knot, Colonel."

Fitz glanced at Omwake. "What's that?"

"Never mind, Fitz. Just don't get angry."

"Oh, hell," Fitz said. "I'm well passed that point." He directed his next comments to the committee. "Gentlemen, if you want to know about me or my wife, ask me straight out. I'll tell you everything I know about myself, but if you think I'm going to drag my wife into this business, you can go to hell."

Fitz heard a gasp behind him, and he noticed with satisfaction that even the clerks had stopped writing.

Wade's gavel crashed down on the block. "Colonel Dunaway, you're out of order. I could have you arrested for insolence."

"Senator Wade, I've been arrested before, and accused of insolence before, but no one has ever questioned my loyalty. I would have found the Januarys if I hadn't been called to appear before this committee, and the moment I pass through those doors, I will set after them once again."

"Colonel Dunaway," Gooch said. "This committee will determine when you pass through those doors, and if you do so fully exonerated or under arrest. There are far too many questions yet unanswered about these two incidents and the role played by the mysterious Robert Owen."

"Would the committee consent to a report written and submitted by Colonel Dunaway?" Omwake suggested.

Gooch would not be placated. "It would not."

Wade joined the attack. "I find Dunaway's attitude insulting."

"Colonel," Fitz said.

Wade looked as if he had been slapped. "I beg your pardon?"

"We agreed, Senator Wade," Fitz said. "I call you senator and you call me colonel. Of course, before this day is over we may be calling each other a great deal more than that."

"I believe, Colonel Dunaway," Gooch said, "that the president's confidence in you was severely misplaced. Let us review the situation. You were dispatched to determine the cause of the explosion at the DuPont Powder Works. You settled on rebel involvement after a brief examination, accomplished through some fantastic means. Meanwhile two officers, well known by this committee as staunch Union men, offer a much more plausible explanation—to whit, it was carelessness at the hands of an employee. Sent by Mr. Lincoln to Quebec City to retrieve and safeguard Mr. Abbott, you did neither. Am I accurate in my recital?"

"No," Fitz said. "But it's yours to do with as you wish."

"That's most kind of you," Gooch said, betraying real emotion for the first time. "Here we are arrived at the elusive Januarys and their co-conspirator, Robert Owen. In addition"—he consulted his papers—"we have your wife, Mrs. Asia Dunaway." He paused. "She was at one time Mrs. Lossing, wasn't she?"

Omwake attempted to divert the question. "Gentlemen, please. To continue to delve into Mrs. Dunaway's past and personality is unseemly. I believe it demeans the purpose and intent of this committee and sullies its valuable contribution to the war effort."

Chandler took his turn. "Wasn't her husband involved in a plot to kill Lincoln? This Lossing fellow. A failed lawyer, I'm told. The very plot, Colonel Dunaway, that you thwarted?"

"She made a poor choice of brothers," Wade tossed out, "but a worse choice of husbands."

Laughter erupted behind Fitz, and he let it settle before he replied. "Here I am, gentlemen. Come at me singly or all at once, but the next one of you jackals who mentions my wife will be able to count the teeth remaining in your mouth on the finger of one hand." Fitz stood and slipped his kepi on despite Omwake's attempts to pull him down.

Wade, as shocked as the others at the table, banged his gavel in a frenzy. "Sit down, sir! How dare you address this committee in that manner."

"He should be arrested," Chandler said.

Gooch was silent, appraising the situation. Johnson glanced about for a spittoon, locating one near the end of the table.

"Colonel Dunaway," Wade shouted, beating the wooden block into submission. The gavel's handle cracked and the head flew above the senator's head. The meager audience erupted in laughter, as Wade threw the handle down in disgust.

"Good day, gentlemen," Fitz said, turning away from the committee table. Omwake stopped him in the hallway just outside.

"That was wonderful. Just wonderful," Omwake said bitterly. "Why didn't you just draw a gun and shoot them?"

"Have you one?" Fitz asked.

"Don't tax me, Colonel Dunaway. Lincoln's going to be irritated to learn of your performance today."

"Then why did you turn me over to them?" Fitz said. "Why recall me when I was close to catching the Januarys?" It was a lie, but it had to do. Fitz had no idea where the actors were, but he was certain he would have found them. Owen was a different matter because of his promise to Asia. Promises or players didn't matter, he was close to nothing— not to solving the mystery of the powder works or Abbott's murder or the Januarys' association with any of it. He had an unfamiliar map with no legend. What he had more of than good sense was a burning desire to see the thing done to the end. And the ability to irritate his superiors.

Omwake pointed to the door. "Those gentlemen have been a thorn in Lincoln's side since they decided to help the president, and please note my sarcasm, Colonel, by forming that devilish committee. He has to deal with them because they are of the Congress, and he needs the Congress."

Fitz wasn't convinced. "They had no business bringing my wife into this."

A moment passed while Omwake judged Fitz's political naïvité. "It was all they had, Colonel Dunaway, until that remarkable demonstration of yours."

"Very well," Fitz said. "Now what do we do?"

"I will go and report to the president," Omwake replied, "and you will go somewhere to await a summons by the committee. There are several possibilities here."

"Which are?"

"You return to face them and are exonerated. That likelihood, to quote Mr. Lincoln, is as scarce as hens' teeth." Omwake gave the matter some thought. "You may be recalled, found guilty of some infraction or suspicious behavior—"

"Suspicious—"

"Oh, Colonel Dunaway, haven't you been in Washington long enough to understand this wretched place?" He returned to his explanation. "Don't trouble yourself. I don't think the committee will waste its efforts on your alleged transgressions. To put it bluntly—you're not important enough."

"Thank God for my inconsequence."

"Let us not celebrate too quickly, Colonel," Omwake warned. "I think it more likely that the committee will neither charge you nor clear your good name. They will, as it were, cast you adrift on an endless sea. Or to put it more bluntly, let you rot."

"What do you mean?"

"Die of neglect, Colonel. You will exist until the deities decide otherwise, suspended between heaven and hell." A notion struck him. "That geography certainly has to be Washington, DC. No matter. You will be officially forgotten until relieved of your misery in one matter or another."

Fitz understood. "Hung out to dry."

"That, too," Omwake said. "Good day to you, sir. I shouldn't expect many more if I were you."

Book 2

Chapter 27

Chapman's Hotel
Fulton, Maryland

"What was that man's name?" Victoria January asked her brother.

He was seated at a table, bent over one of the clockwork mechanisms. "What man?" he replied, distracted by the complex machine.

"That Union officer? With De Brule?" She saw that he wasn't paying attention. "The handsome man with the wound."

He answered without looking up. "Dunaway, as you very well know. I thought you were about to devour him in front of me."

She stroked the back of his head, parting his thick black hair with her fingers. "Not without your permission, brother." She was growing bored. They had been at this dreary hotel for nearly a week, pretending, with a great degree of success, to be husband and wife. The hotel's owner was known to be a Southern sympathizer as well as an agent, when there was money involved. January had produced two fifty-dollar gold pieces and an admonition when they had first checked in. "No questions," he had said. "And no idle talk." To assure the owner of the repercussions of either, he added, "We have friends in the area, and they will not take it well if there are complications."

The owner had snatched up the gold pieces and had smiled with a row of broken teeth. He understood the situation perfectly. Nearby friends or not, if he betrayed this strange couple he would receive no more money.

"Must you work on those trinkets?" Victoria asked.

"Yes," her brother responded. "I must understand them. We cannot rely on Goodwin for everything." He twisted in the chair, finding her on the bed. "And since our dear Mr. Abbott confirmed his reputation for being the most difficult man in America by turning on us, we no longer have his skills."

"If I don't get out of here," Victoria announced, "I shall explode."

January chuckled, setting the mechanism aside. "For God's sake, woman, we're in Fulton, Maryland. Where could you expect to go?"

She lay on the bed, pouting. She turned on her side, her head propped up in her hand. "Tell me again."

January grew somber. "It does no good."

"It does you no good," she said, correcting him. "I find it wonderful. Tell me."

January pretended to interest himself in the clockworks, but he gave up the charade. She knew him too well to accept he would deny her anything. He joined her and she slid close to him, laying her head on his chest, throwing her thin arm over his waist.

Above January was a plaster ceiling, pooled with brown stains from rainwater that had found its way through the roof. "It was a palace," he began, feeling her arm tighten. "Xanadu was nothing to it, nor were the halls of Camelot, or the splendor of Versaille. Art from around the world favored its magnificent rooms. Paintings from the great masters, vases from Italy, jade lions from the Far East, and tapestries from the Kingdom of Persia. The setting sun turned its marble columns gold as it bid good evening to a sight that shamed even Apollo with its vibrancy. Its radiance shown with all that was good in the world, and people, even those not permitted to set foot within its luxurious interior, drove by so they might glimpse Olympus."

"Who lived there?" Victoria asked. "Were they gods?"

No, he thought, but swept the word away. "More than gods, greater in noble bearing than any gods that lived. He was an actor with a voice that made the mountains tremble. He spoke and thunder rolled over the heads of all who listened, and lightning flashed from his black eyes. His wife was an actress and when the footlights washed her soft brown hair and shone from her green eyes, every man in the audience fell under her spell. Her voice was as refreshing as a cool fall breeze, and she moved with such grace that many swore her feet never touched the boards. She was Venus and more, and together they welcomed the very best of society to this wondrous refuge."

She pressed her face into his side and began to sob. "Oh, Royal. I don't remember them. Why can't I remember them?"

"Warriors, artists, diplomats," he continued, stoking his enthusiasm, "and musicians came to the palace."

She looked up at him, her face tear streaked. "I remember now. I remember the music. A piano. And violins." Victoria let her face fall.

"There was always music. Singing and dancing, and laughter. Great crystal chandeliers hung in the ballroom, their brilliance second only to the sparkling diamonds worn about the necks of the beautiful women who came to pay homage to Mother, and curtsy in subservience to Father. Authors read from their latest works, and poets brought tears to the eyes of those gathered to hear them. Actors performed scenes from their latest plays, and Marlowe thundered after Shakespeare, with Dante just behind. There was wine, the best in the world, shipped from France. I remember the squeal of the nails as the crate lids were pried open, and playing in the piles of discarded sawdust used to cushion the bottles."

"I remember," she said, the dream taking hold, "playing in the forest of pine trees. The sun came in through the limbs and washed the ground with light. The shadows were alive when the wind blew, and I knew the trees were enchanted. It was all such a beautiful place."

"We snuck down the stairs and crouched on the landing, listening to the sound of the parties. You were too young to remember, of course, but I took you by the hand and led you down the stairs. I told you to be quiet or we would be found out and sent back to bed." He was no longer in a cheap hotel, his lover lying next to him. He was a boy peering through the banisters, listening to the orchestra, hoping to catch a glimpse of his father and mother among the strangers. He caught the faint scent of perfume interlaced with the stark odor of cigars. People were laughing, and he heard crystal colliding with crystal, and dancers whirling across the hardwood floor.

He felt Victoria, not Victoria the insatiable woman but Victoria the child, stationed on the landing next to him, fall asleep. He knew she would—she always did. She had begged to go with him and watch the party, and at first he had refused because he knew she could not stay awake. But he relented and held out his hand for hers, because he could deny her nothing.

It had ended as it always did. He heard a rustle and felt Victoria being swept up in his mother's arms, and heard her soft voice say to him, "Royal. It's time for bed." He had staggered to his feet and, taking hold of her full skirt in his tiny hand, followed her up the stairs.

January felt Victoria's hand part his vest and push aside his shirtfront, seeking his bare chest for comfort. It was like that night, the final time, when her tiny fingers dug into his chest and her sobs were muffled in his shoulder.

"Mother came to take us to bed," he returned to his story, knowing it would help soothe his sister's mind. "She carried you, always, and I trailed behind her."

"What of Father?" Victoria asked.

"He had guests to attend to," January said without hesitation. He did not tell her of the screams near the slave quarters, or the slave who had begged for his children. The man who drove them to town, Jonas, had thrown himself at his father's feet, pleading.

His father had straightened; he wanted Jonas to know who was superior, who commanded the power at Mayfield. There had been a moment when Royal saw a spark in Jonas, when the driver would have lunged at his father. But it passed, and Jonas had collapsed in defeat.

Royal had seen Jonas the next day. He was seated on his father's coach, dressed in fine livery, as still as a statue, staring ahead with dead eyes. Fine lines of rust seeped through his coat. Jonas had been whipped for his defiance.

"You mustn't allow them to gain the upper hand," Royal's father had told him. "They are property and must be taught to respect their masters. Their betters. Be firm, and if necessary, be violent."

They had been riding side by side through the thick woods that surrounded Mayfield. Royal did not like the woods; there was something about them that even his father's presence could not counter. Even the horses were skittish in the silent forest.

"Pay me heed, boy," John Jacob January had said. He did not want his son's mind drifting off the subject. "You can exhibit kindness to the children, and that is the only time that emotion is to be revealed. Of course, you may have to chastise them—the children, I mean. But it's for your own benefit."

"You mean their benefit?" Royal corrected his father.

His father failed to respond for a moment, lost in a dark world. "What?"

"You chastise them for their benefit? So they'll learn."

"Yes," his father had said, but the correction didn't seem important to him. His mind was on the children. A power had overtaken him, and his eyes were bright with desire.

*   *   *

January did not tell Victoria about their mother and father arguing deep into the night, or Father passing the night in the library accompanied only by bottles of whiskey and the memories of his past glory. Or of the long, unsettling ride in the woods.

A tyrant, his mother had flung at John Jacob January, and all the glory of the magnificent house and the magic of a perfect life had melted away, leaving a macabre skeleton covered in decay. *Reprehensible, she screamed. Any children, John? All children? Our own as well?*

"Will it work? The clocks? Everything?"

The question startled January—he thought she had fallen asleep. "Yes. It is not so complicated as it seems. Goodwin understands it best. The winds trouble me."

She slid her hand farther into his clothing. "What about Abbott's assurances? Don't they count for something?"

"Of course," he said. "As far as they go. But no man controls the winds."

"Don't be a bore," Victoria said. "You know what I mean."

His sister had returned, and the little girl racing through the forest that night had disappeared.

January thought about her question. "We are here because Abbott's mind gave us the weapon we needed. I trust him and his assurances unlike I've trusted any other man. We have nothing to fear, especially failure. When it's done, we sail for England."

Her heard her breathing softly for some time before she said, "Good." He lay still, going over everything in his mind before she asked him, "Was it really as wonderful as I remember?"

His eyes settled on the stained ceiling. "Yes, it was a fairy tale."

Chapter 28

Above the Middle Patuxent River
Guilford, Maryland

Owen watched Goodwin and Mark tend to the mules. The young man knew a great deal about the animals, Owen decided, inspecting their hooves, teeth, mouths, flanks, and withers for sores.

"Can't afford any injury," Mark shouted across the clearing to Owen. "It'll lame an animal." He stroked a mule's back, watching how the animal reacted. "And you can't buy a good mule for a sack of gold nowadays. The army wants them all. Best keep what you got and treat 'em well."

Goodwin said nothing of course, checking the animals first and then the load—making sure the lashings were tight. He examined wear points on the ropes and reseated them if necessary. The ropes slipped as the wagons bounced over the rough roads and rubbed against the sideboards during the journey. The edges of the wooden boards slowly ate away at the fibers until, if they weren't replaced, the ropes parted.

Goodwin ordered Owen to build a fire and fry some salt pork.

"Dig through that bag," he said. "There are some apples in there as well. And potatoes, I think. Fix some coffee."

"I'm no servant," Owen protested, jerking a greasy frying pan out of a stained canvas bag.

"No," Goodwin agreed. "But you're no teamster, either."

"You see," Mark called, unaware of the confrontation between the two, "you gotta check the axletree. Right here." He had taken Owen's request to learn about wagons and driving a mule team to heart. "You check that to make sure it ain't split. All the iron on the axle. Make sure the linchpin ain't loose." He stepped back and examined the wheels, running his hand over the spokes. He tested the hub cover to make sure it was snapped in place.

Mark joined Owen, who handed him a cup of coffee. He watched Goodwin inspect the doubletree on his wagon.

"He don't talk much, does he?" Mark said.

"No," Owen said. He stretched the stiffness out of his legs and rubbed his sore back. He had discovered there was no good way to ride a mule, and even walking frequently did nothing to ease the boredom or pain. His ass was numb and bruised and his back ached from the worthless saddle. How could he learn anything if he were in so much pain? Mark's constant talking, at first a diversion, quickly became an irritant. Would the man never shut up?

"You go to church?" Mark asked.

"Church?"

"Read the Bible. Me and my family's Baptists. You accept the Lord. Don't want to go to hell, do you? Man never knows when he might face death. Might not have time to speak to his maker. A fella needs to set everything straight before judgment."

The subject disgusted Owen. He thought those who wallowed in religion didn't have the sense to think for themselves. Religion was a humbug and those who practiced it fools.

Mark's interest was drawn to Goodwin. "He drives a good team, though. He must have done it before. Did he do it before? He knows his teams and wagons. By gum, the man's not satisfied until he's looked over everything."

"Coffee," Owen urged. The man couldn't talk and drink at the same time. "Do you want more coffee?"

Mark held out his cup, but his attention never turned from Goodwin. "He's good," he said, withdrawing his cup. "What are you carryin' in those crates, anyhow?"

The question surprised Owen. Not because it was asked—Mark had talked through every subject at hand so it was understandable that he arrived at this one—but because Owen had to reply, "I don't know."

"You don't know?" Mark said. It was obvious that he hadn't expected that response. "Truly? You don't know? I always know what I'm haulin'. I don't ever want to be surprised. Might be gunpowder. Somethin' like that." He sipped some coffee, then said with an expectant air, "Could be somethin' real valuable." He fell back to disbelief. "You don't know?"

Mark's questions irritated Owen, making him feel like a child from whom so much is expected and nothing realized. His father had been the same way, standing over him with a disapproving gaze, deliberately failing to acknowledge his accomplishment. It had become obvious that the man who visited his mother every other day was more than a friend. Owen had stood before him, a big man in a black suit, as green eyes took inventory of the boy's faults. Owen felt that way now, with Mark's ridiculous probing.

"Ask Mr. Goodwin," Owen said. He noticed a rip in his pants, near the knee, and realized how tattered he had become on the journey.

"Your pretty suit is all tored up," Mark said, following Owen's gaze. "You shouldn't wear good clothes on the wagon. When I saw you at the creek I thought 'Those clothes won't last a day.' Ain't you got no others? You want me to look in your bag for you to find some others?"

Owen jumped to his feet. "No! Just drink your coffee. That's all." Someone approached.

Neither Mark nor Owen spoke as Goodwin knelt and

poured a cup of coffee. They were like boys caught in mischief by a parent. "We need to tar those axles," Goodwin said, blowing on his coffee.

"Them axles fine," Mark ventured. "I've gone twice the distance without pulling the wheels every day. That's just extra work."

Goodwin's eyes swung to Owen. "Cigar?"

Owen nodded, and waited while Goodwin pulled two cigars from his coat, handing one to Owen. "We've got nearly thirty miles to go. A lot of it's bad road. Some of it is no road at all. We'll tar the axles after we get a bite to eat." He directed his next comment to Mark. "Why don't you go see to the tar buckets?"

The young man stood, stung by the command. "Who is going to help me with the jacks? I can't lift the jacks by myself."

"We'll be along shortly. You just get the tar buckets."

Mark stomped off.

"What's he doing?" Goodwin asked.

"Doing?" Owen said.

"What's got you troubled?"

"He won't shut up. The man is never without words. It's constant. I can't stand the sound of his ignorant voice."

Goodwin sympathized with Owen. "I can't stand a man who talks too much. What does he talk about?"

Owen's exasperation built. "The weather. His family. My clothes, of all things. I know they're ruined. Look at them."

Goodwin wasn't impressed. "Did he ask you what was in the crates?"

"Yes. Several times."

"What did you tell him?"

"Tell him? What was I supposed to tell him? I haven't the slightest idea. You never saw fit to inform me." Owen was disgusted with everything. He wanted a bath, good food, and a suitable place to conduct a decent toilet. He had no idea where they were going or what was expected of him except

Goodwin's cryptic instructions to learn how to drive the wagon. Let Mark drive the wagon—he was being paid to do so.

"Lower your voice," Goodwin commanded. "What's he doing now?"

Owen, confused, realized that Goodwin meant Mark. "He's laying under the wagon. He seems to have some trouble disengaging a bucket." He looked at Goodwin. "A tar bucket, I suppose."

Goodwin slipped his hand under his coattail and pulled out a pistol. Keeping it close to his body, he said, "Here. Take it and keep it out of sight."

The weapon's appearance stunned Owen. "What is this? What are you doing?"

"Take it, and hide it on your person. Don't let him see it."

Owen, his eyes on Mark, took the pistol and slid it into his waistband, pushing it under his coat. The pistol's weight was foreign and ominous—its shape bit into his hip bone. "What—"

"That boy knows nothing about freight wagons."

"But—"

"His pa wants our load," Goodwin explained. "It won't do him no good, but he don't know that. I suspect he means to take it, run it down the river, and sell it to the rebels."

"But we're the rebels," Owen said. None of this made any sense. Surely Goodwin was wrong.

Goodwin's look told Owen he was still a boy. "This ain't got nothin' to do with loyalties. This is about money. It's robbery. Mark's pa sent him along and kept his best men back."

"What is in the crates?" Owen demanded. He deserved an answer. If he was in danger he wanted to know what he was fighting for.

"Iron filings and sulfuric acid," Goodwin said. He glanced at the wagon he had been driving. "Those crates have hoses, couplings, and a mixing box." He waited for Owen to absorb the words. "Makes perfect sense, doesn't it?"

Owen exploded. "What is this about? Arms and ammunition I understand. What are these other things? What devilish contraption have we been hauling about?"

"Something of no value to anyone but us."

"But then why does Mark's father want it?"

"Because," Goodwin said, "it has value to us." He smiled at Owen, as if he found the situation humorous. "You have learned how to drive a wagon, haven't you? Like I told you?"

"Yes," Owen replied defiantly. "I know all about a road wheeler and a jerk line. I've had to listen to that boy's incessant ramblings since we left that vile little settlement."

"Then tell me."

Owen felt as if he had been slapped. He hated being treated like a boy. "The jerk line is attached to the left-hand wheel mule's bit. To turn the team and wagon to the left, you pull the line. To turn right, you jerk it. All of this is accomplished by the man riding the left-hand wheel mule." He remembered Mark's comment. "The mule's know what to do better than anyone." He added, more out of irritation than anything, "Any dolt can drive a freight wagon."

"No, not any. It takes a special kind of dolt." Goodwin wasn't impressed. "Well, you can tell me what to do. I hope you can do it."

Owen stood, angered by Goodwin. He was still stiff from the road and his aching muscles hobbled him. "I can do it."

He watched Goodwin decide before answering, "We'll see."

All three of the men worked to retar the wheels, slipping the heavy jacks under the axles, then inserting the jack bar into the bulky mechanism. It took the weight of two men on the bar to advance the gears that drove the shaft and saddle, but with each clack of the gear, and the fall of the stop, the axle rose. When it was high enough, they pulled the linchpin, slid the wheel forward, and liberally painted the smooth axle with tar. Each night after they had stopped, every wheel had to be lubricated against wear. Owen grew to hate the ritual.

* * *

Mark banked the fire after they finished and laid down next to it. Owen collapsed on his single blanket and caught the stink of his own body. He had not bathed in days, he had to make his toilet in the woods, and he had no way to clean himself afterward. He hoped no civilized individuals happened on them. Goodwin's warning came back to him. Hurlock meant to rob them—to steal the load. It was a ridiculous assumption. They carried iron filings? What possible use could those be to anyone? The wagons and mules belonged to Hurlock and he'd already received half of the contract amount. Everything was understood—once they arrived at their destination and unloaded, Mark would hire another man and they would return the wagons. Goodwin must be mistaken. Mark was barely capable of an intelligent thought. How could he be a party to robbery?

The thought that followed startled Owen with its logic. It would be murder as well if Goodwin was right. He froze, wanting desperately to catch a glimpse of Mark. He might hold a gun on him now. He could be seconds from death.

Owen let his head fall to one side as casually as he could but kept his eyes closed. Maybe Mark would see it as an innocent movement, that Owen was asleep and could pose no danger. When he heard nothing coming from Mark, Owen's eyelids fluttered open.

Mark was laying on his back, mouth open, drawing in gulps of air. Occasionally a whistle escaped his nose, but it was obvious that nothing was going to disturb the boy until morning.

Owen turned his head to the distant white stars. Goodwin was a fool, and he had been a fool to believe him. He had deceived the Januarys. Surely they must have seen the man was incapable of performing any complicated task. He was not reliable. Owen saw an opportunity. It would be his responsibility to see this affair through to its successful conclusion. He would find out where the wagons were to be delivered and take over from Goodwin. What would happen to Goodwin? Owen set that question aside, convincing himself that things would fall into place to satisfy him. He would triumph, he concluded, his mind rapidly assembling the events, and Victoria would be there to meet him. Everything settled into place.

Nothing remained of his concern but the fatigue that tugged at his eyelids and drained his body of strength. He decided to waste no more trust on Goodwin, or the man's ideas. Sleep nudged him.

He was nearly asleep when an errant thought crept into his mind. It had to do with awkwardness, and he was surprised he hadn't thought of it before, but he had been far too irritated with Goodwin, Mark, and the journey to consider it. Why had Mr. Hurlock sent only one driver? Two wagons, two drivers to return them. Certainly he could have been shorthanded, but wouldn't it make more sense to hire a local man to return with the vehicles than to contract a man when they arrived at the destination, hire him to drive a wagon back, and then return him? Part of Owen's brain agreed with his rationale, but most of his mind pleaded for sleep, so he could not come to a consensus on the puzzle's answer.

He rolled to one side, and felt something stab him in the ribs. It was the blasted pistol that Goodwin had given him. He fumbled through his blanket and coat, pushing the weapon out of the way. Sleep had nearly triumphed, darkness covering his mind in a soft mantle, when a single thorn of an idea pricked him to wakefulness. If the mystery of the missing driver troubled him, then Goodwin must be aware of it as well.

Owen's ankle exploded in pain as someone kicked him. He awoke with a cry to find a dark figure standing over him, pointing a pistol at his head.

"Get up," the man said. It was Hurlock.

Owen staggered to his feet, his ankle throbbing. It was still night, but the comforting stars that had fallen to sleep with him were gone, replaced by a slate haze.

"Where is he?" Hurlock said. There were three other men standing just behind Hurlock. One was Mark, suddenly grown dangerous. He held a musket.

Owen didn't understand any of this. Was he dreaming? "What?"

Hurlock jammed the pistol's muzzle in Owen's stomach. "Goodwin."

"He's here," Owen said, helpless to answer. "He's here, isn't he?"

"Let's just kill him and go on," said a round man standing next to Mark.

"No," Hurlock snapped. "I ain't leaving that other fella to come after us. This dandy ain't nothin'."

Owen felt something tugging at his waistband. The pistol. If he could get to it he could fight his way free. They were going to kill him if he didn't. Hurlock was turned to the others while they argued what to do. Mark seemed intent on brushing the dirt off his musket. He could do it now. He could slide his right hand over to the pistol, jerk it out, and cock it in one action. He'd used a pistol before. In a play in Philadelphia. What was it—something about western desperadoes? He'd received no billing but had three speeches and was then required to draw a pistol and aim it at the leading man.

Do it, you fool! His hand was on the pistol and he felt it coming free of the waistband of his trousers. He heard the first shot and saw the top of Hurlock's head fly off, spewing blood and brains into the air. Owen felt a warm spray pepper his face as the man's body fell against him. He stumbled against the weight and fell backward.

The round man shouted and dove under the wagon, but his collar caught on a brace and he hung there, frantically kicking the ground, trying to free himself. It was macabre and horribly funny at the same time—a fat clown entertaining an audience. Two bullets plowed into his back and his body collapsed on the ground.

The other man who came with Hurlock, a stocky man with a thatch of red hair, turned to run but became confused, stopped, and wheeled about looking for safety. A bullet hit him in the neck, a mist of blood jumping out of his throat. He was clutching at the wound when another shot tore into his jacket, setting the wool on fire. He slid to the ground, lifeless.

Goodwin stepped into the faint glare of the dwindling campfire, holding two pistols on Mark. The young man, trembling uncontrollably, had dropped his musket. A dark patch of urine colored his trousers.

"Are you shot?" Goodwin called. Owen realized he was talking to him. He rolled the dead man away and struggled to his feet. He wasn't sure he could stand. He thought he could talk. He had never been so frightened in his life.

"No," he said. He looked down at the gun in his hand. "I never got a chance to use it."

"Wouldn't have done you any good anyway," Goodwin said, kicking the other bodies to make sure they were dead. "It's not loaded."

Rage replaced fright. "Not loaded! What was I supposed to do?"

"Nothing," Goodwin said, turning on Mark. "I didn't want you to shoot me by mistake." He motioned to Mark with one of the pistols. "Anybody else coming?"

"No. No. I swear." He glanced at his father, not out of grief, Owen noticed, but relief. His father was dead, but he was alive.

"Get their guns," Goodwin said to Owen, and added to Mark, "When he gets done, strip the bodies. Money and valuables."

"You're robbing the dead?" Owen said.

Goodwin didn't bother to look at him as he answered, "Yes."

Owen picked up the weapons—two pistols, a carbine, and Mark's musket, his eyes darting from Mark to Goodwin. He noticed gore on one of the weapons. His stomach twisted itself into a knot. When he was finished, he dropped to one knee and threw up. He lifted his head, staring in anger at Goodwin. "You were using me as bait. I could have been killed."

Goodwin nodded to Mark to begin and squatted near the fire, the pistols dangling in his hands. "I wouldn't have let that happen." He didn't bother investing any emotion in his reply—it was a statement of fact that didn't require embellishment. "When you get done," he called to the boy, "drag the bodies into those bushes. Don't bother trying to run. I never knew of anyone who could outrun a bullet."

Mark was sobbing now, a thin stream of snot dangling from his upper lip, swaying back and forth as he searched the bodies for valuables. He stopped and jumped back when he came to the fat man lying under the wagon. He looked at Goodwin in horror. "Mr. Naylor is still alive."

Goodwin stood reluctantly and walked to the wagon. He waved Mark back with his pistol, and then kicked Naylor in the ribs. There was soft groan in reply, but no appreciable movement. "He's not much alive. Get at it."

Owen was overwhelmed by thirst and searched for a canteen. He found it and, pulling the cork, drank greedily. He realized how close he had come to dying. He stepped back and dropped the canteen, gasping. He was alive. He would not die—he would never die. He watched Mark drag the first of the dead men into the bushes, and saw Goodwin waiting patiently near the wagon, his pistol crossed over his chest, as if in prayer. For what? For killing? Or did he pray in gratitude, thanking the Lord for allowing him to triumph over his enemies?

"How did you know?" Owen ventured, certain he would be answered. "When did you know?"

Goodwin's eyes tracked Mark's clumsy efforts to pull his

father's body into the thicket. "Everyone at Saylor's Creek was too obliging," Goodwin explained. "Everyone was good to us." He paused, making sure that Mark properly hid the bodies under a thick covering of branches and dead leaves. "They sent one man to return two wagons—"

Owen wanted to speak, to tell Goodwin that he had thought of the very thing and wondered if it meant something. Perhaps he was developing into a killer like Goodwin. Strangely, the idea excited him. He could still appear in plays, but when he was at liberty he would undertake adventures. He wondered if he should assume an alias.

"You help us get hitched up," Goodwin shouted to Mark. "Then you can go on home."

Mark stumbled out of the thicket, wiping his sleeve under his nose, sniffling like a child. Owen thought, now he truly was a boy and not a child in a man's body. His eyes were swollen; his thick arms fell to his side, the body too weak to hold them.

"You goin' to let me go?"

"Get us hitched up," Goodwin ordered. He shot a glance to Owen. "Help him. Let's see how much you learned."

They began working, removing the hobbled mules, guiding the first span of two alongside the wagon tongue. Each of the other three spans were moved in order to the wagon.

"See, I told you," Mark said to Owen. "They each gotta go in order. Each mule knows his place." He touched on the other subject, letting his voice mellow in regret. "I didn't have nothin' to do about that. I mean, I always does what my pa tells me, but I didn't know that him, and Mr. Naylor, and Mr. Sutherland was going to come down here to rob you." He passed the tack over the mule's back, working without thought to what he was doing. "I tell you, I'm goin' home and I ain't gonna say nothin' to nobody about this. I swear. I'm gonna go home and mind my own business."

Owen was tired of listening to Mark, and thought of things to say—rude things to shut him up. But the boy was scared, had just lost his father, and Owen just wanted this night to be over. The harness was laid in place and cinched tight around the mules' bellies, with the jerk line the last thing tended to. Mark ran it from the lead pair, taking time to speak soothingly to each mule, to the wheeler. He brought up the small mule that Owen had been forced to ride, the tiny creature seeming so forlorn.

"I'll take him back," Mark said, pulling the bullwhip out of his boot and handing it to Owen. "I knowed Billy for a long time, and he can carry my weight easy. I know he was tough on your backside, but I've got more fat on my ass than you. He can carry me better."

Goodwin came up. "Leave the mule here. You can walk."

Mark's face fell, one more disappointment for the boy. "He can't pull nothin'," he explained. "He won't take to the harness at all." He chuckled nervously. "Look at him. See?"

"Leave him be. You can walk home."

Mark looked at Owen for help, but Owen turned away, embarrassed for the boy.

"All right," Mark said. He tied Billy's reins to the wagon's midbrace. "I guess I can walk. I guess that'll be all right." He hesitated, wanting to know that everything would turn out well—wanting to be reassured by the adults. "I'll go on now." He turned and began walking back up the road, the slow, lumbering gait of a boy whose body was too big for him.

Goodwin watched, Owen standing next to him. "Get on your mule," Goodwin said.

Owen took the bullwhip in one hand, twisted the mule's coarse braid in his fingers, and swung into the saddle. He heard a bang, and spun to see Mark drop to his knees and pitch forward on his face, his arms hanging lifelessly at his sides. Owen jumped out of the saddle, confronting Goodwin. "You killed him. You had no cause to do that. He didn't do anything!"

Goodwin looked at him incredulously. "Who do you think was tryin' to kill us tonight? He had a musket, didn't he? You don't think this whole thing came as a surprise to him, do you?"

"You said he could go."

Goodwin was amazed at his companion's innocence. "I lied."

Owen wanted to strike him. He wanted to beat him without mercy for all the hardships he had been through, and for killing the boy. Goodwin had lied to the boy, and Owen had been lied to as well. He wanted romance in his struggle, and heroic encounters, and to be covered in accolades by beautiful women. But his ass hurt, and he saw the true nature of death, and smelled the stink of shit that comes when men die and they no longer have need of their bowels. He had seen a stupid, simple boy killed after having been given hope. He wanted justice, and reward, for all he had suffered.

Goodwin studied him with cold eyes. "We have come nearly as far as we need to. Mr. and Miss January will be expecting us before long, and when we get there we'll have more work to do. You threw in with us, givin' us your word to do what was required. Nothin' says for sure that we'll get done what we hope to. The only thing that will stop me is death." He jerked the bullwhip out of Owen's hand and examined it. "You're a smart boy. I saw you watchin' everything he did. Now get back up on that mule and use this." He tossed the whip to Owen. "Them mules are smarter than you and me. You just give them their lead, and they'll follow the back of any wagon in front of them. If you have any troubles, call out."

"What about—"

Goodwin glanced at the bundle lying on the road and walked to his wagon. The boy is not important, Owen decided—he had never been important, or of any matter. He was just a thing to be left behind. Owen watched Goodwin pluck the bullwhip from its holster, settle into the saddle, and snap the whip over the mules' heads. They started out at a shambling gait, the freight wagon rumbling behind them. Owen's team, taking the signal, began to move. He jumped into the saddle, throwing the long whip over his shoulder. No matter what he did, Owen decided, everything would happen as it was meant to happen.

Chapter 29

The Lossing Boarding House
Washington, DC

Fitz sunk the ax blade into a log, pulled it free, and then swung it over his head with all his strength. The blade buried itself in the wood. He jerked it free and slid his hands along the ax handle, seating them. A stack of firewood lay next to him.

"Every one of you is a damned fool," he cursed as the blade came up, and fell with a flash. "Can go to hell in a handcart." The ax came up. "And kiss the Devil's bright red ass." The blade bit into the wood. "I hope the son of a bitch farts right in your faces." The wood refused to release the blade, and Fitz turned his anger on the tool. "You son of a bitch. Let go of that." He pumped the handle up and down, trying to free the ax.

"Fitz?" Asia called from the back porch. "For God's sake, let William do that. You'll injure your arm."

"My arm is already injured," Fitz replied, trying to jerk the blade free. He hated to rely on the servant's help. "If this son of a bitch doesn't let go, I'll build you a fire right here."

"If you're going to curse," Asia chastised him, "the least you can do is show variety. That's the third time you've used that expression."

He straightened and glared at her. ""I was saving the best for when I become truly vexed with my situation. Would you like a sample now?"

"No." Asia stomped her foot. "You come right into this house and warm yourself. William can finish and bring in the firewood."

Fitz glanced at the ax. It remained still, taunting him. "Stay there, you greasy bastard," he whispered. "When I come back we'll have a reckoning." He brushed the wood chips and dirt from his jacket and climbed the back stairs. Passing Asia he said, "It's won now, but I'll soon change that."

She watched him walk into the kitchen. "You mustn't harm the ax, Colonel Dunaway. I plan to breed it and fill the yard with little hatchets." She heard him growl in reply as she closed the door and followed him into the parlor. She saw him pull his coat off, thinking how strange it was to see Fitz dressed in civilian clothes, and then noticed him hesitate as he drew the sleeve over his left arm. "You've hurt yourself, haven't you?"

"No," he said, dropping the coat on the floor next to the chair he had claimed as his. "Just a little stiff, that's all."

"I told you not to chop firewood," she said. She unbuttoned his shirt and gingerly eased it over his head. The scar on his left arm was an angry bundle of maroon fissures emanating from the swallow depression. A piece of shell, he had told her, or perhaps a minié ball, or even a stone kicked up by an exploding shell.

"How does it look?" he asked.

"What do you care?" Asia asked sharply. He had tried to do too much, despite her protests.

He knew to be patient with her. "It is my arm and I do care, but I can't go about mollycoddling myself." She tossed him a glance. She wasn't convinced. "Now, Asia. I know enough to stop working if it hurts too much. I may be a bit dense"—he added the last part to tease her—"but I'm not a complete fool."

Her eyes flashed at him. "You're not? Well, you come as

close as any man I know." She calmed. "Very well. But please don't try to do too much."

The words stung him as he dropped into the chair. "The problem is, I'm not doing anything." Asia seated herself at the piano and resumed playing. She had begun a Haydn sonata just as Fitz announced he was going to chop wood. A discordant chord told him what she thought of this idea.

Fitz continued. "I thought this business would be over and I could return to my regiment. Or at least those idiots would let me track down the Januarys."

"They're probably in England," Asia said, testing a note with her finger. "Does this sound flat to you?"

"All right, then give me my regiment. Men with worse wounds than I have returned to fight. It's my left hand—not my right. I can still ride a horse and handle a pistol."

Asia stopped playing and sat back, disappointed. "I had a man in here just three months ago to tune this instrument. He assured me everything was fine." She pummeled the key. "It is flat." She slammed the keyboard cover down with a crash.

"Do you want me to fetch the ax?" Fitz asked. "We can burn piano wood as well as hickory."

"I don't want you going back to the war," Asia said, running her hands over the cover. She lifted it gently and laid her fingertips on the keys. "I just got you back and I nearly lost you."

"I can't stay here forever," Fitz said.

She smiled at him as she switched to Beethoven. "Why not, Colonel Dunaway? You have everything you need." Her fingers danced over the keys. "Food, wine"—her smile became demur—"companionship."

"Well." Fitz smiled in return. "There's that." He retrieved a pipe from a stand near his elbow, saw that it had enough tobacco in the bowl to satisfy him, and lit it. "Your brother is safe, you know."

She continued playing, but her mind wasn't on the music.

"The Januarys have gone south. Chances are he has as

well. In any case"—Fitz puffed the pipe to life—"I would do my utmost to ensure that no harm comes to him."

"Don't you have your duty to perform?" Asia asked. The question came as an accusation, but Fitz knew better. She had to be certain.

"I have my duty to you as well," Fitz said. "And at this point, it supercedes my duty to the government. Besides"— he shifted in his seat—"they have cast me loose without a duty to perform."

"What is the matter?" Asia asked, as Fitz dug into the cushion of the chair.

"I'm sitting on something. Oh!" he exclaimed as he pulled Abbott's notebook out of the crevice.

"How—"

"I was glancing through it," Fitz said. "Last night." He flipped the book opened and thumbed through the pages. "I thought—" He shrugged. "Oh well. It doesn't matter. Everything is at an end anyway."

Asia resumed playing. "What are you going to do with that?"

Fitz studied the book.

"Fitz?"

Numbers, equations. Formula of some kind, but for what? He caught a flash of color. The silk swaths. How did they fit into this? The explosion at the DuPont Powder Works, of course. Well, not according to the committee. But did they really? Perhaps the real plot was to kill or kidnap Abbott— he might have been killed resisting the abduction. But how did two similar pieces of silk end up hundreds of miles apart?

"Fitz!"

Asia's voice startled him. "What?"

"I just wanted to see if you were alive. I have been talking to you for the last five minutes."

"Oh," Fitz mumbled. "What did you say?"

She shook her head. "I said, 'What are you going to do with that?' "

"Do?"

Asia laughed at her husband. "The book, silly. That thing in your hand."

Fitz chuckled. "Keep it. My reward, I suppose." He laid the book in his lap, then cupped his palm over the pipe bowl, building a draft. "Still, I would like to know what it says. To my own poor eyes it's nothing but gibberish."

"Well," Asia said, "it's beyond me." She watched as Fitz's finger traced a design over the leather cover. "You can't let it go, can you?"

Fitz said, "It's a little like that infernal ax, I suppose. I hate to have anything get the best of me."

"My God," Asia exclaimed. "You are stubborn."

"Diligent," he corrected her.

She was about to speak, when she hesitated. "Do you have the time?"

"Time?" Fitz replied, fumbling for the pocket watch in his trouser pocket. He snapped open the cover. "Yes, just after eight. Why?"

"Oh," Asia said. "I just had a thought, but I fear it's too late."

"My dear, how enticing. The evening is—"

"Not that, you lecher. I know a man who can translate that book. I least I think he can."

She had Fitz's attention. "Who? Can we see him tonight?"

"Samuel Fuller, and no, it's much too late. He is a keeper at the Smithsonian. Professor Fuller is brilliant. Absolutely brilliant."

Fitz was wary. "I think I've had my fill of brilliant men. One with common sense would suit me fine. What are his politics?"

"Science and history, Fitz," Asia returned. "He barely cares for food and drink and he probably thinks Polk is still the president. He doesn't lift his head from his books for anything but his daughter."

Fitz held up the book. "He can read this?"

"If there is a man alive who can, it is Samuel Fuller."

Fitz mulled over her proposition. He would not be satisfied until he had answered the questions that had arisen over the death of Abbott.

"Well," Asia interrupted his thought. "What is your decision?"

"We can go tomorrow?" Fitz said. "He can help us?"

"Yes," Asia said, answering both questions at once. What she had promised became painfully apparent to Asia—she would begin the investigation anew. She did so for her husband's sake, but she wondered now if she had sacrificed her brother for the sake of Fitz.

The dread of setting off once more on the chase squeezed her chest so that she could hardly breath. She knew, yet she had no reason to be certain, that at the end of it was Robert.

She had lectured herself over and over, each time very nearly convinced that Robert had to be safely out of the country. Sailing toward England, perhaps, or France—settled comfortably aboard a blockade runner, or basking in the warmth of a Caribbean sun in Bahamas or Cuba. Robert had to be safe—far from danger, far from her husband.

"Fitz?" Asia began, her thoughts screaming at her to ask again—and knowing that the man who sat across from her, the man she loved and respected, could not consciously abandon the chase, nor its conclusion.

Fitz couldn't see the turmoil that threatened to overwhelm Asia. "Is it time for bed?"

The sight of the man who gave her so much happiness did nothing to dispel her pain. "Yes." She could not ask it of him—*Will you spare my brother?* She rose and extended her hand. "Shall we?"

Chapter 30

The Lossing Boarding House
Washington, DC

"Would you like to drive?" Asia asked.

"Drive?" Fitz exclaimed. William had harnessed Asia's gelding to the buggy and had it ready for them in front of the boarding house. Fitz went his way to the driver's side, expecting to help Asia into the vehicle, and take his place as a passenger. He shot a glance to William.

"I guess there's a first time for everything," the black man replied.

"Can you drive?" Asia questioned him. She meant his wound, despite healing, might cause him difficulty.

Fitz pointed at Jack. "It's been a long time. That is the horse, isn't it?"

Asia was not amused. "Shall I go off and leave you to walk?"

"No," Fitz said. He seated Asia in the buggy and took the reins from William. He turned to Asia. "Any suggestions?"

"Yes," she said, wrapping the carriage robe around her legs. "Don't dillydally."

Fitz grinned, jerked the whip out of its socket, and snapped it with a shout over Jack's head. The horse dashed forward, throwing Asia back into her seat. The whip cracked again and Jack sprang into a gallop.

"Hang on, Mrs. Dunaway." Fitz laughed.

She leaned over, one hand grasping the iron railing behind the seat, and kissed Fitz on the cheek. "With you, Colonel Dunaway, I can do nothing else."

A servant took Asia's coat, hat, and gloves; deposited them in a cloak room; and returned for Fitz's. It was midmorning, and Fitz and Asia found themselves sharing the Lower Main Hall of the Smithsonian Institution Building with no more than a dozen people.

Fitz was moved to comment, "Magnificent," as he took in the long island of glass cases that ran down the center of the hall and the elegant marble columns and arches that sprang like trees from the floor, spreading to support the distant roof. Alcoves filled the hall, each lined with shelves and glass-front cases. The smells—a ripe combination of decayed fur, stale dust, wood, and harsh chemicals—confused him. One hundred odors had been dumped into a monstrous kettle and heartily stirred. His attention was drawn to a large case. Leaves, unlike any he had ever seen, lay carefully arranged in the case. They were as lifeless as leather, the brown ends curled upward like the fingers of the dead. Name cards, bearing descriptions in Latin, were next to them. Fitz did not like the scene—it was unnatural and sad, and oddly he felt sorrow for the fanlike spray. He had seen nothing like them in this country. To come all that way, he thought, only to be displayed in a dusty case beneath the cold eyes of indifferent visitors.

"I wonder where he is?" Asia posed. "Let us go this way."

"I don't like this place," Fitz said. "Everything is dead."

"Why, Colonel Dunaway," Asia said, leading him down the Lower Main Hall, "you might one day find yourself the subject of an Institution exhibit."

"Pickled or stuffed?" he replied.

They found an attendant in front of yet another long row of glass cases.

"Professor Fuller is most likely in the West Range," the attendant said, pointing out the direction. "His desk is just behind the cases when you first enter." He fumbled for his watch and held it at a distance. "Yes. He keeps to a very exacting schedule. It is always the West Range at this time of day."

This time Fitz led the way, steering clear of the rows of cases. He noticed the interiors of many were empty, or the objects were covered in a thin film of dust. Some of the cases lacked doors, or their glass tops were cracked. Asia, despite Fitz's urging, lingered.

"Look at this, Fitz," she said, slowing him. He saw a dozen porcelain pots and vases, each bearing a colorful landscape of buildings with upswept roofs and spindly trees. "These are from China. Those, over there, are from Japan. Oh, how I would love to travel to China. See how exquisite they are."

Fitz saw a long, thin sword lying next to its sheath. The handle was simple in design, yet elegant, and the blade captured his attention. It was smaller than a cavalry saber but more imposing than an officer's sword. He decided that it was a very deadly weapon and that he would like to meet the warrior skilled in its use.

"See," Asia said, pointing to a row of paintings suspended high on the wall. "Those were done by Antonio Zeno Shindler. He is an artist employed by the National Museum. He has painted every Indian who ever visited Washington."

"What color?" Fitz said.

"I swear to God, Colonel Dunaway, if I had a pistol I would shoot you."

"Who is it?" a voice dry with age called from the depths of the West Range.

"Professor Fuller?" Asia said.

A slight man, with a mass of thick white hair and a face smooth with expectation, appeared from behind one of the large sets of shelves. "Who is it?" he asked again, advancing. "I know that voice."

"It's Asia."

Fitz was startled by a youthful squeal of delight from another direction. A girl, as lithe as a fawn, rushed from nowhere and threw herself in Asia's arms.

"Asia," she cried. "Father, it's Asia." She couldn't decide where to turn her attention. She stepped back in awe. "You're beautiful. Father, look, she's more beautiful than ever." The girl's bun of light brown hair, haphazardly gathered at the back of her head, barely survived her excitement. Strands of hair broke free of their confinement and hung to her shoulders.

"Orchid!" Asia exclaimed. "I can't believe it's you."

She turned up her nose. "Oh, don't use that name." She struck a dramatic pose. "I call myself Gretchen."

Asia smiled. "A rose by any other name."

"Who's this?" Orchid asked, noticing Fitz for the first time. "Is this your husband? Oh, how handsome he is. He is your husband, isn't he?"

"Yes. He is." Asia laughed. "This is Colonel Fitz Dunaway. Fitz, this is Orchid Fuller."

"Orchid Fuller!" the girl said, stung. "What a horrible name. How can I be an actress with such a clumsy name? Don't you think it's a wretched name, Colonel?"

Fitz recoiled in alarm. He had no idea how to answer.

"He's a man, Orchid," Asia explained. "He doesn't think of such things when he thinks of such things."

Professor Fuller's bow tie hung limply at his neck, bouncing with excitement when he spoke. "My dear Asia, what a lovely surprise. And did I hear this is your husband? Wonderful." He glanced down at Orchid's feet in dismay. "Child, where are your shoes? Didn't I tell you to wear shoes?"

Orchid wiggled her toes in response. "I cannot climb the ladders to get your specimens in those horrible shoes. I hate them. They are too confining."

"Perhaps they are too small," Asia offered. "Young ladies your age do grow quickly." Orchid's dress caught her attention. "Who made this dress?"

Orchid looked down, running her fingers over the faded silk. The garment had been repaired, but poorly, and the fabric was beginning to wear in long discolored streaks. "Nobody. I mean, I don't know. Mrs. Wallins gave it to me."

"We must find you another immediately," Asia said. "Do you know Mrs. Frederick on Connecticut?"

Orchid shook her head.

"Well," Asia said, clasping Orchid's hands in hers. "We will go now. Go find your shoes and a coat."

"Now?" Fitz said.

"And new shoes," Asia called as Orchid searched for a coat. "We won't come back until you have everything you need."

Fuller looked up at Fitz. "Who are you?"

God help me, Fitz thought in disgust.

"The book, Fitz," Asia urged. "Show him the book."

Fitz withdrew the notebook from his coat and handed it to Fuller. "Can you tell us what these symbols mean?" he said, certain that nothing would come of the visit.

"Ah," Fuller said, intrigued. He took the book and turned the pages in reverence.

Orchid rushed past and, grabbing Asia by the hand, dragged her down the hall, chattering excitedly. Fuller reached for a chair without taking his eyes off the book, pulled it up to his desk, and sat down.

Fitz watched in disbelief as Asia and the girl disappeared. Fuller cleared his throat and Fitz turned to him, expecting some revelation. It was only a bit of dust irritating the professor. The book had cast a spell over the man, and it would be some time before it was broken. Fitz glanced overhead at the long row of Indians who regarded his predicament with a sense of satisfaction. He found a stool near a bank of shelves, unbuttoned his frock coat, and sat down. The stool cracked in protest, until Fitz found a comfortable position on the noisy furniture. He pulled a large, dust-covered book from the shelf, blew as much of the grime off as he could, and read the title imprinted in gold leaf on the spine—*Fall of the Roman Empire*. "I wonder if it was because their women spent too much time shopping for dresses," he muttered.

Fuller's eyes, bright with curiosity, appeared. "What? Did you say something, Colonel?"

"Nothing," Fitz said. The stool's leg gave way with a snap, dumping Fitz on the floor.

After two hours, Fitz walked outside, relieved to be able to taste air that wasn't laden with dust, age, and the foul stench of chemicals. He knocked his pipe free of ashes, refilled it with fresh tobacco, and walked his post—striding back and forth in front of the red brick castle. He stopped for a time, watching the men working on the Capitol dome in the distance. Derricks swung huge blocks of marble from the muddy field that had once been the beautiful west lawn, high into the air, to be set into place by the tiny figures of workmen. He turned away, remembering his adventure atop the dome.

He found a pastry shop and bought two donuts, deciding after the first bite the baker used equal portions of sawdust and flour. He threw them away and walked parallel to the Canal—surprised he could not smell the putrid soup. *I must be getting used to the town,* he thought in surprise. He discounted the notion. The only interest he had in Washington was Asia. That thought brought him back to the book. What would Fuller find? And whatever he found—would it lead to anything?

What of it? Until the committee calls me again there is nothing I can do. He grew angry with himself. There is always something to be done.

A watchman came through and lit three lamps hung on pillars next to Fuller's desk. He ignored Fitz, who by this time had found a chair capable of bearing his weight, and disappeared into the gloom of the deserted hall. Fitz read his watch as the man's footsteps receded—just after five in the evening. Asia and her newfound friend had been gone for seven hours. Fitz's stomach rumbled and he wished he hadn't been so quick to throw those mealy donuts away. He retrieved the *Fall of the Roman Empire* and scanned the pages.

"This is most unfortunate," Fuller said, shaking his head in regret. "Very disconcerting."

"What?" Fitz asked.

For the first time in a number of hours, Fuller behaved as if Fitz actually existed. "Colonel Dunaway? Whose notebook is this?"

Fitz set his book on the floor next to him. Rome had fallen sometime before, but he was indifferent to the empire's fate. "Abbott. Phillip Abbott."

Fuller gazed into the darkness, rolling his eyes in thought. "He is the fellow who builds those iron boats?"

"Ironclads, yes."

Fuller took the news in disappointment. "This is most unfortunate."

"What?" Fitz stood, his back stiff. He was in no mood to guess Fuller's concerns.

"Oh, this. This," the old man said, waving at the notebook. "This is the most confusing scientific document I've ever seen. There's no logic to it. Sloppy, very sloppy indeed." He turned on Fitz. "A good scientist cannot approach any of his studies in a haphazard manner," he lectured. "Careful notation, legibly written, should proceed and follow every action. I mean, the man might have been brilliant, but this"—he dropped the book on his desk—"this is a travesty."

Fitz was very tired, and he resented Asia running off to buy dresses. Surely the man had more than that to reveal. "Can you read it, Professor? Do you know what it means?"

"Read it? Oh, yes, of course," Fuller said. "Most of it. What it means, or rather what Professor Abbott meant in writing it, is another thing entirely."

Fitz tried again. "What do you understand of it?"

"He is obsessed with diverse and unrelated subjects, for one thing."

"Was," Fitz pointed out. "Phillip Abbott has crossed over Jordan."

"Oh? You mean he's gone to the Middle—"

"Dead. He's dead."

"How terribly unfortunate. Well, in any case, a good portion of his notebook contains very confused ramblings about elements." He stroked the book in thought, seeking to divine clarity from the action.

Fuller was wearing on Fitz's nerves. "Asian or African?"

The question brought Fuller around. "Neither," he said, confused. "Here, look." He opened the notebook to a page so full of penciled notations that it was difficult to see the paper. "These writings are quiet intense," Fuller said. He whispered to Fitz, "I would not be surprised if the man was adjudged insane."

"You don't have to whisper, Professor Fuller. He can't hear you."

"This is very simple," Fuller said, ignoring Fitz's comment. "This symbol is for iron."

"He built ironclads," Fitz reminded Fuller.

"Of course, but here is hydrogen. I mean, the symbol for hydrogen—discovered by Henry Cavendish in 1766."

Fitz was too tired to lose his temper. "I have no idea what any of this means. I need you to tell me why the book is important, or if it is. Thus far you have told me that the man was probably insane and filled his notebook with undecipherable scribbling. This may surprise you, sir, but I was aware of both facts before my visit to you. Is there anything worthwhile, or at least interesting, in those pages?"

The question confused Fuller. "I'm not sure what you mean."

Fitz picked up the notebook. "Professor Fuller, thank you for your time and your hard work. If my wife returns within the next month, kindly inform her that I have gone home to cut firewood." He regretted being insensitive to the man, but the entire day had been a disappointment. He had hoped that the book held some clues to the whereabouts of the Januarys, or if not that, then at least some suggestion of what they had planned. Now it appeared the book confirmed what others had suggested all along—the Januarys' plan was to kill Abbott and nothing else. There was no grand conspiracy, no complex plan—just a madman lured to his death by actors.

Fitz was halfway down the hall when Fuller called to him. "Colonel Dunaway? When you say 'interesting,' are you referring to the balloons?"

Chapter 31

The Fuller Residence
Ohio Avenue, Washington, DC

Fuller slipped into a tattered velvet jacket, lowered himself onto a couch that was minus one arm, and began to study the notebook, yet again. The man's thoroughness taxed Fitz almost as much as the chatter about dresses. Asia and Orchid had returned from shopping to find Fitz firing questions at Fuller in the dark hall of the Smithsonian. It was Asia who came to the old man's rescue with, "Let us have a nice cup of tea." She managed to mix a warm smile for Fuller with eyes that warned her husband to be civil. Fitz understood the look and clamped his mouth shut.

They drove to the Fullers', a modest frame house nearly hidden by a forest of untended trees and shrubs. When they entered, Orchid sweeping through the parlor with a bundle of packages and Fuller walking uncertainly, as if he thought he belonged in the house but had his doubts, Asia pinned Fitz outside.

"Colonel Dunaway," she began, and he knew this was going to be a tongue-lashing. "You must be sensitive to Professor Fuller's way of doing things. He will not jump simply because you bark an order."

"I spent the entire day with the man and got nothing until I was ready to leave," Fitz said. "Why did you go flying off like that?" Fuller was her friend; she should have stayed to intercede.

"For pity's sake, the girl has nothing to wear."

Of the many responses Fitz could have chosen as his reply, he selected the worst one. "I've heard you say the very same thing countless times and yet you manage." He had seen Asia happy, disgusted, alarmed, depressed, joyous, and enchanted. He had never seen her completely devoid of emotion as she was at that moment. She had the look of a she-wolf, deciding whether to eat her quarry's hindquarters or shoulder.

"She has no mother. Her father is brilliant but detached, and she has reached the age when a young lady needs attention. I could not translate the book, you could not translate the book, so I left the only man who could in the capable hands of my darling husband."

"Point well taken," Fitz said, certain she had more to say.

"I plan to assist Orchid with her new things, and I'm sure that you will stand ready to help Professor Fuller, if the need arises."

Fitz crossed his arms in thought, studying Asia.

"What are you looking at?" she asked.

He grinned, hoping he would disarm her. "Why, the woman I love, of course."

Orchid ran back through the parlor, calling for Asia. "Come here. You must come and see these shoes. And the ribbons."

Asia followed Orchid, and Fitz found a battered chair, one leg shored up by a stack of books, next to Professor Fuller. He asked the question that Asia's appearance at the Smithsonian Institution had interrupted. "You said 'balloons.' "

Fuller looked up from the notebook. "Have you any tobacco?"

Fitz pulled the pouch and pipe from his pocket. "Help yourself."

It was the first time that Fuller had shown any emotion but

confusion. He beamed as he pulled a pipe from his smoking jacket, filled the bowl with tobacco, and lit it. Fitz hoped the shared tobacco would stimulate the man's mind. It did.

"Balloons, yes," Fuller said, savoring the taste. "But nothing like I've seen or heard of. Smaller. Much smaller. Did you know the French army was the first to have a Balloon Corps? Seventy years ago. Well before the Union army's efforts. Never mind. You'll see." He flipped through the pages, stopping at a series of drawings. "This drawing shows a gas balloon."

"That's a balloon?" Fitz asked. All he saw was a series of circles covered with a wild mass of interlocking lines.

"Oh, yes," Fuller said, obviously surprised at the question. "Here is the envelope and net. The envelope is usually made of a tightly woven fabric coated in some rubber or varnish solution."

"The pieces of silk," Fitz said, remembering. The whirlwind slowed, and for an instant Fitz thought he glimpsed an answer.

"Yes." Fuller continued. "Generally there is a hemp net that contains the envelope and supports the basket. Things you would normally expect to see on a balloon—a rip panel, suspension rope, drag rope, and that sort of thing—are not illustrated here."

"How do you know so much about balloons?"

"Oh, I don't. Very little in fact. Just a few years ago I helped a bright young man with his balloon. His dream, actually. I suggested that it was possible to cross the country by air. In a balloon, of course." He shrugged. "The war stopped his endeavors, or at least those of a scientific and peaceful nature. The last I heard, Professor Lowe and his balloon were in the army."

"Lowe?" Fitz said.

"Thaddeus Lowe. He and John Wise were rivals in the field of lighter-than-air craft. Professor Henry, Joseph Henry, was involved with both much more than I."

Fitz remembered the name he had heard at the Brooklyn Navy Yard. "Lowell."

"Lowe," Fuller corrected him. "He—"

"Would Abbott have known about him?"

"Oh, yes. If he studied balloons then he surely read about professors Wise and Lowe."

Fitz sat back in his chair. Why hadn't he seen it? "Lowe was with McClellan during the Peninsular Campaign, wasn't he?"

"He was," Fuller confirmed, relighting his pipe. "He made several ascents, observing the enemy fortifications around Richmond. I believe General McClellan went aloft as well."

The *Harper's Illustrated Newspaper* he had found in Abbott's carpetbag. It was dated 1862, the year of McClellan's aborted attack on the Confederate Capitol, and Fitz was certain that within its pages was an account of Lowe's balloons. Why would Abbott have information about balloons in his notebook?

"You said 'small balloon'?" Fitz quizzed Fuller.

"Small," he said, showing Fitz the pages as proof. "They can't be used for anything. Or at least anything that I know of."

"What makes them"—Fitz wasn't sure what he was asking—"go up?"

"Well," Fuller said, placing his thoughts in order. "Some are hot air. That goes back many years. The Montgolfier brothers were the first, I believe. Mostly it's hydrogen. Some people prefer coal dust because it's much less expensive and certainly not as dangerous as hydrogen."

"Dangerous?"

"Hydrogen is very explosive," Fuller warned Fitz, as if the gas were floating nearby.

Fitz took a moment to consider what Fuller had told him. There was nothing lethal or traitorous in any of it. Balloons were hardly a secret, and apparently Abbott had not committed any information about his monitors to the book. "What else is in the book?"

"Oh," Fuller said. "Quite a bit. I've only managed to get through a portion of it. There is certainly no logic to the man's reasoning."

"I wonder if the book has any value at all?" Fitz asked, posing the question to himself rather than Fuller. He was offered an answer only to have it batted aside by common sense. Toy balloons. Exploding gas. The whirlwind descended and blocked his view.

"That is determined by how you define *value*," the old man said. "Let us have some tea, and I will read it as speedily as I can, or as these poor eyes of mine permit."

Fitz stopped Fuller as he struggled to rise. "Where does one find hydrogen?"

Fuller settled back into his chair before answering. "In nature, of course. It is an element."

"Can it be made or mined?" Fitz asked, feeling foolish. Science and mathematics had been elusive subjects for him. So, too, had been the workings of the female mind.

"Made. That is produced, not mined," Fuller answered. "It's a simple process involving zinc or iron and diluted sulfuric acid. The combination of either of the metals and the acid produces hydrogen gas. One only need capture and transfer it to the envelope. That is the oldest method, developed by the French, I imagine. Or you can pass steam continuously over hot iron and by that method create hydrogen." The old man regained his footing, his mind set on tea. "None of these methods is very complicated, nor would it take equipment of any special sort."

"Would iron filings work?" Fitz asked.

"Oh, yes," Fuller responded. "Quite well, I would suspect. More surface area is exposed to the acid, if sulfuric acid is used, so I would imagine that one could produce a healthy supply of gas, depending on the quantities of materials used, in a reasonably short period."

"Father?" Orchid spun around, the skirt of her dress billowing out. "It's ready-made. Asia bought it for me."

"She did?" Fuller said, beaming at his daughter. "My, how lovely you look."

Asia, standing behind Orchid, caught Fitz's attention.

"Yes," he said. "You are a lovely young lady." He remained in the parlor as Fuller followed his daughter into the kitchen. Asia joined Fitz, and from the look on her face it was obvious that she caught his concern.

"Fitz?" she prodded him.

"Well," he said, not certain where to start. "I know why Abbott collected iron filings."

Fitz smoked his pipe as Fuller continued to pore over the notebook. Asia sat sound asleep on a settee, its fabric shredded by age. Orchid, still wearing the ready-made dress, was folded up in another chair, close to the fireplace. The fire had died long ago, leaving only glowing embers. Orchid was barefoot, Fitz noticed, and her innocence amused him. Children and dogs—he found delight in watching them play, exploring the world that surrounded them, or finding comfort in each other's company. The appreciation melted when he thought of Fuller's findings. He had told Asia all the old man had told him, and in doing so realized that none of it made any sense. So Abbott was making balloons, perhaps even toy balloons—bearing what? Toy soldiers? Balloons and exploding gas, but Abbott was dead and chances were the Januarys, and Robert Owen, were far from justice. Fitz glanced at Asia, half-convinced that she had somehow heard him. She slept on, her auburn hair falling across her arm.

"Could there be a way," Fitz began. He halted, wanting to make sure he explained himself properly. "Is there a way to set fire to these balloons?" *A glow,* Gideon had said. *A yellow light that came from above.* Could balloons have set fire to the DuPont Powder Works?

Fuller, his eyes red and swollen from lack of sleep, raised

his head. He may have been old but he had stamina, Fitz decided. "Yes. That's not the problem. You want to keep fire away. I saw one of Mr. Wise's balloons take fire, quite by accident. It was over in seconds. Envelope, netting, basket—all gone in an instant."

"There is no way to prolong the fire? Perhaps aim the balloon."

"No. Neither. The introduction of so much as a spark around hydrogen produces an intense flame that consumes the gas in a flash. The larger the balloon, of course, the longer the flame exists, but the duration can be measured in fractions of a second."

"No way to control the balloon?" Fitz mused. He had no direction, no intention in making the comment—just a need to discover the secret of the notebook. And to determine if he had been mistaken about the Januarys. They were not safely south, as first others, and then he, had assumed. It seemed such a logical assumption. But they were involved in a plot of some sort. The idea of using balloons as weapons sounded ridiculous to Fitz, and yet it nagged at him.

Fuller cocked his head in thought before he answered. "No. Wait. That's not entirely true. The ascent and descent can be controlled by a combination of weights and valves. The rip panel is a last measure in case one wants to descend immediately."

"How?"

"One simply pulls on a rope that tears the panel away from the top of the balloon, expelling all of the gas. Or one can pull the valve rope, releasing gas from the top of the balloon for less extreme measures. The valve rope offers more control, of course. It is for a gradual return to earth."

"You release the weights if you want to rise higher or faster," Fitz supplied.

"Exactly," Fuller said. "Most use bags of sand. Release either a portion of a bag or the entire weight. But there is no lateral control, you understand?"

Fitz nodded. "I thought as much."

"Once aloft the balloonists are at the mercy of the winds unless they take it upon themselves to descend."

Fitz stated the obvious out of frustration. "One does not aim a balloon."

Fuller nodded in agreement. "No more than one aims fire."

Chapter 32

Fitz was amazed that within a span of one week he had visited a museum and a library. The first was on the occasion of Asia suggesting they take the notebook to Professor Fuller. He had managed to translate some of it and promised to return the book, fully deciphered, in two days.

The trip to the library was also instigated by Asia, but began with her suggesting that Fitz was brooding.

They were at home with nothing else to do but wait on Fuller to complete his examination of the notebook. "What?"

"I asked," Asia said, "what you are brooding about."

The question offended him. "I'm not brooding."

"You are sitting there, after having lit three matches, none of which you managed to get anywhere near your pipe." They were seated in the gazebo, enjoying an overcast but relatively warm day. Asia had her book and a cigar—Fitz had his pipe and his thoughts. "Shall I make a suggestion?"

He looked at her, relieved that she had given him a chance to tease her. "Would anything I say prevent you from doing so?"

"Be a gentleman, Colonel Dunaway," she said in response to his question. A tiny smile escaped her. "But not too much of a gentleman. Let us go to the Library of Congress. The library probably has a copy of any book on ballooning that exists."

"Why—"

"The inaction is killing you, Fitz. We must get you out and about."

Fitz shrugged in defeat. "You know me too well, wife. I should be troubled by that."

Asia took his hand in hers. "That should be the least of your worries, my dear."

Mr. Sellers appeared the moment they entered the musty confines of the library, and in a voice as solemn as a parson's, asked if he could help them. He showed a trace of excitement when Fitz told him they needed to learn about balloons. Any balloons, all balloons. Sellers guided them to a table, asked them to wait, and then disappeared.

"He seemed happy to see us," Fitz mused as he pulled their chairs out. He looked around the nearly deserted room. "Maybe he was just happy to see anyone."

"Do you think we'll find anything to help us?" Asia said.

Fitz saw Sellers approach with his armload of books. "It won't be from lack of information."

When he set them down Fitz noticed that his vest, and coat, were covered with a soft, red dust from the ancient leather bindings. Sellers sneezed, adjusted his glasses, and picked through the books.

"I pulled what I could find. We have very little on ballooning. It's a relatively new occupation. I do have some pamphlets. Do either of you read French?"

"No," Fitz said, examining the books.

"Yes," Asia said.

"Very well," Sellers said. "I shall go and get them."

Fitz slid the books with complicated, scientific titles to one side and concentrated on those that were firsthand accounts of balloons and traveling in balloons. They each selected a book and began to read. Soon they were part of the silence that surrounded them. Fitz drifted from page to page, losing interest almost immediately. The answer's not here, he decided, but he had no response to the question that followed—where is the answer? He irritated himself with a logical companion to the first question—what is the answer? *That is what you need to look for.* He argued the point back and forth, stumbling from question to question with no hope of finding a solution.

"You haven't turned that page in ten minutes," Asia said, looking at him.

Fitz flipped the page and began scanning the next.

"Where are you?" she asked.

"I'm reading," he said, vexed she had caught him daydreaming.

"Fitz—"

"I'm reading." His response was too sharp. "I was reading and thinking, and considering what I read."

"Considering your answer, Fitz, I think you're lying."

Fitz dodged the accusation with, "Let us continue to read about balloons." His mind drifted away from the book and over the issues of balloons, and the Januarys and the late Professor Abbott, and settled on the DuPont Powder Works. It was an attack from the sky. Fitz pictured balloons manned by rebels pouring flaming streams of coal oil from the baskets. He was tired, and his mind was reduced to playing silly games.

Hydrogen is flammable, Fuller had said. It ignites in an instant. Any heat source in the basket would fire the envelope. Fitz was pleased he remembered the components of a balloon. He returned to his search for answers.

Abbott made balloons. Small, but if you consider the DuPont Powder Works, effective. Then how are they made effective? His mind fixed on that point, but no answer followed. Or certainly wouldn't until Fuller completed the book.

Abbott is dead. The Januarys are alive and free to do as they please.

"I don't know what we're looking for," Fitz said.

Asia, surprised, looked up. "Then why are we here?"

"No, I don't mean that," Fitz said, and then realized how confused he sounded. "I mean I don't know where to begin. Abbott was designing balloons, but for what purpose?"

"The Powder Works," Asia pointed out.

"If I planned to attack anything, I'd hate to rely on balloons. Even something as large as the Powder Works. You're at the mercy of the wind, so you can't target even something as large as the works."

"It's been my experience that a shotgun works reasonably well," Asia said, "and that's more pointing than aiming."

She failed to see his reasoning, or his dilemma. "You're no help."

Asia rested her elbows on the table and dropped her chin on her hands. "Nonsense. I agree with you only when it's required."

Sellers returned, batting at his coat front as if he had just found it covered with dust. He had several pamphlets in his hand, which he gave to Fitz. "These might be of some assistance. They're Spanish. Observations of the French trials, I believe. "

Asia took the pamphlets from Fitz and thanked Sellers, who returned to a desk in the shadow of a row of tall bookshelves.

Fitz leaned back in his chair.

"Are you going to look at these books?" Asia asked. She waited for his response.

"I think the answer to the question is in Abbott's book."

Asia began thumbing through the pamphlets. "Would you be so kind as to tell me the question that has you distracted?"

"I don't know."

"Husband," Asia said, "you find new ways to amaze me."

"I'm here to serve you, wife," Fitz said. He had an idea. "Who was that fellow—that doorman at the theater?"

"What?"

"When we first met. You took me to the theater?"

Asia smiled. "The Markham. How gallant of you to remember even if your timing is perplexing. Of course you were never adept at when to speak and when not to, or what to say for that matter." Fitz started to speak, but Asia interrupted him with a quick, "Marcus Hall."

"Yes," Fitz said. He stood quickly. There was another way, if the book failed them or Fuller failed them; there was another way to approach this mystery.

"I don't understand," Asia said. "Why are we abandoning our interest in balloons to speak to Mr. Hall?"

"I'm not sure we can find anything here. Professor Fuller has the book and hopefully will discover something before I die."

"Yes," she agreed, but was still uncertain about Fitz's reasoning. "But Marcus Hall?"

"It has to be the Januarys. Everything must revolve around them. You said Mr. Hall was an actor."

"Yes, one of the finest."

"Would he have known the Januarys?"

"I have no idea," Asia said. "He was quite well known in the theater." She hesitated. "Even if he does know them, I don't know what good that does us."

"I don't know, either," Fitz said. "Maybe nothing. But every avenue is blocked and I've nothing to lose. It may be a waste of time, but I can't sit here reading books. I'll explode. I must *do* something."

"Then we must go see Mr. Hall," Asia said. "I would hate to have to explain my exploding husband. Poor Mr. Sellers. What will he think when he finds us gone?"

"Probably that we left," Fitz said, struggling into his overcoat.

Mr. Sellers, looking just like a man who had lost a fortune, intercepted them on the way out. "But you're not done, are you? You haven't completed your research? I'm sure we have more materials."

Fitz didn't know which to respond to first, so he said, "You were most helpful, wasn't he, dear, beyond our expectations."

Asia managed a quick, "Yes, most helpful," before she began pulling on her gloves. Mr. Sellers wasn't about to release them just yet.

"You don't require anything else? Something else besides balloons?" He followed them like an expectant puppy. "We've just scratched the surface, you know."

"There is something," Fitz realized. He pulled a notebook and pencil from his pocket, wrote a quick message, tore off the page, and gave it to Mr. Sellers. "Someone may call after us here. We must go to Markham Theater—"

"Markham Theater," Mr. Sellers said. "On—"

"Yes. Now, listen. It is imperative that the messenger reaches us. Make certain that he knows. Markham Theater."

"And Mr. Sellers," Asia said, trailing after Fitz out the door. "If ever we are called upon to do research again, we shall come to you."

They found Hall backstage at the Markham Theater, armed with a broom and dustpan, tidying up the floor near a pile of sandbags. He was genuinely happy to see Asia, and pleased that she was married, although it was evident from the way he observed Fitz he hadn't formed an opinion about her husband yet. He was startled when Fitz asked him about the Januarys, and his watery blue eyes slipped back to another time.

"I don't know them, you see," he said. "They are young actors well after my time."

Fitz was desperate. He needed something. "Are you sure? You must know them." Fitz looked to Asia to supply the names.

"You knew them, didn't you, Mr. Hall?" she asked. "Royal and Victoria. Please, if you know anything about them, we would be most grateful."

"They were children when last I saw them," Hall said. "Are they in some sort of difficulty?"

"I am if I can't find them," Fitz said. He caught Hall's puzzled look. "They are involved in some action against the government. Probably murder as well."

Hall shook his head, and after a long pause spoke. "They come from a troubled family. Their mother and father were great actors. I knew them."

"John Jacob and . . ." Asia said. She tried to remember.

Hall supplied the name. "Esther. His wife. She was the most beautiful creature on earth."

"But you knew them?" Fitz said.

"Not well," Hall said. "They were featured players. I was at one time, but circumstances—" He moved to the wings on the edge of the stage, as if it were safer to put some distance between himself and his memories. Two white dogs were rehearsing under the critical eye of their owner. They ran feverishly from pedestal to pedestal, springing through hoops before spinning around to begin again. Their yelps echoed in the empty theater, interspersed with their master's sharp commands.

"I don't believe you," Fitz said.

"Fitz!" Asia said.

"Well, a lie is a lie. You're a poor liar, Mr. Hall. Don't you see, Asia, he's only given us half the truth."

Asia wasn't convinced. "Yes, but you don't have—"

"No," Hall said. "He's right. We were very close. Esther, John Jacob, several others, and I called ourselves the Devil's Troupe. I told you the truth about the children; of course, they are grown now."

"We are in desperate need of finding the Januarys," Fitz said. "But we've had little luck. You must help us."

"The sins of the father, perhaps," Hall whispered.

"I don't know what that means," Fitz said.

Hall nodded in reply and said, "Come with me, please. Perhaps if you learn something about the parents it will help you find the children."

Asia took Fitz by the arm. "Don't be so rude to the old gentleman."

"I don't have time to be polite," Fitz returned.

Hall knocked on a door hidden in the depths of the theater. "Odessa?" he called. "I have company."

They entered a small room crammed with costumes, with just enough room for a bed in one corner and a dresser against one wall. A tiny black woman, a gown thrown over her lap, sat on a stool at the foot of the bed. Her wrinkled hands, no bigger than those of a child, held a needle and thread. Glasses were perched on the tip of her nose, and her black hair, streaked with gray, was gathered at the back of her head.

Her brown eyes, frightened, searched from Fitz to Asia. Hall sat on the edge of the bed and stroked her back, soothing her. "These are some people who came to see me," he said. "I've known Mrs. Lossing"—he stopped, embarrassed— "Mrs. Dunaway for many years. This is her husband, Colonel Dunaway."

Fitz watched as Odessa shrunk back. He had seen the look before—men who had endured too much on the battlefield.

"Oh, that is lovely," Asia said. Odessa's eyes flew toward her. "Did you make that gown? Fitz? Isn't it beautiful? Oh, how I wish I could sew."

Fitz watched as Odessa's attention went from Asia to him, and back again. He remained still. "I'm sorry we troubled you," he said. He kept his voice soft, hoping he did not frighten her. "We only came to speak to Mr. Hall."

"I think you're better off speaking to Odessa," Hall said.

Fitz glanced at Hall. He didn't understand.

"Odessa knows more about John Jacob and Esther than I." He slid his arm around Odessa's shoulder, comforting her. "Ask your questions."

"You want to know about the fire night, don't you?" Odessa said in a voice like the rustle of a silk dress.

Fitz said nothing, letting her begin as Hall found a chair for Asia. Odessa's words came slowly, each memory a sharp knife blade drawn across her thin arms.

"I worked for Mrs. Esther as a seamstress. I was owned by Master Calhoun, but after he died his missus didn't want nothin' to do with me. She had evil ideas about me and Master Calhoun, but she was wrong." She relaxed a little. "They brought me up to Mayfield in the spring. It was the most beautiful house I ever seen—big white columns, a big porch— a thousand windows. When the sun hit them, they looked like sheets of gold. I thought everything was goin' to be all right." Her head dropped, and her thoughts were lost in the rich folds of the gray gown draped across her lap. "Mrs. Esther, she was always kind to me, but that house." She shook her head. When she looked at Fitz it was with the conviction of a soul who had seen absolute horror. "You could feel the evil in that house, Colonel Dunaway. Taste it. Smell it like a stink so bad that it closes your throat like you ain't never gonna breathe again. That was the master. He never sleep. You could always hear his heavy steps in the hallway and going up and down the stairs. I had me a room close to the missus so I could help her, that's how I know this about the master. He go out in the night. He got this torch. He never carry a lantern, he always got this torch, and he go out in the slave cabins. I can hear Mrs. Esther cry, but sometimes the pain so bad she take medicine. It's no good for her, but she takes it anyway. And them children, a boy and a girl. I think, maybe, they like the master. But I pray to the Lord they not. But I think they are."

A match hissed as Hall lifted a lamp globe and lit the wick. Odessa smiled at him in gratitude, and he nodded for her to continue.

"It must have been goin' on for a long time before I got there," Odessa said. "The master go for the slave children, and nobody can't do nothin' about it. It come one night. There was a high wind, and it was cold. The windows was rattlin' and the house seem like it was groanin', like it knowed what was comin'. I get up and look out and I see lights, a whole river of lights comin' from the slave cabins. They was comin' after the master, carryin' torches just like he carry when he come for their children. The fire alive with vengeance and hatred, the wind cryin' out for justice.

"I run to get the missus but she gone and so I run for the children, and they cryin', holdin' each other so tight you couldn't get a thread between them. Then I hear people shoutin' and master shoutin' and then he starts shootin'. Then I hears glass breakin' and the missus screamin'. The children pull away from me, but I can't find them because they too much smoke. I get outside and in a little while the patrollers come." She drew a deep breath, and calmed. "I ran away and come to Washington and after a while I met Mr. Hall, and he gets me work here." Something occurred to her and she glanced at Fitz as if he might have the answer. "Do you suppose that master used his children the way he used those little black boys and girls?"

Fitz said nothing. He knew that any answer he could give would be too terrible to consider.

"There ain't nothin' out there now," Odessa said, putting distance between herself and that night. "The patrollers, when they come and got them slaves that killed master and missus and burned down the house, they crucified them, like our Lord and Savior Jesus Christ. Every one."

"No one goes there," Hall said. "Not since that night. I'd been to the house twice. For parties, you understand. John Jacob threw parties whenever we closed a play. I think people knew. I suppose I did as well. Mayfield was decaying from the inside out, like John Jacob. He couldn't keep his hands off black children. I never went back. A thousand acres that stink of death and perversion."

Fitz heard Asia stifle a sob, and he felt sad for the world. How could such injustice prevail, cloaked in respectability? How could anyone harm a child? Why did God abandon those who sought only to protect their children? Why was cruelty triumphant in the world?

"Madam," Fitz said. "I wish I could find the words to express my horror at what you've had to endure, and to acknowledge your courage for surviving it." He held out his hand for Asia to rise. "Mr. Hall, with your permission, we will take your leave. Please accept our thanks for your assistance."

Fitz and Asia wove their way between flats and rigging to reach the stage wings. Asia dabbed her eyes several times before slipping her handkerchief into her cuff. "That is the saddest thing I've ever heard. Don't you think so, Fitz?"

"Yes," Fitz said. "What makes it twice as sad is that I have no idea of what it means."

A boy at the back door doffed his checkered cap. "Are you Colonel Dunaway?"

"Yes."

The boy pulled a piece of paper from his pocket and handed it to Fitz. Anxious to explain he said, "Professor Fuller sent me to the library, but the fella at the library said you were here, and I come to give you the note." He waited expectantly, and then added, "The professor said it was worth a dime."

Fitz unfolded the paper and read it aloud. " 'I have uncovered something of importance—Fuller.' " He realized the boy was waiting. Fitz gave the boy a dime and said, "Where do you live?"

"Ohio Avenue," the boy said, quickly pocketing the coin. "Near Professor Fuller's."

"Well, you can come with us," Fitz said. "That's where we're headed. Did Professor Fuller say anything when he gave you this note?"

The boy thought for a moment and replied, "No." But as they were leaving he tugged on Fitz's sleeve. "But Colonel Dunaway, he sure did look scared."

Chapter 33

Mayfield
Twelve Miles from Washington, DC

Owen slid awkwardly from the mule's back. Everything ached. His back was tight with pain and so stiff that he was afraid he couldn't walk. His arms were numb from constantly tending the jerk line and wielding the heavy whip. He stood uncertainly, taking tentative steps until he was sure his legs would not fail him. He was cold, hungry, and thirsty, but most of all he wanted done with this business. There was no honor in the drudgery of guiding a bunch of dumb animals along a dusty back road. No romance in tight muscles or an ass that burned from sitting on a worn saddle astride a plodding animal. Worse, they had arrived and he had no idea where he was. They were on the edge of a thick forest, the floor long overgrown by sinewy vines and thick patches of brambles. Beyond the forest—west, Owen knew, from the setting sun—was a broad natural meadow that continued on to a distant line of trees.

Goodwin, unaffected by the journey, walked back along his wagon, joining Owen. "We've got to get busy and unload these."

"What?" Owen said. "Now?"

Goodwin turned to go without answering, but Owen wasn't through yet. He laid his hand on the bigger man's shoulder. "Don't turn—"

Something struck Owen's chin a stunning blow. He was surprised to feel no pain, just the dull impact. And then he was flat on his back, looking up at Goodwin. The whole incident happened quickly.

"Don't come up behind me. Don't lay your hands on me," Goodwin said.

Owen rubbed his jaw as the pain appeared. "You struck me."

"Get up and help me."

Owen jumped to his feet and rushed Goodwin. The man stepped to one side as Owen flew past and stumbled into the side of his wagon.

"This won't do you any good," Goodwin said. His voice was flat—as if the incident were so minor he decided not to invest any emotion in it.

Owen spun around, his back against the wagon box. "How are we going to unload these wagons? You killed the boy who was going to help us. We can't do this by ourselves. Where are we? What are we doing here?"

"You do what I say and we can get the unloading done," Goodwin said. "As for the rest, you'll find out soon enough. I'll unhitch the teams. You take the tailgate off your wagon. Move it to one side so it ain't in our way. Take the top sideboards off and lay them so they make a ramp from the floor of the wagon box to the ground."

"Those crates are too heavy for us," Owen pointed out, certain Goodwin had lost his mind. He had thought about the killings as they traveled. Goodwin was a maniac, that's all. Royal probably didn't realize it, and Owen vowed to inform him of everything that had happened. *Goodwin is dangerous,* Owen pictured himself telling Royal January and saw in his mind the Januarys' gratitude for the information.

Goodwin began unhitching the mules, ignoring Owen's

concern. He started with the front span, quickly stripping the animals of their harnesses and leading them to a nearby tree. He hobbled them, and then returned to the second span. He stopped midway through removing the harnesses and stared at Owen. The implication was clear—*do as I say.*

Owen climbed the twelve-foot-tall rear wheels, stepped on the brace ear, and pulled the top pin from the tailgate. He made his way to the other side and repeated the action. The tailgate refused to budge, and Owen stepped off the wheel to take the bottom pins out. He realized that if he did, the gate was liable to fall on him. He studied the situation, climbed back up the wheel, and hopped into the box. Settling his back against the rear crate, he set the soles of his boots flat on the top frame of the tailgate, readied himself, and then pushed. The gate squealed in protest, slipped, and then popped free. Pivoting on the bottom pins it fell with a crash. It swung back and forth until Owen jumped out of the wagon and stopped it.

He knew it wouldn't work. When he removed the first of the bottom pins the weight of the tailgate would jam the other pin in place. He couldn't move it, and he wasn't even sure if Goodwin could move it once it was wedged. Owen stepped from behind the wagon to tell Goodwin of the situation, but changed his mind. He decided that he had enough sense to master this dilemma, and he didn't need the help of a maniac.

Owen climbed back into the wagon and contemplated the situation. The top boards were roughhewn, close to two inches thick and fourteen feet long. A block brace set every four feet, and at both ends, had been pegged onto the board. He tried to knock the first top board loose with the palm of his hand but was rewarded with hot pain and no movement. Using the heel of his boot, and with five or six powerful kicks, he loosened the board. He climbed over the crates to the front and lifted that end. His hands stung, and a sliver of wood pierced his thumb. He cussed under his breath, freed the board completely, and let it slide down the tailgate, one end sticking in the earth. He turned to the other top board and was relieved to find it was less reluctant to be moved.

When he climbed out of the wagon it was with a wild sense of satisfaction. He had bested the filthy machine, and by doing so he had triumphed over Goodwin's animal power. After a moment to celebrate in silence, Owen flipped the board over so the block braces would catch against the edge of the floor, preventing them from slipping when the crates began their descent. He stomped the other ends into the dirt, making sure they were properly seated. After he finished he dug the splinter out of his thumb with a pocketknife.

He would tell January about Goodwin and cement the man's confidence in him. Victoria, too, would be appreciative. Owen could practically feel her hand in his as she gasped in amazement over his bravery. She would see the splinter's ragged scar, and take pity on him.

"That tailgate's goin' to be sprung when we unload those crates."

Startled, Owen looked up. Goodwin, his hands locked in the bridles of two mules and a coil of thick rope thrown over his shoulder, stood in front of him. Lengths of harness were looped over the mules' backs.

"No," was all that Owen could manage, but he feared Goodwin was right. What if he was?

Goodwin led the mules past Owen and stopped them with their tails to the wagon, at the end of the makeshift ramp. He rubbed their snouts to comfort them. "Hold them," he ordered Owen. He examined the top board, hopped into the back of the wagon, and made a loop around the first crate. Tying it off, he threw the remaining rope in the direction of a large tree. It arched through the air, uncoiling until it struck the tree.

"Throw me the harnesses," Goodwin instructed Owen.

Owen, not certain what Goodwin had in mind, tossed the harnesses from both mules to the other man. He waited as

Goodwin wound the harnesses around the crate, tightening them with a grunt. Satisfied, he climbed out of the wagon and said, "Take that rope around that tree three times. Make it tight. You're going to be the stop. The mules will pull that crate out of the box, but you make sure it don't come down that ramp too fast. Understand?"

Owen nodded, afraid he didn't have the strength. His earlier commendation of Goodwin came back to taunt him.

"Don't let that crate get away from you," Goodwin said. "If it does, that means we came all the way here for nothin'."

"I won't," Owen said. He was allied with the big man now, and everything else was forgotten. He ran to the tree, wrapped the rope around it as he was ordered, and waited. Goodwin took up position in front of the two mules, spoke patiently to them, and then tossed a nod at Owen. The younger man's grip tightened on the rope, and he could feel rough fibers of hemp digging into his skin.

Goodwin clicked at the mules and pulled them forward. The animals' hooves dug into the muddy ground, kicking up dead leaves and debris, and they pulled against the weight of the load. Owen's eyes flew from the rope, to the load, to Goodwin, and back to the rope again as the crate inched forward, the high-pitched squeal of wood against wood cutting through the forest. Goodwin encouraged the mules, who responded to his steady voice and strong hands by stiffening their backs to drag the box to the end of the wagon bed. Its leading edge inched over the boards.

The mules fought against uncertain footing, their hooves slipping and then finding purchase. They strained against the burden, swaying as the heavy crate hung on the boards.

"Get ready," Goodwin shouted, and then urged the mules on with guttural calls, not words but a singsong chant.

Owen watched as the crate slid over the top of the board, teetered, and slowly dipped. He planted his heels in the ground, kicking away leaves and twigs, berating himself for not having done it sooner. He leaned back against the rope and prayed that the strain would not jerk him from his feet.

He felt it, an invisible force, first in the rope as it slipped around the tree trunk and then in his shoulders and back. He glanced up and saw the crate fully on the ramp and Goodwin guiding the mules. He felt a sharp pain in his back and realized that his jacket was soaked in sweat. He twisted his heels into the dirt with a grunt, and almost cried out to Goodwin to hurry for God's sake, hurry. He didn't—he threw every ounce of strength that he had into the single, primitive effort of pitting his body against the superior weight.

The rope stopped.

Owen, his arms trembling, looked at Goodwin in relief. The big man began unhitching the mules, stroking their flanks, thanking them. As the mules brushed against him in gratitude, he tossed Owen an acknowledgment. "You done good."

His mouth was too dry to speak, and he wondered how his quivering legs kept him upright, but Owen managed a reply. "Thank you."

It took nearly four hours to unload the first wagon, and Owen was certain after each crate that his strength would fail him for the next. He hated Goodwin, and hated the mules. Goodwin paid attention to them, coddled them in fact, and led them about to breathe after each crate. But to Owen he merely said, "Get some water, but not too much" or "You had better tighten up on that rope." Owen was sick of Goodwin, and sick of his hands being sliced to ribbons by the rope, and the burning that ran up his back to settle between his shoulder blades. When he tired of cursing Goodwin, he turned on January. He had joined him to fight the Yankees, to save the South—now he was being used as a dumb animal. He hated them all.

"We'll build a fire," Goodwin said, waving him in. Owen was so relieved he almost cried out in joy. He threw the disgusting rope on the ground when Goodwin added, "Don't never treat your tools like that. Bring that rope in and coil it up. We've got more work to do first thing in the morning."

Owen did as he was told, not sure if he wanted water,

food, or to just fall to the ground and sleep. Goodwin had a small fire going about ten feet from the empty wagon. He threw a canteen to Owen and concentrated on the fire. Owen sat down, cross-legged, and tipped the canteen back.

A packet wrapped in waxed paper landed at his feet. "Salt pork and bread," Goodwin said. He dug into a grease-soaked bag and tossed Owen an apple. "Dessert."

"Where are we?" Owen managed, more to irritate Goodwin than out of interest.

"Maryland," Goodwin said. "If you look real close"—he pointed to the west with the stick he had been stirring the fire with—"you can see the lights of Washington. Maybe hear the church bells."

Owen stared into the darkness but decided the effort wasn't worth it. "I don't understand—why are we here?"

Goodwin ignored him, peeling an apple.

Owen was too tired to be angry, but he wanted an answer. "What do you have in the crates?"

"Eat your supper and get some sleep."

Owen threw the canteen down and struggled to his feet. "I want to know."

"Ask him." Goodwin nodded into the darkness.

Royal January, Victoria's arm wrapped easily in his, walked into the firelight. They could have been strolling on the most fashionable boulevard in New York. They were a prince and princess of a race that had long since disappeared.

"Ask me," January said, as Goodwin rose. "Come, come, Mr. Owen—you have a question?"

Stunned, Owen could not speak.

"Look at the poor boy," Victoria said. She slid a gloved hand over Owen's brow. She shook her head in pity. "Mr. Goodwin, how you have worked poor Mr. Owen." She stepped back, appraising him. "His clothes! See how ripped and filthy they are, Royal."

Her brother passed a cigar to Goodwin and lit one himself. "Did you have any difficulties?"

Owen looked at Goodwin. Surely he would tell January about the men he killed. And the boy. He waited in disbelief as Goodwin drew a match to the tip of his cigar. He blew it out and spoke. "No."

Oh, but that wasn't true, Owen wanted to say, but he knew it would do no good. Goodwin had Royal January's confidence. Perhaps Victoria—if he had a chance to be alone with her, he could tell her. She would be shocked, of course, but she must be told. She would tell her brother. Then things would be set right.

"We have been working for a very long time," January said.

Owen realized he was speaking to him.

"These boxes—for which you have sacrificed to bring such a great distance—hold the key for retribution." He was a half being in the scant light of the fire, illuminated only when the breeze flicked the flame and picked shards of his features from the darkness. "This is sacred ground, Mr. Owen. This is Mayfair. A thousand acres and more of art, music, progress, and enlightenment." January's eyes shown in the darkness as he spoke. His voice was soft, nearly lost. "We, I say we meaning Victoria, Mr. Goodwin, and I, and others, have been planning this event for some time. It has not been easy, sir. Some were not so convinced, and our chief architect, Professor Abbott, proved himself a false companion. We were very fortunate that he did not betray us until after our scheme was set in motion." He waved his cigar toward Goodwin, the tip a glowing fairy floating through the darkness. "We owe so much to our friend—"

"Our savior," Victoria corrected.

"Our savior," January acknowledged. "It is his skills and determination that enable us to go on. Untutored as he may be, Mr. Goodwin has an innate sense of science and devices."

Owen looked at Goodwin, amazed at the description. He saw nothing but a country ruffian with coarse manners. And a murderer, he reminded himself. He was ashamed of himself, but confused as well. He had seen Goodwin do terrible things, but the man succeeded at everything he put his mind to. His was a singleness of purpose that Owen envied. The Januarys adored him. He felt small, a failure, and hoped that Victoria did not see him as he truly was. He felt a delicate hand slip under his chin, and his head was lifted to meet Victoria's.

"You are so worn from your journey, aren't you, dear Robert. You must know how much my brother and I count on you. We are in your debt."

He wanted to pull away. He knew he stank from his exertions and his mouth tasted vile. Owen dropped his head when he spoke, fearful that his breath would offend her. "I have done nothing." He felt it was the truth, but he knew, because of his battered muscles, the filth that encrusted his body, and the grime forced under his fingernails, that he had done a great deal. His sacrifice should be recognized.

"When this is over," Royal January said at the wagon, "I will spare no effort to reward both of you." He held out his hand, and his sister took it and climbed into the wagon seat. She arranged her skirts, pulled a carriage robe from the dashboard, and draped it over her lap. Owen felt her smile warm him as her brother took his place beside her. *She must know how I feel,* Owen thought. *She smiles at me as if she knows everything about me—as if she can see into my soul. She must know that I would give everything I own to have her on my arm. But she knows this. She can see how I feel.*

Victoria January nodded to Owen in farewell as her brother slapped the reins.

She knows, he decided, his heart buoyant with love. His was a young man's gratitude as well—a fragile vessel filled with hope and yearning, and, according to his understanding, readily accepted.

Victoria slid her hand under her brother's arm and watched pale clouds drift from her mouth. "He is such a boy—is he not?"

January concentrated on the horse. "You're an ungrateful little witch. Don't you know that he loves you?"

Victoria tilted her head and blew a breath into the cold air. "Every man does. Didn't you know that?" She laid her head on his shoulder. "Don't you?"

What was left of the moon peeked out from behind a bank of clouds. "What? Know that every man loves you? You've told me enough times."

She shook him playfully. "No! Love me. You told me." She awakened to her surroundings. "We're nearby, aren't we? Aren't we? It's near here, isn't it?"

"It's late."

Victoria became frantic. "No. No. It's not too late. We must be close by. This looks familiar. Oh, please, Royal. Take me there."

"Now? It's late." He glanced at the scrap of moon. "You can't see anything anyway. Tomorrow. In the morning. I'll bring you out early."

Victoria set her mouth, and her body stiffened in determination. Her eyes flashed in anger at being denied. "No! I said now. Take me there now!"

January ignored her.

She slapped him and waited for a reaction. When he did not concede she slapped him again. Nothing. She doubled up her gloved fist and struck his arm, and then his shoulder. She continued, an angry whine coming from a petulant child. The blows fell on and against January, but he ignored them. It could have been a child's game, but his nose was bleeding, and her shrill cry increased as her fury increased.

January threw the reins down and grabbed her fists. She struggled against him, infuriated that she was trapped. She tried to lash out with her feet but her legs were bound by the robe. He held her at bay and watched amused as she tried to bite him.

"You want to go tonight?" he said, teasing her.

She stopped struggling. "Yes. Tonight." She was wary, and he could feel the tension in her arms.

He opened his hands and drew them back—it was a signal

of acceptance. "Very well." He picked up the reins and snapped them in command. "But you won't be able to see much."

"I'll see everything," she said, relaxing against him.

Victoria January climbed out of the carriage without waiting for her brother's help, awed by Mayfield's beauty. Nothing had changed. The eight columns, gleaming in the moon's light, bright and white, and so thick they must have been made by God himself, ran along the front of the red brick mansion like sentinels guarding the castle. There was the door—*Papa's Door,* she had called it—ten feet tall and nearly as wide with a dozen panels below three tiny windows. The brass knob glowed beckoningly—she had mistakenly called it gold, and Royal, playing the older brother, laughed at her until she ran to Papa who said, *we shall call it gold.*

Victoria counted twelve windows as the house called her closer, twelve windows from floor to ceiling on the first and second floors, for the twelve disciples. That is where they lived—Papa, Momma, Royal, and people who came from all over the world to visit—on the second floor. The first floor was a place of magic. The ballroom sparkled with the lights of a dozen crystal chandeliers and swirled with gay couples in an endless dance. The ballroom opened into the parlor, an intimate room with an air of rich cigars and men's deep voices rumbling against the oak paneling. Next to it was the sitting room—the haven for ladies, who sipped light refreshments and hovered over gossip.

And the dining room with its long table heavy with food and polite conversation. They could not sit with the guests of course, Victoria and Royal. They were fed early by one of the house servants, Auntie Sally usually, and spirited to bed, with the last opportunity to share in the spectacle denied them when the heavy bedroom door closed, extinguishing the light that beckoned from the hall.

She felt herself floating before the broad stairs that led to the front porch. Above her the veranda watched silently as her memories led her back to laughing couples and the soft strains of a string quartet drifting through the open windows. She stopped at the base of one of the huge chimneys and noticed a shattered piece of slate at her feet. That must be seen to. Someone will have to replace this piece of slate from the roof and make sure that the cast-iron stops are securely fastened in place. It was a field of slate, the pitched roof that rose above the stunted third floor, undulating with twelve dormers like the waves of an angry sea.

Victoria looked away. The servants lived on the third floor, and they were never to go to the third floor, Papa had said. He was sometimes required to punish the servants, and they cried out, but all Victoria had to do was dance around Mayfield like she was doing tonight and everything that could have been bad disappeared.

Her arms were outstretched, eyes closed, and she twirled merrily, a spinning fairy in a forest of make-believe. She stopped and opened her eyes, almost fearful that everything before had been a dream.

It was not.

Mayfield stood, a firm reminder of a magic time, grand, indestructible, a brick behemoth so solidly planted in the ground that it must have sprung from the earth fully complete. Its windows were dark, but they would glow with life again.

"Can we go now?" Royal January called.

Victoria knew she could stay longer if she wished—her brother would let her. But it was late and it was several miles to the inn, and the moon that had been so kind to her might become impatient and dash behind a cloud.

"Yes," she said brightly. She was happy now—she forgave her brother for treating her badly, and when she slipped into bed she would fall asleep instantly. He helped her into the carriage and she quickly threw the robe over her knees. Her brother had hardly sat down before she threw her arms around him in gratitude. She had returned to Mayfield and nothing else mattered.

Royal January found it hard to drive with his sister's weight pinning him to one side of the seat. She had fallen asleep, nestling against him, legs entangled in the robe.

He had watched her from the carriage as she made her way around the ruins, past the one remaining column that had inexplicably survived the fire, to the mass of brick mounds, a labyrinth of walls, cast-iron railings, and piles of shattered slate. The forest had invaded the remains before the embers had cooled. Saplings struggled from the house's decaying body, while vines struck from the flanks, piling atop one another and the wall until the silhouettes of the man-made shapes were worn smooth. He always thought it strange that the veranda was nearly intact, swinging from the front wall and falling behind the stumps of the columns. They were candles, he thought, charred at the crown, misshapen and near collapse. When he was a boy he had measured his growth by the columns' distance from one another, standing with outstretched arms, straining, willing his fingers to graze the flutes. He had wondered if Samson had done that as a boy, testing his strength and span until the day, blinded and robbed of his power, he had called out for justice and toppled a kingdom.

He had brought his sister home, and it was all that she really ever wanted. She saw what once was, and he remembered what once was, and together they had decided on a form of revenge. They were to account for not only what happened years before but also a life that was slowly being eaten away by a malignant growth.

It made no difference that what she saw had long since died in roaring columns of fire, in a night pierced with the screams of the dying. What is reality anyway, but one's perception?

Royal January had planned, and undertaken. In the process

he had involved those who were reluctant and soon became unwilling. He had relied on Goodwin, and his dear sister, to set exact revenge. He could deny her nothing, but at times he worried that she asked too much of him.

But aren't you Samson? he heard, and chuckled at his arrogance.

Chapter 34

The Fuller House
Washington, DC

Professor Fuller had been called away, his daughter explained. To the Smithsonian.

"We were summoned here," Fitz exploded. "At his request."

"Fitz," Asia said to calm him. "Did he say when he might return, Orchid?"

"Very soon," the girl said, hurt by Fitz's outburst. She chose to give her attention to Asia. "He said it was very important and we shouldn't worry. Would you like some tea, Asia?"

"That would be lovely, Orchid," Asia said.

"No, thank you," Fitz growled, and got a hard look from Asia. Orchid left to fetch the tea.

"I thought by now your temper would have cooled a bit," Asia said. "Instead it flares up at the most inappropriate times. You should not have been so rude to that young lady."

Fitz dropped in a worn chair near the window. "I'd give my eye teeth for a good cup of coffee. Don't you people in Washington drink anything but tea?"

"Why, we have champagne with every meal," she prodded

Fitz. "Or didn't you know that? What is that strangely quizzical look?"

Fitz brushed aside his coat, searching for his pipe. "Mr. Hall troubles me."

The front door clicked open and Professor Fuller raced in, throwing his hat and coat to one side. The presence of visitors startled him. "Oh dear. I had hoped to be back before you arrived. Please forgive me. Have you been waiting long? Will you have some tea?"

"It's on the way," Fitz said, pushing himself out of the formless chair. "What have you found?"

Fuller stood near the fire and rubbed his hands together, trying to drive away the cold. "Something very odd. Frightening as well. But confusing." He looked at Fitz for answers. "I do not understand."

Orchid appeared, carrying a tray with mismatched cups surrounding a teapot. "Father? You're home. We have guests. Would you like tea?"

Fitz lost his patience. "For God's sake, can we dispense with the tea for one moment?" The room was shocked into silence. Fitz regained his composure, careful to avoid the icy stare from Asia. "Now. What do you mean, 'you don't understand'? If you don't, who will? What have you found?"

Fuller pulled the notebook from his pocket and offered it as evidence of his work. "One-third of the book contains an endless series of observations and calculations that are far too complex for my feeble brain to comprehend. I was able to determine that some of the notations refer to directions, although I have no idea how Professor Abbott managed to reach his conclusions. But then again, I must add it is not an area with which I'm familiar."

"Directions?" Fitz asked. He wanted to be clear. "Instructions? Materials from a manual?"

"No. Compass directions. North, south, east—"

"I'm familiar with a compass," Fitz said.

"Were it that simple," Fuller continued. "But there is more

to it. There are graphs." He opened the book and offered it to Fitz. "Here. See?"

Fitz studied the yellowed pages peppered with numbers and several boxes filled with ascending bars. He looked up. "I have no idea what this means."

"Nor I," Fuller said. He tapped a page with his finger. "This might be time. A particular time or date." He shrugged, unwilling to accept his own idea. "Or series of dates."

"This isn't much help," Fitz said. "You're speculating. I could have done the very same thing."

"Fitz," Asia warned him.

"Oh, but that isn't all." Fuller thumbed through several pages before stopping. He settled his spectacles on his nose and scanned the page. He lifted his head, and his manner became grave. "You know of Greek fire, do you not?"

Fitz was too stunned to answer. It was Asia who asked, "It's a myth, isn't it?"

"No," Fuller said. "There are many myths surrounding it, to be sure. It was said to have been invented by Callinicus, a Syrian engineer, but I believe it to be much older than that. It was a closely guarded secret among the ancient rulers. Its potential as a weapon was incalculable."

"What does it have to do with the book?" Fitz asked. The one class at the Academy he had enjoyed was Captain Lynch's Military History. Lynch was an odd-looking sort, having a mass of unruly black hair and spectacles that teetered on the verge of sliding from his nose. But despite his unkempt manner, and the wandering nature of his lectures, he told a good story—that was all history was, Lynch informed his class, a story well told.

"The First and Second Siege of Constantinople," Lynch had begun his lecture. "And the Fourth Crusade. Did I mention Syllaeum? There as well." He had pulled a worn book from under his arm. He untied a silk ribbon that appeared to be holding it together, jammed his spectacles against his nose with his index finger, and began to read. "It happened one night, whilst we were keeping night-watch over the tortoise towers, that they brought up against us an engine called a perronel." Lynch paused and repeated the word as if it held some mystical quality. He had continued reading, and Fitz closed his eyes, picturing the scene. "Which they had not done before and filled the sling of the engine with Greek fire. When that good knight, Lord Walter of Curiel, who was with me, saw this, he spoke to us as follows: 'Sirs, we are in the greatest peril that we have ever yet been in. My opinion and advice therefore is: that every time they hurl the fire at us, we go down on our elbows and knees, and beseech Our Lord to save us from this danger.' "

"It is recorded in Professor Abbott's book," Fuller offered. "Here." He flipped through the pages. "Here as well. What I take to be Greek fire. Or something very similar to it."

"What is it?" Orchid asked.

"Burning pitch, petroleum," Fuller ventured, "some combination of quicklime, resin and other ingredients. No one is quite certain what its composition is. That knowledge died with the last of the Roman emperors."

"But it would not be difficult to concoct," Fitz said, "for a talented man of letters? If he had the ingredients?"

"Difficult, perhaps. But it could be done. Or, something very similar to it."

"Fitz," Asia said, "I don't understand. Abbott has invented a sort of liquid fire. What has any of this to do with balloons?"

"It makes no sense, does it?" Fitz conceded. "What could be done with these things? What do they have in common?"

Fuller was confused by Fitz's statement. "Why nothing, they just happened to occupy pages in the same book."

"No, professor," Fitz corrected him. "It was in front of me, but I chose to overlook it. This is an instruction manual of some sort, and if we could determine how, everything in its pages are linked, somehow."

Professor Fuller dropped in his chair, gazing at the notebook. "Why would someone resurrect the Devil's own weapon? What good could it possibly do?"

"Is it so terrible?" Asia said.

"It cannot be extinguished except by being completely smothered," Fitz said. "Water won't do it. In fact, it's the worst thing to fight Greek fire with. It increases the flames, causing them to spread." He heard Lynch reading from his book. " 'This was the fashion of the Greek fire: it came on as broad in front as a vinegar cask, and the tail of fire that trailed behind it was as big as a great spear, and it made such a noise as it came that it sounded like the thunder of heaven.' "

"The Powder Works," Fitz whispered.

"Wilmington?" Asia said.

"Remember what Gideon said? Something about a fiery tail coming from the sky? I've seen Indians shoot flaming arrows, so that's what I thought he meant—fire somehow being thrown at the works. That makes me an idiot, of course, because I chose to see what I knew. But suppose it was being dropped. What Gideon saw was a thin stream of Greek fire falling on the Powder Works."

"It has to be ignited," Fuller reminded Fitz.

Asia wasn't convinced. "Falling from one of Abbott's balloons?"

"Far too dangerous," Fuller observed, standing. His mind began working. "An ignition device would probably fire the balloon, as well as the Greek fire. Remember, hydrogen is very volatile."

Fitz flung a glance at the notebook. "Well, the answer may be in there, but if you can't decipher it, I certainly can't."

"Wait a moment, Fitz," Asia said. "If that is a plan for a treasonous act, then there is nothing to worry about. We are in the possession of the book."

"That's right," Fuller cried in excitement. He looked at Fitz for confirmation.

"When I command a regiment," Fitz explained, recalling that was what he was supposed to do, "I give orders to my adjutant, who writes them down in the Order Book, tears out a sheet, and sends it to the appropriate officer. He then makes a copy of that order."

Fuller's face said it all. They could not be certain about copies.

Asia broke the silence. "What do we do now?"

"I don't know," Fitz said. "I dare not go to the president."

"Oh, but you must," Fuller urged.

Fitz dismissed the notion. "And tell him what? Someone has resurrected an ancient weapon and used it on the DuPont Powder Works? Those events are past. According to the Joint Committee on the Conduct of the War, I am awaiting recall at their pleasure and should not be involved in any official activities."

"Husband," Asia said. "I have never known you to do what you are told, unless it pleases you. You have something in mind and I, for one, would like to hear it."

"I as well," Fuller said.

Orchid joined in. "And I."

Fitz glanced at Orchid. "I don't suppose you have any coffee in the house, do you?"

"It's quite old," she replied. "It may be bitter."

"Let's have it," Fitz said. "The same has been said of me."

Chapter 35

Markham Theater
Washington, DC

The door swung open and Fitz read the expression on Hall's face—it was shame. What he had been in the past, what he had done, or chose to ignore, was coming to exact revenge.

"We have to talk," Fitz said, entering the room with Asia at his side. He would return to speak with Hall, Fitz had told the Fullers and Asia, as he sipped his coffee. Orchid had been right—it was sharp. When Asia tried to question him about his reasoning, Fitz merely shook his head. He wasn't sure, and he wouldn't be sure until he confronted Hall again. The old man at the theater may not have told Fitz everything.

He had insisted Asia stay with the Fullers, but she refused. "For God's sake, woman, haven't you seen enough excitement to last a lifetime?" He should have expected her reply.

"Not at all," she had said, with that irritating smile of hers. "I could use a bit more."

Hall was alone, although Fitz suspected he kept himself company with the half-filled bottle of whiskey on the table near the bed. It dulled the memories. "She's at a fitting," Hall said, answering Fitz's unspoken question.

"Good. Then we can talk without reservation."

Asia sat on a stool in one corner of the tiny room. Fitz had not revealed what he expected to find out from Hall, just that he was certain the man hadn't been honest.

Hall reached for the bottle but Fitz snatched it out of his hand. "You can have it when you tell me the truth. When we last spoke, I thought it strange that out of the dozen or so theaters in the city, Odessa would come to the Markham for sanctuary."

Hall was quick to answer. "She knew I was here. She knew I was a good man."

"The only way she would know that," Fitz said, "is if she knew you quite well." He watched Hall sink to the bed. "You were involved with her at the Januarys, weren't you? You could reveal nothing of the horrors at that house without exposing your own affair."

The old man rallied, rebuffing Fitz's accusation. "It was nothing. White men take colored women all the time. Nobody says anything about it. It's a common occurrence."

Asia offered an explanation from the corner. "But you love Odessa."

Fitz nodded his concurrence. "She could have been sold, or sent away. You went to that house many times and saw the monstrosities committed by John Jacob January."

Hall nodded, and found his voice. "If I said anything, I would lose Odessa. She planned to run away and come to me. We would flee to France or England. But the night of the revolt, she knew she had to get away. She came to me. We saw what happened in the papers the next day. We thought we were safe." Tears rolled down his cheeks. "But we could not escape the guilt."

Fitz handed him the bottle. "You can now. I want you to take me out there."

"Fitz!" Asia cried. "What are you talking about?"

"I won't do it," Hall said, cradling the bottle as if it were his only salvation.

"Yes, you will," Fitz said. "You owe that much to the innocents who died there. And you owe as much to those who may yet die."

"What do you expect to find at Mayfield?" Asia said.

"The place was abandoned years ago," Hall added. "People won't set foot on the grounds. It's overgrown—nearly impassible. Some people swear it's overrun by ghosts."

"Victoria January told me I was likely to find them there," Fitz told Asia.

"What?"

"When we were in Canada. She told me they often returned to Mayfield. They drew their strength from the place."

"It's evil," Hall said, finishing the bottle. "The ground reeks of decay. The spirits of the dead live at Mayfield now."

Fitz pulled him up by the shirtfront. "Quit performing. You're taking me out there. Once you show me where it is you can go about your drunken business. But you're taking me. The worst thing that could happen to you is for me to leave you here to wallow in your own shame. I'm giving you a chance to account for yourself, Hall." He felt Asia's hands encircling his arm. "I don't want you to go," he told her.

She smiled, and he knew he was lost. "I have to have a chance to account for myself, don't I?"

"Wife," he said, exasperated. "Don't you recall hearing the word 'obey' in your wedding vows?"

She patted his arm. "Of course, husband. And may I say, you obey me quite well."

"Please," Hall said. "I can't go out there." He was a broken man, his memories having become nightmares that ate away at his soul. His only salvation was liquor, and that was only temporary. Fitz felt sorry for a man who had sunk so low that every vestige of courage fell from his shoulders like a cloak. But he could not find the place by himself. It was growing late—it would be nearly dark when they made their way to where he supposed Mayfield was—and his only guide was a frightened sot.

"Yes, you can, Marcus." Odessa, shrunken and featureless

with the light from the hallway bathing her, stood in the doorway. "We have come a good distance together, you and I, but you'll never make peace with God until you do right."

"I'm sorry to disturb you," Fitz said. Hall was not the only one wounded by Mayfield. Odessa was no larger than a child, and her face was drawn in pain, ebony skin pulled tight against high cheekbones.

She looked at Fitz without expression, ready to accept what came to her. "I'll go. I'll show you the way."

"No," Hall said in horror. He glanced from Odessa to Fitz. "No. You can't let her. For God's sake, man, have pity on us."

Fitz shook his head. "I have none to give, Mr. Hall. I am going to get to the bottom of this one way or another. I need your help. If you can't find courage, even that from a bottle, I'll have to accept Odessa's assistance."

The black woman dropped a bundle of clothes she had been carrying and wrapped her tiny arms around Hall. "Don't worry, Marcus. I'll be fine. Mr. Dunaway is right. It has to be done. That place can't do nothin' to me no more."

Hall, his cheeks wet with tears, his eyes pleading for understanding, looked at her. "I can't go. You understand, don't you? But I can't let you go, either." He choked out a sob and buried his face against her shoulder.

"It ain't nothin' to worry about," Odessa soothed him. She stroked his gray hair and guided him to the bed. He sat, and then toppled on the pillows, crying. When Odessa straightened she gave Fitz a strangely peaceful look, her eyes determined, her body relaxed. She was prepared. "Don't judge my man," she told Fitz. "This ain't him. He's got a disease that he can't help. He's as strong as you or me. Stronger maybe."

Fitz knew there was no reason to respond. "There's a livery just outside. I'll rent a horse and buggy. All you have to do is show us the way. You need do nothing else."

The words seemed to mean something to her. "All of this is because people did just what had to be done and nothing else. Husbands, wives, and babies died because of people doing just enough to get by. I'll take you there. I trust in the Lord to guide us." She kissed Hall on the neck, then led them out of the room.

Fitz let Asia pass and then followed, feeling the weight of the Colt revolver and an extra cylinder at his waist. *The Lord can lead us,* he thought, *but let us go armed for the nonbelievers.*

Chapter 36

Nine Miles Northeast of Washington, DC
On the Laurel Road

The carriage drove into a warm wind, a strong, constant breeze, unrelenting in its efforts to slow them. They rode silently out of town, watching the city sparkle to life with streetlights and newly lit house lamps. Carriages passed them—landaus, rockaways, and phaetons—their lamps glowing a deep yellow, with drivers bundled not against the cold, which should have been biting at them this time of year, but against the unnatural wind that kicked up dust and spooked horses.

Clouds, luminescent from the city's lights, drifted quickly into view and then out of sight, as if they wanted nothing to do with the strange weather. As he drove, Fitz unbuttoned his coat, trying to pull it off. Asia, sitting next to him, slipped the heavy garment off his shoulders as he pulled his arms through the sleeves.

"You should have let me drive," she chided him. "You wouldn't have had to go to all of that trouble."

"Allow me my tiny victories," Fitz replied, happy to break the silence. The wind rushing overhead was now their only companion, with an occasional dust devil spun out of the earth to accompany them. He did not take to the idea of spirits or bad omens, or any of the nonsense that the unseen somehow played a role in man's fortunes. Long ago he determined that if he could see it he could fight it, and if it wasn't visible, it wasn't a threat. But there was something troubling about the night. When they left Washington all of the city's vitality seemed to have fled before the racing clouds—what was left was a somber collection of buildings under a hard, slate sky. The only relief was the warm glow of lamps through windows. And now, in the countryside, shadows as fleeting as their makers rolled over the fields, pastures, and clumps of forests, beneath a moon that appeared too weak to hold its head up. The only other light came from an explosion of stars scattered over the sky, but these only made their appearance by the grace of the passing clouds.

Asia chose that moment to comment, "What a strange night."

"There's nothing strange about it," Fitz said. He glanced over his shoulder. Odessa sat huddled in the backseat, a shawl wrapped around her shoulders, a kerchief covering her head. "How far is it?"

She leaned forward, as if to prevent the wind from hearing. "We go about another mile and then turn down a lane. There were two stone markers, each with a stone ball on top. I reckon they are still there. But they might be overgrown."

"How far is the house from the markers?"

Odessa thought for a moment. "About two miles. Nearly. The lane goes back and forth, like a snake. They said Master January had it cut that way so people got all confused as to where they were."

"Imaginative of him," Asia observed. "I hope he took the same road to hell."

Fitz glanced at her in appreciation. "Why, wife. You have a fighting nature about you."

"I have more than that, husband," Asia said, holding up a short-barreled Remington.

Fitz pushed the pistol to one side, studying it critically. "That won't be accurate at more than ten feet."

"Too true," she said, slipping the pistol into her purse. "But it will frighten considerably farther than that."

"Yes," Fitz said, ready to broach the subject that had been on his mind since they had started out. "Let's talk about that. When we arrive at the gateposts, I want you and Odessa to stay with the carriage."

"Fitz!" Asia objected.

He had his reasoning, and Odessa had given him more. "I'm not going to march down that road so that everyone will see me, which means I'll have to go through the underbrush." He nodded at Asia's voluminous skirt. "You can't travel through briars and brambles dressed in that. Nor can Odessa."

"But you won't know where the house is," Odessa argued from the backseat.

"As long as I can keep the road in sight, I can find the house."

"Fitz," Asia said, and he knew she was frightened about more than the danger that lay in the distance. "What if Robert is there?"

"I am one man, and I don't know how many there are of them." He wanted to offer her more reassurance. "It is likely that no one is there."

"But you have no idea," she insisted. "You don't know for sure." She didn't give him time to answer. "You must keep yourself safe at all costs, Fitz. But I beg of you, and I know how insensible this is—I beg that you do not harm Robert."

"I said I will not, and you can count on that. Will you remain with the carriage?"

"Yes," she said, much too quickly to please Fitz. "Do what you can to prevent harm to Robert, and I will not follow."

"I should go with you," Odessa said to Fitz.

"Stay with Asia," he commanded.

Odessa leaned toward Asia. "He don't have much confidence in women, does he?"

"He just thinks he doesn't," Asia said. "I haven't convinced him otherwise."

* * *

The stone pillars had been captured and held captive by an army of encroaching vines that had slithered out of the forest, wrapping their tentacles around each post. Sometime in the past, separated from its base by the fibrous mass that threaded its way into every crack, one of the stone balls had fallen off to land at the base of the post to the right of the entrance. The vines, in their triumph, had smothered it.

Fitz looked up at the tall, leafless trees, their spindly limbs intertwined in mutual support. The trees lolled back and forth, buffeted by the wind, creaking in the darkness. A branch snapped deep in the forest, a crack as loud as a gunshot, and fell to the earth with a crash, taking other limbs with it.

"It's picking up," Fitz said before he realized it. He vowed to speak no more of the weather or the wind, but as they stood on the edge of the forest, he stared in disbelief as the trees swayed in unison—some sort of unnatural dance. There was something else as well—something that startled him. It was a high wind, well above the ground. Dead leaves and twigs, the debris usually snatched aloft by even a moderate wind, remained untouched. It had followed them from Washington, closely, forcing dust and leaves aloft. They had come to Mayfield and the gale had gone above them, hiding high in the branches, as if looking down in judgment. He stopped, dismounted, and tied the reins to a sapling.

"We have a bargain," he said to Asia. "You stay here." He glanced at Odessa, including her in the agreement.

Asia kissed Fitz deeply, and ran her palm over his cheek. "I will. And you will be careful." She dropped her head. "And Robert—"

"Wife," Fitz said, pulling out his pistol. "Don't worry about Robert or me." He gave her a smile. "I've never failed you yet, have I?"

She stopped him. "You must hear me, Fitz." There was no attempt at levity. "If I haven't told you why I love you it is this—you are the most honest, kind man I know. You do what you say, and have never uttered a falsehood in your life. I could go anywhere, do anything with you, and suffer not the least regret." She kissed him and drew back.

Fitz smiled, and nodded. "I'll do my best not to cause you any regrets."

He set off, picking his way through the forest, circling thickets and the decayed bodies of fallen trees. The wind moaned overhead, bending the tops of the trees to its will, tossing torn branches and limbs into the night. Near the ground, it was as silent as death. Fitz stopped and unbuttoned his frock coat. It had become heavy with sweat after thirty minutes of fighting his way through the underbrush, and he came to the conclusion that he would have to take the road after all—the forest was too thick with obstructions. Vines grabbed at his feet, and toppled trees barred his way, and the intertwined branches of fallen limbs stopped him as effectively as a battlefield's chevaux-de-frise. It would be the road after all.

Asia turned to Odessa. "Help me. Quickly." She pulled a knife out of her purse and pulled up her skirt.

"What?"

"Help me cut this contraption away." She began sawing at the ribbons that tied the hoop skirt to her waist. "I won't get two feet in those woods with this thing hampering me."

Odessa untied one of the ribbons. "But you promised the colonel you'd stay here."

"I did," Asia said. She hacked at the trappings in frustration. "Oh, for the day when women don't have to wear these things."

"Here, let me," Odessa said. "You'll cut yourself wide open." She pulled the cumbersome garment away and tossed it to one side. She looked down at her own skirt. "I have only the one petticoat."

"You can't go," Asia said. "You mustn't go in there."

Odessa grew defiant at Asia's concern. "There ain't nothin'

up there that can hurt me worse than I been hurt already. You're a kind lady. I can't let you go up there alone. I ain't got no gun."

Asia handed Odessa her knife. "Carry this. The minute we locate Colonel Dunaway and the others, you must go and fetch help."

"There ain't nobody around here," Odessa said. "Nearly everyone has moved out or gone off to war."

"You've got to find someone."

"I will," Odessa said. "If there's a soul to be found around here, I'll bring them back."

Asia took a deep breath and smiled at her companion. "Ready?" They set off along the road, and soon disappeared in the darkness.

Chapter 37

Mayfield
Off the Laurel Road

Owen stood dumbfounded as the balloons swayed gently, bloated bodies occasionally nudging one another in a friendly reminder that they were brothers. There were ten of them, no more than eight feet in diameter with wicker tubs suspended below each. Goodwin had staked each balloon down, tested the netting to make sure it wasn't twisted, and then signaled with a wave for Owen to begin ladling iron filings into the glass vats filled with sulfuric acid. Owen did as he had been instructed, quickly dropped the door over the gas canister, and watched with amazement as the hose running to the first balloon began to swell. It filled out, growing until it reached the deflated balloon lying in the pasture. At first nothing had happened and Owen thought the coupling—Goodwin had told him everything—was loose or there was a hole in the balloon, or Abbott's calculations were wrong, and he shouted his concern to Goodwin.

Goodwin had glanced his way, but said nothing. The indication was clear enough—*be patient.* Owen, stung by the man's silent dismissal, had thought the whole thing was a waste of time and he would flee the moment he could.

The balloon had stirred, and then trembled, life having been breathed into it. Waves undulated through the fabric, and Owen saw a strange animal stretching itself awake on the golden field after a long sleep.

"More," Goodwin had shouted, and Owen quickly poured another measure of iron filings into the acid. He watched Goodwin examine the balloon's inflation. After he was satisfied with the progress, he sealed off the valve and switched the hose coupling to the next one. Owen did not understand any of it—the hydrogen, the balloons, the bladders Goodwin handled with great care as he unloaded them from a small crate. The Januarys' arrival just after sunset did not ease his confusion.

Royal January beamed at Owen. "You've done well, Mr. Owen. Quite well. I'm sure Mr. Goodwin is pleased with your assistance." He left Owen with the compliment and joined Goodwin at the inflated balloons. They spoke, too far for Owen to hear what they said, and studied the sky. Apparently satisfied, January nodded and walked to his carriage.

Owen followed his progress, but his attention was drawn to Victoria. She sat in the carriage, awaiting her brother, strangely distant, sad, watching the dark clouds that raced overhead. He wanted to speak to her, to reassure her that, no matter what transpired, he would protect and care for her. Her brother would not always be there for her, and she would need a husband. Owen had rehearsed his performance many times. He would approach Royal January, declare his intentions, and seek permission to ask for Victoria January's hand in marriage.

Royal January walked toward him, Victoria on his arm. Owen jumped from the wagon and wished for a mirror to tidy up. He realized that was the last thing he wanted—he would only see how filthy he was.

"Mr. Owen?" January said. "There is a small box under the seat of my carriage. I wonder if you would be so kind as to bring it to me. Handle it with care, if you please. It contains the secret of our adventure."

Owen ran to retrieve the box, and Victoria turned to her brother. "I can't bear to be gone so long."

"I told you. It's a temporary measure. Once this is done we will have to seek refuge in Richmond." He cupped her chin in his fingers. "Don't worry. I wouldn't keep you from Mayfield for any length of time."

She kissed his fingers in gratitude and forced a weak smile. "You understand that I need this place. That Mayfield is as much my soul as you are?"

"Yes," he agreed. "I understand completely about Mayfield."

"You promise?"

There was no other answer possible. "I can deny you nothing."

Owen arrived and offered January the box, pausing to glance at Victoria. She offered a demure smile in return. "Here it is, sir."

January took the box and called for Goodwin. The big man trotted across the edge of the pasture. Behind him the ten balloons bobbed anxiously at their tethers, ready to start the night's events. Wicker baskets hung beneath them, just inches off the ground.

"Is that them?" Goodwin said, eyeing the box. "The watches?"

Owen couldn't help himself. "Watches? What are we going to do with watches?"

January passed the box to Goodwin. "Don't you know that timing is everything to comedy, Mr. Owen? The joke's success, the impact of a punch line, depends not only on how it is delivered but when it is delivered. Timing rules the stage. Drama as well, sir. A line spoken too early or too late will destroy a scene. Those watches in Mr. Goodwin's hands are the key to our little drama."

"I don't understand," Owen said, looking from January to Goodwin.

January pointed at the horizon. "There is the city, sir. See how its lights shimmer under a cloud-laden night."

"Washington," Owen confirmed.

"More than that. A very large target for some remarkably unwieldy weapons," January added. "Tents, frame buildings, ammunition—a vast field of combustible materials. We'll supply the flames."

Goodwin held up one of the watches. "We will set this clock to nine minutes. Abbott figured the time. At the last second, this wheel here spins against a flint, throwing sparks into the reservoir of fuel."

"Each balloon will explode over some part of the city," January said. "The area affected is dependent on the capriciousness of the wind. The liquid contained in each reservoir, Abbott's Greek fire, will cover hundreds of square feet."

"Yes," Owen said, shocked. "But I didn't think—"

"It's retribution," Victoria said, gently laying her hands on his shoulders. " 'Open thy doors, O Lebanon, that the fires may devour thy cedars. Howl, fir tree; for the cedar is fallen; because the mighty are spoiled; howl, O ye oaks of Bashan; for the forest of the vintage is come down.' "

"Better Isaiah," her brother suggested. " 'Oh that thou wouldest rend the heavens, that thou wouldest come down, that the mountains might flow down at thy presence, as when the melting fire burneth, the fire causeth the waters to boil, to make thy name known to thine adversaries, that the nations may tremble at thy presence.' "

Goodwin had another idea. "To hell with every god-damned Yankee."

Victoria let both comments pass as she smoothed the fabric of Owen's tattered jacket. "Now you must do what Mr. January and Mr. Goodwin ask of you, so we can be on our way."

"Go and get a bladder out of the box," Goodwin ordered. "Place one carefully in each basket. That stuff will burn if you look at it sideways, so be cautious."

Owen moved away from Victoria, wanting to linger in her presence, to feel her touch on his shoulders, but at the same time needing to be away from everyone. They were going to fire Washington from these ten balloons. It was fantastic, and unbelievable. Much of the city was a ramshackle collection of frame houses and wood structures thrown up to house soldiers or government workers. Every lawn not occupied by the statue of some hero blossomed with tents housing soldiers. Fire was a constant threat, but fire from the air?

Owen stared at the vulcanized rubber bladders packed nestled in a bed of wood chips in a medium-sized crate. He picked one up, testing its weight, and decided it was nearly five pounds—perhaps more. It was a foot long, about four inches thick, and nearly a foot wide. This single device could hardly be much of a weapon. He carried it to the line of waiting balloons. But there were ten of them, so the weapon's impact was increased, and compounded by the hydrogen that each balloon carried.

He stopped in front of the first balloon, thinking. He grew up in Washington. He knew the city and its people. He was an agent of the South—he knew he was a part of an action against the North. *What did you think you were doing?* he chastised himself. Not this. He had never considered an action like this. He never thought to ask what was required of him. He had done as he was told—like a good soldier, he added. The notion stunned Owen, and he felt sick to his stomach—the same way he felt when Goodwin had killed those men.

Goodwin reached over the lip of the basket beneath a balloon and laid a leather pad in the bottom. "Put those bladders on the pads. We don't want the wicker piercing the rubber. What's the matter? Are you all right?"

Owen laid the bladder on the pads. Goodwin's hand clamped down on his arm. "This has all been a closely run thing. Do what you're told and everyone will be happy. We have a chance here, Robert." Goodwin's use of his name startled him. "We have come pretty far with just a little way to go. Don't fail us now."

Owen straightened. "I'll go and get another."

Victoria stood near the carriage while her brother walked

down the line of inflated balloons, inspecting the bindings of each. He reached Goodwin as the other man consulted a small booklet. Goodwin looked up to see January.

"The weight is correct, but the wind may be a touch higher than Abbott figured," Goodwin said. "I don't think it will make any difference in the end. I think we ought to leave the clocks at nine minutes and take our chances."

January accepted Goodwin's opinion. "What about our young novice?"

Goodwin turned to see Owen struggling with two bladders. "He's anxious, but ambitious. He's one of those who are eager to help even if they don't know why." He shouted a warning to Owen. "Be careful with those."

"I think when this is over," January said in a considerate manner, "we ought to do away with Robert Owen."

Goodwin nodded without looking up. "Just as soon as it's over."

Chapter 38

A mule's bellow warned Fitz, and he dropped to one knee, peering through the thicket. He could see nothing, nor hear anything except the animals braying, but he knew they couldn't be far off. He slipped the Colt revolver out of his waistband, rose slowly, and advanced, taking deliberate steps. He hadn't expected to find anyone, although he had hoped to find evidence they had been there. As he jogged down the road, stopping to listen for signs of life, he saw the remnants of a large home. Mayfield itself, burned, gutted, its splendor and decadence mingled in one massive pile of debris. He thought of Odessa and the horrible death of those poor souls seeking justice.

He stopped again and slid behind a tree. It was a voice this time, someone calling in the night, off to the left. He listened. Two voices perhaps, men's, echoing in the darkness. He waited for more, and heard a third voice—another man. If Victoria was there, she was silent, or her voice was so faint it was lost in the woods. He counted on her being as dangerous as her brother.

One of the men might be Owen. Fitz decided he would

have to be wearing a big sign hung around his chest that said *I Am He,* before he would recognize Asia's brother. He remembered his promise to her—to keep Robert Owen safe, to do him no harm. What about me? Fitz wanted to say.

No, Fitz decided. Robert Owen was with his comrades, and Fitz had to confront him. Leaving the road he made his way as quickly through the tangle as he could, hoping to weave between the obstructions without betraying his presence.

Fitz sank behind a clump of bushes. He'd heard someone shout a warning of some kind. It might have been about his approach, but he doubted it. At least he had a direction—to his left. He glanced at the tops of the trees, still in the grip of the fierce wind. They rolled back and forth in unison, dancing over the ground beneath them that had seen so much death. He did not like this place. It was despicable.

Fitz listened, rose, and made his way in the direction of the shout. Three men, one woman—the odds were not too bad. He had to make sure he accounted for everyone when he confronted them. A tiny regret stung him—perhaps Asia should have come along. She could handle a pistol, and she had courage. But another thought intruded—her brother was there. What would she do if Robert Owen ran—or tried to overpower Fitz? Better to have her out of this, Fitz decided, than to give her an impossible task, testing the woman's love and loyalties in one moment.

He saw a pasture through an opening in the trees. It ran for some distance, perhaps a mile, ending with a thin line of trees in the distance. The moon floated free of a bank of clouds, illuminating the scene. Fitz knelt near the shattered base of a toppled elm and stared at the massive array before him. Ten balloons floated just above the earth, anchored in place, miniatures of Professor Lowe's balloons that Fuller had showed him. Below the balloons rode small baskets, each of them no larger than a saddle blanket. A man was loading something into the last of them. It looked like a pillow. No, a cask of some kind.

Fitz saw the man's face when he turned to signal to the others. He had seen it once before, in the shop in Quebec City—not in features but in form. He had seen the man embrace Asia, and Fitz remembered the awful feeling of abandonment and betrayal when he thought Asia had taken a lover. It was Robert Owen. He looked older, and his clothes were tattered and filthy, but here was the man who shared Asia's affection, and who might cause her to betray her husband.

There was another man, kneeling over a box near one of the wagons. A mule brayed loudly, startling Fitz, and he heard a woman laugh. But he could not see her. He had to know where everyone was.

He recognized Royal January as he appeared next to the man by the wagon. He was trim, and assured, and he spoke with authority. The other man, kneeling, handed him a device of some kind, and they discussed it. They were too far away for Fitz to make out what was said. He studied the balloons. Their movements mimicked the swaying trees, but they weren't nearly as frantic. Over their rounded tops he saw a faint glow softening the horizon. It was Washington—the lights being lit as they drove out of the capital that evening were now in full bloom. The wind was driving toward the city, gaining strength with each hour.

Robert Owen had been loading parcels of Greek fire. The balloons would be released, rise high enough to be captured by the wind, and be carried over the city. They were going to firebomb Washington, DC. For the first time since setting off from the carriage, the horror of the scheme made itself known to Fitz. This was not war or an act against a powder works. This was a crime—murder on an unimaginable scale. He forced himself to think about the plan, about what they intended.

They had to have a fuse of some kind—something that

would ignite the Greek fire. But what were those machines being handed to January? *Fitz, you fool,* he nearly blurted in frustration. Those are the fuses. They were setting them to ignite. With ten balloons and a trail of Greek fire they could set blazes in a hundred locations in minutes. They could reach any site—the Navy Yard, the Marine Barracks, the Capitol—and anyplace holding explosives would add to the conflagration by a score. And if the Metropolitan Fire Department was anything like the Metropolitan Police Department, they couldn't contain a grass fire let alone a blaze that threatened to consume the city.

Fitz glanced at the clearing again. Owen was standing back while January and the other man loaded fuses into the baskets. Fitz shifted to one side, trying for a better view. She was there—she had to be there. Fitz had heard Victoria laugh, and he didn't want to move on them before he accounted for her. But he was running out of time. They had fuses in half the balloons, and most likely planned to release them all at once. But he did not see her.

He would take a chance. He reasoned he could approach the group from the flank. He should be able to see her the moment he stepped into the clearing and had a clear shot at the others. As he got to his feet, he hoped no one was standing near the balloons. It was a volatile gas, Professor Fuller had warned him, and Fitz didn't want to be the unwilling architect of his own destruction by a badly placed round.

He glanced around once more, trying to calculate all that could happen. Actors.

Fitz slipped into a crouch and eased his way through the thatch of stunted undergrowth. Nearly every plant was dead, which meant that the husks gave way without trouble. But it meant also they were dry, and they crackled as he pushed them aside. He winced as each stalk snapped, and he stopped, listening for any response.

Fitz was just free of a row of decayed bushes, wrapped in the veins of withered vines, when he was knocked to the ground. He fought for his breath and realized that someone was on his back, wrestling with him and shouting at the same time.

He tried to throw the man off and then bring his pistol to bear, but his assailant had his arms pinned to the ground, and the man's weight rested squarely on his back.

"I got him. I got him," the man shouted. Fitz knew it was Owen, and he fought to free himself.

Fitz heard footsteps approaching rapidly, brush and dead leaves being kicked aside. He tried to lift his head, but all he saw were mud-caked boots. He felt his pistol jerked from his hands, and he heard a man say, "Let him up."

"I captured him," Owen said. "Did you see me? I saw him sneaking about and captured him."

Someone grabbed Fitz's arms, someone much larger than Owen. The man's grip was like iron. *I'm not likely to escape,* Fitz thought. Even if he did, he was likely to be shot in the back by his own pistol. The big man turned him to face Royal January.

The only thing that pleased Fitz was the shock of recognition on January's face. "Colonel Dunaway," he exclaimed, in a mixture of surprise and humor.

"Dunaway?" Owen said, looking at Fitz.

"Do you know him?" January said. His manner was pleasant, even mild.

"No."

Had Asia told him?

Owen gave Fitz a defiant stare. "I captured the enemy."

"Boy," Fitz said, "you don't know what you've done."

"We haven't much time," January said to Goodwin. "Bring him with us."

"There are others," Fitz said, knowing the ruse was unlikely to work. "We have this place surrounded."

"I have to admit, Colonel Dunaway," January said. He noticed a tangle of dry limbs. "Watch your step there. I have to admit you are the last person I expected to see. Indeed, I didn't expect to see anyone in these woods. They're haunted by demons. Did you know that? No one comes on this land."

They crossed the clearing, passing the row of balloons, and January presented Fitz to his surprised sister. "Is this our attacker?" she asked. "Just one soldier?"

"Ah," January said. "But it is the tenacious Colonel Dunaway."

"I like to think of myself as inevitable," Fitz corrected him. He was angry at his own clumsiness, and for being taken by a boy. The balloons, trembling with anticipation under the gentle caress of a breeze, mocked him. They would be free soon.

"My God, I thought I was arrogant," January laughed. He turned serious. "The only thing inevitable, Colonel, is that we will all descend into that stygian darkness."

"What's that?"

Victoria chuckled. "And I thought you were a learned man."

"Tie him up," January ordered. Goodwin threw Fitz against the wheel, pulled and cut lengths of rope from the wagon bed, and tied his hands together, running the rope around the wheel and iron tire. To Fitz, January said, "Now pay close attention to what we do. It has taken the efforts of a great many to perfect this scheme."

"I'm to be your audience?"

"You?" January said. "Heavens, no. The entire city of Washington will be our audience, as well as take part in the play. Tonight you will play the role of the critic. And after the play is over I will do to you what I've longed to do to all of my critics."

Fitz watched him walk away. He worked his hands, trying to stretch the ropes, hoping that Asia had heard enough to send for help but knowing that was unlikely—she was too far away, and the woods would have trapped any noise. He pulled at his hands and twisted them back and forth. He felt like he was making progress loosening the rope, but he knew he had little time. He watched as Owen and Goodwin set what Fitz now knew was a clock in the seventh balloon. January and his sister stood.

Fitz saw that the rim of the iron tire was pitted and ragged. He realized if he stretched the rope enough he could pull it back and forth over the rim, cutting the fibers and weakening it. He slid the rope along the rough metal, keeping an eye on the group near the balloons. They were at the eighth balloon, setting the clockwork mechanism. He rubbed faster, the rope tearing at his wrists—certain he didn't have a chance. His fear was confirmed when Goodwin and Owen reached the ninth balloon.

Fitz's wrists burned and blood soaked the rope. He had to hurry.

"Stop, Colonel Dunaway." The whispered command came out of the darkness. It was Odessa, hunched under the wagon. She held a knife. "Be quiet. I'll cut you free."

He shot a glance at Goodwin and Owen. They were at the last balloon. "Hurry. Please." Where was Asia?

Odessa answered his question before it was asked. "Mrs. Dunaway's over there with her gun." She sawed at the rope. Fitz felt it slip. "We got to hurry before we're found out." The rope binding him to the wagon wheel fell away. He dropped to his knees and offered her his wrists. "Cut these." Odessa began slicing. The blade severed the rope.

They ran back into the woods, zigzagging between clumps of bushes, Odessa leading. They heard a low call. "Fitz."

He saw Asia hiding behind a tangle of branches, and he and Odessa joined her. "Give me your pistol."

She saw his hands dripping with blood from the attempts to free himself. "You're hurt."

Odessa started off.

"Where are you going?" Fitz demanded.

"I've already got my orders, Colonel," she said. "I'm goin' for help. If I was you, I'd scat."

As she disappeared, Fitz grabbed the pistol out of Asia's

hands. "Get back to the carriage and go for help. We haven't any time. Those things are to be sent against Washington."

"What are you going to do?" Asia demanded.

Fitz jumped to his feet. "Stop them." He ran through the woods, first parallel to the line of balloons and then straight at the last one. Goodwin and Owen had just finished setting the clock and had joined January and Victoria when Fitz burst out of the trees. He could hit anything with Asia's pistol at less then point-blank range so he had to close the distance before anyone had time to react.

It was Owen who shouted a warning—that damned boy—and then Victoria turned, as calmly as if she had been onstage. Her look was of annoyance, nothing more. By that time Goodwin and Royal January had stepped to one side, trying to see the danger.

Fitz couldn't get into a gunfight with them at this distance—he was still twenty paces away. He hoped it was dark enough to obscure his movements.

"Robert!" It was Asia, calling from the tree line. "Robert. It's Asia."

Asia's appearance startled everyone, and it gave Fitz a moment or two more. *But why didn't she do as I asked?*

"Cut it loose," January ordered Goodwin. He took Victoria by the arm and led her toward the wagons.

Fitz dropped to one knee, his pistol aimed at the actor. But Royal had not drawn his own weapon, and then Fitz realized why—they were too close to the balloon. One errant shot and they all would be engulfed by fire. "Stay where you are!"

"Help me cut them free," Goodwin shouted. Owen hesitated, looking for Asia among the trees. "Help me!"

"Please be careful with the pistol, Colonel," January said. "You could create quite a mess."

Fitz stood. He walked slowly, trying to watch the Januarys and the pair at the balloon.

"You are persistent," Victoria said.

Fitz waved them back toward the balloons with his pistol.

He eased to his right. He wanted to keep everyone in sight. He saw a figure emerge from the woods out of the corner of his eye. His heart sank. It was Asia.

"Robert? Please!" She walked slowly, a spirit in the night.

Owen stopped and watched her advance. "Don't come any closer. Go away. Do you hear me?"

Goodwin knocked Owen to the ground, finished cutting the rope, and then stepped back as the balloon rose, twisting slowly as the wind caught it. It floated westward, a pale imitation of the moon. Goodwin reached down and, dragging Owen by the collar, threw him at the next balloon. "Cut it," he said, sinking a knife into the ground next to the tie rope.

Fitz saw the pistol in Goodwin's hand and dropped to one knee, aiming his own. But Goodwin ignored him and leveled the pistol at Asia. Fitz didn't have a chance. He was too far away. "Asia!" Fitz screamed, and January was on him.

Owen hacked at the rope. What was she doing here? She had to run—she had to get away. That was her husband, the man she loved, but they were going to kill him. He would plead for Dunaway's life. He had captured him; it was only fair.

He wiped sweat from his eyes with the back of his sleeve and saw Goodwin. Why wasn't he cutting? He had a pistol. Owen saw Goodwin's target. "Don't!" He dropped the knife and launched himself at Goodwin, striking the larger man just as the pistol went off.

Asia fell. She regained her senses and knew she wasn't wounded. She checked her arms and legs, just to make sure, and found no sign of blood. She had stumbled, that's all, and now as she climbed back to her feet, trembling with emotion, she saw a balloon, restrained by one rope, twisting wildly over the ground, weaving figure eights in the air. She looked overhead. It was the wind bursting through the tree branches from a different direction. The gale that had buffeted them from Washington had now gone mad.

She ran toward the gyrating balloon, to the two men grappling on the ground. To her brother.

January drove his fist into Fitz's chin, stunning him. Fitz threw him off and tried to regain his footing when January rushed him, driving his head into Fitz's stomach. They stumbled backward, hit the ground hard, and rolled free of one another. Fitz staggered to his feet, gasping for breath. The pistol! Where was his pistol?

January stripped off his coat and raised his hands in the classic pugilist's stance. "Let's make this quick, Dunaway. I have work to do." He ordered Victoria. "Go to the carriage."

Fitz waved him on, his head still ringing from the earlier blow. "Come on, January."

The actor advanced, his legs carrying him lightly across the grass, his fists raised, ready to fight. Fitz struggled to remove his frock coat, as January closed the distance. Fitz dropped the garment on the ground, raised his fists, and smiled.

January hesitated. Fitz kicked the coat into his face and rushed forward. He slammed his shoulder into January's ribs, lifted him off the ground, and threw him down as hard as he could. Fitz heard January's breath rush out, but the man was on his feet before Fitz could react. A fast right fist connected with Fitz's jaw, and a left grazed his belly as he staggered backward. He fell to one knee, trying to keep January in sight. Fitz felt like he was going to throw up. Where was that damned gun?

It was no contest. Goodwin's fists pummeled Owen, and the slighter man could do nothing but try to protect himself. The wind increased, swinging the balloon in a wild arc between the ground and the sky. Goodwin, satisfied he had dealt with Owen, rose, found his knife, and fought his way under the balloon to the remaining rope. Asia rushed to Owen, helping him to his feet.

"We've got to get away," she said, pulling on him. "Robert. Please."

Owen, blood gushing from his broken nose, shook his head. His mouth was swollen and it was difficult for him to speak, but he managed a smile. "Not the best circumstances, eh, Asia?"

Asia tugged on her brother's arm. "Robert. Now. Please."

He shook his head and reached down, retrieving the pistol lying on the ground. He staggered, regained his balance, and cocked the pistol, pointing it at Goodwin. His arm sagged, and he gripped the weapon with both hands. The remaining rope snapped, and as Goodwin stepped back, the balloon rose into the darkness, flying erratically.

"Come over here, Mr. Goodwin," Owen managed.

Goodwin nodded, appraising the situation, and did as he was ordered. Asia saw it, saw the danger and the thin glint of light on the knife blade, and the fact that Owen was too numb from his beating to understand the threat.

"Robert!" she warned, but Goodwin closed the distance quickly, and in one thrust sunk the blade into Owen's chest. "No!" she screamed as her brother fell forward, the pistol gripped in his hand, slumping against the man who killed him. Owen's finger tightened on the trigger, and the pistol went off with a flash. The muzzle blast singed Goodwin's hair and deafened him. He screamed in pain and clasped his ears, stumbling against a balloon.

Owen sank to his knees and fell backward into Asia's arms.

"Oh, Robert," she cried. "Look at you."

Robert Owen shook his head, his eyes searching for his sister's. Blood bubbled around the corners of his mouth as he spoke. "Go find your husband and leave this place. Tell him I'm sorry for everything. I wish you could have seen me onstage."

Asia, careful that her tears did not fall on her brother's face, said, "I did. You were magnificent."

A strange look came over Owen. "How light it seems." His eyes fixed, and his head fell to one side.

The glare behind Asia captured her attention before she

could mourn her brother's passing. She turned to see one of the balloons on fire. In the distance she saw Fitz, struggling with Royal January. "Fitz! Run!"

There was a loud whoosh behind Fitz, and his back was hot. January stopped, his eyes wide in horror.
"No. Not now!"

Chapter 39

Fitz heard Asia's cry. One of the balloons had exploded. The others would follow unless they had been cut loose. Fitz backed away from January. He heard a dull bang followed by a wave of hot air. He turned to see a wall of fire running along the grass toward the woods. This was no time to trade blows with January. Asia raced up to him.

"Fitz! Come on. Hurry. Hurry."

"Yes," he said as January rushed by him. He was going to launch the remaining balloons. Fitz turned to Asia. "I've got to stop him. Run to the woods."

"Fitz—"

"Now, Asia." He broke away and ran after January. He slowed long enough to shout back to her, "Go, Asia. Please." He ran, swerving to the right to avoid the heat of the growing fire. It wasn't the hydrogen. He remembered Fuller's admonition. It was Greek fire, spreading in a blazing pool across the ground. He saw January, cutting away one of the ropes of the first balloon. The balloon twisted in the swirling air currents created by the fire. It had a mind of its own, fighting the man's efforts to cut it free.

Fitz ran into January, bowling him over. The balloon flew

around on its rope, dipped, and struck Fitz in the back. It was a soft blow but it had enough force to toss him to the ground. He pushed himself up and saw January hacking at the remaining rope. The rope unraveled, its ends whipping around and striking January in the face, but the balloon pulled itself free and drifted into the darkness. January ran to the second balloon. He drew his blade across the rope, when there was an explosion.

Fitz threw himself on the ground, covering his head. The air turned molten and he cried out in pain as the wind seared his hands. It was a balloon, he knew, possibly two, and the Greek fire stored in the baskets would be next. He stood and heard the piercing cries of a wounded animal. Keeping his hands close to his body to protect them, he staggered forward, looking for January. Fitz bent forward, as if fighting a harsh wind, but the wind came from behind, fuel sucked into the fire's maw. January. He had to find him. He had to stop him.

A demon staggered toward him, wreathed in fire, hands clasping, blackened skin sloughing off his body. The demon emitted a shrill scream—not of a human being but of a soul tortured beyond endurance.

January. January the Magnificent. He stumbled blindly past Fitz, toward the shrieks of his sister.

There was nothing to be done. Nothing for Fitz to do. But run.

His eyes burned from the streams of hot smoke and his hands ached as he fought to orient himself. He saw the edge of the woods and started out in a clumsy run, shuffling away from the terror behind him. *Faster,* he urged himself, and then ordered himself, finding strength in the command. He stumbled and fell forward. The world exploded behind him with a hollow boom, and he caught sight of flaming trails of debris and Greek fire arching overhead. Into the woods.

Asia was pulling at his coat. "Fitz, get up."

He tried to rise, to get his knees under him.

"Fitz. Get up."

He succeeded, and rocked to a kneeling position.

"Get up." Her face was black with smoke except where her tears had washed it away, and her dress was ripped. Her face was set in determination. Fitz knew that look.

"Hello, wife," he managed, getting to his feet. He cried out when she touched his hands.

"We've got to go."

"Yes. Through the woods."

She looked at him in horror. "What? The woods are on fire."

"It's not a sliver compared to what's behind us." Fitz fought to remain calm. "Besides we have the road." He pulled off his coat, then told her, "Rip that skirt away. We've got to run for it, Asia."

She tore the fabric free, and kissed him deeply. "Come, husband. Let's quit this awful place."

They set out, entering the woods, brushing away vines and bushes, dodging trees. In the distance, in the direction they ran, they could see the soft glow of young fires.

"Lock your fingers in my waistband, and stay behind me," Fitz ordered Asia. "We can't be separated." He led her through the underbrush, wincing as the saplings whipped his burned hands, trying to contain his cries. He had no time for the injuries, and he did not want Asia to take notice. All of their strength had to be directed to one goal—escaping the fire.

But the wind had gone berserk. The gale had turned on it-self, driving the flames into the dry woods, giving the blaze a feast. The woods glowed in anticipation as the fire consumed all it touched. It cracked in delight, spitting out vast clouds of ashes that swirled through the air like snow.

"Up ahead," Asia shouted. "The road."

Victoria's shrieks were lost in the roar of the flames that had killed her brother. She knelt next to his charred remains, crying for his death, and her loss, and the flames that had come into the night again. Mayfield was gone again. All of the beauty in the world—the finest elements of life—were destroyed.

She stood, trembling, and walked without fear, without purpose, away from the heat of the footlights, the thunder of the crowd, the clapping of her adoring audience, toward the woods that had once held Mayfield and now promised nothing. All was lost.

It twisted through the dark woods, a serpentine pathway to sanctuary. It wasn't much of a road, but then they didn't have much of a chance.

As they ran Fitz saw a wall of fire building to their right. "Faster," he said, as much for him as for Asia. Smoke rolled over them, taking away cool air and filling their lungs with acid. His clothes were soaked in sweat, and he heard Asia gasping for breath as they ran.

He wished he had the gun. If it came down to it he could use the gun on her instead of letting her die a hideous death like January.

"How are you?" he called out as they ran.

"The smoke," was all she managed, but Fitz knew what she meant. He felt like he hadn't drawn a decent breath in hours. His throat was dry and his eyes burned so badly from the smoke that he could barely see.

"Not much farther now," he lied. He had no idea where they were. They might have struck the road two miles up from the stone pillars, or a mile, or ten miles. He heard her coughing, a deep, hacking cough, and he felt her hand slip away. He turned, catching her as she fell forward. He helped steady her until she regained her balance and offered him a weak smile. Asia's eyes were puffy, red, and sunken deep in her face. She wouldn't last long at this pace.

"I am all right," she said.

He forced as much strength as he could into answering. "You underestimate yourself, my dear."

She gave him a wry look and grabbed hold of his trousers. "Run, husband, and I shall follow."

They ran. Fitz felt the muscles in his legs tightening. They beat a clumsy cadence on the dirt road, and he stumbled several times. Their pace had slowed, but the fire's had increased. The trees wavered, seeming to drip like candles as smoke whirled around their trunks. Brush, smoldering, sent clouds of sparks corkscrewing into the air to hover over the road—scouts for the fire.

Fitz knew he was failing. He could barely see, and his legs were encased in iron. This was a place of demons—hell in the Maryland countryside. There were ghosts ahead, wavering figures that floated through the smoke.

A dozen spirits sped down the road at Fitz. They were the ghosts of those poor slaves, crucified for nothing more than defending their children from a monster. They shouted at Fitz, calling him by name, urging him to join them.

Soon enough, he thought. Soon enough.

Odessa was at his side with a dozen men and women. "Come on, Colonel Dunaway. We've got to hurry." Someone, a large black man with a boy next to him, poured a canteen of water over his head, as others held him up. "I couldn't find a soul nearby so I had to go to Pigtown. I prayed I wasn't too late."

Strong arms guided him as they ran, and he felt his feet were barely touching the ground. He wanted more water, but he couldn't find the words. He abandoned himself to the men on either side of him.

Fitz was on the ground, and someone was moistening his face. "Asia?" he cried as he saw the stone pillars.

"She's here," a man said. "Right here."

Fitz struggled to rise, and someone helped him.

Odessa appeared. "We've got to walk down the road a bit. We couldn't get the horses to come no closer. Do you want us to carry you some?"

"No," Fitz said.

The fire consumed the forest. Its blaze towered above the twisted bodies of trees that first began to smolder and then burst into flames. White smoke boiled out of the fire, rolling into the sky as embers, rushing on the edge of the wind, glowing with life. White ash, all that remained of living things, floated to earth, covering the ground. Fitz thought of De Brule's snow.

"That ought to have happened years back," Odessa said. "When those poor folk burned that wicked house, this land should have fallen under the torch as well. It never done nobody any good. It's always been sick. Now the fire's come back and done what should have been done long ago."

Fitz knew what she meant. "Justice."

She watched the fire a bit longer before answering. "Retribution."

There was nothing he could say. He had not been a part of it—not even the ending of this terrible place. Fitz knew that his only role had been through happenstance. Well, he decided, that's how most of us get through life, anyway.

He saw a black woman pouring water over Asia's head from a wooden bucket. Asia turned, her hair plastered against her soot-streaked face, and smiled at Fitz.

"What do you say we go for a walk, wife?"

"Any place but those damned woods," Asia answered.

Chapter 40

The East Room
The Executive Mansion
Washington, DC

Fitz pulled at the starched white collar that threatened to strangle him, as silk dresses and evening wear swirled gaily in the large room.

Asia tugged at his arm. "Don't do that!"

"I can't breathe." He dug between the collar and his neck, and decided the only solution was to remove his cumbersome white gloves. Asia clung tightly to his left arm, preventing him from doing so.

"So help me, Fitz, if you ruin this evening for me, I'll shoot you."

He glared at her. "I'm burning up, and I can't breathe, and you know I hate to dance."

Asia leaned in to him, smiling sweetly. "I don't care. I don't care. And you had better learn in the space of three minutes."

"Colonel Dunaway?" a young man with a trimmed mustache said.

"Yes," Fitz replied. He prayed it was not another inquiry about the fire at Mayfield. He had been approached by a dozen people this evening, everyone fascinated about the adventure. Asia, luckily, had taken over the odious task of relaying an account of the event. She was quite good at it—weaving a story of intrigue, spies, danger, and death. Asia did not mention the death of Robert Owen that evening or anytime after they escaped the fire. But Fitz saw the suffering in her eyes. He thought he ought to say something to her, but realized he barely said the right thing when times were good—he had no idea of what to say about her brother's death.

He bore the blame for that, and he knew she felt guilty as well. Fitz knew about hindsight—it haunted him after every action. If only he had called back the men, if only he had not ordered an attack on the enemy position. Those sorts of memories, those tinged with regrets, could eat at a man's soul. Or a woman's.

The man bowed, looking like a boy at his first dance. "I am John Hay. President Lincoln asks if you might attend to him."

"Of course," Fitz said, looking over the sea of coiffed heads for any sign of the president. He knew how easy it would be to locate Lincoln—he towered above most of the partygoers.

"Just look for the clot of sycophants," Hay suggested.

"We will," Asia said, before Fitz had a chance to ask for a definition of the unfamiliar word. She pulled him around the edge of the crowd, toward Lincoln, and informed him, "People who spend all of their time flattering other people in hopes of receiving some reward."

"Well, why didn't he say so," Fitz huffed.

They arrived at a long line, several couples thick, as it made its way past Lincoln and his wife, Mary. She was a short, stout woman with a round face, and Fitz was embarrassed by how much flesh her low-cut gown exposed.

"Keep your eyes focused on her eyes, Fitz," Asia ordered him. "If you look down, you're lost."

Lincoln saw them and waved a big hand barely contained by a white glove stained from shaking hands. "Dunaway. And here with the missus."

Fitz had received an invitation to the reception three days

ago, just two days after the fire. He had no desire to attend, but he thought Asia would be pleased.

He was heartened by Lincoln's wide grin. The president had a knack of making Fitz feel comfortable in his presence. The crowd of hangers-on, taking a hint, parted to let Fitz and Asia approach.

"Mother," the president said, turning to his wife. "Here is that brave man, Colonel Dunaway. And this is his lovely wife."

Asia curtsied, as Fitz bowed, averting his eyes from Mary's bosom. "How do you do, Mrs. Lincoln?" he asked.

Mary Todd Lincoln inclined her head arrogantly and threw a frosty glance at Asia. It was said that she was insanely jealous over her husband's attention and kept women she felt were more attractive than she at a distance.

"So," Lincoln said. "Here you both are in one piece. We can't have you sent on dangerous errands anymore. Dahlgren went out to the woods after the fire had burnt itself out, and"—he chose to be delicate—"things were tidied up a bit. Nothing left of those balloons, Dunaway. A few scraps. A few chunks of melted iron. You did well." Lincoln smiled in gratitude at Asia. "You both did well."

Mary Todd Lincoln cleared her throat. It was a warning to move on.

"Mr. President," Fitz said before they were dismissed. "The Joint Committee on the Conduct of the War—"

Lincoln patted Fitz's shoulder like a father reassuring his son. "Now don't you give that a second thought, Dunaway. You tweaked their nose a bit, but after they had time to cool down, they decided you're just the sort of man the Union needs. They won't trouble you anymore."

"Father," Mary Todd insisted. "You have other guests."

"Yes, Mother," Lincoln said, hanging his head in mock shame. He winked at Fitz. "Lead the way."

The throng swarmed around Fitz and Asia, following the president and his lady. They found themselves alone in a swirl of gaiety, under brightly lit chandeliers. Music floated over the crowd. Fitz stood listening, thinking—of snow-bound Quebec City and the race across the frozen St. Lawrence; of the young face of Robert Owen bursting with pride mixed with confusion at having caught an enemy; and of Odessa, the woman who saw nothing short of the hand of God in the terrible fires that destroyed Mayfield.

"Well." Asia brought him back to the reception. "Do I have to threaten you or are you going to ask me to dance?"

She was his, her intelligence and charm, that quick humor that always seemed to skewer him when he least expected it and was unprepared to defend himself. And her beauty—a smile that never remained hidden for long, green eyes that searched for understanding, and auburn hair that glowed even in the feeble light of a single candle.

He raised her hand to his lips and kissed her fingers delicately. He bowed, and when he rose, said, "Mrs. Dunaway, may I have the honor of this dance?"

Epilogue

Dr. Arthur adjusted the wick on the lamp, filling his tiny office with a soft yellow light.

"Put her there," he ordered his slave Jack, and lit the wicks of two other lamps.

Jack laid the woman on Arthur's operating table and held her down so she wouldn't throw herself off. She was incoherent, thrashing about as if trying to escape the devils that had burned most of her garments.

Walter, Jack's son, and Josephine, his wife, gathered bandages, clean water, and the doctor's instrument bag. They were as devoted to Arthur as he was them, and he would rather have them at his side than all the doctors in Maryland.

"Hush, now," Josephine said, trying to soothe the woman.

"How did you find her?" Arthur asked Jack as he dug through his bag. He set a bottle of laudanum on the cabinet next to the table. He found a bottle of carron oil, decided there was too little in the brown bottle to be of use, and settled on mercury bichloride.

"I saw Watkins out by the crossroads. He was leading a horse and buggy with the lady on the seat. I could tell she was in a bad way."

"It was lucky you happened upon her," Arthur said. "There's no telling what Watkins had in mind." He gingerly pulled back torn silk, examining her neck. Her skin, black with soot, was an angry red underneath.

"She's burned on her arms, too," Jack said, trying to find a way to hold her still without further injuring her.

"Those aren't bad burns," Arthur said. "She might have broken bones or damage to her internal organs." Josephine handed him a pair of shears. "Where is Watkins now?"

"Out on the porch."

"And the lady's buggy?"

"Tied up out front."

Arthur handed the shears back to Josephine. The only way to tell the extent of the woman's injuries was to cut all of her clothes away. But first he had to talk to the man who found her. "Watkins!" Arthur shouted. He heard the door open and close and the clumsy steps of a big man. Watkins, heavily bearded, greasy hair falling over his forehead, his clothes covered in stains, peered into the office. He seldom spoke unless he had to. He was uneducated and ignorant, but cunning.

"You found this lady?" Arthur said. He knew how to deal with trash like Watkins.

"Yes," Watkins said, looking from Jack to Arthur. "Out on the road. Didn't your nigger tell you?"

"I'm asking you," Arthur said, brusquely. "What Jack told me is of no concern to you."

Watkins's big shoulders jumped in an answer. He gave Arthur a sullen look.

Arthur ignored the man's insolence. "This is what I'm going to do—I'm going to give you that horse and buggy—"

"I found it already. I figure—"

"Shut up!" Arthur snapped. "I'm giving them to you. But on the condition that you tell no one about this woman. Do you understand me? You can have them if you keep your mouth shut."

Watkins stared at his feet in reply.

"You know who my friends are?"

The man's head came up. Arthur saw real concern on his face for the first time.

"You know how they treat traitors, don't you?" Arthur waited for recognition on Watkins's part. He saw the man's eyes dart about. That was enough for Arthur to continue. "Good. You go wait on the porch. Jack, you and Walter get our guest something to eat while he waits."

"I could use something to drink," Watkins said hopefully.

"That's fine," the doctor said. He nodded at Jack. "Make sure Mr. Watkins has plenty of water. Go on." The men and the boy left, closing the door behind them. Arthur nodded for the shears, and then began cutting away the woman's dress. He indicated her face with his shears. "That's the worst of it, I'd say. I can't speak for her mind. Lord knows what she's undergone."

"She looks mighty bad," Josephine observed. She searched through the cabinet, finding a bottle of chloroform, a strainer, and a cotton patch. Placing the cotton patch over the strainer, she covered the woman's mouth and nose with the strainer.

Arthur continued cutting. "Chloroform," he said to Josephine. "Just enough to ease her suffering. I don't want her completely unconsciousness."

The slave sprinkled a few drops of chloroform onto the cotton, gauged the reaction, and repeated the procedure.

The woman's movements stilled until her body relaxed. Arthur cut the laces of her boots, removed them, and threw them in the corner with her charred clothes. He listened to her breathing, was pleased at what he heard, and began examining her arms, legs, and torso for broken bones or any sign of swelling. He pressed his hands on her stomach, feeling for any sign of distension. The burns may be the worst of it, he decided cautiously. He searched through her hair for cuts or contusions. When he first saw her irrational activity he was convinced that she had suffered a blow to the head.

He'd seen such injuries, sometimes nothing more than a scalp laceration, result in death.

"Help me roll her over," Arthur said.

Josephine slid her hands under the woman's shoulders and rolled her on her side. Arthur searched for signs of injuries but found nothing. He nodded at Josephine, and they let their patient down.

"What do you think?" Arthur asked Josephine. If she were a white man, Josephine would have been the finest doctor in Maryland. Arthur had taught her to read and was amazed at her remarkable ability to comprehend medical text and journals. He relied on her skills and intuition.

"I don't see nothin' more than you. Those burns on her arms and neck should clear right up once you treat them. That on her face—" The woman moaned and began to stir. Josephine applied chloroform onto the cotton patch cupped over the strainer. The woman settled. "That on her face will scar. The rest of it I guess is being scared, thirsty, and tired. No tellin' what this has done to her mind."

Arthur nodded, accepting Josephine's diagnosis. Even covered in soot and grime, the woman was remarkable. "She is exceptionally beautiful, isn't she?" He remembered his duty. He reached for the chloroform. "Fetch soap and water and clean her up. Get one of your gowns as well. When we get done with her, we can move her to the little bedroom."

Josephine hesitated. "She's the lady, isn't she? The one from the fire?"

"Victoria January." There was a newspaper account three days ago. The story was quickly pushed aside by the second day—another disastrous day for the Union army. "When she's well, we'll make arrangements to send her south. I suppose she'll want to go to Richmond."

Victoria heard the dull drone of waves rolling against the shore and saw figures in the crisp flash of a hundred tiny stars. There was a man tending to her, and a woman—a slave. The black woman's closeness frightened Victoria, and her skin flinched when black fingers touched her. Then she was enveloped in clouds, pure white clouds in a clear blue sky, and she relaxed. She flew in and out of the clouds, an angel gliding, arms outstretched, across the heavens. She felt herself dip and soar, and during the flight she heard bits of words. *Richmond.* She rose well above the clouds and felt the sun's warmth on her face, and she knew that soon she would be safe.

Royal was dead. Goodwin was dead, and the boy who had hovered around her was dead as well. Everyone was dead, and Mayfield was lost forever.

Her mind, satisfied she was beyond danger, now set about listing accounts to be settled. The colonel and his lady. Fitz Dunaway.

Victoria January was sliding into darkness, searching for the deep slumber that repairs wounds, and eases pain—refreshing the body so that when one awakes, one is renewed.

The colonel and his lady, Victoria thought before sleep overtook her—accounts to be settled.

GREAT BOOKS,
GREAT SAVINGS!

When You Visit Our Website:
www.kensingtonbooks.com
You Can Save Money Off The Retail Price
Of Any Book You Purchase!